S. J. MORDEN

GALLOWGLASS

GOLLANCZ
LONDON

First published in Great Britain in 2020 by Gollancz
an imprint of the Orion Publishing Group Ltd
Carmelite House, 50 Victoria Embankment
London EC4Y 0DZ

An Hachette UK Company

1 3 5 7 9 10 8 6 4 2

A CIP catalogue record for this book is
available from the British Library.

ISBN (Trade Paperback) 978 1 473 22854 2
ISBN (eBook) 978 1 473 22856 6

Typeset by Deltatype Ltd, Birkenhead, Merseyside

Printed and bound in Great Britain by Clays Ltd, Elcograf S.p.A.

MIX
Paper from
responsible sources
FSC C104740

www.simonmorden.com
www.gollancz.co.uk

GALLOWGLASS

Writing as Simon Morden for Gollancz:

Down Station
White City

Writing as S.J. Morden for Gollancz:

One Way
No Way

For Sam, who designed both the *Coloma* and the *Aphrodite*, and was a source of invaluable advice and delta-v calculations throughout the writing of this book

Part 1

Escape Velocity

1

Climate change has done more good than harm so far and is likely to continue doing so for most of this century. This is not some barmy, right-wing fantasy; it is the consensus of expert opinion.

Matt Ridley, 'Why climate change is good for the world',
Spectator, 2013

No child – no good child – wants their parents to die, and no parent – no good parent – wants their child to die. Jack's misfortune was to live in a time when those benign, dream-like wishes could become hard reality.

Pap and Mam Van der Veerden had recoiled from both the bitter succession wars that split families and consumed fortunes, and the outside world that had become so difficult and dangerous to navigate. It was a reasonable, sensible reaction, but they had gone on to decide, tentatively at first, then with an increasingly fervent conviction, that they would solve all their problems and protect their only son and their immense fortune by all three of them living for ever.

At first, he'd wanted it to be true. Because he wasn't a terrible child: he was a dutiful, loving son. Only when they started behaving as if it were true – investing in and enjoying the benefits of the latest medical advances that were the sole preserve of billionaires, controlling diet and activities and even the air they breathed – did he begin to question their wisdom. And when he realised that they were absolutely serious, that his memories of them from when he was five and the memories of them when he was fifteen were interchangeable and they hadn't aged a day? That was when he'd begun to hate the idea.

This urge, this reaching for immortality, this godhood, this transhumanism. It repelled him. But at fifteen, there was nothing he could do. So secretly, silently, he'd made a plan, one that would spin out over an entire decade. If he triggered it early, he wouldn't have the skills to survive in the outside world. If he left it any longer? The first appointment at the clinic was next week. He was in perfect health. He was the age everyone dreamed of being, for ever. It didn't matter that the treatments might not work – it was an article of faith that they would, and the process was not to be questioned.

It had to be tonight. It had to be now. It had to be absolutely secret. No one could know. Not Pap, or Mam, and certainly not Mesman, who was his shadow, his bodyguard, his loaded gun, his trigger finger. Her job, her very existence, was to make certain that he stayed safe.

For the hundredth, the thousandth time, he felt the cold, stomach-clenching fear that he was calling this wrong and making a terrible decision. And like all those times before, he faced his fear down and showed no outward sign of his inner dread. If he didn't go, this very moment, then he never would, never could. This was his first opportunity, and his last chance, to make a choice by himself, for himself.

Deep breath. Outside the window was an expanse of tightly mown lawn under the full scrutiny of motion-triggered floodlights and human guards. Enclosing it was a high wall with laser trip wires and anti-drone turret defences. Getting past those was only the start: they were predictable, and therefore defeatable. Outside the wall, things were very different. More chaotic, more risky. But if everything went right, Jack would never see this room, this house, ever again. If it went wrong, he guessed he'd be seeing nothing but this room and this house for a very long time.

So he took a moment to look around him, to feel the hard-wood floor, oiled and varnished under his feet, to breathe the cool, filtered and subtly spiced air, to look at the framed original movie posters from the fifties with their bold fonts and urgent straplines, one last time. He wasn't coming back. He wasn't going to fail.

He used his burner phone – his first burner phone, because he was going to need more than one – to load up a VPN and log on to a server somewhere in the lawless East. Jack tapped out, lo-fi, a message to his crew, using his hidden online identity.

Croesos: If you're ready, I'm ready.

Jack wasn't ready. But he was as close to ready as he might get, and time wasn't on his side, which was ironic, considering he was running away from immortality. He looked at the roster at the top of the message board. His thumb hovered over the screen. His crew, his ridiculous, cobbled-together crew, with their stupid idents and their incongruous avatars. TBone. The History of the Decline and Fall of the Roman Empire (by Gibbon). WhitetailDeer. They knew it could be tonight. They were waiting for him. They were also taking risks. Unquantifiable risks. Potentially fines and jail time. Depending on how vindictive the Van der Veerden family were feeling, it could escalate all the way up to accidents-that-weren't and outright assassinations. He'd made that clear, given them an easy out. And his crew were still doing it: because they could, because they enjoyed a challenge, because they were sticking it to the Man. Because they thought it'd be funny, doing it for the lulz. Whatever reasons they had: they were helping him, and he was going to take that to the bank.

Jack shouldered the pack at his feet and pressed the send button. A disconcerting feeling of anticlimax followed because absolutely nothing happened, but that was good because the plan was supposed to be on rails and any drama would provoke

5

a lock-down that even he couldn't get around. Still, something should have shifted: his perception of reality, if not the ground under him.

TBone: Okay, my friend. Let's get you moving.
TBone: I have the house cameras up.
WhitetailDeer: You weren't kidding about your real estate.
WhitetailDeer: That's some floorplan you have.
History: Go go go.
TBone: Radio fucking silence.
TBone: C, walk out, turn right.

Jack's real phone, lying on the corner of his white linen bed, chirped. The screen bloomed and, simultaneously, the earbuds and the glasses and the wriststrap he'd left on the dresser jiggled. He hesitated, then walked to the bed.

Croesos: It's Mam. She wants to see me.
WhitetailDeer: You want to abort?
TBone: Shit man we got this covered.
TBone: You did the shitty 30 min mindfulness thing every
    night for 4 months. Routine.
TBone: She calls you. You make her wait till you're done. Stick
    to it.
History: Doitdoitdoit.
TBone: C. Now or never. You want to be that lab rat?
Croesos: Sorry. Nerves. Let's roll.
TBone: Out. Right.

Jack opened the door and no, there was no one there. The house would have registered his door catch, just as it would register his presence in the corridor. TBone couldn't do anything about that. Their trick was to make the house not care, not to trip any indicators or alarms, to pacify the house and tell it everything was okay and normal and there was nothing to see and certainly nothing to worry about.

He closed the door behind him, walked down the hallway and took the right turn around the central courtyard. The floor changed from wood to terracotta tile. Through the glass wall, he could see lights, a mirror pool, smooth stones and sand: a Zen garden maintained by servants for a family who never stopped to consider it. A square of night hung above the courtyard.

TBone: Still a clear run to the power room. Go.

Did everyone imagine the Van der Veerdens had an army of staff, cleaning rooms, cooking meals, running errands, fixing things, just hanging around and waiting to be called on? Maybe they did, and maybe they got that idea from those shows where people who needed constant affirmation paraded their sycophantic and disposable entourages in front of the watching millions. Those shows, those people, were always so noisy, as if they had to always be saying something, being something, and if they were quiet and reserved for even a moment, a fickle world would forget them and look away.

His house was a monastery in comparison. Quiet. Ordered. Calm. Nothing showy about the Van der Veerdens. Yes, they had some staff, but those staff had tasks they were expected to do without interacting with family members. Speak only if spoken to. Always defer. Do the job silently and well. Stay out of the way. For the very great part, Jack didn't know who these people were, and couldn't find out. Mesman dealt with that side of things with her usual cold efficiency and they were terrified of breaking rank. They were staff, and that was that.

The door to the power room should have been locked, and Jack half-expected the handle not to turn. It opened, and he pushed through. The lights came on – automatically, because the house knew he was there – and the machinery that powered this particular Van der Veerden compound was laid bare under sharp white light from the ceiling. Battery stacks, CHP plant and attendant pipework, inverter, arm-thick cabling heading in and out of the building, foil-wrapped water pipes, manual breakers and fail-safe valves. It was a double-garage-sized space in a place he'd lived in, on and off, for twenty years, and it was the first time he'd ever seen it.

He pushed the heavy door shut behind him, and it *shumph*ed closed on its seals. The ceiling was two storeys up, and the big air intakes and exhaust manifolds loomed above him, but the only sounds were a low bass hum and his own heartbeat. He should probably breathe now, before he turned blue and fell over.

Croesos: Power room. So far, so good.

History: +1

TBone: House is nominal, but you have an external security detail on the north-east quadrant of the garden. They're moving. Slowly.

WhitetailDeer: Clock time is 5:23. Transport is seven minutes away. Can't speed it up, can't slow it down. I can make it go round the block again, which will give you another ETA in 13.

TBone: Let's not do that if we can avoid it.

TBone: Go to the external door, C. Wait on my command.

Croesos: k

Jack felt he should tiptoe through the machinery. Even his clothes were loud. But there was no one there to hear him, and getting this far without tripping an alarm was trivial compared to what he had to do next. He clenched his jaw. This was his house, and he was having to sneak through it like a thief. The necessity of being protected from all the things that could happen to him outside of the walls had inevitably turned his paradise into a prison. He could go almost anywhere and do almost anything. Except that. And that and that and that. Always for a good reason. Always because it wasn't safe enough.

He checked that the bright, abstract image pinned on the back of his bag was still in place, and quickly fixed one to his front as well. If he screwed up now he'd never have another chance and—

TBone: C, go.

Jack pulled the handle down, and the door was sticky enough to give him the momentary panic that it was still locked, but it gave and he was out in the warm night air, warmer than it was inside, for sure. There was the garden beyond, designed to look aesthetically pleasing but also so that there were a great many sight-lines and very little cover, just subtly lit open ground with no pools of shadow to hide in. Jack was going to have to cross the whole hundred-metre distance to the boundary wall in full view of the cameras.

Certainly, the house would see him, but TBone had the house neutralised. There was always someone in the control room, but unless the house flagged up the movement, he wasn't going to be spotted – the patterns he wore front and back should convince image recognition that whatever he was, he wasn't a human.

Run, Jack, run. A hundred metres. Ten seconds. Not for him, obviously, though he was fit enough. Twenty-five seconds, then, spent fully illuminated with a small rucksack bouncing wildly on his back and only some stupid print-out to protect him. If anyone was actually looking, they'd hit the button and that would be that. The house would turn into an impregnable fortress: it would slam the shutters down, lock the doors, go onto battery power and canned air and cisterned water. The boundary wall, which was only two metres tall on his side – with a five-metre drop on the other – would abruptly be heightened with another two metres of steel plate topped by electrified wire. Such overzealous, defensive security was justifiable because most of the world outside was poor and on fire, and sometimes people wanted to get in, really badly.

He closed on the wall. He'd practised this. He tucked the phone into a pocket because like an idiot he was still holding it. He zipped the pocket up, and mentally prepared himself for take-off.

He jumped, not breaking stride. He'd visualised this moment so many times, so, so many times: the moment he was really going to get into a shitload of trouble. Sometimes, in his dreams, he missed and face-planted into the ground. Today, when it really mattered, he executed it perfectly. His hands tapped the top of the wall and he twisted his hips so that his legs cleared the top in a single, fluid arc. On his way over, he broke the invisible infra-red beams, and maybe the house was going to call that in and maybe it wasn't, but it didn't matter because there was the car that WhitetailDeer had hired, just about rolling to a stop by the side of the road.

All Jack had to do was land without breaking something. On the other side of the wall was a ditch, a moat, that was brimful of water, and he went in, feet first. The water – freezing cold – closed over his head. He splayed his arms and legs, kicked out, forced his hands down to his sides, and he surfaced again with a gasp. Salt. Seawater. He hadn't realised there'd been a dyke breach somewhere. Or he had and this was still the remnants of last week's flood.

He reached the far side of the drainage ditch and jammed his fingers into the bank, clawing at the soil until he gained purchase. Then he hauled himself up, sodden, filthy, and scampered to the car. He opened the back door, threw himself in across the rear seat and saw a phone – his new phone – sitting on the left-hand front seat. Jack snatched it up, and tried to type at the same time as pulling his legs in and slamming the door shut.

Croesos: In car.

The car pulled out from the verge and in its unhurried, self-guided way, joined the dead-straight road that headed north across the polder. Jack lay back on the upholstery and pushed his sodden hair away from his face. The first stage was over. Now he had to travel, undiscovered, seven hundred kilometres to the spaceport.

2

'There has been a little bit of warming,' as he puts it, 'but it's been very modest and well within the range for natural variability, and whether it's caused by human beings or not, it's nothing to worry about.'

Myron Ebell, quoted in *Vanity Fair*, 2007

He peeled off his wet clothes and piled them in the footwell, intermittently checking the chat for any updates. He knew not to speak, because the car's voice recognition would automatically try and log him on as a user, and he was certain that Mesman had her fingers all over his public data. But he was cold and naked, and leaned forward through the gap in the seats to dial up the aircon from a comfortable-when-clothed eighteen degrees to something more suitable for dunked-in-a-sea-filled-ditch.

TBone: @Croesos, you've been rumbled.
TBone: You have controlled panic. They're conducting a room-to-room search for you.

Jack checked the phone zipped in his waterlogged jacket. It still worked, its brief immersion too shallow for any moisture to seep in. He opened the back with his thumb and prised the battery out, throwing both parts into the footwell. He was starting to warm up, and he should probably think about getting dressed. He unclipped his rucksack and pulled out the sealed plastic bags containing a change of clothes and a dry pair of trainers. The seat was still very wet, though, so he climbed through to the left-side front seat and kicked it all the way back.

WhitetailDeer: Clock time 8:54. We need to change this car
   asap because it's the obvious pick. Let me get you across
   the bridge and I'll dial up another.
Croesos: I'm not wearing anything yet.
WhitetailDeer: Dumping you on the side of a busy road in your
   birthday suit is not going to worry me.
History: I'm getting traffic. None to the policía yet. But yeah.
   Get dressed. The weather is holding. P is clear.
TBone: @Croesos, I'm going to try something to buy you a
   little more time. Hold on.
TBone: Hah. The house did not like that.
TBone: Unmasked my port and it threw up its shields faster
   than a fast thing. It thinks it's under attack so now the
   security teams are busy for at least another 5.
Croesos: You did what?
TBone: I showed my hand. House shut me out. It's okay. I'm
   untraceable.

Jack rubbed his feet one at a time to take off enough of the residual moisture for him to get a pair of socks on. The road ahead arched up towards the swing bridge. The control tower and the lights loomed overhead, but the cantilevered section of the roadway remained down, and he passed unhindered. He pulled on a pair of shorts, and then cargo pants. The car moved right, off the main road, and began to track down towards the roundabout at the junction under the elevated expressway.

WhitetailDeer: Take this phone with you. Get ready to bail out.
   I'm going to stop you at the white line for a second.

Jack glanced behind him at the pile of clothes: no time to collect them. He fastened his rucksack and gripped the phone in his hand. The car reached the bottom of the ramp where it pulled over towards the right-hand verge and pulsed its hazard lights. He opened the door and stumbled out into the carriageway. The moment he pushed the door shut again, the car was off, turning right, heading inland. He instinctively looked up, not just to the dark sky but to see if there were cameras. He stepped onto the verge and pulled a hooded sweatshirt over his skinny white ribs. If anyone else was taking exception to him dressing by the side of the road, he didn't know or care. Just as long as the cars drove on past him.

WhitetailDeer: Take a left along the N352. Under the A6.
    There's a car park on the north side of the road. You're
    looking for a blue Qoros.
TBone: Lower car park is under water.
WhitetailDeer: Then it'll be in the upper car park. On the right
    of the turning. Go.

Jack hooked a finger in the heel of one of his trainers and squeezed it on, then the other. He folded his hood over his head and tugged it low over his eyes. It sprang back slightly, and he hunched his shoulders to compensate. He set off briskly towards the underpass, the occasional car on his right whipping by almost silently. He slung his bag onto his back, and dug his hands into his pockets. He walked purposefully, head down: under the roadway, between the concrete pillars, he could see the first sign of tents.

    Some of them were actual tents, nylon, provided by charities or individuals. Some of them were just pieces of fabric hoisted over whatever frame the sleepers could cobble together, and they were probably grateful for even that meagre shelter. In between the flapping flysheets were figures, lit from above and below by the bright sparks of electronic light. Black faces, brown faces, white faces. That was them over there. This was him over here. They didn't see him, or they ignored him. Either was fine. That was under the northbound carriageway. The southbound was similar but different. A unique mosaic of colours representing the same circumstances. Displaced people. Refugees. Not like him. He had somewhere to go, something to be.

Away from the encampment, he crossed the road. There was a bus stop that looked like it hadn't been used for its intended purpose for a while, because its glass sides had been lined with cardboard and its front staked out with a tarpaulin. Behind it, on the semi-submerged cycle path, was an impromptu kitchen, and someone called to him, two, three times, in a language he didn't understand, and he quickened his pace to a run.

There was the car park, and there was the car. But someone was already there, peering through the windows, hands held to the sides of their face to bat away reflections. They looked model-thin, their threadbare clothes hanging off them like bags caught in branches. Jack kept on walking by on the grass. He didn't look round, just held his phone down to his left and typed.

Croesos: Someone by the car. Interested in the car, not me.
WhitetailedDeer: Go to the entrance. It'll meet you there.

The lights came on, and a warning beep came from under the bonnet. The man – gaunt, large-eyed – stepped quickly back. The car neatly reversed out of its space and headed for the entrance. Jack sprinted after it, and as it slowed, he went for the left-side door. He slung his bag in first, then himself. As he closed the door behind him, he found himself staring over the length of the car park at the man, who was staring back.

What was his story? How far had he travelled to get here, to a makeshift campsite under a Dutch flyover and next to a drainage ditch that was more a river than a sump? Jack had seen everything fall apart at one step removed, knowing that it would never affect him. And now? He could still go back home ...

The car pulled away, and headed back to the expressway. Those large, luminous eyes followed the car lights for as long as they were able. Then he, and the camp, was behind Jack. The world was full of people like that man, for whom there was no *back* to go. And there wasn't anything anyone could do about it any more. Jack leaned into the upholstery and lifted the phone.

Croesos: I'm okay.

TBone: Halle-fucking-lujah.

History: The polícia know you're missing. I'm guessing ten minutes for them to find car#1. Then they'll start looking for car#2.

WhitetailedDeer: Obvious place to throw some chaff is the A6/ A32 interchange. Stand by.

Croesos: What's the house doing?

TBone: I lost my feed the moment I flashed my ports. You tell us.

Croesos: Mesman will try and work out where I'm going. She'll know it's me who injected the code. Maybe P isn't the best place.

History: P is the only place you can get to.

Croesos: She'll work it out.

History: I will get you on that rocket.

Croesos: kthx

WhitetailDeer: You got 20 before we do some more gymnastics.

TBone: You should probably eat and drink something.

Croesos: yes mam.

Jack dragged his bag over to him and opened it up, rummaging for a bottle of sports drink and a foil-wrapped chew bar. The drink was blue. He had no idea why. He swigged half of it, and demolished the bar: there was a picture of an astronaut on the side of the wrapper, along with 'Mars approved' in ten different languages. So there was that. He brushed the crumbs from his lips and pushed the empty, sticky wrapper into the drinks holder. TBone had been right. He did feel better.

The car made a broad left loop at an interchange, and he could see lights off to one side. A town. Half dark. If anyone knew how to keep the sea back, it was his people, the Dutch, but even they were losing more than they were winning. Breach, repair, pump. The cycle went on, faster and faster. The water boards were at breaking point. Plans that had been made to cover a sea-level rise of fifty centimetres had to routinely cope with twice that. Storm surges were now guaranteed to top the barriers. He was looking out at the past: it couldn't possibly stay like this for much longer, even here.

Had all this influenced his proposed destination? Yes, it had. While he rationalised it as not being able to escape his family's reach anywhere on Earth, not being anywhere on Earth right now was more appealing than somewhere hidden on it.

TBone: Time we swapped servers. See you on the other side.
TBone: [has left the chat]
History: [has left the chat]
WhitetailDeer: Delivery at my door. brb.
WhitetailDeer: dfdffghlhaytdsgf
Croesos: [you have left the chat]

Jack stared at the screen, and mouthed a single word, still very careful not to voice anything that the car might hear. He dabbed at the icons, and moments later was in another, equally private chat room. The others were already there, logged on, avatars glowing. But not WhitetailDeer. He waited, and waited. Nothing.

Croesos: I think we lost WTD.
Croesos: He had a delivery just as you all logged off. brb then asdfghjkl.

TBone: Fuck. Was it this? Or was it some other shit he was pulling?

Croesos: idk

TBone: We have to assume WTD is down, and we're being traced. Fuck.

TBone: server #3 now

History: [has left the chat]

Croesos: [you have left the chat]

WhitetailDeer was his transport guy. And there was a car waiting for him at the next junction. If he didn't pick it up, he was stuck with this one. No, he was stuck *in* this one. He had no idea where it was actually heading, and whether a third car was waiting for him at all. And without WhitetailDeer to tell him how to make the exchange, it wasn't going to happen. He swapped servers.

Croesos: What do I do?

TBone: Don't panic.

History: I'll take over from WTD.

History: I mean, I'm a 15yo kid in Rio, but how hard can this be?

History: You want a car at the cloverleaf north of Heerenveen? That right?

Croesos: Yes.

Croesos: If this one stops.

TBone: History. Tell me you're secure.

History: I'm in a chip shop in Zona Norte. It's public, so, I guess?

TBone: You should move. Get the car done and shift locale. You've got 12 minutes.

History: I'm gonna need all of them.

Croesos: What do we do about WhitetailDeer?

TBone: He's gone. If this is your Mesman, then I'm ready for her. I got iron.

TBone: @History? You sure you got this?

History: Yeah. But don't @ me. This isn't going to be pretty, but it'll work.

Jack felt his heart flutter, and he took a series of deep breaths. Breath in. Hold. Exhale. It wasn't supposed to happen like this. WhitetailDeer was someone who he'd known on and off for years, and knew absolutely nothing about, age, sex or location. He – on the assumption WhitetailDeer was a he – kept his private life private, and always seemed willing to help a soul out with tech advice or a little light hacking. That's why Jack had approached him, but WhitetailDeer's motivation in all this was opaque.

And now, on the face of it, he'd gone. Maybe the knock at WhitetailDeer's door and his sudden offlining was the result of some other shady good turn he'd offered: that was the best spin Jack could put on it. If it was Mesman – it'd be a hired hit, not her – then … Jack had just killed one of his friends. He put his hands to his face and dragged his fingers down his cheeks. This wasn't the plan any more.

Whatever arrangements had been made for transporting Jack to P were void. History was on it now. A fifteen-year-old kid was on it. Even if they weren't fifteen and living in Rio, then the situation was still dire enough to make his pulse race and his skin feel slick with sweat. Jack looked behind him, and saw only headlights and the red dots of scanning lasers grazing the road surface. No polícia yet.

History: Okay. @Croesos I need you to override whatever WTD gave as the destination.

History: New postcode is 8448EA.

History: Do it now or you'll miss your exit.

Croesos: How do I enter it?

Croesos: I've never done this before.

TBone: Jesus fuck, C. k. Normally voice command, but don't

be tempted. Should be a screen halfway across the dash,
showing your current loc. Tap it.
TBone: That'll bring the menu up.

Jack tapped the dull screen, and it grew instantly brighter. A
little car-shaped sprite was heading down a yellow road, and
below it was a range of options. One was Destination, so he
dabbed at that. A touchscreen keyboard popped up, and he
transcribed the numbers and letters History had given him
into the dialogue box. He pressed Enter, and the address was
repeated to him.

Croesos: A McDs?
History: There's a car pool in the lot.
Croesos: Do I confirm?
History: Confirm. Now.

Jack hit Confirm, and the car immediately started tracking right,
off the expressway. He'd cut it fine. He was on the downslope,
then on a road that ran parallel to the elevated section. Across a
river, and then round in an arc. The lights of the town burned
bright, and in the distance, the upraised yellow arches beckoned
to him. He repacked and refastened his rucksack, and looked at
his phone for the next set of instructions.

3

Sea level continues its centuries-long slow rise – about a foot a
century – with no sign of recent acceleration.

M. Ridley and B. Peiser, 'Your Complete Guide to the Climate
Debate', *Wall Street Journal*, 2015

Jack half-expected a welcoming committee in front of the sur-
prisingly modest but functional passenger terminal. But there
was nothing apart from the illuminated sign 'Peenemünde
Spaceport'. He quickly scanned the rows of waiting cars, but all
of them seemed to be high-end sedans, potentially armoured,
possibly even armed. Mesman could already be here. She could
be half a continent away, chasing a shadow. The car pulled into
a bay in front of the broad plaza festooned with flagpoles, and
his hand hesitated over his bag. Then his fist closed on the
strap, and he left the car with it slung over one shoulder.

Croesos: Out of the car.
History: I'll send it somewhere else. Even if it won't make any
    difference now.

He glanced behind him. There were another couple of vehicles,
lights bright, coming down the access road. With mandatory
self-driving, it was impossible to gauge anything from how they
were handling: no erratic turns, screeching wheels or excessive
speeding. Probably just people coming to catch the same flight
as him. He turned away and tracked diagonally to the leftmost

set of doors, trying not to run and draw attention to himself, trying not to freeze with anxiety.

He typed with his thumb, keeping one eye on the glass front of the building he was about to walk into.

Croesos: In the terminal.

The door didn't open for him. He frowned at it, before realising it wasn't automatic and that he needed to open it himself. He heaved it aside, felt the sudden change in temperature as cool air billowed out, and he was in. He sent his message and started forward, keeping the wall on his left. The departure hall looked like the atrium in an average office block. Pillars. Squeaky lino. Ceiling tiles. Shuttered concession stands. He looked again at the time, and only then registered that it was half past three in the morning.

He felt exposed. So very exposed. He started to walk along the line of pillars, quickly in the open space, more slowly when hidden. His mouth was dry, and his stomach had knotted. Breathe. Breathe. He was going to have to cross part of the main concourse to get to the red line. But he could at least see the red line, a fat stripe across the floor, the width of the security check. Regular police, suited and booted, machine guns cradled in their arms, barrels pointing at the ground, ambled from one side of the atrium to the other. No one was paying him any attention.

His phone buzzed in his hand.

History: I could have stolen all your money.
History: That amount would be life-changing for me and my fam.
History: And there'd be nothing you could do about it.
History: Here's your ticket. Have a good flight.
History: See you on the other side.

When he looked up again, a hand was already flat against his chest. He followed the sleeve to the shoulder to the neck. The face. Fenna Mesman. Her expression was a mixture of admiration – that he'd got quite so far – and sadness at his betrayal. He was leaning against her hand, and she was propping him up. Two suited men stepped out from behind a pillar and stood a little way back from them. Noises off indicated that he was now completely surrounded.

'Jaap,' she said. She inclined her head ever so slightly. 'Are you ready to come home now?'

Jack finally managed to roll back on his heels. The presence behind him solidified. He could smell cheap cologne, and possibly mint. He glanced at his phone again: *here's your ticket*. He could see the red line, barely twenty metres away. The two police officers were ambling back again. He didn't trust himself to say anything. He clenched his jaw. The men she'd brought with her were really quite big, but it was her he was terrified of.

There wasn't any point in him asking how. She knew him. She knew him inside and out, better than he knew himself. He'd been stupid to believe he could ever get away from her, and now he never would. She knew he'd come here, the nearest continental spaceport, and she'd been waiting for him to show for hours. All History's trickery with sending cars here, there and everywhere, tracing routes across countries to the north and south and east, had been for nothing. She'd been here all along, sitting patiently in that compact, legs-tucked way she had, barely moving, with her gaze on the drop-off point outside. Waiting for his inevitable appearance.

More than that, she'd let him think he could succeed. She'd held back until the last possible moment so that his rising hope was so totally crushed, he'd never try anything like this ever again. The longer the fall, the harder the impact. Clever Jack, but cleverer Mesman.

She was standing between him and the red line. She always would. Whichever way he turned, she would be there. She

23

would either go ahead of him, if it was permitted, or bar his way if it was not. And this? This mad, decade-in-the-planning dream? He was not allowed it, so now he had to go home and suffer whatever indignities his parents wanted to inflict on him. Soft, gentle, disapproving punishments, to show that they understood his desire for free will and personal autonomy, while still managing to convey the sense that they were utterly unwilling to give him either. Jaap van der Veerden needed to be safe, and he could only be safe if he followed instructions. If he followed the treatments. If he became transhuman, like they were.

'Jaap,' she asked again. 'I think we should go to the flier. We can talk there, if you want, but this situation is making me nervous. I don't like that.'

When the world wasn't as Mesman wanted it, the world had to change. Seeing Mesman in her full, unrestrained glory was like watching the Angel of the Lord. Beautiful. Terrible. Never forgotten. Her nervousness wasn't the issue, but the means she used to stop feeling nervous. The Van der Veerdens employed her for precisely that reality-shifting ability that seemed to know no limit.

Jack was beaten. He had lost before he'd started. He and his little crew, one down already, and he ought to save the rest of them in case sometime between now and eternity Mesman decided to pay either of them a visit. He logged out of the server and closed the app. The already encrypted data would be inaccessible now. He lowered the phone, and he realised she'd let him do that. She didn't care about the little people any more, only that they'd failed.

He looked towards the red line, and wondered under what circumstances he could have made it across. His gaze in-advertently brushed across one of the police officers. Her eyes momentarily narrowed, and he could see her weighing up the scene with professional care. She would have seen him, this tall, pale young man, in the middle of taller, broader, well-dressed

24

guards, and in front, a slim white woman with a blonde, bob-bing ponytail.

She continued to look. Jack felt himself flush afresh with cold sweat. He shook his head so slightly that it was barely a movement at all. She looked … nice. Normal. Plain. Decent. The body armour and the helmet seemed to wear her, rather than the other way around. Her colleague was an older, greyer, jowly *heeren*. He'd seen it all before, but she hadn't.

'Jaap,' said Mesman for a third time. His attention snapped back to her. 'We're going to go now. I'll take you to the flier. You can call your parents from there.' She nodded to the men behind Jack, and one of them took his bag, just slipped it off his shoulder and arm and held it by its strap. The other rested his hand at Jack's elbow and nudged him to indicate the direction of travel. Back to the doors. Back outside. There'd be a car waiting to take them to a helipad, one of many in the spaceport complex, and they'd be in the flier and off back to Flevoland in a matter of minutes.

No fuss, no complaints. He'd been caught, and he had to pay the price.

'*Mein herr?*'

Mesman effortlessly slipped into German. She didn't even bother to turn around. 'We're just leaving. Have a good night, officer.'

The hand at Jack's elbow tightened slightly, and began to steer him around.

'Wait, please.'

The female police officer approached them, and the male hung back. His gun hadn't moved from its at-ease position, but it was evident that his attitude had shifted. The security detail around Jack moved closer to him, hemming him in, leaving Mesman to do the talking. The two women sized each other up.

'Can someone explain what's going on here?'

Mesman was used to dealing with local law enforcement. She

was just as used to having them defer to her. She glanced over her shoulder, gave a little nod and Jack found himself being frog-marched away. Mesman would give her reasons, but there was no need for her plan to be interrupted in any way.

'Halt.'

Another two policemen stepped around a pillar. They were out of breath, and they weren't as particular as the first pair as to where they pointed their guns. The security men in front did stop, but one of them inadvisedly touched his jacket lapel with the fingers of his right hand. He found himself staring down a rifle barrel. He froze.

'Sir? Yes, you, young man. Step out here, please.'

Jack didn't move for a moment, cocooned between muscle and soft fabric. Then he pushed his way through and stood outside of the tableau. Another two paramilitary police were trotting across the atrium, and they were being followed by two civilians in suits. He looked down at his phone. He could still see the words burned there, even though he'd terminated the app: *see you on the other side.*

He had a ticket. He had an actual ticket. He wasn't a criminal. There was no reason for him to be detained. But once the suits got here, he'd be ushered into an office, and when they found out who he was, he'd never be allowed over the line. He realised that these cops, these ordinary bored cops were his only hope.

'They're trying to stop me from boarding my flight,' said Jack into the silence. 'I have a valid ticket, here.'

He swiped the screen on his phone and showed the police officers the glow of the e-ticket. He waited. He felt sick. He looked at the back of his trembling hand in case he caught sight of Mesman. If he did, he'd be undone. He'd fold. He knew it, and she knew it too. He could feel her willing him to just look at her, the comforting certainty that she represented, the going home, the endless security behind high walls, the endless life.

'Then go,' said the officer. 'Go.'

Mesman said, started to say, 'You need to leave this to me,' but got only part of the way through before she found herself interrupted. That some *smeris* would challenge her was unthinkable, but Jack scooped up the last of his courage from where it lay haemorrhaging and started for the line on the floor.

Mesman tried to intercept him, and the officer deliberately body-checked her. Jack swerved around them, kept walking. He was in danger of cracking the case on his phone, he was gripping it so tightly. There was the line. There it was, ahead of him. Then he was over it. The security screen was next. He looked up at the overhead cameras, and saw himself reflected back a dozen times. He looked small and uncertain.

He paused, then started down the tunnel packed with scanners. He had nothing but what he stood up in and the phone. That was it. Whatever was happening behind him was now, literally, behind him.

Mesman called after him: 'Jaap, we'll get you back. Don't worry. We'll get you back.'

It was a promise. It was a threat. They would try very hard. This wasn't the end of it. This was just the beginning.

4

It has been 30 years since the alarm bell was sounded for man-made global warming caused by modern industrial society. And predictions made on that day – and ever since – continue to be falsified in the real world.

R. L. Bradley Jr, *Climate Alarm: Failed Prognostications*, Institute for Energy Research, 2018

Jack sat hunched over a coffee that someone had poured him – a cardboard cup, and the whitener had never so much as seen a cow. Given the paper cost of his ticket, one of those little biscuits would have been nice. But the coffee was decent enough, and its aroma reminded him that, despite everything, he was still alive and in one piece.

He felt battered, even though no one had laid a rough hand on him, and all he'd done was sit in a series of cars while other people did the hard work. He kept on thinking about WhitetailDeer. Maybe some tech news aggregator would push something about a notorious hacker arrested or killed, at some point in the next twenty-four hours, but most likely his disappearance would go unremarked and, as for family, perhaps he, TBone and History had been it.

They were there at the last. He hadn't been alone. That had to count for something.

Jack raised his head again. As had so often happened since he'd emerged from the other end of the security screen, he looked up to find two people talking to each other, but stealing glances at him. He hadn't anticipated just how often he would be recognised – his billionaire family weren't one of those billionaire families. Pap and Mam paid good money to someone whose sole job was to spike stories about them. They were probably working overtime right now, but he guessed things would be leaky for a while.

It would calm down. He wasn't the first billionaire to head into space, and it wasn't as if the money was even his. It just followed him around like a burr, and he'd been able to use it, within limits.

That money had just become a finite resource. He'd have to budget. He didn't know how to do that. He didn't know the cost of anything. No, that wasn't true: he'd never had to care about the cost of anything, because everything – literally everything, every service, every object, every piece of land, every body – had been within his grasp. He'd squirrelled away what he'd thought of as plenty, and he wasn't going to need much of it anyway. The second part of his plan would see to that.

'Mr Van der Veerden?'

Unseen, a man had appeared at his shoulder.

'Yes.' Jack blinked. 'That's me.'

'My name is Rahim. I'm responsible for making sure you have everything you need, and to take you through flight prep.'

'Flight ... prep?'

'Preparation. Check your documentation. Pre-flight medical. Briefing. Emergency drills. Answer your questions. Flight prep.'

'You're not here to say I can't fly?'

Rahim frowned as if he'd never heard of the name Van der Veerden. 'No, sir?'

'Oh.'

'The pilot is bringing take-off forward. There's a deep depression developing east of the Hebrides, and as well as a storm surge, winds are forecast to be over our usual operating parameters, so if you'll follow me, please, we'll do what's required.'

Jack stood, then bent back down for his phone and his coffee.

'Do you have any luggage, Mr Van der Veerden?'

Jack looked round for his rucksack, and remembered it had been taken off him. 'No. Sorry.'

'No need to apologise, sir. I appreciate that every kilo is costed.'

'It's not that I can't afford the rates. I ... meant to have luggage, but it, I. Lost it.' He shrugged, mindful not to spill his drink. 'It's a long story.'

'One that will, I'm afraid, have to wait. Please, sir?' Rahim gave a half bow and indicated the direction that they needed to go. Once in the small office cubicle, the attendant slipped behind the entirely functional desk and pushed an eye scanner across towards Jack. Jack put what he was holding down, and lifted the scanner to his face: left eye, right eye.

There was some legal boilerplate to sign, which he did without reading it. Rahim took the tablet from Jack, and checked the forms.

'Thank you. I have confirmed your identity, and your fitness to fly. I do have an open police report here, filed yesterday at 21:46, indicating that you are a missing person.' Rahim put the tablet down on the desk. 'Can you explain this report? You're clearly not missing any more.'

Jack ran his finger down his nose, and decided to drink the rest of his coffee before answering.

'If I could have hidden who I was, I would have done. But I, we, concluded that if I tried to use a false identity to travel, my parents would tell you and I would be arrested before I left the ground. I've done nothing illegal. I'm just running away from home.'

'You're,' Rahim glanced at the screen, 'twenty-three.'

'Don't judge me.'

Rahim lifted a finger. 'You're ... okay. Mr Van der Veerden, can you at least confirm that you paid for your ticket out of funds that are either your own or that you lawfully control?'

'Yes,' said Jack.

The man did things to the tablet, tap-tap-tap. 'You are on the manifest.'

'Thank you,' he said. 'For not making a fuss.'

'You're going into space. Fuss is the last thing we want. Any questions?' asked Rahim. 'Anything at all?'

'Just one,' said Jack. 'Which point is the point of no return? I mean, if the pilot was ordered to return here, or somewhere else, without going to the transfer station.'

Rahim pursed his lips. 'You want to know when you're safe.'

'Yes.'

'Part of the concept of the space plane is that it's safer. There are more exits from any given failure mode throughout the flight profile. In a rocket, there are very few. Even after we finish the boost phase, the pilot can just push the stick forward and our trajectory becomes ballistic. You're not safe until you reach the transfer station. However, if the pilot aborts for any non-technical reason, the penalties on the company would be ruinous. Even if you puke your guts up and your eardrums explode, that's not enough reason for us to turn around. You know that passengers—'

'Are an afterthought, sure.'

'Not an afterthought. Economically secondary to our main business. You'll be in a person-rated capsule, but that's only a small part of the lifting body. We make far more money taking material into orbit than we do taking people.'

'I don't think you quite realise just how rich my family is.'

Rahim seemed irritated at the implication. 'I don't think you quite realise that no one is going to abort the flight just because you're on it. Some of these parts are just-in-time deliveries. In space terms, that means if they don't get where they need to go, people will die, and that would swallow up the company, everything it owns and more. Once we taxi down the runway, unless part of the plane falls off, we go.'

'Okay. That's good to know.'

'I know you're in some kind of trouble. That really isn't my problem. But it's you who's our customer: the plane will get you where you want to go. You need to change into your flightsuit and we can carry out the final checks.' Rahim's expression softened. 'You don't have a flightsuit. We'll find you one.'

'Do you know what happened out in the departure lounge? To my … bodyguard?'

'If you want, I can find out for you. I might be able to get a message to him if they're still landside.'

'Her. I, no. I don't want that. I just wondered if you knew what had happened afterwards.'

'I've been busy back here. Again, I can try and find someone who does know.'

'Judging by the number of people looking at me and whispering behind their hands, you won't have to search for too long. I suppose I could have asked them myself.' Jack shifted in his seat. 'I'm not sure if I want to know. Perhaps that's your answer. Sorry, I'm not used to this level of—'

'Independence?'

Jack played with his empty cup, then put it down. 'I have a job lined up. On the Moon.'

'Good. Have you or they arranged a transfer shuttle from the transfer station?'

'I … no. They don't know when I'm coming. I was going to contact them when I was—'

'Safe? Okay. You realise that the transfer station is exactly that? Just a transfer point.'

'Yes. They can look after me for a few hours, though. Until we get the shuttle sorted. I didn't know it was going to be today. It'll be fine. It's just a temporary job – I've trained to be a navigator, so I'll move on to something more suitable once I'm there.'

Rahim blinked, tapped at the tablet, then pushed his chair back. 'It's time I got you on board.'

They left the small office, and stopped by a store cupboard

for a flightsuit. It was dark blue, with the company logo. Jack held it up against himself and decided it would do for now. He changed in a toilet cubicle, with Rahim tapping his foot on the tiles outside.

'Where are you from, Rahim?'

'Here. Hamburg.'

'No, I mean ...'

'Before that? I was born in Hamburg. I'm German.' He sighed. 'My parents came from Syria in the first part of the century, they married here, they had me and my brother and my sisters here, I went to school here. I watched the walls go up and everything go to hell, and I am so grateful I'm not still in the Middle East that I thank God for the war that had killed millions and forced us from our homeland, because it means I'm not there now. Mr Van der Veerden—'

'Jack.'

'Mr Van der Veerden. I'm a child of refugees. I'm ten years older than you. Those are the least of our differences. Our lives have run in parallel. We have nothing in common. When you are gone, flown off to your first space job, I want to still be here, doing mine. I need to put you on the plane, or I will lose that job, and my home, and my family will become destitute. So please hurry.'

Jack finished dressing in silence, and when he opened the cubicle door again, Rahim was holding open a clear plastic bag waste bag. Jack jammed his clothes into it, and his phone, and was allowed to tie up the top and carry it the rest of the way to the covered gantry.

'I ...' he started.

'I need to stow your luggage and strap you in, Mr Van der Veerden.' Rahim directed Jack through the circular door – not an airlock, but a heavy, single disc of composite that opened inwards.

Jack ducked under the upper rim, and simultaneously stepped over the lower one. There were three chairs bolted to the floor, one behind the other on the midline, even though there were anchor points for half a dozen. The front two were already occupied, so he took the last in line. There were no windows in the passenger compartment, because windows were a weak point and an engineering luxury. He had a screen on the bulkhead ahead of him.

Rahim had adjusted Jack's seat – lengthening the back, positioning the headrest and the angle, the feet stirrups, every-thing – and fixed him in with a five-point harness. He also told him how to punch out of it, because no one at the other end was going to do it for him. Rahim was brisk, professional and courteous throughout. Jack thought that maybe, just maybe, he might have been a little more gentle in ratcheting up the harness straps, but he didn't want to float around the cabin, and a little discomfort now was worth the opportunity to do something this expansively grand under his own initiative.

He wanted to tell TBone and History he was on his way. That no one had stopped him. But he'd have to wait: he'd try and find them online in their usual haunts when he'd arrived on the Moon and settled in.

The two other passengers ignored him, and each other. They didn't talk at all. Perhaps they were as restricted in their move-ment as he was. Perhaps they were conscious that they were just cargo, and the important business lay both fore and aft of the pressurised cabin. Perhaps they were mentally preparing themselves for launch. Perhaps they were terrified.

The bulkhead screen flickered, and showed a windy runway overlooking the Baltic Sea, from the viewpoint of just behind and above the pilot. Every so often an arm came into view, from both the left and the right – the co-pilot or the flight engineer or both – to flick switches on the console on the cockpit ceiling. It looked compact, almost cramped. Even the forward-facing windows were small. Everything was in reach.

The runway started to move, the lights either side and set into the ground scrolling by. The noise in the cabin barely altered, but the vibrations increased, with the occasional bump as they rolled over a joint in the concrete. Low buildings slunk past, and he wondered if Mesman was still at the spaceport, watching the plane taxi to the threshold. Making sure that he actually left, so she could report back to his parents, that yes, the disobedient wretch has slipped the surly bonds of Earth to touch the face of God.

He wondered how much pressure had been brought to bear on the space plane company. How many messages had been left on his email and social media accounts. How far the news had got, despite his parents' best efforts.

The runway was ahead of them, and they rolled to a stop. The intercom – tinny and indistinct, and almost certainly an afterthought – snapped static.

'Final checks. Cleared for take-off.'

The runway blurred, then the familiar surge of acceleration pushed him back into the upholstery.

'Airspeed. Rotate.'

The nose came up, and the screen showed nothing but a white haze with a supporting strut bisecting the view. The thrust increased, and the nose stayed firmly up. The airframe shook and rattled and Jack's hands clenched on the arm-rests. This, this wasn't normal. In an airliner, the seat-belt light would already be out and the stewards would be moving through the cabin. Here, it was relentless. He was almost lying on his back, and the engines were still rising through the notes. The gross vibrations got worse, and then they were through the cloud layer. Bright sunlight struck the plane and everything ahead was blue sky and wisps of ice-clouds at the very top of the atmosphere.

Jack forced his hands to relax, and looked at the backs of the heads of the other passengers. Astronauts. The other astronauts. He should really start thinking about them that way, about himself that way too. A man, probably, in front of him, perfectly still, not moving, and beyond him a woman if he was only judging by the hair. She appeared to be inexplicably asleep – her head was lolling at the least. Asleep, or sedated. Perhaps she really hated flying, and this was the only way she could travel.

But to be able to sleep through this? The flight was now extraordinary and terrifying. They ploughed on, up and up, banking but always the same way, describing a perfectly drawn spiral as they ascended. The engines were a high-pitched throbbing whine. The sky was getting darker.

The horizon rose on the screen, white below, azure above. The pilot reached up to flick some more switches.

'Altitude twenty-four point eight kilometres. Airspeed eighteen hundred fifty-two metres per second. Switching to closed-cycle engines. On my mark. Three, two, one. Mark.'

The engine noise dipped a whole octave, and a weight settled on Jack's chest. The horizon swung out of sight again, and the sky above was turning from zenith blue to black. He hauled in air, and tensed his muscles to keep his blood pressure up. He knew how fast the plane had to go, and how long this phase was going to last for, but accepting that was what was happening was impossible.

The weight on him receded, but he was still almost lying down. Then a curious sensation began to steal over him. As if he was falling. His hands instinctively gripped the arm-rests again, and he scrunched his toes, as if that would help him to hold on. He was on the verge of panic, his breathing uncontrollable, his skin flushed and sweating.

The plane was moving from a ballistic trajectory to an orbital one. He was becoming weightless. His sight-lines were telling him he was still sitting down. His inner ear was telling him something completely different. His stomach contracted, and he dry-swallowed against the acid-tasting wind. Outside, as viewed on the screen, was perfectly black. The only lights came from the instrumentation.

'Orbital insertion complete. Altitude one one zero kilometres. Manoeuvring for apoapsis burn.'

And that was it. He was in space. He'd travelled seven times that distance in the last day, and yet it was only the last hundred kilometres that was significant. The shadows on the screen moved, and barely filtered sunlight scoured the cockpit as the plane rotated about its axis. Weight returned for a handful of seconds, then it dissipated again. He was ready for it this time, and his querulous stomach held its peace.

The flight had been perfect. No hitches, no problems. Nothing had fallen off. He was in space and there was no one else he could blame for this. This had been his idea, his plan, his execution, and now it was real. He was on his own. What happened next was up to him, dependent on his ability and his work ethic. It was a hundred k straight down and there was no safety net. He felt dizzy again at the thought, and waited out the sensation, swallowing and holding his breath.

He told himself he had it covered, that he wouldn't have left Earth if he didn't have something to leave Earth for: that it was all very well running away, but it was better by far to run towards something.

A white dot appeared on the screen. It looked tiny. It was tiny, barely two tennis courts across. A private transfer station, run partly by the space plane company, partly by one of the big Moon corporations as part of its infrastructure network. A drum of a satellite, its solar panels becoming more evident as the dot resolved: long spars with flat-black panels that continually turned towards the Sun.

It grew larger and larger, a bright white disc, surface features of grabs, aerials, dishes, panels and hatches all visible. It slid out of view as the plane rotated. He felt himself tugged this way and that, subtle pushes and nudges as the airlocks meshed. The fuselage shuddered, and all was finally still. No one else was unlocking their harness, so Jack didn't either.

'ESTA-5 docking seal confirmed. Equalisation of pressure.'

5

There is a high degree of uncertainty over the timing and magnitude of the potential impacts that man-made emissions of greenhouse gases have on climate.

Exxon Mobil advert, *New York Times*, 1997

From somewhere behind him came a sound like a whale blowing. He should have been ready for it, but he still jumped. As the residual hiss faded away, the woman in the front row twisted her harness catch, and reached up behind her for the handles behind the headrest. She executed a backflip, and planted it perfectly on the floor. Except it wasn't the floor any more. Up and down had ceased to mean anything.

The circular hatch they'd entered through unsealed itself and hinged inwards. There was no ladder, because there was no gravity. The woman, clearly experienced in zero-g manoeuvres, pushed herself gently towards the hatch. Her hair was a halo, and she seemed to fly so gracefully. She caught the lip of the hatch, and pulled herself through using only her arms.

The man ahead of Jack unbuckled too, and swung himself around, holding onto the arm-rest. He looked at Jack, perhaps wondering what this kid in a borrowed flightsuit was doing in a spaceship. Perhaps he was wondering why Jack was having so much trouble with his harness.

'Jaap van der Veerden?'

And perhaps he recognised him after all. 'Uh, yes.'

The man unzipped the front of his coal-black flightsuit and slid out a business card: Park Min-gyu, Attorney-at-law.

'You're intending to take a shuttle to the Moon, to start work with Selenothon, in the Peary crater?'

'Yes?'

Park's mouth formed a tight-lipped line. 'They filed for bankruptcy at midnight. I'm here to wind them up and inventory the assets.'

Jack stopped trying to remember what Rahim had told him about the buckle, and looked up.

'What?'

'They've gone. One of the big corporations will pick up the infrastructure and some of the personnel, and the rest will have to float home.'

'They've gone,' echoed Jack.

Oh, he knew how. He didn't have to ask. Selenothon had a solid prospectus and employees and a habitat at the north pole of the Moon. But compared to VdV Holdings? He should have seen this coming.

He twisted his buckle once more, and as the parts fell away, he found himself drifting up from his seat. He wasn't sure that he liked that, and hung onto the loose straps as they writhed around him. 'I need to make some calls.'

'Whatever you feel you need to do.' Park let go of his arm-rest and tapped at the floor. He rose slowly to the hatch, where he grabbed on. But he didn't slip through completely. He inverted himself and slid his legs out of sight, leaving only his head and shoulders visible. 'I don't work for your parents directly, so here's some pro bono advice: just stay on board, and the plane will take you back to Peenemünde.'

No. No. This wasn't going to happen. He could still make those calls. He was in space. He could live at the transfer station for a while. Or the Moon. They had hotels on the Moon. He could go and stay there. Possibly. He'd need to see how expensive they were. He needed to find a job up here, from someone

39

willing to resist the Van der Veerden fortune. He wasn't just some spoiled little rich brat having a tantrum. He was an adult human being who was within touching distance of his hopes and his dreams, and he was never going to be in this position ever again.

'Okay,' said Jack. 'Thank you for your advice. I'm going to try and make this work. I don't know whether I can, but I can't go home. Not now, not like this.'

'No charge,' said Park. 'But I have to go.' He hesitated for a moment longer, before ducking away. 'Good luck.'

Jack realised that he couldn't stay on the space plane any longer. He didn't know how long the turnaround time was, but he was guessing that it wouldn't be substantial. Shipping companies got paid by how quickly they could get their goods from one port to another. The economics of it only worked by spending as little time as possible dockside. He knew that. That was his family business.

He let go gingerly, and nudged himself towards the exit hatch. His pace was glacial, but once he'd lost contact with anything solid, there was no way to correct either speed or direction. That, in itself, was a valuable lesson. He stretched out his hand for the grab rail, caught it well enough, and didn't know how to counteract his momentum. He ended sprawled across the ceiling, but fortunately, no one seemed to be watching. He pulled himself through into the clinical white interior of the transfer station.

A dark-skinned woman in a StarLift jumpsuit and beanie hung by her ankles from a cross-connecting corridor. She was called Kirui, according to the flash on her top pocket.

'You're Jaap van der Veerden?'

More confident this time. 'Yes. I am.'

'You know you've got a problem, right?'

'Yes, yes, I know. Mr Park was just explaining.'

'Park is expert. I'd pay attention to him.'

'I need to call some people, get this situation sorted out.'

The woman laughed at him. 'Selenothon has gone. All assets seized, all tickets void. Do you have credit?'

'I have credit.' Less than he had, but still a substantial amount. 'Sorry, who are you?'

'The other person who has to make some calls. The people who own this can? They also own the air you're breathing, and that's a consumable you have to pay for. Water, food, watts, everything has a cost.' Kirui jackknifed to orientate herself in the same plane as Jack. 'There are no passengers in space, and for sure, no room for freeloaders.'

'I have credit,' reiterated Jack. 'But just as a theoretical question, what—'

'You go out the airlock. Bear that in mind when you choose who to call.' Kirui kicked off and travelled back up the corridor she'd emerged from.

In the absence of any other instructions, Jack clumsily moved along until he could see up the tube. Kirui's legs were just disappearing out of view. He touched off and drifted after her. His heart seemed to be fluttering, and he realised that this was what panic felt like. No one was going to throw him out of the airlock. He needed to stay calm.

She showed him the terminal from which he could make his calls, a keyboard and a monitor bolted to a side wall. He expected live video and a headset at the very least, and she just snorted at his naivety and ignorance.

'That's not how it works. That's not how it can work. Lag is everywhere, so we do it with text. You'll need to sign up to the network. If you're not using a corporate or government account, it'll cost, so I hope you remember your bank details.'

'Can you not just log me in as you?'

'No. I don't want to find myself floating home.' She fixed him with her unflinching gaze. 'And no one else does either, so don't ask them. You pay. That's it. The company will work out how much it'll cost you to be here by the hour, and you'll pay that too. Or you go home. Which will also cost you. No favours. No nothing. Got that?'

'I understand.'

'I don't think you do. I'm sorry that your job has evaporated, but there's nothing I can do about that. I have to run this can, and currently, your CO_2 is fouling up the filters.'

Jack took a deep breath of someone else's air. 'Let me just sort this out. If I talk to StarLift and pay them for what I'm using while I'm here, will that get you off my back?'

Kirui gave a conciliatory shrug. 'Not my call. I still want you out of here as soon as. This isn't a hotel.'

He knew when to be assertive, and when to be diplomatic. 'I know, and I'm grateful for your concession. I'll be out of the way just as soon as I can arrange an alternative place to be. Which might be a hotel.' The terminal came with a fold-out bar he could hook against his back while he typed. 'Can I get regular Earth internet too?'

'Data transfer costs apply,' she said, then finally relented. 'Yes, you can. It's all pretty straightforward. Look, if you can square things up with the company, you can stay, as long as you don't get in my crew's way. This is a transit point: sometimes people have to wait here, a day, a couple of days, for their shuttle to come over. That's okay. But we all know it's temporary. I don't know why you're here, and why you won't just do the sensible thing and turn around now you know there's nothing here for you.' She reached over his shoulder and tapped the screen on. 'Do what you do. Just realise if something goes wrong on board, I'll be too busy saving myself to save you.'

He started typing. He was there a while. Negotiating a price per hour with StarLift was the only easy part – they told him how much it would cost, and he agreed to it.

Eventually, he did the only thing left to him.

Croesos: I'm here. I'm in space. That's the good news.
TBone: Do I want to know?

Croesos: My parents took out Selenothon. I don't know how they found out I'd hit Dimakos up for a job. Nothing ever went in writing. No e-trail.

TBone: C, I don't know how to put this but.

TBone: Dude was only your friend because you stood to inherit a mountain of money.

TBone: If your olds are serious about this transhuman shit, that's never going to happen.

TBone: You are never going to take over the company. No point in sucking up to you anymore.

TBone: Your olds are always going to be there. And everyone's just worked out what that means.

Croesos: It gets worse. They've taken out most of my bank accounts.

History: Is that even legal?

TBone: Laws are for little people, my child.

History: What are you left with?

Croesos: Crypto.

History: They can't trash that, can they?

TBone: It might be the one thing bigger than they are. But they can probably force its price down.

Croesos: I just can't believe that after all that hard work, this is what I'm left with. Do they think this will make me love them more?

TBone: The long game, C. They can afford to wait a decade or two for you to come around to their way of seeing things. You can't. When do you run out of cash?

Croesos: I've got a week. Roughly. They're charging me by the hour.

History: Cheaper on the Moon? Being there would mean you could ask people straight up for a job.

Croesos: I've costed it out. There's nowhere I can stay except hotels. I can't afford them. I just can't.

He dragged his fingers through his hair. Jack van der Veerden couldn't afford it. He'd never had to say that before, ever.

Croesos: I'm screwed, right? No one is going to take me on. They'll hear what happened to Selenothon and back away. It's not like taking it down would even have cost them that much.

Croesos: Somewhere south of 500 million.

Croesos: If they sold on the infrastructure and the mining licence, they'd probably make a profit.

History: Cheaper to throw your man D 50mil and he voluntarily winds the company up.

TBone: For a kid, you are evil.

History: Thanks I think.

TBone: What you going to do, C?

Croesos: I'm not giving up.

Croesos: I've got seven days.

Croesos: I'm going to hustle. See if I can find anyone up here who owes me a favour.

TBone: Far be it for me to tell you not to follow your dreams but.

TBone: Reality check: you got skills but zero experience, and your name was your biggest asset. TransH has fucked you. Your parents will still be around into the next century and beyond and they'll torch anyone who helps you now. Maybe not today, maybe not tomorrow. Maybe in ten years time. Or twenty. Their revenge will be served cryogenic.

History: We did what we could, C. We got you out. But this is too big.

TBone: Worst case scenario – you had fun storming the castle, but you didn't get through the front gate.

TBone: You run out of money, and your parents collect you from the spaceport and surgically graft Mesman to your butt.

TBone: You are still alive and worth billions.

Croesos: Something will come up. It has to.

TBone: Okay. I tried. WTD got swatted, btw.

Croesos: Was it this?

TBone: Could have been anything. We'll never find out the truth, but yeah. We know.

Croesos: You guys have to stay safe.

History: They know we can't do anything for you now. You being up there means we *are* safe.

That penetrated Jack's black mood like a needle through his skin.

Croesos: I got to get to work. I'll keep you in the loop.

TBone: [has left the chat]

History: [has left the chat]

Jack logged off and cleared the dialogue. He stared at the screen, at his own reflection in it, listening to the rattle of a loose fan somewhere close by. The lights were too bright, unshaded, and the air had a tang of acid sharpness behind its chill.

Seven days to save his dream, and potentially his friends' lives.

6

Resolved: that we consider proposals to regulate CO_2 and other greenhouse gas emissions based on a maximum acceptable global temperature goal to be very dangerous, since attempts to meet the goal could lead to a succession of mandates of deeper cuts in emissions, which may have no appreciable effect if humans are not the principal cause of global warming, and could lead to major economic hardships on a worldwide scale.

Southern Baptist Convention resolution, 'On Global Warming', 2007

Four days into his frantic job search, he'd come up with nothing. It was as if the entire inner solar system was boycotting him. No, he didn't have an EVA certificate, which would have allowed him to work in a vacuum, or any number of other highly specific qualifications that would have let him operate heavy machinery, refill fuel tanks, service spacesuits, drill, mine, smelt, sinter, weld, even do filthy-dirty hazmat stuff.

And he wasn't a doctor or a dentist, a paramedic or even a plumber, whose services seemed to be inexplicably in demand. Science stuff was done dirtside, as all the experienced spacers called it – he was picking up the lingo from the brief conversations he had with Kirui – and it was technical skills that cut it on the High Frontier.

He'd talked to recruiters, using assumed names, but he guessed they knew who he was by now, and that someone, Mesman probably, had let it be known that the Van der Veerdens' extreme displeasure was going to fall on anyone who offered him work. What he needed was someone who didn't care about that. Someone either richer than his parents, or crazy enough not to care about the consequences.

He had just over three days to find them. Halvorsen, the granite-faced electrician and Kirui's second in command, loomed behind him, and he moved out of the way, drifting off down the corridor towards the sleeping quarters. He was spending a lot of time in his bunk, the other side of the thin curtain, because he was unequivocally not interfering with the normal operations of the space station while he was there. The moment he showed his face, he was risking a confrontation with Kirui, Halvorsen or Petrescu, the third member of the crew, and despite the competition, the least likeable of all.

In his bunk – no more than a slot in the wall, a mummy sleeping bag and some straps to stop himself from floating away – he wondered how ESTA-5 managed to keep working without turning itself into a short, bloody horror movie. The three worked eight-hour shifts, with the handover meetings at start and finish measured in bare minutes, but they were all on call if something specific broke and needed fixing. The contact between them might be minimal, but in that time they appeared to exhibit such levels of sociopathic hatred for each other that any cooperation between them was only ever ruthlessly efficient.

Perhaps that was his answer. That they didn't have to get on, despite being confined in such a small volume: what actually mattered was professionalism. They lived or died together, and that was enough.

Given that dynamic, precisely what was it that he had to offer? He was smart. He had a degree in astronomy and mathematics. He could run calculations in multi-dimensional space and didn't have to look up equations before he used them. He could speak six different languages fluently. He was good with computers and a couple of the usual programming languages.

He was highly socialised, and trained from a very young age to make small talk to his peers and not offend. He was confident. He could bluff competence in things he wasn't good at – that was his defining trait, the defining trait of his whole class.

The realisation was slowly taking hold that out in space, bluffing was absolutely the worst thing he could possibly do. For any company, finding a complete bastard who could nail the job every single time was going to be so much better for everyone than picking an affable muddler who got things wrong. That would kill people, fast.

Even if he were supremely qualified and didn't have the Van der Veerden name, he lacked all experience. He couldn't fake that. He couldn't actually 'do' anything. He'd been relying on Selenothon and a handshake, and now he had neither.

The walls of the station rang. The first time it had happened, Jack had thought they'd been hit by something. He didn't know any of the emergency drills, and he didn't have his own suit. If they'd been punctured, and the hole couldn't be sealed quickly, then, depending on where it was, he'd die. It would have bothered the crew not at all, because they'd be fine. They had spacesuits. Repair the breach, repressurise the hull, check the systems.

There were bulkheads, and they were supposed to automatically close. There were also an unconscionable number of cables and ducts running down the corridors and over the lips of the seals of the airtight doors, rendering their fail-safe status moot.

Part of him was still clinging onto the fact that nothing bad had ever happened to him, because any difficulty evaporated with extreme wealth. 'How much will it cost to make things right for me?' wasn't a question he'd ever had to ask, like the merely rich. All he'd ever had to do was to tell someone to make the problem go away. The cost was immaterial. It didn't matter. And another part of him remembered the few times when people and situations were immune to that. His first and so far only serious girlfriend breaking up with him because she didn't want someone like him. Losing his cousin, Ruben, from what he later found out was an overdose but was to this day strenuously denied. And his grandparents on his father's side. And his favourite uncle, Oom Peter.

Death and heartbreak. The unavoidables. And now, with the right treatments, only heartbreak remained a certainty.

He thought about it some more, enmeshed in his webbing straps, the cold dry air rasping in his throat and chapping his lips, and conversely, making his nose drip. StarLift weren't about to throw him out of the airlock because that wasn't what his parents wanted. But they would force him home. He had seventy-six hours left on the clock. Seventy-six hours to learn the lesson that nowhere was out of reach.

It was a bitter taste in his mouth, but he was absolutely not going to go home until he had exhausted every avenue. There had to be something he could do up here, even if it was just work-for-resources, until he'd picked up some certificates and could start to market himself.

He was having trouble sleeping, because he was so inactive. He was forbidden to use the limited resistance equipment – Kirui had made that quite clear – and there was nowhere else to go except around and around the station, always running the risk of bumping into the duty crew member. There was no reading matter, no music, his phone had died and he didn't have the correct charger for it.

He'd think of something. Something soon.

Against expectations, he dozed, and woke up to a slapping sound on the outside of his bunk. Jack pulled the curtain aside and revealed Petrescu's lumpy features. Zero-g had temporarily given Jack a puffy face, but Petrescu permanently resembled a misshapen potato. Jack tried to redraw the curtain, but the man put his hand in the way, and silently beckoned Jack to follow him.

Unhooking himself and rolling out into the corridor, Jack propelled himself along behind Petrescu's feet. He was still a

49

novice, and he rarely let go of one handhold before targeting another, so made slower progress. Petrescu turned and parked himself next to the extractor fans that continuously whirred, and sometimes clattered, taking the dust and debris and CO_2 out of the air. Their hum filled the whole station, and their absence would spark an immediate response.

Jack caught up, and Petrescu folded his bony fingers around Jack's flightsuit to hold them closer together. They both smelled of antibacterial gel, but Petrescu's scent had an underlay of unwashed stale sweat. The proximity to the fans made it necessary to shout, but it also ensured that their conversation would be secret.

'Dutch boy,' said Petrescu – never Jack, or Jaap, or even Van der Veerden, even though he knew well enough – right into Jack's ear, 'you know we don't want you here. We don't like you here. We get grief for you being here. Yet you don't go home. You don't go home like a smart boy would.'

'You know why.'

'I know why, but I don't understand why. You have all the money you ever need, and it can buy you anything. You want fancy watch, fancy boat, fancy house, fancy woman, fancy man, whatever, then,' and he rubbed his thumb and forefinger together in front of Jack's eyes, 'that's all it takes. Why you want to give up that, I don't understand. You were dropped on your head as a baby?'

'Not that I know of.'

'Okay. So we don't want you here, and you won't go home. So here's what Vasile will do for you to get rid of you. I give you a name of someone. You call them. That's it. That's what I'll do, and then you forget who gave you the name. Deal?'

Jack tried to ease himself away from Petrescu, who maintained his grip on the front of Jack's flightsuit. 'Are you *helping* me?'

'No, no. I'm helping me, and getting you off my station. That you might be persuaded to go is easier for me than

50

smacking you around and forcing you to leave. Or making you float home.'

'This name. This person. He – they – have a job?' Jack's eyes narrowed. 'One that I could do?'

'Talk to him. See what he says. If he likes you, if you can do the job, maybe he hires you. If he says no, you get in that plane and go home. No argument, no fighting. Just go.'

'How do I know this isn't another set-up?'

Petrescu reeled him in again. 'This is, how do you say, a grey area of employment. No certificates. Not regulated.'

'Cowboy outfit? Wild West?' prompted Jack.

'Yes, Wild West, keep them dogies rolling,' said Petrescu. When he laughed, it was unpleasant to look at, and Jack stared through the gratings at the whirling fan blades until he'd stopped. 'You go one way or the other: doesn't bother me. Just that you go.'

'Is this illegal?'

'No, no. Not illegal. This is outside of the law, where words like legal or illegal do not apply. If you don't like that, if you're scared, then okay, why are you even here? No one else will help you, Dutch boy. Not Kirui. Not Halvorsen. Only Vasile Petrescu. Take it or leave it.'

Jack was down to those two options. Forget for a moment that this was someone that Petrescu knew. Either he took it, and maybe it would work out, or he left it, and he'd be back on the plane.

'Why are you really doing this?' asked Jack.

'Why? Okay, listen to me, Dutch boy.' Petrescu tightened his fist on Jack's flightsuit and shook him. They oscillated backwards and forwards like the two ends of a spring. 'I hate you. I hate you so much. You are everything and everyone I hate in this world or off it. I look at you and I want to vomit. It is not envy: no, it is rage. You could have done so much with your money, done so much good. Instead you have sat on it like a dragon sits on a huge pile of gold. Now, in the stories I read as a child, I learned not to worship dragons, but to kill them, yes? With a sword to the heart. That is how I would deal with your kind.'

'That—'

'Shut up, Dutch boy. Vasile is talking. I cannot get to your family. There is nothing I can do that can hurt them. But you are here, and I think, maybe, maybe I can hurt them after all. You want life away from your parents?' Petrescu dug in his top pocket with his free hand and pulled out a torn strip of lined paper. He pushed it into Jack's own pocket, methodically feeding it in until it disappeared from sight. 'You want adventure? Here is adventure. Maybe you live, and maybe you die. I don't care. This is my revenge.'

Petrescu let go, and pushed Jack against the fan grilles, using the transfer of momentum to float back to the wall. Then he flipped over and headed like a spear down the corridor. He didn't even look back.

Jack peeled himself away from the suction of the fans, and pulled himself back to his bunk. He drew the curtain, then fished out the strip of paper. It had three words on it, Mikkel Andros – NovaS, followed by a string of numbers.

Petrescu had promised Jack adventure. And death. And life. How much did he want this? He wavered. It sounded dangerous, but it was either NovaS or the space plane home. Running out of money meant running out of options. Soon, he'd not be able to choose between anything.

He pulled the curtain open and made his way to the terminal, slip of paper clutched in his hand.

The string of numbers looked like a server address. Where that was located was anyone's guess, and where it was being accessed from was another, different matter. He tapped out the numbers in the browser, and the screen slowly loaded up. It was a private chat room, occupant currently him.

ESTA-5: Hello?
Andros: [has joined the chat]

52

Andros: Van der Veerden?
ESTA-5: Yes. Are you Mikkel Andros?
Andros: Yes.
ESTA-5: I was told to call you.

Jack screwed his face up and looked around to check who else was about. Petrescu was on duty, but that didn't mean either Kirui or Halvorsen couldn't appear at any moment. This was as sketchy as hell.

Andros: I'm looking for crew. What's your competence?

His competence? What was he good at? What did he want to be? What, in fact, was the answer that Andros was looking for?

ESTA-5: Navigator.
Andros: Is that true or just bullshit?
ESTA-5: I can do the delta-v calculations on both chemical rocket and continuous thrust manoeuvres. I can plot Hohmann and bi-elliptic orbits and I know my way around the ephemeris.
Andros: Intercepts? Matching velocities?
ESTA-5: If you want it path-constrained, I can do that.
Andros: This is all theoretical. You've no experience.
ESTA-5: Mr Andros, I appreciate that. But there's little difference between the theory and the practice. It doesn't matter to the software if it's a simulation or a real spaceship. The course is the same.
Andros: I need someone with experience.

It was getting away from Jack, and he had to bring it back.

ESTA-5: I've plotted courses all over the solar system, thousands of times. Fast, efficient, whatever the payload or thrust parameters. I can get your ships where you need them to be, when you need them to be there. Every time. Without fail.

And he could. He'd just never actually done it before with an actual piece of hardware, that might get lost, or burn up, or crash. But that was what simulations were for. Computers could model all the bodies in space, and all the ships that might want to fly to them. It was complicated, but he had studied for it. That part at least wasn't bullshit.

Andros: I know who you are, Van der Veerden. I'm taking a
    hell of a risk just talking to you.
Andros: Nothing can go wrong here. We have one chance.
ESTA-5: One chance is all I'm asking for, sir. Nothing will go
    wrong. I guarantee it.
Andros: Absolute secrecy. Talk to no one. I'm booking a place
    on the next shuttle to L2 for you. Be on it. You'll be collected
    from L2.

He was doing it. Andros was hiring him. Fear and relief washed over Jack in equal measure, and he could barely type.

ESTA-5: Can I ask what the job involves?
Andros: No. Only that you will be crew. You'll get your briefing
    when we're on our way. Secrecy, Van der Veerden. Tell me
    you understand.
ESTA-5: Yes sir.

Crew. He was going to be crew. A navigator. *The* navigator. Now was not the time to hyperventilate.

Andros: Be ready. Wipe the log when you log out.
Andros: [has left the chat]
ESTA-5: [you have left the chat]

He scrubbed the history and closed the session. Then he glanced down the corridor. Petrescu just happened to be passing. Of course he was. Jack gave the tiniest of nods, and it was returned before the engineer vanished again.

Jack pressed his hand over his heart, to feel it beat slow and hard against his ribs. Not illegal or legal, was what Petrescu had told him. He was going to take that on trust, though he had no idea why. He'd done it. Whatever *it* was.

7

'You're saying the Intergovernmental Panel on Climate Change is misleading humanity about climate change and sea levels, and that in fact a new solar-driven cooling period is not far off?'

Interview with N. Axel-Mörner, Sky News Australia, 2019

Kirui was on duty when the shuttle docked. Jack was already there, waiting, clutching his waste-bin bag that held his now completely dead phone, and the clothes he'd arrived in at the spaceport. It was all he had.

She spun the pressure release valve. Air hissed, and when it had died away she cranked open the hatch. She waved at the connecting tube.

'I never thought you'd do this,' she said.

'Do what?' asked Jack.

'This. When they find out that you've gone, they are going to be pissed. I don't know where you're going or what you're doing, and I don't want to know – but they will try and claw you back. They're expecting you on the plane down in three days' time. Be somewhere else by then.'

'Thank you.'

She snorted. 'For what?'

'Not throwing me out the airlock.' He lined himself up with the hatch, and nudged his belongings through, into the shuttle. 'Not tying me up and putting me on a plane. There were lots of things you could have done to me, and you didn't do any of them. So thank you. I'm sorry, too, for all the trouble I've caused you.'

'You're going to cause us a lot more trouble when your people realise you've gone.' Her hostility slipped for a moment. 'Take the flight back to Earth, Van der Veerden. Anything that Petrescu's involved in is ...'

'It's this or nothing. I am not going back. I am not.'

'Then good luck. You're going to need it.'

Jack held out his hand, and Kirui looked at it like it was something dead and nameless. He pulled it back in, and aimed his feet through the hatch. Her face dwindled, lit from behind like a saint, just before she slammed the door shut on him. Jack emerged from the transfer tube and took stock of his surroundings.

A cylinder that was barely three metres long, with some bolt-down chairs and internal lighting that could only be described as moody. Jack's bag was gently drifting around the cabin, knocking against the tops of the chairs, threatening to spill his socks. He snagged it and sat in a seat, looking at the single waist strap and trying to figure out how to clip it together.

'Hey.' The intercom crackled. 'Hatch light is still red. Unless you want to breathe hard vacuum, you should probably close that.'

Jack let go of the seat and pulled himself towards the hatch. He held onto the ceiling grab with one hand and swung the door closed with the other. There was a lever, and he pushed it away from him so that the handle travelled from the open circle to the filled square. Each symbol was raised, so he could even feel them in the dark.

The lever appeared to work some bolts, which locked the hatch in place. There was also a handwheel for tightening the seal, and Jack cranked it around until it wouldn't turn any more.

'Light's gone green. Get in your seat, and stow your grip.'

The voice, he presumed, belonged to the pilot, and they wasted no time in disengaging from the transfer station. Jack

57

scrambled into a seat, any seat, as the clamps holding the shuttle in place released. He tucked his bag behind his knees, and repeatedly mashed the two ends of the seat-belt together until they went click.

He pressed his back against the seat, and the acceleration, when it came, was so mild as to be barely anything at all. Just manoeuvring away from the station, and its solar panel array. He looked around, and was disappointed to find there were still no windows. For good reasons, yes, but just outside the hull the Earth would be taking up almost half the sky, in blues and greens and browns. He would have liked to have seen it with his own eyes, but there wasn't even a screen he could watch.

As he got used to the gloom, he could make out more detail in the cabin. Everything seemed very basic. Really very basic. Spare parts basic. More than that: recycled. He was in a modified fuel tank. The rounded bulkheads fore and aft would contain pressurised liquids as well as they would air, and the hatch was simply welded into place. He could see the weld marks around the frame. If what was happening inside was also happening outside, then there'd be some strap-on engines, gas cylinders for life support and low-pressure thrusters. And a flight deck to control it all, which didn't seem likely to be just thrown together out of bits and pieces.

'Excuse me, Pilot?'

'What do you want?'

'Can you tell me how long this is going to take?' There were no toilets, no food, no water in the cabin. He had no idea if he ought to have brought any of those on board himself.

'It takes as long as it takes. I've got a seven-klicks delta-v burn scheduled after I pick up another passenger from ESTA-8. Then we pull in to L1 in a couple of hours.'

'I thought we were going to L2.'

'You got a ticket that'll get you to L2?'

'Yes.'

'This bucket is going to L1. You get another shuttle from

there to L2.' There was dead air, followed by, 'I'm coming up on my mark, so I'm going to ignore you.'

He needed to be at L2 before his parents realised that he wasn't in Low Earth Orbit any more. The pilot probably didn't think Jack was anything but another warm body to get from one place to another, in a routine and predictable way. No sense of urgency, and Jack had no way to instil one, unless he was willing to break cover.

Andros wanted secrecy. If word got out that Jack was heading away from Earth, then his progress would be watched every step of the way. If? When. L1 was the Earth-facing lunar transfer hub. It was going to be busy. Someone would see him. Why couldn't the shuttle go straight to L2? Couldn't he just pay the pilot to ignore his route?

No. Not any more. He could no more give the pilot an inducement than he could book himself into a Moon hotel. He couldn't even call ahead. Comms on the ESTA-5 could be made secure, but he had no access to anything in the shuttle. Perhaps he could contact Andros from L1.

He felt another thrusting manoeuvre, longer than before and of greater magnitude. Without any indication of a horizon, nor a direction, he was completely lost, but at least he hadn't spent every last minute feeling nauseous. It looked like he was one of those people blessed with the ability to cope with zero-g.

The ship fell silent, apart from the ubiquitous fans and the occasional tap from the hull. Something microscopic hitting the outside, possibly leaving a hole in the insulation layer. The engines were off, and they wouldn't fire again until they needed to dock with ESTA-8. It was boring. Nothing to look at, nothing to do. He had no music, no movies, no games, no reading matter. His old phone, the one he'd left on the bed, had all of those things, and the ability to get him whatever he wanted.

All he had now was the inside of his head. He had three days to get to L2 before he was expected home, the same time Apollo had taken, a hundred years ago, and for all the advances in technology, it was still the same distance from the Earth to the Moon, up the same hill, using substantially the same means of transport. Something that squirted hot matter out the back, and got pushed forward in an equal and opposite reaction.

It would be less than that before his parents realised that he was missing from ESTA-5, assuming that one of the crew hadn't already sold that information to Mesman. He wouldn't put it past Petrescu to play both sides. Then again, Petrescu spoke with the conviction of a zealot, so maybe not. Either Kirui or the Norwegian, then.

If he could get past L1 and make it to L2, then it would be okay. He was back to worrying, and thinking that he could never escape the long, powerful reach of the Van der Veerden name. Once he was on the ship, for certain. He screwed his face up. All this anxiety. He should have phoned home, explained to Pap and Mam what he was doing and why, and that he still loved them but he needed to do this for himself, and for his own sanity.

But he hadn't. This was what he'd signed up for. Independence. No phoning home, no tearful goodbyes, no time for feelings. If he was miserable, then he'd better make sure he did all his chores. If he was happy, he'd better make sure he did all his chores. No one cared about his motivation or his mood, they just cared that he did things right.

Manoeuvring. He felt the ship spin around, and reverse thrust applied, then back again, and the slight vibrations of the thrusters. The clang of docking was louder than it ought to have been: something had been offset and forced back into alignment. The ship shuddered and shook, then the hatch sounded, one, two, three times, a distinct, heavy impact. The handwheel turned and air hissed before the hatch door swung down.

A head slid into view: a woman, scalp cut to a fine fuzz. She scanned the capsule, much as Jack had done, then the rest of her followed. Her bag, a small red plasticised drawstring affair that reminded Jack of nothing more than a school shoe bag, was tied around her ankle. She flipped over, and closed the hatch without being reminded by the pilot.

Then she dropped herself in the next-but-one seat, and strapped in.

'We're good to go,' she called.

'Okay,' replied the pilot. 'I'll give you the mark when I make the L1 burn. Detaching.'

The ship rattled again, and without any ceremony, it was under way.

'Hey,' said the woman. She looked at Jack's hair, then at Jack. Her eyes narrowed. 'Okay then.'

His anonymity had lasted the length of the flight from ESTA-5 to ESTA-8. Jack sighed. 'Yeah. About that.'

'You don't look much like you do in the clips.'

He had no choice but to concede. 'No? Uglier? Shorter? Poorer?'

'Less well dressed. That flightsuit.' She leaned across. 'You either borrowed it, or it was part of your disguise.'

She seemed highly amused to find herself in the same cabin as him. That did, at least, give him something to work with.

'I'm Jack.' He leaned across and offered his hand.

'May Engineer.' She ignored his hand, just as Kirui had done. 'So. I'm going to ask you where you're heading, because Earth's the other way.'

'I'm still running, and I could do with your help.'

'Everybody has a theory as to what you're doing, and why,' she said.

'Honestly, I've been too busy to keep up with what they're saying about me. What's your take on it?'

'Mine? A kid's allowed his freedom, right? You've got as many friends up here as you do enemies.'

'Can I count you as one of my friends?'

'Sure. Why not? I've never been friends with a billionaire before.'

'Ex-billionaire. I'm determined to earn my way in the world. Just that people are making it very difficult for me. Which is where I need your help, May.'

May Engineering sat back in her seat. 'What do you need? I can only say no.'

'Are you likely to say no?'

'It has been known that I say no occasionally.'

Jack chewed at his lip. 'I have to rely on you. I can't—'

'Spare me the bullshit, Jack. I'm not one of your starry-eyed Pretty Girls. I'm an engineer on a spaceship. I'm crew. Tell me what you think you need. If I can help, I'll help.'

She laughed at his sudden discomfort.

'Oh, come on. You haven't washed for days, your face looks like a balloon and you smell of desperation. I've had far better offers in my time, but I'm feeling sorry for you because half the world wants to see you dragged from the space plane in chains.'

Jack stared at the blank bulkhead ahead of him. 'The usual rules don't seem to apply.'

'Welcome to space, Jack. So where is it you think you can run to that you can't be brought back from?'

'I can't tell you.'

'Oh, come on, Jack.'

He could make it to L2 without help, probably. But she seemed sure of herself, confident in a way that he used to be, but that had deserted him. Maybe it was easy to behave like the world owed him, when in fact, he was behaving like he owned it.

'I need to get to L2, with as few people knowing as possible.'

She pursed her lips. 'I can do that. I'm going to L2 too. Late call from a mining corp.'

'And you're definitely not working for my parents?'

'I work for one person, Jack. Me.'

The intercom interrupted. 'Prepare for burn to L1. T1 is three hundred seventy-five seconds. Acceleration, acceleration, on my mark. Three, two, one. Mark.'

Down pitched to the back of the cabin, but it wasn't the hard acceleration of the space plane. It was something more than nothing, but still barely anything. The vibrations from the engine were loud, though. Not cold gas thrusters this time: a chemical rocket was flaring out behind them.

They waited it out before resuming.

'Okay,' she said, loosening off her waist strap. 'There's only one reason why anyone goes to L2. They're joining a ship.'

'I can't—'

She held up her hands. 'I'm not asking. What's your competence?'

'My ... it's navigation.'

'Jack, there's no nav up here. You're Jack Astrogator from now on. That's how you introduce yourself to other crew. To civilians, you can call yourself whatever the hell you want. But to crew, it's who you are and what you do. I'm May Engineering, you're Jack Astrogator.' She made a fist of her right hand, then brought it towards Jack, and encouraged him to do the same. They bumped knuckles. 'When you're in a suit, you can't shake hands, so you dap, like that. Crew don't shake hands ever. Astrogator? Seriously?'

Jack put his hand back in his lap. 'Yes?'

'How did you manage to do your training and get your certificates? Difficult to hide that from billionaire parents.'

'Maybe I skipped a few steps.' He looked away, and studied the welding instead. Then thought better of it. No, he was good enough for this. 'I can do the job. I've got the know-how.'

She stared back at him. 'We've all got to start somewhere, but this is baptism by fire stuff. Crews work on trust, you know that.'

'I know that. I've seen it.'

'Have you seen it go wrong?'

'No. Not yet. I know what you're thinking, that I've got this far on my name and my charm. I think you've already proved neither of them counts for anything up here. But I can actually plot courses and do all the things I said I could do.'

'Someone's taking a big risk all the same, picking up a dirt-foot. A dirtfoot with an already difficult rep like yours. Look,' she said, and pulled up her sleeve. She was wearing a fancy watch, big analogue dials and metal bezels. Jack had never worn a wristwatch. He'd never had to. She twisted her arm so that he could get a better look at it. 'Swiss-made, shock-proof, mechanical, rated to zero atmospheres and a temperature range that will either freeze me or boil me. It'll survive an impact that will kill me, keep working long after I've died of radiation exposure, and the advertising has it that it'll take aerobraking from LEO. That last thing is so much bullshit, but despite that it's still a good timepiece.'

'There's an analogy coming here, isn't there?'

'Yes. I wear it because I can rely on it to do the things I need it to do. If it fails and I'm still alive, I will just go out and replace it. I'm not sentimentally attached to it. And any time you think a crew are different, you remember my watch. Got that?'

'I got it.'

'Good. Now, let's make you look more like crew, and a little less like a billionaire playboy runaway.' She kicked up her luggage on the end of its short tether and delved inside. She came out with electric clippers.

Jack's hands instinctively went to his head. But he could see the wisdom in this, and he slowly withdrew them.

'Okay. You're smart. Smart enough to learn, at least. Hold still.'

8

Ocean acidification – the evidence increasingly suggests – is a trivial, misleadingly named, and not remotely worrying phenomenon which has been hyped up beyond all measure for political, ideological and financial reasons.

J. Delingpole, 'Ocean acidification: yet another wobbly pillar of climate alarmism', *Spectator*, 2016

The L2 waystation was a rotating wheel-type station. It gave one lunar gravity at the outer circumference, which was enough to stick things to the floor. It had a sort of canteen, where crew could buy food and drinks, and bolt-down tables where they could consume them, if they learned to compensate for the Coriolis forces.

On the assumption that anything Jack paid for might be traceable, May stood him a coffee.

'L2,' she said. 'Are you going to tell me where you're heading yet?'

He looked at the other people – the other crew – sitting in pairs or on their own around him. Five of them. They all looked wildly different. Older than him, mostly, though in a range from maybe thirty through to fifty. Wherever he ended up, he was going to be the baby.

Not that it mattered: she'd impressed on him there was no room for individualism: space was about cooperation, about everyone having the same set of ethics and the same set of goals. Stand-outs, misfits and renegades might take centre stage in popular movies, but real spaceships ran on soviet lines. Any captain was always going to need all the crew's consent to make decisions.

The coffee was entirely synthetic. He was used to the best, but he drank it anyway, because it was polite, because it had been bought for him, because it meant that he didn't have to answer May's question.

'Thank you for this.' He raised his cup to her. He couldn't tell whether the prices were ridiculous or merely steep, because he didn't know the price of anything comparable. 'What I'd really like is to see outside. I want to know this is real. The last time I saw further than the front wall, I was looking out of an airport window at the Baltic Sea. I've been in space nearly a week, and part of me thinks I'm still on some sound stage somewhere, being moved from room to room to room.'

'Okay. That's absolutely normal, but here's a protip: you can't fake low gravity. That's how you know you're in space.' May glanced at her watch. 'They'll use the tannoy to call either of us if we're needed. Come on.'

He quickly drank some more, and left the rest on the table. The way it tasted, he could more or less guarantee it'd still be there when he got back. Except that May swept it up and sent it through the recycling as soon as they stood. Nothing was ever wasted.

It would have been sickening to view the outside from the rotating sections of the station, given the speed at which it turned to produce gravity, akin to sitting on an old-time fairground ride: so the window was a tiny observation cupola on the axis. The glass wasn't chipped, but it was abraded, chains of microscopic bubbles embedded deep in the transparent material, implanted by colliding dust.

Each one made a rainbow halo, and as Jack pulled himself up into position, almost wearing the window as a hat, they shone with reflected light.

His first sight was of the utter dark of space, nothing but a black shroud dragged over the sky, no stars, no guides, nothing. How was he supposed to navigate in that void? Then, as his shoulders properly filled the gap below and his eyes adjusted, he began to see the lights outside. Stars didn't twinkle. They burned, constant and eternal. Even though he knew all the reasons why that wasn't true, it still looked as if they were holes in a veil, and beyond was the greater truth.

But behind him, a bone-white glare attracted him, and he turned. The Moon, a half-skull made of stone, hanging in the night. He was both fascinated by it – it was far larger than he was used to seeing it – but also felt a twinge of disappointment: it wasn't overwhelmingly close. There was no expectation of reaching out and touching it.

There were lights in the shadows of the craters. Pinpoint and sharp. There were people down there, in the cold and the dust. He watched them for a while. A blue haze drifted over the limb of the Moon. The edge of a bright marble. Earth. His throat closed and, for a moment, he thought he'd never be able to breathe again.

It was real. It was undeniably, perfectly real, and yes, he'd run away to space. He was about to join a ship, and people, people like May, would be relying on him to keep them alive, and there'd be no second chances, no apologies, no bluffing, no rich-boy confidence tricks. He should go home, and go home now, before he killed someone.

He was almost corpse-like as she pulled him down from the cupola, frozen in indecision, in panic, in fear. Shut-down almost total, unable so much as to turn his head, he could barely even blink. May turned him around, his head towards the access tube, then spun herself to face him. She pressed her hands on his cheeks and spoke almost into his mouth.

'It's okay. There's another reason why windows aren't a great idea on spaceships, and you've just discovered that. We call it getting a touch of the Nietzsches. Too much perspective is a bad thing. Take a moment, put it to the back of your mind and get on with the job.' Her brown eyes searched his blue ones for signs of life. Then she moved the infinitesimal distance between them and kissed him.

He came to, his lips still holding the memory of hers.

'I—'

'Something's just docked. It'll be for you, or for me. Crew are always on time. Crew don't delay departure. Crew don't waste resources.' She released him and pushed off down the axis towards the docking ring, down at the far end, a straight journey of fifty metres.

Jack followed her feet. She didn't touch the walls as she passed, but he had to hand off a couple of times to correct his course. He had after-images of the blackness of space burned onto the backs of his eyes. He tried to will them away, and was only partially successful. But there was that kiss, and he didn't know whether it was simply an effective way of snapping him out of the Nietzsches, or something else.

The capsule before the docking ring widened the corridor into a space a few metres across, punctuated by five hatches – one at the far end and one in each quadrant of the wall. Grips and straps protruded from the padded surfaces, and Jack took hold of one and brought himself to a halt without colliding with either May or the other crew gathering there.

The airlock light was red; then, as the pumps began to chug, it turned amber. After it turned green, the wheel fastening spun and the seal cracked with a small plosive pop.

The man inside the airlock – small, sallow, with a long thick monobrow like a soot stain – looked at them looking at him. He glanced down at his tablet and began to reel off a list of names.

'May Engineer, Julia Cryogenics, Patricio Mining, Marta Mining, Kayla Life Support, Arush Medic and Jack Astrogation.'

Jack caught May's sudden intake of breath by his ear. All that shit-talking about being able to navigate in the deepness of space had just got real for both of them. When he looked at her, she was already looking at him, jaw clenched, eyes narrow. She was, for now, the only one that knew. The others would probably recognise him in time, and realise that this boy, this dirtfoot, was their navigator. Maybe he should just get it out of the way early, but there was something about May's expression that told him that would be a bad idea.

The others filtered through the airlock to the waiting capsule, pulling tiny packs on leads like obedient dogs behind them. May unobtrusively caught Jack's flightsuit with her finger and thumb and held him back.

'Tell me this is going to be okay, May,' he whispered.

'I really hope this is going to be okay, Jack. Do not answer any questions about your past, your experience, anything. Not until you've proved you can do the job, and even then, maybe not.'

'They're going to work out who I am.'

'Of course they are. This would have happened on any mission, you naive idiot. Do the job, Jack. Do the job. That's all I ask. That's all anyone asks.'

She pushed him towards the airlock, and he put his hand on the edge of the hatch. The transfer tube was open all the way to the far end. He could see lights.

'Go. I'll close up behind you.'

He slid inside, head first, and palmed his way into the cramped capsule that was waiting for him. Patricio showed him where to fix himself to the wall, up and to the right of the occupied pilot's seat. He half-expected May to cut and run, but she followed him in, and Julia closed the last hatch behind her.

'Sealed. When you're ready, Pilot.'

The capsule was absolutely rammed with people, arranged at all angles and at all levels. If he was ever going to be claustrophobic, now was the time he was going to find out. In front of everyone. His crewmates.

The pilot fired up his screens and tabbed his target with his finger, distant enough to be no more than a white spot, a few pixels wide. He pressed some buttons, checked his readings and settled his hands onto the left and right control columns.

'Disengaging.'

Jack saw, on the left-hand monitor, the hatch he'd just crawled through flare with unfiltered sunlight. It shrank in size, and the rotating wheel of the L2 waystation resolved around it. It turned, silently, steadily, and then it too began to lose definition.

But as it did so, the image on the centre screen grew, the ship they were heading for.

They were coming at it side-on. It looked ... ridiculous. Most deep-space vessels did, being built entirely on the ethos that form followed function, with aerodynamics an irrelevance. This ship simply didn't seem large enough. A fat tube – engines? – tapered to a narrower one – crew? – and part of that forward section was geared with four hammer-ended arms about its circumference: artificial gravity areas. Also crew area, then. Ahead of that was a still-narrower tube. The main feature, however, was the vast halo of solar panels, or perhaps radiators, arrayed like a peacock's tail around the engine segment, each long stalk extending far beyond the ship itself.

A dandelion seed. That was what it resembled. Tiny core, huge feathery train to catch the wind and propel it across the sky.

They docked at the narrow end, with the pilot displaying such lightness of touch that there was barely a correction needed. He killed their forward velocity, rotated the capsule along two axes simultaneously, and lined up with the docking clamps with the merest twitch of his wrist. All the more impressive given that he was reversing into place and translating everything on his screens into its mirror image.

'Engaging clamps.' A light went from red to amber, and stubbornly stayed there until the pilot pressed some more buttons. It finally turned green. 'There. Seal achieved.'

Julia had been last in, so was first out. She slid through,

and Patricio followed. The air had grown stale in that short journey, the filters overwhelmed by their collective breathing, and no one wanted to hang around. May wanted Jack to follow her, to keep him close, to prevent him from saying anything to anyone. Perhaps she thought it would reflect badly on her if it became known she'd been aware this was his first trip out, and had never said.

Ships worked on trust. Of course it would reflect badly on her.

Then it was just Jack and the pilot.

'Runihura Pilot.' He held out his fist to be dapped. 'Runi.'

'Jack Astrogation.'

They sized each other up. Jack tried to exude confidence, something he could normally do as easily as breathing, but he was screaming internally and trying not to let it show. Maybe everyone was. Had the last chance to back out and bolt for home already passed?

Runi was powering the capsule down, no longer paying any attention to Jack, who took the opportunity to scuttle away. Access to the ship led directly into the command module. Many of the consoles were dark, but some were active, scrolling information, showing schematics. A pit in the middle had a proper chair that swivelled a full three-sixty, able to access a penumbra of screens.

Beyond that was the axis that ran the length of the ship. Part way down were open hatches that led to the four arms, and all the sound was coming from one of them. Jack fed himself in, and emerged in the crew quarters: a thin concave arc that would become the floor, and facing it from each side, a row of five narrow doors.

'May?'

She opened the door she was behind and beckoned him in. Inside was a cabin that would be barely long enough to lie down in. Jack made absolutely sure the door was shut behind him. If he held out his arms he could touch both sides of the cabin

71

simultaneously: a fold-down bed was stowed against one of the walls, with a locker fixed to the floor underneath it. A tiny part of it was for personal items, the rest held stores.

'Do not bug out on me,' she said. 'You're here. You've made it. Now you have to be crew.'

'But I don't even know what the hell I'm supposed to be doing or where we're going.'

She pushed her trailing bag into the locker and unclipped the lead from her ankle. 'It's a mining ship, Jack. So we're going on a rock hunt.'

'Asteroid-mining?'

'Yes. Get all the stupid questions out of your system now, please.'

'Look, you know all this. I—'

'By the time we get there, you will know all this too.'

'Where is this asteroid?'

'I'm guessing the asteroid belt somewhere, but it could be a trojan or an outlier. All that matters is that you can put us alongside it. Can you do that?'

'Yes?'

'Then stop worrying. You wanted this, so you have to front this out, no matter what.' She listened to the ambient sounds, of the crew making their way back up the access tube to the command module. 'You're in number four, just across the corridor. Stow your gear. Meet in Control in five minutes.'

She was right. This was what he'd wanted. This exact thing. Why was he suddenly so panicky?

Jack slipped out and he didn't have to stretch to open room four's door. He stuffed his bag into the small drawer at the head of the bed. He braced himself against a wall and opened the main locker, stared for a moment at all the packages, which were themselves packaged in tens and twenties in clear bags with QR codes and serial numbers and embedded RF tags, and closed it again before anything floated away. This was his room, for however long this was going to take.

Jack heard the door across the corridor close, and he waited for a moment to let May make her way up the tunnel to the axis. He was part of this crew in his own right now, and he couldn't be seen forever trailing around after the engineer. He had to somehow manage to keep a grip on what he was supposed to be doing.

There it was, the source of all his fear: there was no one who was going to bail him out, could bail him out. Unlike some, he'd never tried to be the kind of person who deliberately made a mess, just to see how fast they could make others run in their haste to clear it up. But the safety net had always been there, subconsciously. It hadn't mattered if he'd screwed up before. And now it did.

The thought that real people were going to solely rely on him, now and in the future, to keep them alive and bring them home again made his stomach twist. He wasn't anyone's deputy or apprentice. He was the astrogator. And he had to demonstrate to the assembled crew that he could plot a course at a briefing that started in the next couple of minutes.

He backed out of his room, closing the door behind him. Then he pushed himself along the transfer tube, into the axis.

9

Greenland is losing about 0.1% of its ice per *decade* – that is, about 0.01% per year. At that rate, it will take a century for it to lose 1%.

E. Calvin Beisner and J. C. Keister, 'Lying with Statistics: The National Climate Assessment Falsely Hypes Ice Loss in Greenland and Antarctica', *Watts Up With That*, 2014

When he entered the Control module, it looked like he was last to arrive. He acknowledged silently that it wasn't the best start he could have made, but as he checked, he saw that they were missing their captain. He was good with names, from years of being introduced to people he'd only ever meet once, and he was good at reading a room for the same reason. He was able to tick off his mental list who was who and what their roles were from the off.

Who else here could he learn from, how to comport himself, what to say and what not to say?

'Patricio Mining,' said the oldest man in Control, his face like tanned leather, his hands like a cotton glove. He held out his fist, compensating for Jack's over-rotation. Jack took the dap and steadied himself on a ceiling grab bar. 'What do you reckon?'

'Rock hunt,' said Julia Cryogenics, not giving Jack a chance to answer. 'Big one. May be enough to retire on if the assay's good.'

Patricio gave her a non-committal shrug. 'We will not know until we get there. I hear rumours, though.'

Marta interrupted. 'Gallowglass.'

Patricio made the Devil's horns with his right hand, down by his side, but ostentatiously enough that everyone saw it.

Jack glanced at May, hoping for an explanation, but she wasn't looking at him. He supposed it was one of those things he ought to already know, and he'd be giving himself away if he asked.

'So it is a big rock,' said Kayla. She was the only one there with any length of hair, tight cornrows, with a blue bead tied to each strand. They clacked as she turned her head. 'Cycler, too. And we're going for a capture, not just a dismantle?'

'It's the future,' said Julia. She looked directly at Jack, as if he was supposed to add something, but he affected a non-committal look, and then someone he assumed was Andros arrived out of the axis, and the speculation ended.

He stopped at the hatch and his gaze alighted on each of the crew in turn. It lingered long on Jack, before moving on to Patricio, and then May. He had bright, almost fevered eyes, and the way they glittered in the subdued lighting of Control made him seem not quite human. Jack worked his jaw and reined in his imagination.

Then Andros pulled himself over to the pilot's chair and gave Runi a nod. 'Bring it up.'

Runi tapped a screen, and all around the module images flickered at workstations. Curved, coloured lines: Earth in blue, Moon in white, Mars in red, and one extra, in yellow. Numbers ticked over at the bottom of the screen. Universal Time.

'The target is called 1998-KU2, a Cg-class asteroid. It has an estimated mass of two times ten to the power of fourteen kilograms, is approximately four and a half kilometres across, and contains metals and volatiles worth somewhere in the region of one hundred trillion dollars. Any questions?'

'That *is* one big-ass rock,' said someone, and Jack was too busy looking at the orbits to see who it was.

'Our job is to park KU2 at L4 within the current solar orbit. No excuses and no delays.'

'Is that Lunar-L4 or Terra-L4?'

'Lunar.'

Jack, half-listening to the conversation, snapped back to attention. 'You want us to put a nearly five-k asteroid in a Lissajous orbit at Lunar-L4?' Then he realised he'd said that out loud.

'Yes.' Andros fixed him with a stare. Every screen seemed to be reflected in his eyes. 'Is that a problem?'

Everyone else was now looking at him, and waiting for his response. He shrank inside, remembering what he'd told Andros: that whatever the payload or thrust parameters, he could get his ship where he needed it to be. He hadn't expected the ship to be accompanied by a two-hundred-billion-tonne lump of rock, though.

'Is that a problem, Astrogator?'

'Not … necessarily,' he ventured, and started to pick his words very carefully. 'I'm sure the numbers add up.'

'Thank you for your input, Astrogator.'

Jack caught the slight shake of Runi's head that stopped the instant Andros turned back to him.

'Our launch window is closing rapidly. We have enough delta-v to close on the target and match orbits only near aphelion. Familiarisation with ship systems will take place in transit. Manuals are on the computer and components are standard. Astrogation will plot an intercept with KU2. Captain will pass it. Departure will be no later than zero hours UT. Any further questions?'

Patricio cleared his throat. 'I agree with Jack. This seems an impossible flight profile.'

Jack eased himself further into the shadows.

'The *Coloma* is a state-of-the-art mining vessel, Miner. It has a two-hundred-gigawatt laser for ablation-powered manoeuvres. The generated thrust will depend on the thermo-mechanical responses of the regolith, but there is a calculated margin of error that will be more than sufficient. The job is expected to take twenty months, but perhaps we can get it back even earlier.

There will be bonuses for the crew in that event.' Andros turned back to Jack, who was now reeling at the thought of almost two years in space. 'Pilot will give you the flight data. I will run the simulation. You can do what you like in between. I'm not interested in your workings-out. All I want to see is the final course. Understand, Astrogator?'

He didn't trust himself to say anything else, so he just said, 'Yes, sir.'

That was it. That was their briefing. Andros headed aft, and Jack let go of his handhold long enough to wipe the prickling sweat from his forehead into the unexpected stubble where his hair used to be.

Patricio waited for the captain's back to disappear. 'Jack?'

'It'll be fine.' He scanned the wall consoles, the flip-out seats, the elastic straps to hold someone in place. In the absence of any further instructions, he picked one at random, pulled out the plastic seat and fastened the strap over his thighs. He stared for a moment at the console, not knowing where anything was or how to turn it on, or even which buttons he couldn't press for fear of making something go boom. 'I will get us there. I will get us back.'

'Now is the time to say if you think this is too much. Do not let your poverty or the greed of others control your choices.'

It was such an odd thing to say that Jack looked at Patricio properly. He was an old man in space, and if he knew anything at all, it was the aphorism that there were no old, bold spacers. His face was deeply lined, exposed to too many unfiltered suns and freezing vacuums.

'If we say no to this, then that is the end of it. This ship goes nowhere without the consent of its crew.'

'Hey, just hold on a minute,' said Julia. 'Some of us need the money.'

And Jack was now one of those people. As he sat there, he started to see a familiar configuration in amongst the stripped-down, almost naked equipment. He turned the gesture-recognition camera onto himself, folded a keyboard down and felt behind the monitor for the on switch.

'I ... look. You're going to have to give me a minute or two. Getting there, what have we got?'

Runi loaded the information onto his screen. 'We have a rest mass of nine point four times ten to the four kilograms.'

Jack sat back with a surprised grunt. 'Ninety-four tonnes? Did you misplace the decimal point?'

'Ninety-four tonnes.'

'What the hell is this ship made of?'

'Composite. It's designed to be light, because if it was heavy, it'd take more fuel than we could carry to get the delta-v.' Runi turned back to his console. 'All this must have cost someone, or someones, a fortune. Our power generation is point one six seven gigawatts at one AU. Nine Vasimr engines, thrust of up to one thousand newtons apiece at twenty megawatts, continuous.'

'Okay. Okay.' He scrubbed at his head. 'That's ... I'll need to plug in the figures, but we can get there. It's the getting the asteroid back.'

'Jack?' asked May. 'What's the problem?'

'It's how much fine control we have. Getting anything to stick at a Lagrange point is ... it's delicate. You're talking relative velocities of centimetres a second. These things are like threading a needle at the best of times, and that's with something of a few hundred tonnes and the ability to vector. A mass like KU2? It's going to be like threading a needle that's moving at several k a second with thread that's also moving at several k a second but on a different trajectory.' The silence stretched on, and Jack felt he should add something. Quite what, he didn't know. 'I mean, theoretically it's possible.'

'Will it kill us to try?' asked Arush.

'No. I mean, no, unless you know something I don't.'

'It's a big rock,' said Marta, looking around Control. 'The biggest that's ever been moved, as far as I know.'

'No reason we can't do it. Someone has to be first, right?' Julia's bright voice was full of an optimism that Jack didn't share.

'We don't get paid anything unless we go,' said Kayla. 'That's the bottom line. Hell, that's my bottom line. I say we take a look at this KU2 and make our minds up once we see it. We'll have ten months' pay in escrow by the time we get there.'

Patricio in particular didn't seem convinced. He rumbled low in his throat. 'I have heard things about KU2. About how it was acquired. The fight over it was vicious.'

'They were fighting over trillions. What do you expect?'

As the conversation washed around him, Jack stared at his screen. He pushed the current window aside with a two-fingered slide. He loaded up Orbital, which he was already familiar with, and flexed his intertwined fingers while the program interrogated the ephemeris. Planets and their orbits appeared, one by one, and he stared for a while at the screen, watching them in real time, numbers flickering fast but the points seemingly stationary. There, out there, was KU2, far beyond the orbit of Mars, with the distance still increasing. By the time it started to head back towards the Sun, they needed to be on station, having matched its orbit, its speed, its inclination.

'This gallowglass is a murderer. She killed people, for money. That is inexcusable.'

'I can't afford to have your scruples. I have debts to pay and mouths to feed. And look, you're here. We're all here. None of us would have taken this job if we'd had an alternative.'

Jack started listening again, while pretending he wasn't. It was Kayla speaking.

'This is a top-of-the-line ship. Seriously, look around you. Some of this shit is so new, it's still wrapped in plastic. We have, what, a two-hundred-gigawatt laser hanging off our tail? Yet, we're all here on the down-low. Am I right? Yeah, I'm right. This is no standard job, but I'm not standing down.'

'We land this at a refinery,' said Arush, 'we'll never have to work in space again. Even at fractions of one per cent of the royalties, our bonuses for the next decade will be enough. More than enough.'

'I will never work with a gallowglass,' said Patricio. 'They are capitalist mercenaries. Pure and simple.'

'Nothing is ever pure and simple,' Marta interrupted him. 'We – you – got blacklisted. This is the only work you've been offered for half a year. It's this or you float home.'

'Why don't we break this down?' said May. 'We're all here, for whatever reason we're here. No one needs to say anything about that. We have our competences.' She paused, and Jack knew she was thinking of him. 'The ship is new, and we can shake it down on the flight out, for which we get paid, no matter what. No one knows what will happen when we get there, the state of KU2, anything. But if we don't go and look, we'll never know and, assuming commodity prices don't crash in the next two years, we'll all get a life-changing amount of cash.'

'Dregs, compared with what the capital interests will get.'

'Patricio, you're here.' Marta looked ready to strangle the man. 'You're here because this is the system we have to work with. Wishing it otherwise will not feed you and keep you in air.'

'Is there a chance we can pull this off?' Julia said. 'That's all I need to know. Jack?'

Could he learn all he needed to learn in the ten months of going, that would mean that they could drive the largest asteroid ever moved, into Earth orbit, to the precise point ahead of the Moon where the refineries were, and bring it to a halt relative to everything else that was still moving at thirty kilometres a second?

If he said no, it wasn't possible, at this point? What would happen to the rest of the crew? What would happen to him? Could they refuse to fly? From everything that May had told him, yes, Patricio was right: the captain needed the crew's consent. But no one else was going to give him a job though, not in the next day or so before his money ran out. And it looked like Patricio was in the same position. For all their obvious differences, he felt an odd kinship with the man.

He looked at the clock in the corner of his screen. Assuming it was working on Universal Time, he didn't have that long in which to calculate a course that would satisfy the captain. Quite what would happen after zero hours, and why, he couldn't work out. Neither, why all the secrecy.

He pushed it all to the back of his mind. He had a job, on a spaceship, that would take him out of his parents' orbit for almost two years. It was selfish, but it was enough.

'I can get us there,' he reiterated. He pressed his fingers to his mouth, then dragged them away. Could he really do this? Sure. Why not? Continuous thrust manoeuvres were easier to finesse than single big delta-v burns. Even if he got it wrong to start with, he could get them on track without too much difficulty. 'I can get us back. Whether we can bring KU2 with us, I don't know, but it seems as if no one does.'

'Okay. We go,' said Julia.

'Go,' said Kayla.

'Go?' said Arush, less certainly, but a declaration nevertheless.

'Go,' said Marta, and elbowed Patricio in the ribs.

He sounded weary, but he assented. 'Go.'

'Go,' said Runi.

'Go,' said May.

'We have a go for launch.' Julia twisted herself around and pushed off towards the axis. 'About bloody time. I've got some reading to do, and some hatches to lift. We should probably leave Jack alone to work his magic, right, Jack?'

'Something like that,' he managed. He looked at the screens, at the thread of gold that he had to weave into a pattern.

Eventually, it was just him and Runi. A feeling up and down his spine told Jack that the pilot was regarding him with ... concern? Scepticism? Outright distrust?

'Tell me honestly, can you do this?'

Jack gripped the edges of his keyboard. Now was not the time for a confession. He swivelled round. 'Can you? Can anyone here? We're strangers to each other and the ship. On top of which, none of us knows what's waiting for us up there.'

Runi demurred. 'If you can lay a course, I can fly it.'

'It's a deal.' He turned back to his screen. Ad Astra was common navigation software, and he fired it up, along with a cobra console for some off-the-books calculations. 'You can tell me about the gallowglass, though, if you want.'

'You know how mining licences work?'

He thought about asking, but didn't. 'I know how they work.'

'That the gallowglasses have to physically land on an asteroid in order to stake the claim?'

'I know that.' Well, he did now.

'But do you know that there is a period of dead time between sending in a claim to OSTO, and OSTO verifying that claim and confirming it with their digital signature? The gallowglass can be light minutes away from the Earth-Moon system.' Runi talked to his back. 'Time in which, if something happened to them or their fragile, one-crew ship, their claim would be void.'

'And did something like that happen at KU2?'

'A dozen gallowglasses set out for KU2 when it was at closest approach. It was a race, and a battle. Whatever happened, one of them landed and registered their claim. Shortly after, the first claim was voided. Someone else was still alive to replace them.'

'And Patricio thinks that they killed the first claimant and ended up staking their claim instead?'

'What happened to the other gallowglasses? It doesn't take much to disable a ship that small. EMP, rocket, kinetic weapon. Whoever is on the surface is most likely a murderer at least once over.'

'Wait, they're still there?'

'Still there, Jack. On the rock. In their ship, in a sleep tank. It's part of our contract that we wake them up and bring them on board, assuming they're still alive after nearly three years under. Share the voyage home with them. Do you see why no one wants to deal with this gallowglass?'

'NovaS have the mining rights. So someone clearly does. And we're still here. No one refused the mission.'

'You could buy whole nations with the wealth KU2 represents. For such, we all hold our noses with one hand, and reach out with the other to take our share. But we have to be seen to object first, even though we are complicit in the act. Our wages are soaked in blood.' Runi sucked the cold air of Control in through his teeth. 'But we will spend them all the same. Plot your course, make it fast and true. If it was not us, it would be someone else, and that is all there is to the matter.'

Jack took a deep breath, leaned forward to his screen and tried to forget everything else.

Part 2

Prograde burn

10

Whose asthma attack has been traced to ozone? I challenge
Sheffield et al. to produce a single medical record of an asthma
attack that can be linked to the ambient air of today. If there
are 675 annually, surely they can produce one or maybe two?
Please?

S. Milloy, 'Global warming causes asthma?',

JunkScience.com, 2011

Sometimes, when he woke up, he didn't remember where he
was, and he was gripped by vertiginous fear and disorientation.
This was one of those times, when everything felt wrong,
sounded wrong, smelled wrong, like he was in a waking dream
he didn't know how to escape from. Mesman had chased him
not just across Europe, but across the emptiness of space and
was lying next to him, the only way she could keep him safe
from harm.

It was May. It was only May. It was May, not *only May*, because May wasn't a substitute for anyone. He kept still in case
his thumping heart hammered too heavily into her back and
woke her. He breathed, in in in, and out. He remembered the
rest of it. He was under the one-fifth gravity of the rotating
section of the *Coloma*, they had left the Moon two hundred
and thirty-eight days ago, and they were three days away from
intercepting the asteroid 1998-KU2.

Night-lights illuminated the floor, and cast a faint pearl
glow up the walls that Julia had drawn on. At first, it was faux

frames and cartoon reproductions of the great masters of the Renaissance – her speciality – but the blank space between had slowly filled up with other decorations. Floral motifs, curving vines and bunches of grapes, jagged acanthus leaves and rambling roses. Her pens were almost exhausted, but she'd managed to make Jack's room not look like the sterile closet it was.

He didn't know what the ship's time was, but since he was awake, he assumed that it was time to get up, wash, eat, and sit in Control to stare at the numbers for a while. If there'd been an emergency, or even not an emergency but Andros just wanting to get him out of bed and run the figures once again, then someone would have pinged the intercom.

Orbital mechanics were literally predictable. What needed constant checking was their position against the stars. A minute change in exhaust temperature or mass ejection could, in a matter of hours, alter the ship's trajectory sufficiently to mean they'd come in too high or too low, or too fast or too slow, and trying to hit a five-k asteroid as it barrelled around the Sun was as difficult as he'd first said it would be.

He disengaged his arm. Had she been there when he'd gone to sleep? Their shifts didn't always coincide, and her call-outs were more of the 'fix this immediately or we die' variety than his – he could send them spinning out into space for a long, lingering death, but he wasn't going to rupture a module or have the radiators feed back their prodigious heat into the life support, both of which would be instantly and explosively fatal.

She was naked, and so was he. Seconds, measured off in precise fractions on the main clock, meant everything, but actual days and weeks and months bled together. So maybe she had, and maybe she hadn't. She didn't always come to him, and she didn't always wake him when she did, but often. Skin-to-skin human contact held back the presence of the void. It was warm and real and the opposite of indifferent.

He shrugged the thin covers off. With the exhaust running hotter than the Sun, and the powerplant enough to keep an entire city going, heat was the problem, not the cold. He eased himself over her curled-up form, and got his feet to the floor. Once, he'd found it difficult to balance in one-fifth-g. Now, he wondered if he could possibly ever survive the full force of one Earth gravity again.

He pulled on some shorts, then shrugged on his flightsuit taken down from the back of the door. He bent down to drag on ship slippers, and took one last look at May lying in his bed before slipping out the door and pushing it gently shut behind him. She hadn't stirred, just as he hadn't when she'd come in. Life on board was exhausting, if not physically, then mentally. He hadn't really known what to expect, but thought that boredom rather than continual bone-tiredness would have been one of the factors.

Jack climbed up the ladder – now that the rotating section was spinning, once every twenty seconds, there was an up – and reached the axis, where he weighed nothing at all. He flipped over and descended the opposite shaft to the kitchen area. Arush and Marta were there, drinking reconstituted fruit juice and eating their breakfast bars. Whatever time it actually was, it was their morning.

Arush ran a critical eye over Jack as he stood at the rehydration point, filling his pouch of powder with the regulation hundred millilitres of water and kneading the paste until it dispersed and became exactly the wrong shade of orange.

'You're losing muscle mass,' said Arush. 'You need to put in more time in the gym.'

'I've been concentrating on not getting us lost in the vastness of space,' said Jack, not turning round but going to the hopper for his carbohydrate- and fibre-rich, calcium-enhanced breakfast bar. 'I can catch up on exercise later.'

Arush folded the empty silvered mylar packet neatly into three and pushed it into the disposal canister that sat at the end of the table. 'I don't care if you break your promises, but I care if you break your arm.'

Jack leaned against the counter and drank his juice. It was acidic and sweet and wrong, but he'd been drinking it every morning for months now and he barely tasted how wrong it was. To think he'd once had fresh oranges, juiced in a machine by an anonymous kitchen hand. He sucked the last of the liquid from the packet and disposed of it in the approved slot.

He didn't feel weaker, but Arush was probably right. It was, after all, Arush's job to keep them in one piece, at least physically, until they got back to Cis-lunar space and could see a proper doctor. Exercising involved bands and straps and discomfort and, above all, time and energy. He had been fairly disciplined for a while, but as the weeks turned into months? They were all slacking on it, and Andros didn't give much of a lead. Just as long as they could still do their jobs, he didn't seem too bothered about anything else.

'Maybe he doesn't need to worry, with all the press-ups he does.' Marta didn't have a filter. Jack didn't find it an endearing trait. She knew his feelings on the matter, and he waited until the perpetual hum had put some distance between her words and his.

'I'll put in some time later,' he said. 'It's ... been difficult.' Manoeuvring the *Coloma* into the exact same orbit as KU2, a few kilometres off its presumed polar region, had eaten up most of his waking moments, and now they were close, he was constantly tweaking the thrust vectors and running the results through the computer before applying what he hoped was the right correction. Then he'd spend the next few hours watching the numbers to make sure he'd made the right call.

By the time he was satisfied, he'd have missed a meal, so would snatch something in the kitchen before going back to the screens for one last look and then crashing into bed, with or without May. Quite how this would work in a proper ship, with a proper shift system, and some actual discipline and a command structure, was something that he sometimes dreamed about, along with ploughing the *Coloma* into the only rock for a million miles in any direction.

He could still kill them all, but he had almost delivered on his first assertion that he could get the ship to the asteroid: it was there, within touching distance now.

He shook himself out of his daydream. Arush couldn't tell him what to do. Marta would shortly be too busy to make pointed remarks about his sex life. That he had one was something else he hadn't considered for a while. Earlier, it had been new and startling, but now it was just normal. Some of the crew had paired up. Some of them hadn't. And others appeared to maintain a network of fluid relationships that seemed to suit them, though not necessarily everyone in their orbit. He didn't feel it was his place to comment, just as long as work was done competently. He'd begun to think like crew. He hadn't, and now he did.

He ate his breakfast standing up, but there was something unsatisfactory about leaning in low gravity, in that it didn't have the same slouchiness as he was used to. Marta tidied her debris away and climbed the ladder, going hand over hand without bothering to use her feet. She was replaced by Kayla, the life support specialist.

She absently dapped with Jack as she passed, and took the insulated cup off her belt to make herself yet more coffee. Jack caught Arush's expression as she poured near-boiling water on the granules, and rather than listen to another medical lecture – this time, on Kayla's resting pulse rate – he headed up to the axis. The voices behind him, low and concerned, higher and fractious, faded away.

He pulled himself through to Control, and installed himself at an empty workstation. Andros was there, and Runi was in the pilot's chair, possibly asleep, but it was difficult to tell as he had a habit of sitting very still and just watching the streams of information, looking for anything anomalous, as if the ship was an extension of his body and he could feel its pain. Patricio, at the next station, was intent on his screen where the software was stitching a three-dimensional model of KU2 from the raw radar data. Jack leaned over and took stock of the new information.

'Resolution?'

'Two metres. Good enough to accurately determine rotation.' Patricio had grown pale in captivity, and oddly taut. Fluid retention, potentially oedema. Arush had given him specific exercises to counter it which, like the rest of the crew, he wasn't doing. He gestured to the screen, and the model began to rotate in real time. 'We have ourselves a tumbler.'

'I guess that's going to make things difficult. But not impossible?'

'We can use the laser to change the moment of inertia.' Patricio glanced across at the back of Andros's head. 'Our burn pattern is going to be baroque, given we still intend to land.'

The plan – splitting the ship in two and anchoring Control and the crew modules to the asteroid – had always struck Jack as an unnecessary complication, but it would make the surface accessible for EVA, and anyway, the *Coloma* didn't have the reserves to keep on station for months. 'So are we definitely doing that?'

'Yes.' The miner tapped the statistic-rich side bar. 'We have the major axis of rotation with a period of six point eight hours, which is precessing at an angle of thirty-seven degrees with a period of forty-eight hours. Minimum ground speed at the pole is a little over five centimetres a second. It is, as you say, difficult, but not impossible.'

'At least it's roughly spherical. Though that, if it's not an artefact, is a big-ass cliff.' He pointed at the line marching around the displayed object, and the computer interpreted his hand in a way that caused the image to shrink to almost a point. 'Sorry.'

Patricio sighed and brought it back. 'It's about a hundred metres high. It may be the edge of a separate body, but we won't know until we take some seismic soundings. How close are you planning to get?'

Jack pushed back to his own workstation and brought up his simulation. 'There may be a tail, and I don't want to get into that. We're pulling in parallel, and applying lateral thrust to vector in sideways. I'll get us to a hundred k, we can properly scan the surface, then bring it down to twenty-five, when Runi can do ship separation.'

'When?'

'The countdown is fifty-six hours for the hundred-k insertion.'

'I'll get Kayla to run suit tests in the next period.' Patricio studied the spinning asteroid. 'I know I can't look through the exhaust with the spectrometer.'

'I can't help that. We're down to the last few decimal points.'

'It'll mean a delay in deploying the laser.'

'By a few days.' Jack watched his own numbers. 'We have to get down there first.'

Andros stirred. They could hear the creak of his seat, followed by his throat clearing.

'Update me, Astrogator.'

Sometimes, it was easy to forget that the captain was there. He didn't take part in any of the crew's discussions, didn't take the lead, didn't veto any of their decisions. He didn't seem to have any competences of his own, and he didn't appear to understand much, if anything, of what was going on around him. Yet he was there, in deep space. Jack wasn't sure what to make of the man.

'The asteroid is behind us as we decelerate. We'll let it draw up alongside us – in two and a half days' time – and as we move closer, we can map the asteroid accurately as it rotates: visual, radar and spectroscopy.'

NovaS might have sent someone who could at least pretend to care about the crew, but they'd got Andros, whose sole concern seemed to be the interests of the people he referred to as 'our investors', and then only to use the concept as a threat. If their investors were real, then to a man and woman, they were no better than gangsters.

'When will we have a preliminary surface assay?'

'Three days?' Jack glanced at Patricio, who nodded his confirmation.

'Sooner, Astrogator.'

Jack realised that Andros was anxious to find out just how much the asteroid was worth, and therefore the price of his NovaS stock. If they found strong signatures of iron, nickel and cobalt, then every shareholder could pretty much write their own pay cheque. If it was nothing but dull rock, they could all end up with a lot less than what they wanted.

But the wait wouldn't hurt them, and no one could have got the ship on station any quicker. Jack was getting used to Andros's unreasonable demands, and, under Patricio's expert tutelage, used to either deflecting or defying them.

'I'll see what I can do, Captain.' Jack knew he'd do nothing, because his course, his best course, was already laid in, and Runi was following it. He waited for Andros's seat to creak into quiescence again. 'Can you see the gallowglass's ship?'

Patricio shook his head. 'Resolution isn't good enough. These things are tiny: central core of two, two and a half metres across. If they ditched their panels on final approach, or they came off, or they were hacked away, then we won't locate it until we get a visual.' He froze the image, and zoomed in with a finger-and-thumb gesture. 'The hull is supposed to be a ceramic foam. Like *pómez*. Pumice. It won't show up as any different from the rock. Also, it might have unused weapons on the outside. Retrieving the gallowglass may not be straightforward.'

'Okay. And I'm sorry about the approach.'

'It would take seven hours' observations to map ninety per cent of the surface. We need those seven hours to slow ourselves down. I understand.'

94

He wondered if pulling up within a hundred kilometres of the surface wasn't showing off a little, doing it because he wanted everyone to see how good he was, because he wasn't just some ultra-rich kid having a jaunt on a spaceship that his Pap could buy out of loose change, because he wanted – deserved – praise.

A hundred k was well inside the Hill radius. He could go for three times that and still make orbit. But given that he could make a hundred k, and that controlling the ship would be significantly easier at that distance, with less chance of just wandering off out into space again, then a hundred kilometres it was. Runi might appreciate his artistry, but he doubted anyone else was going to.

Definitely not doing it to be lauded. Doing it because it was safer than all the other options. Doing it because he was crew, and he wasn't going to be the one to kill them all.

These people, these contradictory, infuriating people, these brothers and sisters in adversity.

'Why not stand down? Get some sleep before the real work starts,' said Jack. He flashed a quick grin. 'I'll call you if it hatches.'

It was a space joke. Asteroids looked like potatoes, or eggs, or seed pods.

'Sure. Keep the radar on target, yes? More data is better data. I'll take another look next shift.' Patricio unstrapped himself from his seat, and used Jack's shoulders to push himself towards the axis.

As the miner's feet disappeared, Jack turned back to his screen. He watched the numbers: deceleration constant, velocity decreasing, distance to KU2 falling. If he concentrated, he could feel it, the very slight notion of down in the direction of the engines. If he took something out of his pocket, it would drift towards the nominal floor.

Andros was staring at him, and Jack could feel it without even looking.

'You could have stayed at home, Van der Veerden. You

could have stayed on Earth with your parties and your drugs and your drink and your whores.' He did this sometimes. The ammunition he used was different for each of the crew, but it was consistent to the person. That was how Jack knew Patricio was blacklisted labour, chased out of meaningful work for unionising, and fighting: so many fights. And how he knew Runi was a former child soldier, responsible for God knows how many deaths. But Andros habitually picked on Jack, presumably because the target was so easy.

And yes, he was right, of course. Jack could have stayed on Earth. But he was also wrong: Jack's parents were puritan when it came to the pleasures of the flesh. The world was burning, yet it was the integrity of their genetic material that concerned them most. All that money, all that opportunity for great good or greater excess, and it was their health and their wealth that they guarded fiercely. Like dragons, just as the ESTA-5 technician Petrescu had said.

Jack had soon stopped trying to defend himself to his captain, justify why he'd given up what he'd had then for what he had now.

The dark. The light. The cold and the heat. The ever-present hum. The terrible food and the sleeting radiation. The bone-thinning, muscle-wasting low gravity. The water that passed, endlessly recycled, through their bodies. The fractious interpersonal bonds between disparate, ill-matched people with dubious motives and dirty pasts. May. Threading a ship through the emptiness of space to exactly the right place at exactly the right time at exactly the right speed.

'Yes, sir,' said Jack. 'But then I would have missed all this.'

11

Sea level rise, which was occurring long before humans could be blamed, has not accelerated and still amounts to only 1 inch every ten years. If a major hurricane is approaching with a predicted storm surge of 10–14 feet, are you really going to worry about a sea level rise of 1 inch per decade?

R. Spencer, *Forbes*, 2016

Jack was desperate to eyeball the asteroid, just to confirm to himself that it was there and this wasn't some giant immersive simulation game. He had all the read-outs, the stitched-together maps, and for the want of some transparent plastic, he doubted any of it was real.

He confessed his sins to May, who ruffled his hair – he refused to get it buzzcut after the first time, even as the rest of the crew kept theirs suede-short – and showed him once again that it was real. After they were done, and she was lying on top of him, he was left wondering what it would be like to really feel her weight, five times what it was now, pressing against him, cutting off nerves and blood supply.

He stroked her spine, feeling the ridges of the vertebrae as his finger moved from coccyx to the base of her skull and back, counting the bones. They were all getting thinner.

'We should really exercise,' he said out loud, mainly to the ceiling.

'This again?' she murmured.

He turned his head slightly. 'I'm starting to forget what the inside of the gym looks like.'

'Arush.'

'He mentioned it.'

'He doesn't have eighteen-hour days making sure something doesn't fall off.'

'Has something fallen off?'

'It shows how good I am.' She raised herself up and rested her forearms across his chest. 'The ship's well made, well fitted out. It's fresh out of the can. Sure, it's a hell of a commissioning voyage, but it'll get us there and back. Everything is routine maintenance. Which, unlike exercise, I can't skimp on.'

'What's the time?'

She glanced down at her watch and read the dial in the half-light. 'Oh five thirty-eight.'

'I need to be in Control. Three hours to first approach.' He waited for her to move. 'That was a hint?'

'I know.' She rolled off him, and lay on her back. She lifted one arm and rubbed her scalp, running her fingers from back to front, against the grain of her hair. 'I'm exhausted. And not just because of that. If I haven't shown my face in a couple of hours, hit me up on the intercom. And take a shower. You smell of me.'

'Has someone said something?' He sat up and swung his legs out. He held them straight, for as long as he could, but was eventually disappointed with the result.

'Someone's always saying something. Usually on the lines of why I find sons of multi-billionaires attractive.' She pulled the quilt over her body and buried her face in the pillow. 'Ignore them. I do.'

'You know I'm not going to see a cent of that. Not now.'

'It's not why I sleep with you.' Her voice was muffled, drowsy. 'And I'm soon going to be rich myself anyway.'

Jack pulled his shorts on. He thought back to the message he'd sent when they were three days out and already moving at a thousand metres a second. A message that had, so far, gone unanswered.

He hadn't tried again. There were even times when he'd forgotten he'd sent it. Snoring noises came from behind him, and he shrugged his way into his flightsuit without doing it up, and put on his ship slippers.

He stood by the open door for a moment, looking back into the room. His room. It wasn't love. At least, it didn't feel like love. His experience was so incredibly limited that maybe it was and he couldn't tell. She hadn't said she loved him, nor he her. Something told him that she wasn't an undying-declaration sort of woman.

Shower. Breakfast. Work.

Jack climbed up to the axis, then down towards the gym. Not *to* the gym, of course, but to the shower cubicles that were next to the gym area. There were two stalls, one of them occupied, and whoever had last used the other hadn't wiped it down properly with the squeegee. He could feel himself get annoyed, and consciously told himself to let it go. After all, he'd used to have people invisibly cleaning up behind him, and he'd not given that a moment's thought until he had to do it himself, which he did because it turned out he liked things clean.

Sure, he expected he did things that other people didn't like, so they were cutting him slack on that. They were all crew, and it was how they got along.

He squeaked the rubber blade over the inside of the stall, shaking it every so often, watching the fat, slow drops of water bounce on the hard plastic and slide like gel into the drain. The reclamation plant in the next unit gurgled. Then without seeing who the other showeree was, he clicked the stall door shut, stripped off and ran the hot for five minutes.

For that exact length of time, the ship was fine, and he was fine. He turned the water off and turned on the blowers. The humidity rose to uncomfortable levels, then dropped again. He squeegeed the ceiling, the walls, the floor, and gave the blowers another blast, just to dry the bottom of his feet, and his hair again. He got dressed, and by the time he'd done that, the other shower was empty.

It was like that. He could go for days without seeing the same people twice, something that he hadn't anticipated on such a small ship with nine crew.

He grabbed a breakfast bar and some juice from the kitchen module. Kayla was there.

'You ready?' she asked.

'As ready as I can be,' he said, changing his mind halfway through his sentence from 'ready as I'll ever be', because that wasn't true. The next time, he'd be better. 'I'll take it in slowly. An extra few hours, even another day, isn't going to make any difference.'

'Suits are ready when you need them.' She saw his less than thrilled expression. 'You don't have to EVA. Astrogators generally don't.'

'I want to do it.'

'To prove to us you can do it, or to prove it to yourself? Or is it your mother and father?' She gave him the look over the top of her coffee.

'If I'm going to spend any time in space, I have to know how to do this.'

'As much as we need you, if you float off, no one will come and rescue you.'

'I've been told that too. By everyone.'

'Even May?'

'Especially May.' He binned his wrappers. 'All this way, and it comes down to the last few k.'

'Don't fuck up, Jack.'

'I've got this.'

'I hope so,' was her parting shot.

Jack climbed up the shaft and pulled himself into Control. Runi was there, as ever, and Andros, and Julia, since she was in charge of the fuel systems. He nodded to his captain, and dapped Julia and Runi, before settling in his usual seat and strapping in. He loaded up his screens and looked at the lines and the numbers. They were as good as they were going to get. He'd planned this, over and over again, and now they were finally here.

He cleared his throat, and swallowed the last crumbs of his breakfast bar. 'Okay,' he said. He examined the radar model of the asteroid. 'Okay.' He leaned forward. He frowned. 'That's not okay.'

'Talk to me, Astrogator,' said Andros.

'We ...' Jack spun the model around, and played with some of the error correction values. 'Give me a minute here. Runi, hold your position.'

He switched from the deconvoluted data to the raw signal and back, flicking the images in real time.

'I think we have a debris ring.'

Andros rumbled, 'Is that a problem?'

'Yes. Yes, it is. I'm going to need some time on this. I'll call Patricio.'

'More delay?'

Jack caught his tongue between his teeth until he was ready to speak. 'We could drive the ship through a rotating field of rock fragments without knowing exactly what's there. Personally, I'd rather not go anywhere near it without working out a profile of particle size. It shouldn't be there on an asteroid this small, and yet here it is. Runi, can you put us in some kind of holding pattern so we can take a look at this, minimum approach of seven hundred k?'

'Triangular orbit?'

'That's fine. No closer.'

Runi leaned towards the intercom. 'Acceleration acceleration.'

'How long is this going to take?'

Andros really was being a dick, and Jack clenched his jaw, then deliberately relaxed it. 'I need to map this out, find out whether the radar targets are large enough to put holes in the hull, or the radiators, and how defined the band is. There'll be a clear zone towards the surface, and an outer limit beyond which the disc is too dispersed to matter, but it only needs a couple of hundred-centimetre blocks hiding in amongst all that to hit something critical, and we're all floating home.'

'We're not in university now,' said Andros. 'All I asked you was how long this was going to take.'

Jack again had to clamp down on his irritation. 'Once we're over the polar region, we can scan the whole disc. The longer we look, the more likely it is that we can spot potentially damaging debris—'

'Van der Veerden. How long?'

'I'm trying to explain—' He gave up. 'In four hours, I'll have a better idea of how much longer I'll need. You, inexplicably, made me the astrogator of this ship, and I am doing my job keeping the ship and all of the crew safe from a potential navigation hazard that I have just spotted. And since I know about orbital ring systems from that fancy university I went to, I am trying to make sure that not only can we land the crew part of the ship on the target, but also ensure that the laser system doesn't get damaged, which is, after all, why we're here. To conclude: this ship goes absolutely nowhere near KU2 until I'm satisfied it's safe to proceed. Captain.'

Julia gave him some serious side-eye, but he wasn't backing down. The four of them sat in silence for a while, and finally Andros stirred.

'Astrogator has the helm.'

He unclipped his strap and pushed off his console, falling down the axis head first. Julia leaned back to see if he'd truly gone, and Runi shook his head slightly in warning.

'Jesus, Jack,' said Julia.

'What, you think we should plough a spaceship into a cloud of rock too?'

'God, no. I'm proud of you. I mean, good spot and every-thing, but telling Andros to go fuck himself was the icing on the cake.'

Jack swigged some water from a bulb, and tagged it back under his console. Confrontation always made his heart race. 'I'll take that as a vote of confidence. Right: Runi, forget about the orbit. Can you put us in a polar station, seven hundred k, keep it as stable as you can. Julia, I need the optical feed pushed into the plotting software. I'll get the radar sweep set up. Everyone know what they're doing?'

'I'll warn everyone again,' said Runi. 'Acceleration acceler-ation.' His tone was far calmer than Jack felt, but he needed to follow it, to slow right down and get this right.

The ship started to turn. He could feel it at the start, and again at the end of the manoeuvre. He zoomed his screen in on the graphics, that told him where the *Coloma* was in relation to the asteroid. The numbers were falling.

'Runi, can you yaw plus ten degrees on the x-axis?'

The ship shifted, and Jack was able to get a full radar picture of the asteroid, front-on. He looked at the data, at the fuzzy ring that surrounded the potato-shaped rock in the middle. There were potentially a couple of brighter spots inside of that, and he tracked them for a while. They kept winking in and out of existence, enough to make him think they might simply be noise, but their presence was annoyingly persistent.

'It has moons,' said Jack. 'Pretty certain it shouldn't have moons.'

'Tell me why it shouldn't have moons,' said Julia. She was aiming the optical telescopes, both the narrow-field one and the wide-field that Jack used for star shots.

'Too small, too unstable, and it should get cleared out every time it does a close approach to the Sun.'

'And yet it has moons.'

'They're a metre across, two at most. One at roughly two-fifty k, and the other at three-fifty.' He brought up a spreadsheet to the side and tapped in some numbers. 'The second one is a two-to-one resonance with the first. If we've anything to be grateful for, it's that they've cleared the inner orbits of debris.'

Patricio appeared on deck. 'Did someone call me? We have a visual?'

Julia turned her screen towards him, and he hung from the nominal ceiling to see it better.

'What is this?' He waved his finger in a circle around the bright central dot.

'Dust ring.' She cut off his objections. 'We've done that. It still has one, whether we like it or not.' She drove the telescope lenses to enlarge the image. 'This is, I guess, what we're calling the north polar region.'

Where the sunlight hit, it was white. Where it didn't, it was black. It looked lumpy, cratered, with several pits appearing to be deeper than they were broad, though that was probably just a trick of the shadows.

'It's an ugly place,' he said.

'I can get some more definition on that,' she said. 'Where's Marta?'

'Preparing the lab equipment.'

Julia dialled down the contrast on the image and boosted the brightness. Space still looked flat black, but the surface of the asteroid became a more familiar greyish colour. The crater bottoms resolved, but Patricio was right: it was ugly. 'Jack, you're very quiet.'

'I'm looking for something. A needle in a haystack.' He shoved a duplicate of his window onto Julia's screen. 'You see how there's a distinct gap here in the dust? That's at the four-to-one resonance, or two-to-one with the second moon. There's dust further out than that, but it's very diffuse. Then nothing. Then a more distinct band.'

'How far out is that?'

'Six hundred and thirty k. Anything orbiting at that distance will have a period of about three hundred days, so it's going to be moving slow. Around fifteen centimetres a second.' He scowled at the screen, trying to force it to give up its secrets. 'We could be here for a while.'

'We don't want to run short on cold propellant,' said Runi. 'I'll have to turn the ship every half hour and boost us back up with the main engines.'

'I'll keep an eye on it,' said Julia, whose job it was.

Patricio drifted over to Jack's console. 'What do you think? About all this?'

'I'm disturbed by the fact it's here at all. But we have to account for it somehow. An impact, maybe in the last couple of years, with something, enough to make the ring, but ...' His voice trailed off. 'Okay. I'm just going to check something.'

'What?'

'So, I assumed that the reason why the asteroid was roughly where we thought it would be, but not exactly, was because whoever measured the orbit the first time, or the second time, didn't do it quite accurately enough. As the ship got closer, I continually adjusted the intercept based on actual data, not on the predicted path. I've been doing that for months. If I lay the asteroid orbit as it really is on top of what it was supposed to be, three years ago, then—' Jack's fingers clattered across the keyboard and a new image appeared.

Two lines, clearly divergent. Ever so slightly, but in terms of orbital mechanics, significant.

'Does this make it easier, or more difficult, for us to get this rock to the L4 refineries?'

'I don't know yet. Since we're here to steer it, a bit more or less steering should be easy enough to factor in. The difference between the orbits isn't that great.' He looked up into Patricio's peculiarly plump face. 'I should have realised earlier. I could have predicted this.'

Patricio made a rumbling sound deep in his chest. 'If it was an impact, if the rock is broken, into two or more pieces, and it falls apart when we try and move it, then we may have to choose which fragment to take. Our haul could be significantly less than either we, or our mysterious investors, would like. Then there is also the question of the gallowglass.'

Jack had been so concerned with the technical aspects of the debris ring that he'd completely forgotten that there ought to be a live human being cocooned on the surface of the asteroid.

'They could be dead.'

'They could be dead. They could have been buried. Their ship could have been thrown off into space and be lost for ever. Or,' he said, 'it could be one of these moons.'

12

Around the world, environmentalism has become a radical
movement, something we call the Green Dragon, and it is deadly.
Deadly to human prosperity, deadly to human life, deadly to
human freedom, and deadly to the gospel of Jesus Christ.
Cornwall Alliance for the Stewardship of Creation,
Resisting the Green Dragon, 2010

Now they were all in Control, and Jack had been awake for
twenty hours. If only he'd inherited his parents' ability to need
next to no sleep and still function at a high level – but if that
was in his future, he was still dragging his teenage past with
him, and he wasn't doing so well, no matter how much caffeine
he'd drunk. Kayla was beginning to fear that the ship's dried
coffee stores that she'd come to see as hers wouldn't last the
trip home.

From where they were, balanced precariously over the
asteroid's pole, they couldn't see more than a third of the
surface of the rock with the narrow-field telescope. Patricio
and Marta had been over those images with their own eyes and
pattern-recognition software, and couldn't spot the gallowglass
ship bolted down anywhere. Resolution was good – they could
image anything over the size of a house-brick – but what they
could see made them nervous.

The cliff Patricio had seen on the radar looked too sharp,
too new, as if there was a fault-line running all the way through
the heart of the asteroid. The only way to tell whether that

was true or not, or whether it would fracture completely when they started the laser ablation, was to go down and do a proper seismic survey. That would take more time.

Andros, as ever, was the one who wanted to just go ahead, to deploy the solar arrays, to land the crew section, to start the laser, and worry about whether his prize would fall apart underneath them later. The crew were united that they weren't going to do that. Sure, they all wanted their bonus, but they all wanted to be alive to spend it.

But that wasn't what they were arguing about. It was that the second moon, the one orbiting at the three-fifty-kilometre mark, bore a striking resemblance to a gallowglass ship. Jack had assumed that it would be easy to tell, but May had found some schematics to show him that, stripped of their solar panels and their external sensors, and their ceramic hulls pitted by collisions both deliberate and accidental, they'd quickly start to resemble a smooth, pale sphere of plain rock.

There was also a chance that if it was a gallowglass, it wasn't their gallowglass, just a remnant of the fight over the mining rights to the asteroid. The competing gallowglasses would have converged on the rock from various trajectories, then fired projectiles at each other, launched bomblets and EMP weapons, potentially even rammed each other. The rewards – a fraction of a percentage of the overall wealth represented by the resources – were still enough to motivate someone to kill, and only one of the gallowglasses had successfully staked a claim out of the many who had set out.

So the gallowglass ship, if that was what the object was, could simply be a casualty, a coffin, of a skirmish that happened back when the rights were grabbed. Or it could be the ship that had made it to the surface, and the one they were contractually obliged to retrieve, even if the pilot inside was dead.

May zoomed in on the moonlet. 'Once we start pushing the rock we'll accelerate the dispersal of the debris ring anyway. Ideally, we'd use the laser on the larger bits of debris to turn them into vapour, and take them out before they could spiral in and threaten the infrastructure. But I'm not going to be party to vaporising something that's potentially got a human inside, even one that's a gallowglass.'

'They're not crew,' said Marta. 'They'll never be crew.'

Jack said nothing, because he knew that the next comment would be from someone saying something about 'your girlfriend'. Supporting her now would undermine her, and honestly, he was a little surprised by her stance, given he knew full well her feelings on the untrustworthiness of gallowglasses.

'We risk the ship, and the mission, if we try,' said Andros, 'and that is unacceptable. The *Coloma* is not equipped to retrieve objects from space.'

Runi shifted in the pilot's seat. 'We can get close enough to it to identify it for certain. Ten k away to resolve the surface features. We'd see the engine cone, and external pylons.'

'Since we cannot retrieve it,' said Andros, 'there is no point going closer.'

There was a profound silence. The crew each thought about being entombed in a sleep tank in a ship slowly draining of power.

'Can we use the shuttle?' asked Jack. 'It's got some propellant left, and the ship doesn't have to get within a kilometre of the object. We can orbit above the ring, and our delta-v will be effectively zero.'

'We cannot retrieve it,' reiterated Andros.

'If we could work out a way to retrieve it, we could then discuss whether it's a good idea to try.' Over-caffeinated Jack struggled to keep his temper. 'What's the mass on this?'

'Couple of tonnes,' said May. 'Most of that is the thermonuclear pile.'

'If we can't physically tow it, can we just drop it? Kill its orbital velocity and let it fall?'

Kayla snorted: 'You'd scramble whoever's inside.'

'Escape velocity is three and a half metres a second. That's a third of what it would do if we dropped it just one metre back on Earth. It won't hit that hard, and even if it does, it's clearly already been through worse. It was tethered to the asteroid, and now it's orbiting it.' Jack was convincing himself, and now he wanted to convince the others. 'We just have to nudge it. The shuttle has more mass than two tonnes.'

'At the risk of putting a fly in the ointment,' said Kayla, 'you've studied elastic collisions, right?'

'Yes,' he said slowly.

'What's going to stop anything we drop on the asteroid at over a metre a second from just bouncing off it, given surface gravity is a millimetre per second squared?' Kayla demonstrated with her hands, and then had to reattach herself to the ceiling.

Jack felt his plan unravel. 'Hope?'

'Come on, Jack. We're deorbiting something that might have a human being in it. If it doesn't land in a bed of sand, it's – at best – going to bounce all over the rock and have multiple impacts, any one of which might crack the shell, disrupt the electronics or break the life support.'

'She's right, you know,' said Arush.

'And we don't have three hundred and fifty kilometres of cable to gently lower it to the ground, either.' Kayla tried to soften the blow. 'I know that sucks, but it's just not going to work.'

'Okay. So it wasn't the best idea I've ever had.' Jack went back to staring at his screen.

May frowned. 'If we tie it to the shuttle – securely – then dock the shuttle back onto Control? As long as our max acceleration is within tolerances, we can just land with it. It'll need an EVA to strap it on.'

'Shuttle's not exactly made for that, but this is low gravity, low acceleration,' said Runi. 'What's its orbital velocity?'

'Twenty centimetres a second,' said Jack. 'Barely moving.'

'I'll go out,' said Marta. 'If only to get the mission back on track.'

Jack raised his eyebrows. 'I thought you wanted her to rot?'

'I'm an EVA specialist,' she said, 'and you're young and stupid enough to think you can do it yourself even though you have no experience at all, and I'd like to go home and be rich, thank you very much. For that, we need you alive.'

'We cannot retrieve it,' said Andros for a third time.

'It's in the bloody contract.' Julia had developed a twitch under her right eye. 'It's in the contract that we revive the gallowglass and bring them home. This is the only gallowglass we can see, so even if they've managed to get themselves launched back into orbit, then that's where we're going to have to get them from. Let's take a look. If it is a gallowglass, give them a tow back to the surface. If we screw it up, or they're already dead, no harm, no foul, we tried.'

'Do you really want a gallowglass on board?' asked Marta.

'Fuck no, but we're the only ship that can help them, can ever help them, and I might be a cold-hearted, money-grubbing bitch, but really? If it was me left out there one day, whatever the circumstances, I'd like to think someone passing by might lend a hand.'

'This is simply more delay,' said Andros. 'The mission, and your bonuses, depend on us deploying the laser on time.'

'You will blame us for your failure, and take credit for our success, no matter what,' said Patricio. 'You are a contemptible man, and this mission cannot be over soon enough.'

Andros appeared as a technological demon, malevolently lit by coloured lights and glowing screens against a backdrop of pipes and wiring looms. Even though he was impotent, and the threat he represented merely conceptual, Jack still worried about him, and what he might be capable of if he continued to be so thoroughly ignored by the crew.

'So we're doing this?' Julia turned to Jack. 'Run the numbers. See how much fuel we have to spend.'

'Trivial, given how little gravity is local to here. Less than we're using keeping on station, that's for sure.' Jack tapped

111

some keys. 'Okay. If we combine a prograde burn of plus point two with a two-stage manoeuvre to put us in the ecliptic. Call it one metre a second.'

'We can do that. I'll go with Marta to suit up and depressurise.'

'If anyone needs the can, do it now.' May looked content with the outcome. 'And if you've got loose shit in your cabin, you've got five minutes to stow it. After that, rotation will cease. Jack? You know what you're like.'

'Especially after all that coffee.'

'Thanks, Kayla.' He ported the course to Runi, and undid his strap again. He floated to the axis, but in turning around, met Andros's gaze full on.

All he could think about were how the walls were very thin, and the vacuum outside very hard.

He showed Control his heels and drifted down the axis to the rotating section. He slid down the ladder to the gym section, and locked himself in a cubicle with his flightsuit down around his ankles. It gave him more time to obsess about how the ship was the only habitable place for a million kilometres, how on Earth it was still the case that simply stepping outside the door wouldn't kill you, and that human beings had no business trying to move into space without fixing the mess they were leaving behind first.

Yet here he was, asteroid-mining beyond the orbit of Mars, and his motivation for being there was no more or less pure than any other crew member's, and he couldn't judge any of them for it.

And he was now definitely crew. Quite when he'd made that transition, he didn't know, but he was absolutely crew in a way that Andros wasn't. He was valued for what he did, not for what he might potentially be worth – which was currently nothing, if they didn't successfully park this asteroid at a refinery.

Someone hammered on the door. 'There's a queue out here.' Arush.

'Sorry.'

112

Jack pressed the buttons that evacuated the bowl with a suck and a thump, and pulled his flightsuit back up to his shoulders. He disengaged the lock and stumbled out.

'You shouldn't need any me-time in there,' said Arush, already unzipping.

'I was ... thinking,' said Jack at the already closing door. 'That space is big and scary and we must be mad to be out here so far from home.'

'You'll be fine once you get some sleep. Nothing but water or juice from now on. But if you'll excuse me, I don't like talking to people while I'm taking a dump.'

Kayla emerged from the other cubicle, zipping up her flightsuit. 'You ready, flyboy?'

'I mean, sure.' He squirted water on his hands, and finished up with some alcohol gel. 'There's no way this can go wrong. We have all the problems of working in a gravity well while having all the problems of working in zero-g. Maybe Andros has a point.'

'Fuck Andros. Seriously, fuck that man. No one likes a gallowglass, but we're better than that.'

Jack offered the ladder to Kayla first, who took it, and he followed. Back in Control, Runi was ready with the course profile, and Marta and Julia were inside the shuttle, suiting up. May was at a console, staring at a screen, and Andros ... he was just sitting there. And perhaps, if he'd tried to order the crew to retrieve the gallowglass, they would have swung the other way and this – using the crew's enmity towards him – was the only way to get what he actually wanted.

Was he that calculating? Jack couldn't tell, and he was past the point where he cared. Gallowglasses were still people, and the *Coloma* was the only ship that could save them. He strapped in, checked his course, checked it again, and waited for Arush to re-enter the module. May, next to him, pulled up a checklist on a new window.

She talked to the intercom. 'Arush, we're going to need you out of there soon, or we'll miss the burn.'

He appeared as if summoned, head first out of the axis. 'I'm here.' He found a seat and tied himself down. Patricio slid everyone the optical feed, and overlaid it with the target. It wasn't even a pixel wide.

May worked her way down her checklist, before finally announcing, 'Rotation rotation,' and telling the motors that turned the spinning section to slowly power down.

'Rotation stop.' She glanced at Runi. 'Ready when you are.'

'Acceleration acceleration. Burn in ten. Five. Three, two, one. Mark.'

The ship had already turned. The acceleration was tiny, but sufficient.

The lines on the screen twisted, and began to converge. They were deliberately moving closer to a ring of debris: that was a risk, but it was a calculated one. They could orbit above the main disc, and they would be moving at the same speed as it was. If anything did bang against the hull, it would do so very gently. May had her eye on the radiator stats which, given each panel extended nearly a hundred and twenty metres out from the hull, presented a much bigger surface area to hit than the profile of the hull. If damage was going to occur anywhere, it would be out there.

They closed in, and halfway through the burn, Runi turned the ship to kill some of the inward vector. It rendered the moon unobservable for a minute, but once he'd turned the ship again, the narrow-field camera hunted down the target and brought it to their screens in much sharper resolution than before. They were twenty-four kilometres and five hours away. When things outside moved so incredibly slowly, they had to too, and there was no margin for error.

'That ... looks like a ship,' said May. It was pale, quite smooth over most of its surface, but with regular protrusions around its circumference. 'That's where the panels were anchored. And here, that looks like the plug-in for something bigger on the hull.'

They waited for the object to rotate, which it did, just very slowly, creeping around like it was an hour hand.

'And that's the exhaust from the drive. The bell's missing, but that's what the hole is.'

'Where's the hatch?' asked Jack.

'Under the skin of the hull. They literally seal them in, and the only way out is to chip them out. Standard mining tools will see to that.'

Jack baulked. 'Can they not choose to get out on their own?'

'Technically, yes, there are explosive bolts, but if you're shaving grams off, they can get missed. That's what the sleep tank is for.' May raised her voice. 'So, do we agree? That's a gallowglass. Whether it's our gallowglass is impossible to tell, but do we tow it or not?'

No one objected, not even Marta. Given that Andros stayed silent, Jack thought that his suspicions were confirmed.

'Decided. We're here, so let's do it,' said Julia. 'I'll even make notes on how we do it, so we can show everyone what a bunch of big damn heroes we are later.'

13

Amongst other birds were those which men in the Indies call *doddaerssen*. They were larger than geese but not able to fly; instead of wings they had small flaps, but they could run very fast.

V. Evertsz, survivor of the shipwreck of the *Arnhem*,
Mauritius, 1662

'Ready for separation.'

'This is it. Hang onto your hats.'

'I'm not wearing a hat.'

'The hat is metaphorical.'

'Can I concentrate here?'

Jack listened to the conversation, the banter, as the English would say, without joining in. The gallowglass ship was attached by ratchet straps to the shuttle, which was docked to the docking ring at the end of Control. They joked, while he sweated bullets. Perhaps they trusted Runi not to drive them into the asteroid's pole – an inconstant place at that, given that it was itself moving at five centimetres every second. That was okay, but while he was doing that, Jack was inexplicably in charge of the business end of the mission, steering the drive section into a parking orbit.

With the drive, they could abort. Without it, they couldn't. Simple.

Jack had the course plotted. A tiny boost to move it clear of the crew section, and then a longer burn to get it up to the required seventy-five centimetres a second to maintain its twenty-five k orbit above the surface. He was used, theoretically, to designing trajectories in the kilometre-a-second band. This seemed simply surreal, and he had to keep on checking his calculations for a rogue decimal point.

If he lost the drive section because he'd got confused, they were probably never getting home again, let alone claiming their bonuses, and they'd be tethered to an almost five-kilometre-wide asteroid as it headed inexorably inwards on its three-year journey around the Sun, while they slowly ran out of supplies.

They'd used the main drive to kill any remaining drift. They were now falling towards the asteroid. They were also pointing the wrong way up.

'Separation in three, two, one, mark.'

Control gave a little shiver, and Jack used the remote connection, endlessly tested, to nudge the drive back. The cameras on the hull – both parts now – showed that there was an increasing gap between it and the crew section.

'One metre,' he called. Some thirty seconds later, 'Two metres.'

They were on their way. No rush, though. When separation had got to two hundred metres, the cameras on the crew section showed the drive's huge radiators as a sixteen-pointed star surrounding a slim cylinder.

'Pretty,' someone said, but Jack had more or less blanked out his surroundings. He used the gyroscopes to turn the drive section, and the ephemeris to check on its position in space. It was where he needed it to be, and he lit the drive, the million-degree exhaust momentarily bright against the black backdrop. He watched the orbital velocity increase, and when it hit the magic number, the drive shut down in a ghost of glowing vapour that expanded and cooled and darkened.

'Drive section orbital insertion complete,' he said. 'Runi, your turn.'

'Acceleration, acceleration.' The pilot spun the crew section over smoothly, so that the landing legs and the anchors and grappling hooks and targeting cameras were now pointing down.

'Descent is point one five. Ground speed is point zero seven.'

At which rate, they would arrive at the surface in around two hours. It would give them time to look properly at the surface, find the best landing spot and fix any problems that might occur. It was also a very long time to stare at a screen with total concentration. Jack rubbed his eyes, drank from a bulb of water and tried to massage some life into his face.

They could go quicker, but that only meant that the bad things would happen faster. On Earth, the same fall would be over in seventy seconds, which was no time at all. Barely enough for the Lord's Prayer.

'Landing lights. Test.' May leaned forward, the screen giving her face a pale blue wash. 'Four green lights. Ground anchors. Test. Four green lights. Grapples. Test. Four green lights. Landing shocks. Test.'

She stayed silent long enough for Marta to say: 'Am I going to have to go outside again?'

'Three greens and one amber. Deployed but not locked. Julia, can you get me a camera on leg three?'

'Leg three. Okay.' Julia swung the camera from straight down to pointing along the bottom of the crew section, looking from the outside of one of the non-rotating rotation capsules. She zoomed it in. 'It's extended fully.'

'I'll try it again.' May dabbed at her screen. The legs re-tracted, then re-extended, as smooth as a spider. 'Still getting three greens.'

'It looks ... fine?' offered Julia. 'Can we not land on it and hit it with a hammer when we're down?'

Andros intervened. 'We will not abort because of this.'

Patricio stiffened, but May got in first.

'If I don't get a green light, yes, someone, probably me, will have to go out and fix this. We need all four landing legs, because the hint is in their name. Once more for luck.' May repeated the operation, folding the legs back in, then out again. 'Four green lights.'

Marta shrugged. 'Good.'

'I'll EVA and take a look at it before we spin up,' said May. 'Might be a sensor error, but we don't want it failing.'

'How's our passenger?' asked Arush.

Instinctively, they looked up to where the shuttle was docked.

'Attached,' said Kayla. 'Something else we'll have to do before spin.'

'Has anyone given any thought to how we get it down from there? Something about mass and inertia still remaining?'

'Arush, leave the physics to the physics people, okay?'

'I'll remember that when I have to perform an emergency appendectomy on you.'

'I don't have an appendix. Or half the junk that's supposed to be in my lower abdomen. I swear I rattle sometimes.' Kayla's hair beads clacked. 'He does have a point, though. How is Rapunzel getting down from her tower?'

May already had the solution. 'Put a couple of tight lines to the surface from the top of the shuttle, and roll it off down those. Maybe another line to the back in case to act as a brake. Probably need a winch to start it off.'

The cabin fell silent again.

'So is that it for the next couple of hours?'

'Pretty much. If you wanted exciting, you should have signed up to Space Force.'

'Super flying / Death defying / There when you need them most / Heroes coming / Planet spanning / Spaaaace Foooorce.'

'Enough,' said Andros. 'Enough. Concentrate on landing the ship.'

They fell, slowly, inexorably, towards the asteroid. As they descended, the downward-facing cameras picked up more and more detail. Every last centimetre of the surface was pitted. There was a largish crater – thirty, forty metres across – in the

119

polar region, but that was overlapped and eroded by dozens of smaller ones, endlessly overwriting the earlier marks. Until now. Now it appeared frozen in time, ancient, for ever.

The cliff they'd seen from further out was invisible from their position. A feature that large on an asteroid so comparatively small didn't bode well. Taking his attention away from his own figures to glance at Patricio, sitting over to his right, Jack watched the miner as he stared at his screen, like a hovering hawk would watch its potential prey.

'What do you see?' Jack whispered.

'I see the Beast. Abaddon, the Angel of Death. Apollyon, the Destroyer.' Then he shook himself. 'It is a rock, that is all.'

Jack had never seen Patricio look so haunted. Angry, passionate, comradely. But never scared. There was something here the miner didn't like.

It went on, and on. Sinking further and further into the well. Their descent was now at two metres a second. Half an hour in. Jack's attention began to wander, and he snapped it back. This was where mistakes would happen, where something would have gone wrong earlier, and no one had been awake enough to spot it. He rubbed his face, stretched his arms above his head, checking he wasn't getting tangled in any wires, and drank some more water. Though not too much, or he'd be using a vacuum toilet, and frankly, they scared him.

The numbers rolled over: the metronomic tick of the time elapsed, the slow tumble of the altitude, the gentle rise – it could never be called a rush – in descent rate. Two and a half metres a second. Three. An hour and a half since they started the manoeuvre. Still ten kilometres from the surface.

Jack slapped himself. Hard. His cheek stung. Everyone else turned to look at him, then back to the screens they were monitoring.

'Bored?' asked May.

'I ran out of adrenaline, and the coffee is off-limits.'

'It's time we called it,' said Runi. 'Engineering?'

'Go.'

'Life support?'

'Go.'

'Power?'

'Go.'

'Landing site?'

'Go.'

'Telemetry?'

A pause. 'Jack. That's you.'

'Sorry. Yes, go.'

'Flight is go.'

'Captain?'

Asking Andros was a formality. If they hadn't wanted to go, then they wouldn't be going. And it would be extraordinary if he called off the mission at this point. 'Go.'

'Landing is go,' said Runi.

The ship carried on just as before. Patricio ported his proposed landing site to the other screens. There was no such thing as flat ground on KU2, just a choice between what was less and more broken. It seemed to be a real rubble pile of a body, held together by a combination of impact melting, tenuous gravity and vacuum welding. The closer they got, the more it looked like one good shake would break the whole thing apart.

Patricio shook his head, and Marta's expression grew grimmer by the minute.

They not only needed a rise on which to park the lander, with enough space around it to swing the rotating section freely, they also needed to be able to anchor the ship firmly to the ground, otherwise the torque from the rotation would send them flying off into space again. The face of the asteroid wasn't presenting itself as a safe harbour.

'We might need to find alternatives,' he finally said.

On the basis that several pairs of eyes were better than one, they all went through the nearby options, but there was nowhere better, and lots of places that were far worse. With the drive section powering the laser, they had to land to wait out the months-long voyage back to Cis-lunar.

It was this or nothing.

'One k,' said Jack, a little belatedly, because they'd just passed the kilometre mark. The cameras gave them no sense of scale. A crater that filled the screen might be a metre across, or ten metres, and it looked the same. A subsurface boulder might be an obstacle, or it might be something that was just fist-sized. Everything was rendered in black and white.

'Landing lights active.'

The starkly shadowed land beneath them flushed in yellow. The darkness fled, and they were left with a diseased, distressed landscape.

'Proximity radar to audio,' announced Julia, and Runi looked up as a low, rattling hum, like a distant road drill, filled the cabin.

'Eight hundred metres,' called Jack. 'Descent three point five. Ground speed point zero eight.'

The sound pitched up, to a more angry wasp noise.

Marta's hands moved across her screen. 'Arming grapple.'

'Five hundred metres. Descent three point five. Ground speed point zero nine.'

'Firing grapple. Grapple away. Grapple impact. Tensioning. Negative negative. Reeling in.'

'Four-fifty metres. Descent three point six. Ground speed point one zero.'

'Arming grapple. Firing grapple. Grapple away. Grapple impact. Tensioning. Negative negative. Reeling in.' Marta dry-coughed into her hand. 'There's a lot of loose aggregate, and I seem to be finding all of it.'

'Four hundred metres.' Jack glanced at Runi. 'Descent three point six. Ground speed point one one.'

'Arming grapple,' said Marta. 'I'll try a different attachment.'

'If you can't plant this,' said Arush, 'maybe we should try another site.'

'There is no other site,' said Patricio. 'Keep trying.'

'Three-fifty metres?' offered Jack. 'Descent three point six. Ground speed point one two.'

Marta took in a deep breath, and held it. Atheist Patricio crossed himself. 'Firing grapple,' she said. 'Grapple away. Impact. Tensioning.'

There was a pause while she slid a window to Patricio, who eventually nodded. 'One grapple in target.'

'Let's do it again,' she said. 'Arming grapple.'

'Three hundred metres. Descent three point six. Ground speed one point zero.'

'Firing grapple. Grapple away. Impact. Crap, it's rebounded. Cutting cable. Brace brace brace.'

Somewhere outside, a harpoon, unaimed and loose, was coming back off the asteroid and into space, with as much velocity as it was sent. It could punch through the hull, or simply collide with it, or miss completely. The seconds ticked by.

The ship rang like a gong, and there was a simultaneous twitch that rattled every loose thing in Control.

'Fuckity fuck.' Julia's fingers were already skimming across her keyboard. 'Damage report.'

'Pressure is falling,' said Kayla. 'Lab section.'

'I'll seal it.' Patricio unstrapped himself from his seat and jackknifed away down the access tube.

'We're yawing on our y-axis,' said Jack. 'Runi, can you correct for that?'

'Power is good. Fuel is good. Systems are good,' reported May. 'Pretty certain it missed anything critical. What the hell did you hit down there?'

Marta glared at her screen. 'Must be metal.'

'Try not to kill us, okay?'

Marta glared at May. By way of an answer, she said deliberately, 'Arming grapple. Runi, we're tilting. I need this level.'

A beat.

'Runi. Level us off.'

'There is something wrong with Pilot, Medic,' said Andros. 'Fix him.'

'Two-twenty metres. Descent three point six. Ground speed one point zero.' Jack twisted in his seat, to see that the pilot had frozen at his controls. The proximity warning tone was a rattling note somewhere above high C. 'Impact in sixty seconds.'

Arush launched himself across Control and caught the grabs above the pilot's chair. He pushed himself down and held onto Runi's shoulders. The man had just stopped, apart from his lips, which were mouthing ancient incantations.

'What the fuck is wrong with him?' It was a small space and Julia was very loud.

'It was the bang. It set off his PTSD.'

'Ah, terrific. We've got about thirty seconds left on the clock here. Anyone? Jack?'

'I am not a pilot,' Jack managed. 'I can ... wait.' He dabbed furiously at his screen, working his way through the menus. There were powered gyroscopes. 'I can get us level.'

He eyeballed the image of the surface and guessed.

Right.

Marta shot out her hand. 'That's enough. Firing grapple. Grapple away. Grapple impact. Tensioning. *För i helvete.* Negative. Negative. Reeling in.'

'One eighty metres. Descent three point six. Ground speed one point two.'

'Arming grapple.'

'Do we need two?'

'Yes, we need at least two.'

'One-seventy metres. Descent three point six. Ground speed one point three.'

'We could really do with our pilot back,' said May.

Arush had his arms around Runi, and was whispering in his ear.

'Arming grapple.'

'Pressure is holding,' reported Kayla. 'Not that that'll mean jack in a minute.'

Jack glanced up at Andros. He was stone-faced, gripping his seat with whited knuckles. His crew, his hand-picked, sometimes fractured crew were about to plough their spaceship into the asteroid, and whatever desires had driven the captain out into the depths of space were about to crash along with it.

'Firing grapple. Grapple away. Grapple impact.' Marta cracked her knuckles. 'Tensioning. Tensioning. Hold, you bastard. Okay. Two grapples in target. I'm quitting now. We need to kill our descent before it kills us.'

Jack unstrapped. They were anchored to the asteroid, and they could plant this if he could buy them a little more time. The proximity radar was making a sound only dogs could hear, telling him he had bare seconds to do this.

Runi's right hand was clamped around a joystick. It appeared to be in a neutral position, which was good. The pilot's thumb was over the larger of two red buttons. 'Someone give me telemetry,' he said, and he folded his own hand over Runi's.

He didn't move it to the left or right, he just pressed lightly on the pilot's thumb.

May called out. 'Descent two point nine.'

Jack pressed again, harder, longer.

'Descent point eight. We're drifting. Ground speed one point five.'

Julia growled with exasperation. 'Jesus, Jack. Don't try anything fancy.'

He hit the button again.

'Minus point three. We're going up again. Fifty metres.'

Jack held his hand very steady over Runi's. 'Marta, can you reel us in?'

'You want me to damp the ground speed using the grapples?'

'It's either that, or you've got me flying this. I want that less than you do.'

'They might not hold.'

125

'Then do it really slowly. I've got nothing else here.' He used his spare hand to wipe the sweat from his eyes, and looked at the screens and graticules around him. Beneath them, the ground was glittering. He hadn't expected that.

'Fifty metres and closing,' said May. 'We're going down again.'

'Slowing to five centimetres a second,' said Marta. 'Ground speed?'

'One point two.'

'It's working.'

'Forty.'

'Trays to the upright position.'

'Shut up.'

'Thirty. Ground speed point eight.'

'Twenty. Ten. Five. Four. Three. Two. One.' May checked her other screen. 'Ground contact. Four green lights.'

There was a slight shudder, but no other discernible difference between before and after. Jack waited for something to happen.

'Are we down?' he asked.

'Everything tells us that we are.' May took her own water bulb from the holder in front of her and held it out to her side. She let go, and it looked as if it was hovering in mid-air.

Then it started to fall, as slow as a turning tide. She put her hand under it and waited patiently for it to drop into her open palm.

Andros's chair creaked as he unclamped his hands from it, and uncharacteristically he gave some orders. 'Take Pilot away, Medic. Miners, prepare for EVA. Fix the ground anchors. Engineer, liaise with Life Support to fix the hull breach. Cryo: full systems check.'

Jack eased Runi's fingers away from the joystick. He didn't resist.

'What do you want me to do?'

The captain loomed over him as he headed for the axis.

'What I want you to do is count yourself lucky any of us are still alive.'

Then he was gone, and Jack was left wondering what he meant.

14

An atmosphere of that gas [CO$_2$] would give our earth a high temperature; and if as some suppose, at one period in its history the air had mixed with it a larger proportion than at present, an increased temperature of its own action as well as from increased weight must have necessarily resulted.

E. Foote, *American Journal of Science Articles*, 1856

Jack had worn a spacesuit before, but he'd never been out in the vacuum of space. Kayla had gone through everything again, but his mind had been elsewhere, and he'd just nodded. He knew all the things he needed to remember to do, and he had to trust that muscle-memory would eventually kick in. Sitting in the shuttle, being decompressed, he went over again and again the details of the descent, and whether any of them could have done anything different.

Runi was not just apologetic, but mortified. But he was, as events had proved, their only pilot. And Arush was neither apologetic nor mortified, but defiant and defensive, insisting that patient–doctor confidentiality extended to his role. Jack didn't know if that meant that Runi was already taking medication, or was now taking medication, or that they absolutely had a problem that their pilot could go offline at any random loud noise.

They'd landed, just. Julia had repaired the damage to the lab section, and Marta and Patricio had fixed the ship to the asteroid surface with lines and anchors. Now it was his turn to go outside.

He stared at his booted feet through his plexiglass visor. Three other pairs of boots were visible, but he didn't look up. He listened to his breathing, watched how the fans demisted the inside of the visor almost instantly. He flexed his fingers and curled his toes. He worked his jaw and popped his ears. He burped and farted. He was sitting still, and it felt like he was climbing a mountain.

The air inside his suit was changing. From a sea-level standard pressure to a third of that, and from a fifth of every lungful being oxygen, to one hundred per cent. No naked flames from now on. The air in the shuttle was being depressurised, too, otherwise it would be almost impossible to move in the suit enough to get into the airlock.

He could have chosen music, or a book to listen to. He didn't feel confident enough to do that. He wanted to concentrate on what his suit was doing, and work out what was normal or abnormal. This wasn't his suit – both Patricio and Marta had their own – and Kayla had made the adjustments to a standard-sized one as best she could. He was quite tall, and that in itself could have caused problems. But she was happy enough to let him go outside in it, and he ought to trust her judgement. This was the price of not fully doing that: him sitting in the shuttle, staring at his feet and listening to every creak and rustle as the suit stretched and settled around him.

May would see him right. The world outside, the surface of an asteroid of uncertain solidity and possessing enough micro-gravity to really screw things up, was as harsh an environment as anyone could encounter. Orbital velocity could be achieved by simply walking too vigorously. They needed to be tethered at all times. Yet most things that went up – or around – would eventually return, minutes or hours afterwards, and absolutely when anyone was least expecting it. And as everyone was at pains to state, repeatedly, lack of gravity didn't mean lack of inertia.

Patricio in particular had returned from his EVA with an

ashen expression, and he was by far the most experienced crew member of them all.

'Okay. Time's up.' Julia was too loud in his ears, and he used his chest controls to dial her down a notch. 'EVA order is Marta, Patricio, May, Jack. Let's be careful out there.'

There wasn't room for all of them to stand up at once. Marta got to her feet, bracing one hand on the ceiling to stop herself from rising from the floor, and took the handholds either side of the airlock. She spun the wheel, undogged the door and pulled it towards her. There was just enough room for her and her suit, and she wedged herself in. Patricio, equally careful to not bounce around the cramped cabin, closed the door behind her, engaged the clamps and tightened the seals.

The light above the airlock went from green to amber, and the pumps scavenged the air from inside, adding it to the cabin. The light went red.

Marta's voice said: 'Opening the pod bay doors.' Then: 'Tethering and exiting.' A period of silence followed. 'Closing outer door.'

Patricio hit the pump controls with his fist, waited for the green light to show again, then followed Marta outside.

Then it was May's turn. Before she entered the airlock, she grabbed Jack's helmet and made him look at her. Her eyes narrowed as they scanned his face. She raised her fist out to one side, and Jack hit it with his own.

'Hell of a way to earn my certificate.'

'You'll be fine, noob.' She slapped at the pump controls and waited, back to Jack. The airlock door opened, and she pulled herself across the threshold.

In order, then. Reach up and brace against the ceiling. Reach out and close the door. Take the two handholds and settle. Dog the airlock, spin the wheel. Wait for the red light, and wait some more for the amber to show again. Open the valve for the air to fill the airlock. Green light. Spin the wheel, undog the clips. Open the door. Go in backwards. Last man out goes backwards.

Pull the door shut. Spin the wheel, dog the door. Start the pump.

This was it. The ambient sound drained away. All the noises he'd heard for months vanished as if they'd never existed. Pumps, motors, fans, the baseline electronic hum of the ship. Silent. It was just him, and his suit.

He didn't hear them open the door behind him, but only their words.

May: 'Back up, Jack.'

One of the tethers was taken from his waist belt and clipped to the outside of the ship.

Marta. 'Secure. Easy breathing, Jack. Handhold to your right.'

He backed out further. It was all but impossible to tell where the step was in his thick-soled boots, and he was abruptly over the edge before he realised. He didn't fall. Marta guided his right hand to a hoop on the outside of the shuttle, and let him hang there while he got his bearings.

Below him, imperfectly seen, was the curve of the shuttle and then the cone of Control. Above him was a shape, a boulder, held in place by straps. And a hint of raw, unfiltered space. If he turned his head, his visor didn't move, and his field of view was the internal workings of his helmet. Looking up and down, left and right, wasn't a thing in a spacesuit.

Patricio, from somewhere that Jack couldn't see, said: 'Rappelling to the surface.'

'May, I'm going down too. We'll set out some lines. Be ready for you in three zero minutes.' Marta vanished as a presence at the edge of Jack's sight-lines, and it was just him and May, on opposite sides of the airlock.

'Closing the door,' she said, and pulled herself into position. She reached in and brought the door against its seals, and afterwards spun the wheel to tighten it. 'Jack, we're climbing to the top of the shuttle. Remember, two tethers at all times, except when you're swapping one out. Then it's one and a handhold.'

'Kayla's done all that.'

'It's really easy to forget, so you won't mind me telling you again. Will you?'

'No, May. I won't.' He was chastened. Reminding people of safety procedures was standard, and backchat wasn't.

His two tethers were patterned differently: diamonds and stripes. He was fixed by the diamond tether to a rail. Parallel to it was another. Still holding onto his handhold, he reached down for the stripy tether, and pushed the carabiner at the end over the second rail.

'Secure.'

'Secure too. Nice and easy to the top. Don't bang your helmet on the gallowglass ship.'

Jack reached up and took the left and right rails, and started to pull himself up. He weighed next to nothing, but everything felt so incredibly cumbersome now. The bulk of the suit resisted his movement, and the life support pack that hung off his back was most definitely there, a swing when he moved his shoulders.

The carabiners slid up the rails until they reached the support pylons, when he moved them along to the next section, left then right. He carried on. The curve of the shuttle's hull started to flatten, and now he had to watch out for the gallowglass, balanced on top, and not get caught up in the straps that held it in place.

He leaned back a little against his tethers, just to get his bearings. The view hit him full in the faceplate.

The universe was there, not just above him like the sky, but all around him. The ground – ash grey, blood black – curved away from him in a way that ground only ever did on the highest, sharpest mountain peaks. Their ship, their tiny ship, was stuck to this broken boulder, this ragged rock, and the pin-bright stars were wheeling about him.

He was incontrovertibly in space. The Sun, obliquely behind him, cast shadows that were razor-edged. Blocks and slabs and

132

shards broached a surface made of dust and aggregate, in some post-industrial wasteland pocked by craters, debris excavated and piled up and abandoned. It was a demolished factory of an asteroid. It was surprising that they had found anywhere to land at all.

'You okay, Jack? I can't hear you breathing.'

'I'm fine. I'm fine. Just that it's ... very raw. Unfiltered. This place is a mess.'

'Classic rubble pile. Let's hope it's just the surface that is loose, and the rest of it is solid. We need it to hold together when we start moving it.'

The shadows had already changed, and were still changing, as the asteroid turned about its inconstant pole. The stars turned, and there, there was Earth, barely a dot and yet definably blue. If he squinted, he could maybe see the Moon, too. This was what he'd wanted. To be so far out of the reach of any help, any advice, any favours, that at last he could call himself his own man. It finally felt like catharsis. To live and die out in space, surviving as part of a crew – a crew who cared only about what he could do for them, and not for the number of zeros in his bank balance. All the money in the world couldn't save him now.

He twisted round, so that his back was to the shuttle hull. Below him, on the thrown-together surface, Marta and Patricio were laying out lines: screwing in anchors with broad, flat threads, and attaching cables to them from reels. The horizon was so close, and the curve of the asteroid so great, that it really did look like they were working on the top of some great mountain.

The miners were working at the dangerous end of protocols. They were laying out double lines, in parallel and a metre apart, but there were places where the anchor posts wouldn't grip the subsurface properly. One of their tethers was always on one or other of the lines. The second was permanently attached to a third line, unanchored along its length but fixed to the ship's hull.

133

They extended the path to some fifty metres beyond the potential sweep of the rotating section. They worked as if they were not walking on a horizontal surface, but hanging from a vertical one, like climbers. Their touches on the cliff face were ephemeral and temporary, in an attempt to keep themselves away from the friable, powdery rock as much as possible. If they accidentally kicked loose debris, it flew from the toes of their boots, straight out in all directions like a spray. It would spin and fly, rebounding if it struck an obstacle, possibly coming back at the astronaut. The debris that didn't hit anything soared away until it was lost from view.

Lost from view, and potentially from mind, but even a gravity as ephemeral as KU2 possessed never forgot. They were very careful not to kick up loose debris. Mostly, they succeeded. Whatever they did stir up could so easily become lethal, hours later, and the last thing they needed was something else banging against the hull.

'We're done,' said Patricio. He and Marta had fixed a spare post in the middle of the path, and attached the free end of a spool of cable to it.

'I'm ready,' said May.

Patricio turned his back to the ground and threw the spool in the direction of his feet. It glided away from him at the same time as he floated backwards, and his tether tightened and held him in place until he could take hold of an anchor post again. The cable paid out, and the spool sailed in a straight line towards May, positioned on the other side of the shuttle from Jack. It did neither of the things a thrown object usually did. It didn't describe an arc. It didn't slow. The spool was occluded by the curve of the shuttle, but she announced she'd caught it.

She locked the reel, and fixed it to the outside of the shuttle.

Then it was Marta's turn, and Jack's.

'I'm ready, too.' He wasn't sure that he was, but he should be able to catch something with an entirely predictable trajectory.

The reel left her hands, and he watched it come towards him, chest-height. He held his hands out in front, fat, gauntleted fingers splayed. The roll of cable hit his hands, tried to bounce out of them and he snatched at it. He got the cable, not the reel, but that was enough to let him quickly gather the rest of it in to his midriff.

'Elegant,' said Marta.

'Effective,' countered Jack. 'I've got it.'

He wound in the excess, applied the brake and clipped it onto the shuttle, just as May had.

'Let's get the ship unstrapped and lower it down.' May shortened her tethers so that she could use them to stand in tension against the hull. 'Nice and easy. Let's not drop it.'

They undid the constraining cables one by one, always checking on each other. One false move could potentially put them in orbit, and their air would run out by the time they were due to come back round again. Always two tethers. Always certain that the gallowglass ship was stable. Always with a sufficient margin of safety in their suits. No mistakes. It was slow, tedious work. In air, in something resembling proper gravity, they'd be done by now. Half an hour. An hour. Jack was tired. He stopped to drink some water and take a rest.

They had one more strap to unfasten, and they'd already hooked up the safety cable. May was going to take the lead, and Jack was going to get out of the way, in case anything bad happened. Such were the conditions that anything that wasn't supposed to happen was going to be bad, just varying in degrees of bad, from not great to catastrophic. But they'd taken all the precautions they could.

He climbed down to the surface, his first contact with the asteroid itself. His feet were instantly surrounded by a cloud of dust that only very slowly fell back to the ground. He tried stepping, lifting one leg and bringing it down. The impact of his boot sent loose debris spinning out, pattering nearby rocks, then, in an ever-expanding wavefront, everything else. Marta and Patricio turned their backs on him.

'Sorry.'

'Keep everything low,' said Patricio. 'No sudden movements, nothing unplanned. This place is not a good place to be, okay? Hand over hand. Minimise your time touching the surface.'

Jack imagined himself abseiling, little touches with his fingers against the rock to keep himself away from the hard surface. He swapped his tethers one at a time when he reached the anchor posts, and he managed to not kick up any more rock as he belayed himself.

'You're doing good. Now May brings the ship down, and we can go back inside. Spin up the crew quarters. Tomorrow we get the gallowglass.'

'Not today?'

'Not today. We're at our limit. They can wait another day.' Patricio waved to May on top of the shuttle. 'Let it go.'

May undid the last strap, and for the longest time, nothing appeared to happen.

'It's definitely moving,' she said. 'Don't think that it's not.'

The nearly spherical ship started down the two taut guide wires. It picked up speed, enough now to be obviously in motion, although still very slow. It slid down, well away from the hull of the *Coloma*, and the wires barely sagged at all. With some ten centimetres between it and the surface, it started to slow, and at its lowest, barely kissed the dust.

'If you know the initial conditions of all the elements, everything is predictable,' said Patricio. The gallowglass ship had rebounded on its restraining cable to some five centimetres above the asteroid surface. 'We tie this down, and we finish.'

Marta screwed in a second anchor behind the gallowglass, and they looped a strap over the top – easier said than done – and fastened it down. The hull scrunched into the surface, with debris squirting out, pattering against Jack's legs and making him fearful of punctures. The suit stayed perfectly intact. He was learning about what might harm him and what might not.

May released the brake cable when they were done, and Jack

136

spooled it in, clipping the reel to another anchor. The gallow-glass wasn't going anywhere.

'Are we done?'

Marta pulled on the line, and let the tension back off it slowly. 'We're done. Jack, you have the lead. Back to the ship.'

Another awkward transit, a slow-motion glide with moment-ary pushes against the surface, back to the *Coloma*. Anything they kicked up now would also hit the hull. No. Just no.

Jack slowed himself down as he reached the ship, and moved his tether from the wire to one of the rails on the hull.

As his mind tried to readjust as to which way was up, he happened to glance behind him, in the direction that he'd tem-porarily thought of as down. There was Patricio, and Marta, and the gallowglass ship, all in a straight line. And behind that, nothing. Space. Stars. If he fell, he'd be falling for ever.

The vertigo hit him square in the gut, like he'd been winded. He was on an overhang. There was nothing supporting him but two insubstantial strips of woven fabric and a couple of metal clasps. He froze, clinging to the rail.

'Jack? Talk to me, Jack.'

Abruptly as it had started, it was over. When he opened his eyes again, the ground was beneath him and he was hanging off the side of the ship. Just a touch of the Nietzsches.

'I'm okay. I'm okay.'

No, of course they weren't going to get the gallowglass out today. They'd done enough for now. Rest. Sleep, if it would come. And definitely no dreams about scrabbling with his fingertips at a fast-moving rock face that would suddenly end and leave him plummeting towards the abyss.

15

The estimate of Dr Arrhenius, based upon an elaborate mathematical discussion of the observations of Professor Langley, is that an increase of the carbon dioxide to the amount of two or three times the present content would elevate the average temperature 8° or 9°C, and would bring on a mild climate analogous to that which prevailed in the Middle Tertiary age.

T. C. Chamberlin, *An Attempt to Frame a Working Hypothesis of the Cause of Glacial Periods on an Atmospheric Basis*, 1899

Jack opened the door to the inflatable airlock they'd set up, and had that same rush of vertigo as he'd had outside the shuttle. He held his breath and swallowed, and waited for everything to reorientate itself. He wasn't hanging over a star-pointed drop, he wasn't about to fall into the void. There was still that slight pull towards his feet, and that was, despite all his senses telling him otherwise, down.

He clipped his tethers to the guide wires, left and right, and pushed himself out into the white sunlight, black space, grey rock. Arush was ahead of him, a pressurised ball containing medical supplies strapped to his thigh. Jack had oxygen cylinders on his. Behind him, waiting their turn, Marta, carrying a percussive rock drill, and Patricio, with the spacesuit the gallowglass was going to have to wear.

Jack glided and clipped, glided and clipped, face down over the loose surface. Some fragments appeared to be almost hovering, the slight vibrations echoing down the anchor poles sufficient to dislodge them from the main mass. Having had time yesterday to appreciate just how lethal the environment outside was, they were going out again to free the gallowglass.

He wasn't sure why he'd been picked for EVA twice. Perhaps Andros was feeling mean. Perhaps, having done it once, he was now experienced in the working conditions and less likely to fuck it up. Perhaps both. More likely both. But with Runi still an uncertain quantity, and Andros never seeming likely to take a turn, that he had no actual navigating to do until they fired the laser up was the most likely explanation of all.

Even though they had months of hard driving ahead of them, Andros still wanted results now, something he could use to settle the NovaS investors' nerves. Fortunes were being made and lost even while the crew were risking their necks for a measly percentage. And it was a distraction, as was any news from Earth. Crew didn't look at the news. They actively disdained it. And they resented that their captain was so driven by what was happening millions of kilometres away, it was affecting how they organised their work.

Even messages from home, from parents, from friends, weren't welcome. It had surprised Jack at first: now he understood it. The crew ways were wise, and it allowed everyone to concentrate on the mission without every twist and turn of personal or civic life being played out in a small, inescapable environment.

Unclip, clip. He was coming up on the gallowglass's ship. Arush was already there, tethered to the lines and standing under their tension on the hull. Jack closed his fist on the cable and brought himself to a dead stop. He aimed his legs down and shortened his tethers so that he too could feel the press of the hull against his feet. He moved to one side, and Marta replaced him.

What they were doing on KU2 had been done before, but nowhere near often enough to become routine, and never quite on this scale. They were trailblazers: some of the tech was, if not experimental, certainly untested in the field. If the others harboured similar reservations, they, like him, kept them quiet. They were all here, one way or another, for the money, and they were glad it was them with the opportunity to get it, rather than someone else.

Patricio arrived behind Jack, and together the four of them set about searching the hull for where the access hatch might be buried. May had the schematics up back in Control, and was comparing the abraded features she could see over the video feed with the plans. If they picked the wrong place, they'd crack the hull, and it'd be impossible – no, not impossible, just very, very difficult and Andros would complain some more – to get the sleep tank out and into the airlock.

'Just there. Where your left foot is.'

Marta used a piece of coloured chalk to mark the pitted hull with an X. Then she started up the drill. Pieces of ceramic were going to break off. Arush and Jack were supposed to catch them and net them before they could cause problems. Like all tasks in microgravity, it was easier said than done. Especially when they were both encumbered with essential pieces of kit that, in Jack's case, might act as rockets.

Marta touched the drill bit to the hull. Dust bloomed in an expanding cloud. As she pressed it home, her feet lifted free. She stopped, tightened her tethers and tried again. This time it was better, and she got more contact. The drill started to cut into the ceramic, and when she'd gone a little way in, she engaged the hammer function, working the drill into the hole at the same time as using it as a lever.

A fist-sized piece broke off and sailed towards Arush's faceplate. He instinctively batted it down. It bounced, and came Jack's way. He used both hands to intercept the fragment and closed his fingers around it, trapping it. It was impossible to tell its weight, but beneath its smooth exterior the inside was all bubbles, just like pumice. He bagged it and waited for the next bit.

Marta worked her way around her mark, spalling off pieces

and letting her catchers collect the debris. She went deeper, and even though nothing could be heard, she evidently felt the quality of the vibrations change.

'I think we're there. Let me make this wider.'

She chipped more of the pumice-like shell away, and gradually revealed a circular pattern inscribed in the ceramic inner hull. She used a brush to dust it off – more bright clouds of glittering sand in the unfiltered sunlight – and there it was. A hatch, but seemingly with no way of opening it.

Jack fastened his collected bag of rocks to the line behind him, and did the same for Arush's. 'May? What are we supposed to do now?'

'There should be recesses on the cover. Inside are bolts that will release the seals. There's something here about a key.'

'Tell me we have the key, because otherwise we're a long way from anywhere that's likely to have what we want.'

There was a conversation off-mic, and when she came back, May said: 'We don't have the key.'

Marta: '*Fy fan.*'

Patricio, who was clasping the spare spacesuit like a salsa partner, leaned over and assessed the situation. 'Either we can jury-rig something, or we go through the hull. We need to make a decision soon.'

'Can we just leave them in there until we get back to Cis-lunar?' Arush bent down and brushed the hatch with the back of his hand. He found the holes May had mentioned, and tried to clear one of them out. His gloved finger was too large. 'It's tethered securely, and it's not going anywhere again.'

'If it was you, would you want out?' asked Patricio.

'They're asleep. Whoever's inside doesn't even know we're here. Another few months won't matter. And we still don't know if this is our gallowglass or not.'

'These are old, tired arguments,' said the miner. 'Basic decency says we should try.'

'I think we should too,' said Jack. 'We don't know anything

141

about the state of their life support, and they could die in the next few months.'

'Right answer,' said May, over the radio. 'See what shape the bolt heads are.'

Arush took Marta's brush and wriggled it in the first hole. As he excavated, he uncovered a triangular-shaped plug in its centre. 'That's non-standard.'

'Hold your camera over it for a second?'

Arush looked straight down, and held his thumb next to the hole for scale.

'Ten mil hex socket? I'll put the heads for a few sizes inside the airlock, but someone's going to have to come back and get them.'

'I'll go,' said Jack. 'If someone can look after these tanks.'

They tied the oxygen cylinders to Patricio, and Jack hauled himself back to the *Coloma*, collected the bag of tools and hauled himself back again.

'Do we have enough time to complete this?' asked Marta.

Kayla replied: 'If you're not started in thirty minutes, I'd call it a bust for today. Problem is, once you start, you'll depressurise the capsule, and as far as I know, sleep tanks don't work so great in a vacuum. It's all or nothing.'

'We're the people on the ground. We make the decision,' said Patricio. 'Call it.'

'Do we see if the tool fits first?' asked Arush.

'If it does, it will alter our perception of the job. Call it first.'

'Open it up,' said Marta. 'If we crack the seal but can't open the hatch, we break the hull and get them out that way. Never liked sleep tanks anyway.'

Arush looked up from the circle of broken stone. 'If it means not coming out again, and we can do it all now, open it.'

'Jack?'

'Sure. I mean, I don't really know what I'm doing apart from holding stuff for you guys, but getting the gallowglass out is in the contract, and I'm good with that.'

Patricio nodded. 'Then we do it.'

Jack opened the bag, tethered the electric wrench to himself and tried the first head. It didn't quite fit, so he swapped it over, making certain that nothing flew away. He tried again, and got a lock.

'Clockwise or anticlockwise?'

'Righty tighty, lefty loosy.'

He pulled the trigger, and the torque started to turn him.

'I need to brace either me or the wrench somehow.'

Marta stepped in with the drill, pushing the bit into the hatch cover. Jack wedged the wrench against it and tried again. The bolt simply held fast.

'Has this got any more settings on it? Can I get a bigger gear?'

'That bolt hasn't been turned for over three years. Hit it with something.'

'Is that going to work?'

'Percussive maintenance. It always works.'

'It never works,' said Patricio, but Marta pushed the drill bit down into the recess and twitched her finger on the actuator. Dust bloomed, and Jack tried again.

The bolt spun out.

'Okay. I was wrong.'

They tried the same trick with each of the subsequent three bolts, and each one twisted out. Arush caught them and bagged them.

'Now what?' asked Jack.

'You have to equalise the pressure. There should be a vent. Look for a valve ... it's central. Try there.'

Arush brushed the middle of the hatch, and under the dust was a push-button. He held it down, and moisture-laden air squirted out from tiny vents around it. Ice instantly crystallised and coated every exposed surface, and even though the amount of gas escaping was small, he struggled to keep his hand in place.

'Use the drill bit. Just push it, don't turn it on.'

Marta depressed the button again, and the air plumed away. It died off, and she tapped at the lid with her foot. The hatch moved fractionally downwards, and Jack, better positioned, pushed it enough that he could get his hand around the rim. He used that as a lever, and pushed the hatch in the rest of the way.

He peered inside. There was one light, burning blue in the darkness.

'It still has power,' he said. 'They might still be alive.'

'Clock is ticking, people,' warned Kayla. 'I'm not saying move faster and take risks. I'm saying you can't afford to sit around on the stoop and shoot the breeze.'

Arush turned his suit lights on and carefully moved over the open hatch. 'I'll go in, you pass me the kit.'

He dipped down, and entered head first. The lights showed a tiny cabin, barely large enough for one, let alone two.

'So this might have been a mistake. When they built these things, they really didn't care about retrieval.'

'Gallowglasses were, and always will be, expendable. They know the risks,' said Marta.

'That doesn't mean we have to agree with how they're treated, or how they treat themselves.' Patricio unstrapped the spare spacesuit, and with Jack's help fed it down to Arush. He followed it up with the first of the oxygen cylinders. 'Do you need the other?'

'Send it down. If I need it, I'll need it inside.' Arush pushed himself back as far as he could against the dead control board. 'I don't think I can reach back far enough to close the hatch again. Jack?'

'Hold on.' Jack put his hand in and found the edge of the hatch. Where the pilot's chair should have been was a sleep tank, designed into a sitting position. Almost every bit of space inside the cabin was occupied by something, and now Arush was in there too, in his suit, with all his equipment, it was a claustrophobe's nightmare. 'You going to be okay?'

'Fine, fine. Close the lid and don't go anywhere.'

Jack hauled on the hatch, and Arush was able to push it back shut.

'The next time someone does this, they need to bring a bubble and inflate it around the ship.' Arush's breathing was loud over the comms. 'Someone make a note of that.'

'Do I seal the hatch back up?'

'No, don't. I'm going to pressurise the cabin, and deal with any leakage with squirty foam. Quick and dirty, much like my sex life.'

Outside the gallowglass ship, Jack, Patricio and Marta waited, watching the Sun turn and stars wheel. Even though the *Coloma* was less than a hundred metres away, Jack started checking his air gauge. The alarms would kick in long before he could get into trouble, but the inactivity was both uncharacteristic and unnatural. EVA was purposeful, and time carefully accounted for. Standing around seemed dangerous.

Inside, Arush had more than enough to do. He had to check that the sleep tank was, in fact, registering it had someone alive inside. Then flood the cabin interior with most of the contents of a tank of oxygen, and in doing so turn the little ship into a potential firecracker. Then get the tank to give up its contents without killing its occupant.

'Is everything okay in there?'

'Trying to do this with fat fingers is hard, okay? I can't take my suit off, and I'm not exactly certain how whoever this turns out to be is supposed to put this suit on with me still in here. It's like trying to extract someone from a coffin while being in a very slightly larger coffin that's built around it. But I think I've got the sequence right: things are happening. Slowly, but they're happening.'

More minutes passed.

'I've got some green lights. I'm cracking the seal.'

'Three years asleep. They've got some catching up to do.'

'They haven't missed much. The news is just a steady diet of shit.'

145

'What do we know about them anyway?'

'I don't even know if we have a bio. I assume Andros has, maybe, but he hasn't seen fit to share it with us.'

'Read-outs are fine. Gods—'

'Arush?'

'It's a girl. I mean, an actual girl. She's tiny.'

'You mean a child?'

'Teenager, maybe. I'm going to hit her with a Vitamin K shot. Done. Oh, she doesn't like that.'

'She's right there in front of you, Arush. Your bedside manner is terrible.'

'She can't hear me yet. She's wearing a cold cap.'

'How does she look?'

'She's staring at me. I'll take the cap off. Hey. Hey! Don't fight me. Take it easy. I've got everything you need right here. Water. Something to eat. And a spacesuit. And crew outside who are going to get you to our ship.'

'You should probably say who you are and where you're from.'

'Right. Right. My name is Arush. Arush Mukherjee. I'm from the *Coloma*. She's not saying anything. Maybe the sleep tank has scrambled her head.'

'Arush, tell her she'll be okay, and show her the suit. We don't want to have to rush this, but the only way to get you both out of the gallowglass ship is if she's suited and booted. We can't do anything else now. Got that?'

'I get it, I get it.' He tried again. 'Okay. It's 2072. Three years ago you claimed the rights to the asteroid KU2 on behalf of NovaS. We're here now, somewhere outside the orbit of Mars. We need to get you into this suit, get you over to the *Coloma*, and then we can start pushing this rock around. Did you understand any of that?'

There was a pause.

'She's nodding. We're good.'

16

When we have dominion over nature, it is not ours, either. It belongs to God, and we are to exercise our dominion over these things not as though entitled to exploit them, but as things borrowed or held in trust, which we are to use realizing that they are not ours intrinsically.

F. Schaeffer, *Pollution and the Death of Man*, 1970

Three years was a long time to spend asleep. It was close to the record – close to the known record at least. There were a couple of documented cases in which a gallowglass had claimed an asteroid but then, for economic or technical reasons, the rights to the asteroid had lapsed. No one was going to pay for a mission with no guarantee of reward, so they were there still. And there were rumours of more: how many more depended on who was telling the tale, and how gullible they thought their audience.

Her name was Catherine – Cat – and the crew took it in turns to peer at her in the lab, where Arush had her wired up to various instruments. It looked as if he knew what he was doing, but he was just following checklists: if this, then that, if the other, this treatment. She took his mechanical care silently. Not that she couldn't speak, just that she chose not to. No more than a dozen words in the two hours since she'd been eased into the *Coloma*'s airlock.

She'd spent a lot of that time eating and drinking, like a caterpillar, except she'd already emerged from the cocoon. A

147

butterfly in reverse, then. She stared at Jack from her seat, not dropping her gaze between mouthfuls of energy bar, and he became acutely aware that she wasn't some animal in a zoo, and he should be ashamed of treating her that way. He, too, was silent throughout what was their second encounter.

The first had been different, with him towing her, and Marta taking up the slack behind, for the journey along the guide wires to the airlock. He had been alone with her while the air pressure equalised, and he'd kept up a constant commentary about what he was doing and why and how, just so that she'd know that she was no longer alone.

Then, she'd just been a figure in a spacesuit, weak and disorientated. Now, she appeared as a small ball of barely contained energy. He wasn't going to be the one to release that, accidentally or otherwise. He turned away, blushing, and mumbled something about how he was glad she seemed to be doing so well. He hurried back to the axis, and his habitual seat in Control.

'So what do you make of her?' asked May.

Jack feigned indifference. He could still see the gallowglass, her glare. 'I don't know what sleep tanks are like. Do you know time's passed, or is it just like an edit? One minute, you're going to sleep, and the next you're waking up. That must be, I don't know. Terrifying?'

'She went under when she was sixteen.'

'Fifteen when she launched.' Jack pulled a face. 'I mean, fifteen.'

'Do we know where she's from, what her story is?'

'I don't. Only that she had the mining rights. It's funny.' He glanced back down the axis. 'She doesn't look like a killer.'

'What do they look like, Jack?'

He immediately thought of Mesman, and didn't feel happy about that. 'Different to her, that's all.' He stared at his screen, and watched the numbers change for a while, and then Andros appeared from aft.

'Astrogator. When can we start?'

'Test firing? Tomorrow. As scheduled.'

'I want it today. Something to say we have the laser in position, it works, and that we can alter the orbit.'

'This is about NovaS investors again?'

'They're the people who are paying your wages.'

May started to speak, but Jack got in first. 'Okay. I can do the first two, but not the last. That will take sustained firing over several hours, if not days, before we get a measurable effect. The only way to prove orbital change is using the star charts, and our cameras aren't sensitive enough to register anything under a tenth of an arc second.'

He guessed that Andros probably wouldn't know what that meant, and even though he was absolutely right, he didn't want to have to explain himself any further.

'Do it,' ordered Andros.

'How much debris is this going to throw up?' asked May. 'If it's too much for the seismometers to be planted properly, I'm going to say no.'

'I'll just flash it, low power. Not a full two-hundred-gigawatt blast.'

'We'll still get chaff.'

'Once the trench has been dug, it'll be all out into space.'

'And the solar panel arrays?'

'It'll work.'

'And Runi?'

Jack looked at the empty pilot's chair. 'You know what the surface is like. If we warn him, I'm sure it'll be fine.'

'It doesn't work like that, Jack.' She gave in. 'Okay. You break something, you can come out with me and fix it.'

'I'll need to spin out the panels,' said Jack, giving Andros a timeline. 'Park them, bring everything online. Four, five hours.'

'Call it six with breaks,' said May. 'Jack will need breaks.'

'Yes. Sure. Tell NovaS that.' He looked back to his screens. 'I'll start plotting the manoeuvres.'

'Good,' said Andros. 'Don't disappoint me.'

'Because this'll make my work so much easier.'

'What was that, Astrogator?'

'He was just saying how well he works under pressure,' said May. 'I'll keep an eye on him.'

'As long as you two don't go off to fuck halfway through.'

The air scrubbers failed to cover the abrupt and lengthening silence.

'If,' said May, 'you're implying that either my work or his is somehow compromised by what we do or do not do when not on duty, then you're going to need to provide proof of that accusation. Otherwise, you know where you can shove it. Sir.'

Andros paused, and not for the first time, Jack wondered which of them would be first to drag the captain to an airlock and send him into space without a suit.

'Just do your jobs,' he said eventually, heading back towards the axis. 'That's what you're paid for.'

May snorted, and Jack started typing.

The physics of it was sound: fire a massive laser at a small area of rock, melt it into an expanding cloud of plasma and use the force created by the gas as a proxy rocket. Keep it up for long enough, and that rocket could be used to steer an asteroid into a different orbit. In this case, one that would park it near L4. The asteroid would lose mass throughout the journey, but nowhere near enough to make any significant dent in the company's bottom line.

Powering a laser that big, though ... They had solar panel arrays, kilometre-sized grids printed on mylar, which themselves had microwave lasers to transmit the energy they collected to the laser. If they put too many holes in those, then the laser wasn't going to work at maximum efficiency, and they wouldn't get maximum thrust. That itself was just one of the problems that Jack had to try and solve – the further out he put the arrays, the less likely they were to get damaged, but then they'd potentially end up in a debris ring that already existed, and were more likely to get holes.

He was going to have to use some of the power generated by the panels to hold them in fixed positions around the laser, just as he was going to have to keep the laser in one place. He couldn't afford the luxury of putting them in orbit. And while the fuel requirements for station-keeping were low, to keep them in position for months? He'd run his figures by Runi, and see if some straightforward calculations would ease the pilot back into his seat in Control.

The next piece of the puzzle was to calculate KU2's orbital characteristics which, as he'd discovered, were different from the published ones. They'd gathered enough data over the last few days to tighten up the numbers, and he spent some time checking the equipment used to give him those numbers.

Lastly, he knew where he needed to get the rock, and then it was just a matter of how much thrust was required to change what was to what would be. The final number wasn't huge, but it represented a vast transfer of energy. No one had ever tried to move an asteroid as big or as valuable as KU2 before.

'You need to take a break,' said May, and Jack became aware of her still sitting next to him. Had she been there the whole time? Yes, why not?

'I'll go to the can, get something to eat.' He looked at the last figure the computer had spat out. Could he get that much thrust? If the subsurface material was as loose and friable as the top layer, then the laser might simply blast material out without necessarily turning it all into superheated plasma. If the seismic survey didn't come back showing there was solid rock below, then the whole asteroid might fall apart.

NovaS would go instantly bust, and the crew would be a long way down the list of creditors. He knew how this worked. Andros would almost certainly order him to fire the laser and damn the seismics. May, Patricio and Marta would almost certainly tell him not to, as the resultant cloud of debris would endanger the ship and potentially shatter the asteroid completely.

'Jack? Break.'

Sometimes, he needed to be told. He unbuckled himself from his seat and floated free.

'Before you go, there's something we need to discuss,' she said.

'You're leaving me?' He was joking, but the mere mention of the idea gave him an odd tightening, right in his chest.

She gave him the look, and he grabbed hold of a ceiling bar.

'Runi.'

'What about Runi?'

'He nearly killed us. We – the crew – have to think carefully about what that means for the mission. Opinions are being gathered, and I said I would ask you.'

'I don't get it,' said Jack. 'What do you mean?'

'It would be difficult to do without a pilot at this point. He's the only one who can fly the shuttle, and we need it to lay out some of the infrastructure and plant the seismometers. But after that, you're more or less in charge of the course, steering by the laser, right?'

'You think we should relieve him of piloting duties? That's ... okay, I can understand that. He's normally very safe, though.'

'That's not what I'm talking about, Jack. I'm talking about spacing him.'

'What? I mean, what the actual fuck?'

'He's already nearly killed us all once. Are you willing to give him another chance to kill you, or me, or any of the others?'

'I'm not voting to space him. Not now, or ever.'

'Ever? We're outside any and every jurisdiction. We're on a voyage that takes almost two years to complete. We can't go back to port. We can't risk the ship, or the crew, for the sake of one person. Jack, come on. Join up the dots with me here. Remember my watch, and how replaceable it is.'

'No.' He underlined his objection with a gesture. 'No.'

May made her lips go thin. 'Can we trust Runi again? If he freezes at some critical moment, or starts breaking stuff because of the noises in his head, it's not just our pay that's on the line – it's our lives.'

'If it comes to that, we can just give him a corner to sit in and tell him not to touch anything. As an alternative to being pushed out the airlock, I'd find that a little more acceptable.'

'Don't get pissy, Jack. This is part of being crew.' She looked away, then back. 'It's not like this conversation hasn't happened already once this voyage.'

'What do you mean?'

She carried on looking at him.

'Me? You've all had this conversation about me?'

'Jack, you were asking a lot of the crew when you came on board with no experience. Some of them expressed concern. Concern that you'd get cocky, make a mistake and kill everyone.'

'But how did they know I had no experience? Was it that obvious?'

'Yes, but I still told them. It was my duty as crew to tell them anything that was going to affect the safety of the ship. We kept a close eye on you. There was a vote. You passed. It turns out our trust wasn't misplaced, so thank you for that. And now it's your turn to exercise your duty as crew, and decide whether one of your colleagues is fit to continue.'

Whatever Jack had thought about life in deep space had just been obliterated in an instant. The honeymoon was over. This was the harsh reality of living in an easily breakable tin can with nine – now ten – other people. He blinked hard, and swallowed.

'The answer to your question. Yes, I trust him. He's a bit damaged, but we're all aware of that now, and what sets him off. He'll recover. And as you've already pointed out, we need a pilot for this phase of the mission, and he has as much at stake as we do. If we can get him home, he'll never have to go into space again.'

He took a deep breath. He was aware that he might just have

saved Runi's life. He didn't know how this worked, whether his was the first vote, the last vote or the deciding vote. But he wasn't going to have him die on his say-so. The idea was monstrous. He had to sleep at night. He also had to sleep at night next to people who had already voted on whether to kill him or not.

He felt nauseous. His stomach seemed to contract and flood with ice-water at the same time. He especially didn't want to look at May. May, who he'd not just slept next to but with, who had been closer to him than his own skin, who would have thrown him overboard if he hadn't shaped up.

It was going to take some time to come to terms with this revelation, and his own naivety.

His head came up. He knew that she knew how he was feeling, from her expression of mild – only mild – concern. She would have spaced him, to save her and the others from the colossal fuck-up he could have made of astrogation. Was that fair? He was in deep space. Fairness, along with law, was a suspended concept. Whatever got people back home was what mattered. It was him who wasn't playing by the rules now, letting his squeamishness override his pragmatism. He could be endangering the crew by voting for Runi, not against him.

'I'm going to take that break now,' he said.

In that moment, he collided with the gallowglass, coming hurtling down the axis. He spun out into Control, flailing for a handhold. May reached out and missed him, and he collided hard with the instrumentation. As he bounced back, he caught a grab rail and arrested his movement.

May was already out of her seat. 'Fuck.'

The gallowglass looked out from her childlike face, and Jack couldn't see a hint of regret in it. Behind her, Arush was signing something that approximated to 'sorry, couldn't stop her'. She was upset, angry even, and the reason for that hadn't gone away.

'You don't have permission to be here,' said May, hand out

to bar her way. 'You're not crew. You're not on duty. And that was dangerous.'

The gallowglass spun around, looked at Arush and turned again to confront May.

'I ...' She cleared her throat. 'I have to talk to St Ann's.' Her voice was hoarse and unnaturally low.

'St Ann's?'

'My government. I have to talk to them.'

'The contract was we retrieve you. Not that we let you import your shit into our ship.'

Jack shook himself out. He was going to have some bruises shortly, and Julia was going to need to give what he'd fallen against a once-over. But he instinctively found himself moving next to May, banding together with his crew against the newcomer.

'My government,' the gallowglass repeated. She looked pointedly at the empty workstations, and back at May, who she'd evidently decided must be in charge. 'There appears to be no reason why I can't.'

Andros pushed past Arush in the axis and unfolded himself next to Jack. The three of them made an impenetrable wall. 'We are busy. The crew are busy. And Earth is nine light minutes away. Talking to anyone is out of the question.'

She glared at them, and seeing she would not get her way this time, she eventually retreated, turning about and knocking Arush aside much as Andros had done.

'She's been frozen for three years. Why not let the girl phone home?' May didn't look at Andros when she said it, but Andros certainly looked at her.

'Her government know she's survived. NovaS have passed that on.'

'I'm sure they did. Is there any reason she can't tell them herself?'

'There are several good reasons,' said the captain, then

changed the subject. 'Astrogator. How is the work progressing?'

'He's taking a break,' said May. 'I think he could do with one.'

17

Present thinking holds that man has a time window of five to ten years before the need for hard decisions regarding changes in energy strategies might become critical.

J. F. Black, *The Greenhouse Effect*, Exxon Research and Engineering Co., 1978

'Firing in three, two, one. Mark.'

They were all in Control, even the gallowglass, because if something went wrong they could seal the rest of the ship, and the rotating section had been stilled for the test.

'I didn't feel anything,' said Andros.

'Good,' said Jack. 'It's still running.'

'This was supposed to be a short test, low power. That's what you said.'

'I didn't want to cause problems. So I modified the burn. Still low power, but for longer.' He brought up a picture of the target. At the centre there was a glowing spot.

'You melted it,' said Marta.

'Gently. Hoping that surface tension would keep the material in place.'

'How does this prove that we can steer the asteroid?'

'Because it proves we have a working laser, and we can turn that molten rock into plasma any time we want.'

'Show me that.'

'I haven't programmed that in. And it would take some time to do so. And it would be irresponsible to try it until after the results of the seismic survey come in.' Jack wasn't going to meet Andros's gaze, so he looked to see if all the laser components had stayed where they were supposed to be, relative to the asteroid.

'We're already behind schedule. The survey should have been done by now.'

Patricio stirred himself. 'Going out onto the surface is exhausting. It is difficult and dangerous. If we stir up the rock, we might put it out of bounds for hours and potentially days, all the while risking the integrity of the *Coloma*, let alone our suits. Your schedule is stupid because it makes no allowances for the actual work.'

'The investors expect you to keep to the schedule.'

'The investors are not here. If the investors had accurate reports on our progress, rather than what you tell them, they would understand. If the investors were here, they too would see that hurrying now would mean more delays in the future, and possibly the failure of the entire mission. If the investors wanted to put on a suit and go outside and try to navigate around an asteroid with virtually no gravity but all the inertia, then they would most likely decide to leave EVA to the trained personnel.' He paused. 'Perhaps the investors would like to hear from us instead, on how you, the captain, are jeopardising their capital?'

'I'll do it,' said Cat. 'I'll go outside now.'

Patricio looked at the gallowglass, floating by the axis tube. 'No.'

'If you show me where and how to install the seismometer, I'll go and do it right now.'

'No,' he repeated, only louder. 'This is not a job—'

'For a girl?'

'For an untrained—'

'Girl?'

'This isn't about girl or boy,' said Marta. 'We know how to do this. You don't. And it'd take us longer to tell you how to do it than it would for us to do it ourselves.'

'What does it matter what the seismics say?' she asked. 'You want your money. You want your bonus. You'll do it anyway.'

'The hell we will,' said Julia. 'We split this rock up with us on it, none of us is going home. I don't know about you, lady, but I'm pretty much already at the extreme limit of my risk–reward ratio.'

'Then why are you here?'

'I can't speak for everyone else,' continued Julia, 'but for me, there might be a small but quantifiable chance I come out of this both alive and rich. But there is no point whatsoever in being rich and dead. That shroud's got no pockets.'

'You're not the people I want. You're not the people I need.'

'Well, sorry. We're the people NovaS hired.'

'Maybe NovaS are the problem, since you're the only people NovaS could get.'

Everyone in Control shifted at the same time, and May fixed the gallowglass with her best stare.

'Tell me again who promised the rights to one company, took money from them, had them fund your ship and then sold them out to NovaS at the last possible minute? While you're telling us that, why don't you explain what happened to the first gallowglass that landed on KU2, the one that went inexplicably silent between sending their claim and getting it confirmed?'

And she was gone, the axis tunnel empty.

Kayla arched an eyebrow. 'She's fresh.'

'Fresh, for someone who's been in a can for three years.'

'If she wants to EVA, we should let her. If she's got her certificates.'

Now they all looked at Runi.

'She's not crew, Runi. She can't be trusted. Hell, as far as we know, she's already killed at least one poor bugger.' Julia folded her arms. 'I'm not going out with her, and that's a fact.'

'As fascinating as this discussion is,' said Andros, 'you have work to do. I expect a better test from Astrogator at the earliest opportunity, and I expect those seismometers in place by to-morrow at the latest.' He unbuckled and headed for the axis. 'Time we waste now is time we cannot make up later. The viability of this mission – and your pay – depends on putting this asteroid where it needs to be, when it needs to be there.'

The crew let out a collective sigh when he'd gone.

'Who do you think our investors actually are?' asked Jack. He wondered momentarily if his parents had bought in. Perhaps they had. Perhaps they thought it a way of controlling him.

'Kleptocrats, banksters, climate billionaires, vulture capitalists,' said Patricio.

Marta ground her teeth. 'And thousands of people like us who've risked everything they have on this one roll of the dice. They'll be the ones who really suffer, while the already-rich will have hitmen on speed dial. We're hard on Andros, but he's going to be the first one to die if we come back without this rock.'

'You're joking.' Jack looked at the crew's expressions.

They weren't.

'And the rest of us?'

Julia pursed her lips. 'We shouldn't go anywhere dirtside for a few years. These people have long memories and short tempers.'

'I suppose that makes Andros right,' Kayla said. 'Now we're here, we have to do what we came here to do. If NovaS goes under because we're being too cautious, where does that leave us?'

'Technically, in command of an asteroid-capturing deep-space vessel. We will have seized the means of production.'

'Patricio, we can't do that,' said Julia. 'We have to go home some time before the food runs out, and at that point, the *Coloma* will belong to whoever bought the assets. And our asses get thrown into jail.'

'Space jail? Is that even a thing?' asked Arush.

'We're more likely to just get buried in debt for the rest of our lives.'

160

'We could still do this,' said Patricio. 'Cut our own deal with the creditors.'

'Look, if we play it straight, we all still stand to make several mil each,' said Kayla. 'What's wrong with that?'

Patricio growled. 'This asteroid is potentially worth more than the entire US national debt. Why are we giving it to these investors who are already rich?'

'We don't have the mining rights, Patricio.' Marta jabbed her finger at him. 'And NovaS do. That's what counts. They can enforce it.'

'NovaS didn't start off with the mining rights,' he said. 'Perhaps we should take them for ourselves. Do some good with it.'

'This is not a conversation I want to be having. We don't own the ship, we don't own the rights. That's the end of this.'

'But what if we did?'

Jack excused himself and pushed his way into the axis.

'Just start the rotation. I need the can,' he called. Being part of an argument about money was the last thing he wanted. Not because he wasn't broke – as far as he knew he was, although the situation was far more complicated than that – but because he didn't want to think about it.

His parents could wait him out. They would still be alive in five years, and in ten years, and in twenty years, and forty years, and potentially, if medical science kept ahead of their ageing bodies, well beyond that. They could play the long game and realistically expect that Jack would break before they did. Access to billions, and eternal life. As far as incentives to be a compliant son went, they were persuasive.

Not necessarily now, in his twenties, but would *he* feel the same way in his forties, his fifties? They would still be there, unchanged and unchanging, ready to welcome him back into the fold. He shivered.

'Rotation rotation.'

He hung by the junction to the crew section until the arms

had got up to speed, and then headed down to the toilets. He didn't need to go. He wanted to clear his head, and it was about the only excuse anyone had without making a scene.

Except he wasn't alone.

The gallowglass was sitting on the floor in the gym area, looking confused and angry and just a little bit broken. Her flightsuit was several sizes too big for her, making her seem even more like a child dressing up in grown-up clothes. But she'd piloted a ship single-handed across the void, and whatever had transpired over the crumbling surface of KU2, she'd planted her own flag long enough to register a valid claim.

She looked at Jack across the tops of her knees.

'Can I get you anything?' he asked.

'Have they sent you here to check up on me?'

'If they had, I wouldn't be the one they'd send.'

'No. I don't suppose you would.'

'Okay. I just asked.' He took a right angle to the toilet cubicle.

'Who are you?'

'Jack. Jack Astrogator.'

'How long have you been doing this?'

'First mission.'

'You see? Why are you even on board? NovaS should have hired experienced crew for a job this difficult.'

He rested his hand on the door catch. 'You'll have to take that up with them.'

Her head came up, and eyes narrowed. 'I will.'

'I didn't mean to be here. I don't know if any of us did, except Andros. We were told what we had to do after we came on board. We're the crew that you got, for better or worse.'

He flipped the catch to the cubicle and closed the door behind him.

After a while, he could hear her padding about outside. Pacing. She was pacing the floor. He'd rather she leave, then he could end this pretence, but he went through the whole rigmarole of unzipping, zipping and pressing the buttons, before

162

exiting and making a show of washing his hands thoroughly.

There were no mirrors by the sink, but he could tell she was behind him.

'I'm sorry,' she said, the first sign of a crack in her armour. 'I don't know what to do.'

He continued to wash, interlacing his fingers, circling the palms of his hands with his bunched nails, as if he was scrubbing up before a surgical operation. 'Being asleep for three years must be a difficult thing to take. You should cut yourself some slack.'

'I did all this because there wasn't an alternative. We needed the money. This was the only way to get enough of it, quickly enough.'

Jack thought about his own parents' billions. 'What were you going to use it for?'

'Saving my people. My homeland. My ... island.'

Oh. Jack turned the tap off, and rested his wet hand on the edge of the basin.

'I thought we had the time,' she said. 'That I'd make it back home before ... That we could do something. And your medic tells me that St Ann's is gone, and no one is letting me call Earth to find out if that's true.'

'He told you what?'

'It's gone. It's just gone. Abandoned. Two years ago. I don't know where anyone is. My father. My cousins. My friends. My culture. My everything. We had a plan. We had a plan, and it's all gone wrong.'

'Arush shouldn't have said anything.' He moved to the dryer. He had to wait for it to stop before resuming talking. 'He knows better than that.'

She didn't respond, and he glanced around to find her trying not to cry. Her face contorted, and she turned away.

'I was told,' he said, 'when I came on board, that we don't phone home, we don't read the news, that we cut ourselves off because everything is turning to shit and we don't want to bring

163

that with us, because one way or another, it'll kill us. So that's what we've done. We've not looked at anything from Earth for months. Easier now we're light minutes away, but I found it so hard to start with. We're so used to being connected, all the time. But the ship is the world right now. That has to be enough.'

'I can't do that. I can't. I've been away too long.'

'There's nothing you can do about what's happening on Earth. Not from here.'

She regained her composure, swallowing down all the fear and dislocation and bottling it up inside. 'I don't believe you,' she said.

'We're *here*.' Jack stamped his foot down, even though the actual rock surface was somewhere at right angles to where he stood. 'We're a hundred million kilometres from anything. If you want to help anyone, you can help us get this rock back, because while no one's admitting it, we're starting to struggle. You'll get royalties from the refinery, yes? Every ingot of ore they cast, you – and your people – will get a percentage of that, which will add up to a vast sum of money over the next decade.'

'That's the deal.' She was listening.

'Our interests coincide. We want what you want. Like I said, you can't affect anything that's happening on Earth right now, but you can make a difference in the future, and you will be there to see it, because we're taking you home at the same time.' He jammed his hands into his pockets, because he was waving them around too much. 'I appreciate that we're not necessarily the crew you were expecting, or even wanted. But we're the crew you're going to have to work with to get what you do want. How about it?'

She thought about it, then nodded. 'What do you need me to do?'

'Can you ... fly?'

18

Altogether the evidence that the earth is warming by an amount which is too large to be a chance fluctuation and the similarity of the warming to that expected from the greenhouse effect represents a very strong case. In my opinion, that the greenhouse effect has been detected, and it is changing our climate now.

> J. Hansen, NASA Goddard Space Institute, testimony to the US
> Senate Committee on Energy and Natural Resources, 1988

In order to place three seismographs on the surface of KU2, Cat took Patricio and Marta out in the shuttle. Using the craft was the only possible way they were going to cross kilometres of broken, barely attached surface before their suits became depleted of oxygen. The miners took reels of cable with them, and spooled them out along their routes, only fixing the cable at either end. Putting in anchor posts could be done later, during the burn phase, or not at all, depending on the requirements.

The surface rotated below them at sixty centimetres a second, no faster than a standard escalator moved, but that meant some difficult flying for the gallowglass, and some equally tricky manoeuvring for the miners, hanging upside down over the asteroid and trying to screw in posts while tethered to a free-running wire. Contact with the rock was unavoidable. The shuttle returned with all three of them, but with less paint than when it left.

Marta came through into Control first, and she looked

as shattered as the rock itself, hollowed from the inside out. Patricio came next, his face grey and his expression locked into one of joyless determination. The smell of gunpowder and sweat drifted off them like smoke.

'We did it,' he said. 'We'll put them online, later.'

Jack watched for Andros's reaction. More delay, more nervousness from the investors. But even he had the sense not to argue: Patricio looked both utterly exhausted and ready to swing at someone.

'How was the girl?'

'The girl has a name,' said Patricio. 'She was a good pilot, in testing circumstances.'

Andros ignored the positives, as ever. 'How are you going to provide the sound wave?'

'I can do that,' said Jack, deflecting the conversation away from the miners. 'You wanted another laser test. I can just fine-tune it to produce an explosive impulse. A small one. And then I can vary the impact point by moving the target. We should get all the readings we need.'

'And the debris?'

'These will be tiny explosions, halfway around the asteroid. Whatever gets thrown up won't have enough energy to pierce the hull. I'm barely heating the surface at all, just a few watts. But if I pulse it in the microsecond range, there'll be explosive thermal expansion. The results we get will be far more accurate than going outside again and hitting something with a hammer. We've got it covered.' He added: 'We do, you know, talk to each other and plan how we do things.' But he muttered the last part and gave himself some plausible deniability. Six months ago, he wouldn't have dared. Now, he'd joined in. Being rude to Captain Andros was becoming something of a national sport. Nothing, short of endangering the ship or the crew, seemed to be out of bounds and, inexplicably, their captain was following the same unwritten rules just as closely as they did.

'The wait is unacceptable, and yet entirely predictable,' said

Andros. 'The sooner the seismic readings are taken, the sooner we can begin the steering burn.'

'The sooner the stock rises,' said Marta.

'Without the investors, this ship would not be here, and you would not have the opportunity to earn a life-changing amount of money. We all take our own risks. Theirs are of a different type to yours.'

'We risk our lives. They risk a portion of their capital,' rumbled Patricio. 'Very fair.'

'We will not have this conversation again at this time,' said Andros. 'Go and do what you need to, and bring the seismometers online at the earliest opportunity.'

Patricio grunted, and pushed Marta towards the axis.

Cat pulled herself through the shuttle hatch and into Control, towing her borrowed spacesuit and clattering it against the hard surfaces. The first thing she did was glance towards the pilot's chair, and the man sitting in it. She didn't seem the sort of person to crow over another's weaknesses, but Jack still held his breath.

'You would have hated it,' was all she said to Runi, and he looked so relieved, then so ashamed that he turned away. She was momentarily confused, then drifted across the rest of Control to the other end. She hesitated when she got to the axis. 'Have I earned my call home yet?'

'This is not something we do, Gallowglass,' said Andros. 'I believe the astrogator has made that clear.'

'You talk to NovaS. You talk to these investors of yours all the time. All I want is one call home. To talk to my father.'

'If it was just your father, I would permit it.' Andros folded his arms. 'I'm not made of stone, Pilot, so take the look of condemnation from your face. There are complications, are there not, Gallowglass? Complications you're hiding from the crew, in order to manipulate their support for your cause against good practice and common sense. Do you want to tell them, or shall I?'

She said nothing, and he continued.

'The truth of the matter is that your father is also the Prime Minister of St Ann's, and his decisions are critical to the fate of your country which, thanks to our loose-lipped medic, you already know more about than you should. Order will be maintained on this ship, and if that means denying you 'one call home', as you disingenuously put it, then that is what I'll do. I trust my crew to follow those instructions.' He seemed very pleased with himself, that he actually had some captaining to do. 'Are we clear on that, Pilot? Astrogator?'

'Sir.'

Cat Gallowglass left in a way that made it quite clear that if Andros thought he'd won this particular battle, there was a whole war still to fight.

Jack went back to pushing windows around his screen in a desultory manner.

'Astrogator.'

'Captain.'

'What's your opinion of the gallowglass?'

'My opinion?'

'There is no echo in space, Astrogator. She is currently an asset: she is a skilled astrogator. All singleship pilots are. She's also a pilot. Engineer? Some training, likewise life support, ship systems and medical emergencies. The only roles I don't think she could cover are the geotechnical ones. But she won't let this idea of calling home go. At which point does she turn into a liability?'

'I still don't get why it's such a bad idea,' said Jack. 'One brief call home to settle her, and that's it.'

'I know things you don't, Astrogator. I know that one brief call home will do the opposite of settle her, but there's no way of telling her that without making her more dangerous to this mission and its crew.'

'You want me to space her.'

'I want you to consider the possibility. You're squeamish.

You need to get over yourself. And think about what's best for you. So I ask you again: if she was at one end of a tether, and you at the other, would you trust her not to throw you into space?'

He didn't know what the answer might be, so he flipped it. 'What makes you think she trusts us?'

'She doesn't. She's made that quite clear, and she's right not to. If it's decided that she shouldn't be on board, are you going to do the stupid, noble thing, or are you going to do the sensible, low thing?'

Jack was no more going to space her than he was Runi. 'She can be integrated into the crew. She has a wide skill-set, so she can relieve or help several of us. She also has more at stake here than we do. We're just here for the money, but she's here for her whole nation's survival. She'll work with us to get the asteroid.' There was also the matter of having Cat act as the shuttle pilot, and shielding Runi from any further outings on the asteroid. But he didn't say that, not with Runi sitting there.

He ran his hands over his face and into his unruly hair. Runi was watching him carefully, almost in adoration: he'd clearly guessed.

'We'll revisit this discussion when necessary,' said Andros. 'For now, it appears the gallowglass stays.'

At the back of his mind, though, Jack was already constructing scenarios where spacing one of his colleagues might be necessary. The unthinkable was now thinkable: the idea was firmly planted in his consciousness. This was what being in space was actually about. This was what he should have been prepared for. This was what he'd wilfully ignored for too long.

The captain left via the axis, and Runi waited until he and Jack were properly alone.

'Thank you.'

'Don't mention it,' said Jack. 'Really, don't mention it. Just … just let her do the flying, okay? We'll get you home. You'll get your share. But you're going to have to retire afterwards. You can't put another crew in this position.'

'I know, I know. This was ...' he struggled to get the words out, '... reckless of me. I thought I could do one last trip, and then I could stop, but Andros didn't say what it was until we were on board, and by then it was too late to back out. I tried to keep it all down. And I did, for so long, and then. I'm sorry. I've made a terrible mistake coming here.'

'I know you've already had to vote on me. And you know we've had to vote on you. Now we're voting on Cat. I don't think you're the only one who's made a terrible mistake coming here, but there's no reason why we can't all make it home. You have to ...' Jack scrubbed at his face again. 'I'm not comfortable telling a man with whatever your problems are to pull yourself together, but Runi, you have to. Get Arush to give you whatever it takes to get you through the next few months.'

'I don't want to die, Jack.'

'I will protect you as long as I can. We should all be protecting each other, and forgetting this whole Darwinian mindset that we seem to have got caught up in.' He unstrapped himself from his seat and headed for the axis. 'I'm going to warn Cat. Get her to, I don't know, play by the rules or something. Okay?'

He held out his fist, and Runi dapped it.

Cat Gallowglass wasn't in the gym, nor the cans, nor the galley. Inevitably, she was the last place he checked, the crew quarters. He knocked on her door, got no response, and decided that he was going to try again because he wasn't going to have this conversation through a layer of plastic.

'Who is it, and what do you want?'

'It's Jack. Jack Astrogator. And I want to talk to you.'

'Do we have anything to say to each other?'

'Yes. I think we do.'

'And have they sent you here?'

'The answer is still, if they were going to send someone, they wouldn't send me.' Jack took a step back. 'I'm not going to open the door on you. But if you don't then I'm walking away with the information you definitely need to know.'

The rooms weren't big. She could reach the handle by sitting on the bed. It still took an interminably long time for her to give in.

She sat cross-legged on the mattress. He stood in the gap between the bed and the door.

'Say it, then get out. I'm not in the mood.'

'Did you know that whether we live or die is decided by the crew voting on it?'

She didn't move her face, but she did look up and sideways at him.

'So, earlier on in this voyage, they decided, despite the fact it was my first trip out, I was competent enough to not endanger the ship. They let me live.'

'Lucky you.'

'And now I'm crew, I get a say in whether other people get tossed out the airlock for being too big a risk to have on board.'

'Don't put yourself out on my behalf.'

'You don't understand—'

'I understand perfectly well. It's the only reasonable way to run a ship. Tell your captain I'll behave myself from now on. I'll fit in, do the work assigned to me. No more talk about calls home. No more news. No more *drama*.'

'I already told them that. I said we could trust you.'

'Did you?' She sighed, and rocked from side to side, adjusting the position of her legs. Her voice was flat. 'St Ann's deserved to survive, Jack. None of this was our fault. If there was any justice, Africa would be full of European refugees and your countries would be on fire or under water, like mine apparently is, instead of the other way around. If you'd had any sense of shame, you'd have given us land and restitution for what we've lost and are still losing. Instead, we were reduced to this: chasing rocks across the solar system in the hope we can keep back

171

the tides, preserve our culture and our community, and not be scattered to the winds and forgotten by history.'

He took a moment to think about his parents' billions, and his upbringing, and the houses they owned, and the flights he'd casually and liberally taken, that he'd never been too cold or too hot or left in the dark, and then asked: 'What will you do?'

She shrugged. 'I will rage, silently and secretly, while appearing to be a good crew member who is safe and conscientious and not at all the kind of person you want to throw out of an airlock.'

'I just wanted to warn you about that.' Jack made to leave. 'I'm sorry.'

'You don't even know what you're sorry for,' she said.

'It's a general expression of regret and empathy. Everything is just a little bit shit right now, but maybe if we get the rock back home, it'll be less so.' He was halfway out of the door, almost beginning to close it behind him, when she spoke again.

'His name was Castor. We were rivals, but we ended up as friends, because we were there for the same reason, even though we both knew that only one of us could register a claim. We both hoped that if it wasn't us, it would be the other. There were so many gallowglasses, some independent, some sponsored, some corporate-backed, and we were just ... left to fight it out amongst ourselves. The odds of the last two being me and Castor were literally astronomical, and so it was inevitable that we were.'

'You don't have to say any more.'

'I killed him. He managed to cut his delta-v before I could, fired his anchors into the regolith and hauled himself down. He sent the claim. His country – his landlocked, central African country – must have thought they'd been saved. But I hadn't come all that way, in years and distance, to see my own nation lost to the sea. I fired my anchors into his ship and cracked it open like an egg, then landed on the wreckage. His body was under me as I registered my own claim. I don't know whether he's still here on the surface, or if he ended up in orbit like I did.' There was a long silence. 'Tell me if you find him, please?'

Jack pulled the door shut and rested his head against the frame for a second, before scaling the ladder back towards the axis.

19

It is very probable that by 2010, i.e. within another 15 years, there will be at least another 25 million such refugees.

N. Myres and J. Kent, *Environmental Exodus*,
Climate Institute, 1995

Their laser was powerful enough, focused enough, to evaporate rock and turn the resulting plasma into a plume of gas moving fast enough to change an asteroid's orbit. It fleetingly crossed Jack's mind that it would make a formidable weapon, able to hit a target at thousands of kilometres with sufficient energy to punch a hole in any structure. Or ship. And here it was, not just in private hands, but his hands. He could, if he wanted, end the mission by pointing the laser at the *Coloma* and pulling the trigger.

No one could stop him. No one would even know until the hull tore itself apart, the energy pack exploded and the rotating sections were flung into space. Just a few coordinates tapped into the computer to bring the device around and they'd all be dead in less than a second. If they were lucky. They might live a few moments longer if they survived the initial blast.

Then again, he realised, all the rest of the crew were bright people, more than able to figure out how to redirect the laser themselves, and there were absolutely no locks or deterrents or passwords on the subsystems that he was about to use. And if he thought that one of them might just do that, what could he do to stop them?

'Jack. Jack?'

'I'm fine. I'm … fine. No problem.' He clasped his shaking hands together and peered at the numbers on his screen, making sure he hadn't accidentally altered any of them. The entire crew were in Control, except Arush and Runi, who were sitting down next to the spacesuits, just in case. 'Is everybody ready?'

May looked sceptically at him. 'Yes. Are you?'

'I was just thinking. That's all.'

'You have to concentrate,' she said. 'On this. Not on anything else.'

'I know,' he said, biting back on his irritation.

'All seismometers are online and running,' said Marta.

'First point.' Jack typed in the figures as he spoke them. 'Zero degrees by fifteen east. In three, two, one, mark.'

They all felt the shudder, as if someone had kicked the chairs they were sitting on.

'We have data.' Patricio leaned over and tapped Marta's screen. 'It's ringing like a bell.'

'Is that good?' asked Jack.

'Deconvolution is technically difficult, and is more of an art than a science,' he said. 'However, the more solid the object, the more reflections there'll be. It's a hopeful sign.'

'I'll target the second point.'

'Wait until the sound waves have attenuated.'

They all waited. There was a patter of debris against the outside of the ship, over almost as soon as it started: a passing rain cloud and no more than that.

'Damage report,' ordered Andros, and May ran through the systems.

'All systems nominal.'

They waited some more.

'Are we ready for the second?' said Jack.

'We're still ringing.'

'Is that still good?'

'It's an asteroid. There's nothing to damp the vibrations but

175

the interstitial space between the solids. But yes. The rock may be less fragmented than the surface conditions suggest.'

'It's just that target two is rotating out of frame.'

'Recalculate?'

'Okay.' Jack's fingers flew across the keyboard, and he sent the new coordinates to Patricio. 'That do?'

'Give me another sixty seconds. The decibel level is finally attenuating.'

The counter clicked round.

'Second point. Forty north by twenty-five east. Firing in three, two, one, mark.'

Another, firmer jolt.

'We're closer this time, so it could be louder, or it could miss us altogether.' Jack eyed the hull beyond the electronics, the cabling, the screens and the people. Julia had a stash of patches ready, from micro-meteorite size all the way up to that'll-evacuate-all-the-air-from-the-ship-in-ten-seconds dinner plates. Crew had to see holes in the ship as an occupational hazard, and one they were prepared for.

The hull crackled, and was then quiet again.

'Damage report.'

'Still nominal.'

'Data is streaming. We probably have more than we need, but we'll take the third target for completeness' sake.'

Jack thumbed the preset to the third point on the surface, and glanced at May. She was frowning at her screen, and she nudged Julia.

'Problem?'

'Could be. Pressure fluctuation in the nitrogen tanks. Looks like a sticky valve. I'll shut it down, and test it when we're done up here. It's internal. Nothing you've done.'

Jack waited on Patricio's say-so, then triggered the third hit on the surface. Out there in the darkness, the laser flashed and rock fractured. They barely felt it this time, and Jack checked that everything had worked as it should.

'The energy went somewhere,' he said.

'How far away was the target?'

'Just over two k.'

'We hit something loose.'

Julia was already reaching for her patches when something significant smacked against the hull.

Instinctively, they all looked up.

'Damage report?'

'We ... have a leak,' said May. 'Shuttle's been holed. Pressure at ninety-five per cent and falling.'

Julia hit the buckle on her seat strap and pushed herself up to the hatch. She grabbed the handwheel and turned it. 'Equalising pressure.'

Jack's ears popped, and she hauled on the hatch. Everyone in Control could hear the thin, whistling noise.

'Lights are out. Give me the emergency circuit.'

May dragged the control panel open and hit the screen. Green light flooded the interior, and Julia pulled herself through.

'Okay, you bastard, where are you?'

'Coming up on fifteen seconds.'

'Got it. Some spalling. Big hit outside, then.' The squealing cut off abruptly. 'Sealed.'

'Re-pressur— except I won't be because I've disabled the N2 tanks. Everyone will have to cope with decreased pressure until I fix it.'

Julia re-emerged. 'This fucking asteroid. I swear I will cheer when the last of it goes into the furnace.'

'We have the seismic data,' said Marta. 'We'll take it down in the lab.'

'Seal the hatch,' ordered Andros. 'No one enters the shuttle until after an external inspection and report.'

'Aye-aye.' Julia closed both the shuttle hatch and the *Coloma*'s own.

'Pressure is stable,' said May. 'I'll bring the shuttle systems online one by one and check them. Who's suiting up and taking a look?'

'I'll go,' said Kayla. 'I'll need a second.'

'Me.'

The cabin fell silent. They'd all but forgotten the gallow-glass, crouched beside Runi's pilot chair.

Her confession of murder loud in his ears, Jack opened his mouth to speak, then closed it again. She'd done what she'd done to get the mining rights. She wasn't going to jeopardise the safe return of the rock. They were safe with her, surely, and hadn't she already proved herself with Patricio and Marta?

Kayla blinked, and flicked her hair beads. 'Okay. Why not? Let's get suited up.'

They were queuing to enter the axis: Marta, Patricio, Kayla, and finally Cat Gallowglass. When the logjam cleared, and enough time had passed, the remaining crew in Control wondered who would be first to say something.

'We're starting to accumulate mistakes,' said May. 'We can't afford many more.'

'It's gash out there,' said Julia. 'We just have to be extra careful, that's all. No unnecessary EVA. Just close the hatches and ride the lightning home.'

'I didn't know the surface would explode like that. No way I could have predicted it,' said Jack. 'Could have hit some volatiles or something. I don't know.'

'We should have stopped at two soundings,' said May. 'We had enough data.'

'Our investors—'

'Seriously? Are we doing this now? For the last time, your investors are not here. Your constant hurry-ups aren't a solution to the problem: they are the problem.' They stared at each other, May furious and finally scared, and Andros implacable and inscrutable. Eventually, she turned and closed down her console. 'I'm going to fix the N2 valve. Julia, can you ride shotgun on that up here?'

178

'No worries.'

'And on the assumption that the asteroid will stay in one piece, Astrogator can plot our path back to Cis-lunar space.' Andros unstrapped and drifted across Control. 'I need first sight of the seismic data.'

But Jack did notice that their captain rested his hand on the closed shuttle hatch, just for a moment, before floating down the axis.

Julia opened some windows, closed them down again. 'Can you do this, Jack? Can you make it work?'

'That's what we're here for, right?'

'History is littered with costly failed enterprises. This could be one of them.'

'The theory is sound. The laser is big enough. We'll get enough thrust.'

'But will we survive the experience?'

'The surface isn't stable. Once we've got a trench, then the exhaust materials will go up and out, but we have to get to that point. I ...' Jack lapsed into silence, thinking back to the first laser test. 'I could melt the surface rock into a lava sheet where we want the trench to be. Literally melt the top layer and let it freeze. Then drill through the middle of it. That would minimise flying rock. I could probably do that in one rotation period, five hours.'

'Then do it.'

'Do I need to ask anyone's permission?'

Julia shrugged. 'Run it by the mining team. If they can spot a problem, then you have to talk it out, but otherwise no. It's your call. You have the authority. I'm not going to ask anyone about my stuff: it's not a collective decision.' She shrugged again, and turned back to monitor what May was doing down below. 'It's mine.'

'I should test it out first.'

'Then do that.'

Jack started to lay in the coordinates for a target. 'I'm not

179

used to making decisions. Important decisions, that is. I got to choose between two safe, pre-approved options and it took me far longer than it ought to have done for me to work that out.'

'You know what, Jack?' said Julia. 'Don't talk about this. We already know too much about your past, and anything else is dangerous. You know what I'm saying?'

'But I don't know anything more than where you came from, and a few other fragments. We know more about the gallowglass than we do about each other.'

'And that's the way it should stay. Shipboard friendships? Not for me. I like you, Jack. You do your job well, and I trust you to get me home. I'd be happy to crew with you again. But don't mistake that for anything else.'

'As I'm discovering. Can you watch the laser stats at the same time as the N2 tanks?'

'Sure thing. About time we gave it a proper work-out.'

Jack zoomed in on the asteroid's surface, somewhere he was likely to need to fire at anyway, and with a press of a button, turned it from a loose assemblage of discrete rocks to a pool of molten lava five metres across. In accordance with his programming, the laser focused at points in a widening spiral. The process took seconds, and when he shut the laser off, the orbital cameras showed a shining, oscillating mass that slowly dulled and set to a glass-like finish.

Julia peered at her screens. 'Needles barely moved.'

'I'll give it a minute or two.' He could literally sign his name on the surface. In fact, he might just do that at voyage's end. 'Kayla and Cat are in decompression, yes? Not EVA yet?'

'You've got another forty minutes. If you break something else, I guess they can repair it while they're out there.'

Jack's console pinged, and a translucent three-dimensional model appeared in a new window. It was coloured in sections to show the differences in the speed of sound, and he found he could slice it and turn it however he wanted. The asteroid contained three discrete masses, and the brightest, bluest mass was at the north end, under where they'd landed.

'I have no idea what I'm looking at.'

'Then it is a good job,' said Patricio, 'that someone is here to explain it to you.'

He pulled himself out of the axis and next to Jack's screen.

'The more solid the material, the faster the sound waves travel. This is colour-coded – bluer is faster, red is slower. This gives us no indication of actual material type, although we have a database of speeds-of-sound for various rock types, including ice and metal. This mass here? Five thousand metres per second? All iron-nickel. It's much larger than we expected. Bigger bonuses when we get back. It explains why the asteroid has got a pronounced precession, and also why Marta could not get the grapples home. We were firing them at a slab of iron covered with a few loose rocks.

'These other masses. They could be cometary. Rich in volatiles. Also good. There is interstitial material surrounding them. Chondritic or differentiated, it's broken all the way down, but there's good transmission of sound through it, showing at least some evidence of welding and cohesion. I am content with this. It's less worse than I initially feared.' He almost, but not quite, smiled.

Julia looked up from her screen. 'When you say bigger bonuses, just how much?'

'Ten, perhaps twenty per cent for us. For the jackals who own this ship, more. Jack, we can work with this, yes?'

Jack explained his proposal regarding the laser trench to Patricio, who immediately agreed. That was it. That was all the oversight Jack was going to get.

'Let's find out.' Jack tabbed the intercom. 'Test firing of the laser. You may feel it, but it shouldn't puncture anything.'

He lined up his target. The cameras would show him nothing while the laser was on, beyond an incandescent spot.

'Firing in three, two, one. Mark.'

The centre of the solidified circle of rock remelted, grew brighter, then flashed as it turned from liquid to a gas. The laser kept on heating the gas, tearing the molecules apart, and then the very atoms themselves. All that energy in such a concentrated place could only go in one direction: outwards. The exhaust plume grew, and fogged the picture.

'Can you feel it?'

'No?' said Julia. She put her hands out to touch her monitor stand. 'No. Nothing.'

'Okay. Let's take it up a notch.'

'I thought you were at full power.'

'Nowhere near it. Above the threshold, yes, but about a quarter watts.' Jack pumped more energy into the laser. 'I think we can safely say this thing is grossly overpowered. Can you feel it now?'

'Yes? It's like a noise in my guts. I can't hear it, but there's something.'

'Let's take it up to half. If it goes pop, we know one way or the other.'

'Systems are nominal. Barely warmed up. Go for it, Jack. Give those investors something to cheer about.'

'Thirty-five per cent. Forty. Forty-five.' There was a tremor, a quivering, in the deep. 'Fifty per cent. I'll have to shut off in ten, as the target's becoming oblique. But feel it. That's a hell of a kick. Enough to steer by.'

He ramped the power down. The movement ceased, and everything was still again. He pressed his hands to his cheeks and slid his fingers down towards his chin.

'I think we're actually on our way.'

20

Based on these relative risk estimates, a rise in the 1-h daily maximal ozone from 84 ppb to 160 ppb was associated in this group with an increase from 20 to 28 (+/- 2) in the expected number of unscheduled medications administered/day, and from 29 to 41 (+/- 3) in the expected total number of chest symptoms/day.

(G. D. Thurston, M. Lippmann, M. B. Scott, J. M. Fine,
'Summertime haze air pollution and children with asthma',
*American Journal of Respiratory and Critical Care
Medicine,* 1997

Three days later, Jack initiated the first full burn. Vast canopies of solar panels rotating slowly beyond the debris ring, permanently illuminated by the Sun, beamed their power inwards to collectors on the laser. The laser turned that unceasing energy into a five-metre-wide column of invisible light that tore at the rock, first melting it, then evaporating it and turning it into a jet of million-degree fundamental particles.

Where the laser touched, it burned. Cameras on the outside of the hull registered an incandescent plume a kilometre tall. Scattered green light flickered in the gas clouds before they dispersed, an aurora born of unnatural processes.

The ground shook. It trembled and quivered. The full effect was felt in Control, and was only slightly damped by the bearings of the crew quarters. It manifested as an inconstant bass rumble throughout the *Coloma.* After half an hour, Julia pronounced it bloody annoying, and told Arush he needed to fix her up with some ear plugs.

It was a sound that bypassed the ears, though. It resonated in the gut and echoed in the skull. It was the sound of progress, that the mission might be successful, that they might all become rich, but it was also a sound that was going to take some getting used to, if they ever could. It was a sound that had to be continuous for months.

They lived with it for the rest of the day, while Jack made careful observations of the stars. The amount of thrust produced was only measurable by the distance it moved the asteroid, and any changes in course could only be plotted out in the minute angles of the ephemeris. It would take a while to find out how long and how hard they needed to drive the laser: the longer the observations lasted, the more accurately their path could be judged.

He didn't sleep or eat until the first results came in.

'We need a delta-v of three hundred and eighty metres a second in order to park this at the Earth-Moon L4. Neither fuel nor time are the limiting factors in reaching that value. What is, is whether we can get there in this orbital period. Rather than taking three years to do this, let's assume that everyone wants to go home in five months.'

He brought up a graphic and posted it to everyone's screen.

'We can give continuous thrust. That means we need to average zero point zero three millimetres of delta-v a second. Given that we're pushing two times ten to the power fourteen kilograms, we're looking at six gigawatts of useful work.'

'That seems like ... a lot?'

'We get a force multiplier from burning the rock in a trench, so that the exhaust is partially directed. It turns out that we need less thrust than the first stage of the Saturn V, and we can keep our engine running all day, all night, for as long as we want it.'

'So we can do it?'

'Yes,' he said. He felt surprised he was able to give the answer. 'Yes. We can do this. I mean, it's not a trivial task. But we can produce more thrust than we need.'

'How much more?' asked Andros.

Jack was about to answer when he caught the unspoken question. 'It doesn't work how you think it does. Everything is moving: us, the Earth, the Moon, L4. It's not a question of speed, but of timing. If you're asking me can we get there sooner, I'm saying no, absolutely not.'

'If you were to go faster—'

'The boy said no.' Patricio was firm. 'He is the astrogator. He plots the course.'

'A month earlier would give everyone here a significant increase in their bonus.'

Jack waited for someone else to back him up, and it was Runi who came to his defence.

'I've worked with Jack on this, and this is the safest way of bringing the rock in. We need to factor in downtime, maintenance, and everything that might go wrong. You're asking us to pretend that everything will go right, and that hasn't been our experience so far.'

'The limiting factor is where L4 will be at any given moment.' Jack highlighted the point on the model. 'What I've done is optimise for our minimum delta-v. If we arrive late, there'll be complications. At that point, our orbit will match that of Earth's, but if we're behind L4, it could take weeks or months to push us from an unstable point across to L4. We could even lose it completely at that stage. If we get there early, we'll have had to add more delta-v, only to take it off again at the other end, and I don't want to be doing any kind of complex deceleration manoeuvres in Earth's gravity well. L4 is moving at thirty kilometres a second. That's eighty times more than our entire delta-v budget, and we cannot do anything about that.'

The crew had stopped working out what to spend their extra money on now. One or two of them looked disappointed – Kayla,

Arush – but the others seemed content with his analysis.

'We have a narrow window we can hit. The reason we're out here now, is because this is the only time in the next few periods where it's easy. The next time it's this good is 2085, and I'm guessing our investors won't wait that long.' Jack tapped his screen. 'This is the course I recommend.'

'What he said,' said Runi. 'We're moving a mountain, and it's not going to hurry for us.'

'Okay. Whatever,' said Julia. 'Just as long as I can sleep through this godawful noise.'

'Can you guarantee that we arrive at the refinery on schedule?'

Again, Jack felt the question begged the answer. 'When do you expect us to arrive?'

'April the fourteenth, 2073.'

'No. It will be April, sometime. If you ask me again in three months' time, I'll be able to tell you the day. Another month after that, the hour. I'll have to fine-tune both the laser's power output and the burn angle to keep us on course. The thrust will vary because we're burning different rocks with different melting points. This is … look: this is not a spaceship. This is an asteroid. No one has brought something this big home before.'

'Enough of your bullying, Captain,' said Patricio. 'This course is the course that is possible, is the safest, with the largest margin of error that allows us, the crew, to fix things that will inevitably break. You, you haven't worn your spacesuit even once this whole journey.'

'Our investors like certainty,' said Andros.

'Something tells me that your interest in the share price isn't as detached as it should be.' May frowned at her screen, rather than turn round. 'You're an investor, aren't you? You've got a bigger stake in this than any of us. That's why you're here.'

Andros didn't say one way or the other.

'I'm going to ask you straight. Are you actually NovaS? Is this your company?'

He remained mute.

'You idiot,' she said. She looked directly at the gallowglass, sitting quietly by Runi's chair and absorbing everything. Then she unstrapped herself. She was at the axis hatch before she spoke again. 'You fucking idiot.'

'I don't get it,' said Arush.

'It's very simple.' Patricio also unbuckled himself. 'We are out here, risking our lives, doing our job, for a fee. We can only complain impotently amongst ourselves. They are back on Earth, hanging on every tiny message that Andros sends them, watching their fortunes rise and fall with our successes or setbacks. They can only complain impotently amongst themselves. And while NovaS remains a distant, faceless corporation, we can safely hate them, and them us. Balance is maintained.'

He drifted across Control to confront Andros. He laid his strong hand on his captain's shoulder, and Andros tried to shrug it off, but Patricio's grip had turned as iron as the asteroid beneath them.

'Are you dissatisfied with your pay? The percentage of your bonus? How it is calculated? It seems our captain is the person to negotiate with. If something goes wrong with the ship, or with one of the crew, then who is to blame? Our captain. Perhaps the selection of food or the provision of stores are not as you would wish. Captain Andros has personally made those choices for you. It is no longer "us" against "them". It is us against him.'

'I want to renegotiate,' said Cat.

'Here we bloody go.' Julia bailed, and headed down the axis. One after another, the crew left, until it was just Andros, Cat and Jack.

'I should go too,' said Jack.

'No,' said Cat. 'I need a witness.'

'This ... this has nothing to do with me.' Jack felt his courage loosening even as he unbuckled his seat strap. 'I ran away from home to the one place my parents couldn't drag me back from.

I'm here to get my certificates, and maybe a reference, and if I get paid, that's actually extra as far as I'm concerned. If you want my share, then you can have that. I just need enough to live on.'

She appeared genuinely taken aback by his offer, and he abruptly realised that she had no idea who he was, or who his parents were. Of all the people on the ship, she was the only one who was reacting to just him.

'That's ... generous,' she said. 'But that won't be enough.' She turned her fire on Andros. 'Now we've proved we can deliver on the asteroid, I want more money. Another five billion. Euros or dollars. It's a fraction of what you've just made on the share price: you won't even miss it.'

Andros shifted in his seat. The background rumbling did nothing to cover the fact that he still hadn't replied.

'My country needs this. My people are refugees. They need land. They need a home.'

The captain's face remained a mask.

'You'll earn tens of billions from this, and the only reason you will is that I took the risk. I flew here. I landed here.' She choked on her emotion. 'I killed my friend for this. You owe me.'

'You have been paid in full,' said Andros finally. 'Every last cent you asked for, you have received. You have an agreement with NovaS.'

'I'm tearing up our agreement.'

'You sold NovaS the mining rights. NovaS paid you for the mining rights. I do not doubt that that contract will be defended, successfully, in court.' He remained entirely impassive. 'NovaS paid the Government of St Ann's the initial tranche of ten billion three years ago. That should have been sufficient to see your people properly resettled, had it been properly managed.'

The words caught in her mouth.

'What ...'

'Sufficient to pay off the loans it took to get you trained and get you a ship, sufficient to buy land somewhere above the Arctic Circle. They could be there by now, safe, rebuilding their lives. Instead, your own government, your own father, wasted your sacrifice, your life, your friend's life, so now there isn't enough left to do anything useful with it. That your people are scattered and lost is not a problem for NovaS.'

Sometimes it was easy to forget her youth, her arrested development. Other times, it wasn't. Jack had seen enough. 'Cat, this isn't going to go the way you want it to.'

'You'll receive legacy payments as the asteroid is dismantled. Not a cent more.'

'I demand to talk to my father.'

'So you can ask him what he spent ten billion dollars on? I can tell you that. Drink and whores. The rest he wasted.'

Jack couldn't prevent Cat from launching herself at Andros. Neither could he get in the way in time. Slight as she was, she clung to Andros like a burr, scratching and gouging and biting whatever she could, absorbing his blows and not caring if they hurt her.

Jack tried to pull her away, taking a fistful of flightsuit between her shoulder blades and bracing himself against a handhold, but she simply dragged Andros along with her. She was doing real damage to him. There was blood in the air, quivering droplets of it that bounced and splashed.

'Hey. A hand in here,' he called. If he let go, and got to the intercom, then it might be over sooner, but she could have put out Andros's eye by the time reinforcements arrived. 'Hey. Anyone. Emergency.'

Andros and Cat were thrashing. They were hitting consoles and controls, and things were going to break, if they hadn't already. Jack was the only other crew there, and he needed to stop pulling his punches and end the fight now, before they wrecked Control.

'Okay,' he told himself. Zero-gravity combat wasn't anything he'd trained for. But he had at least trained for something, so he improvised.

He hit Cat in the back of the head with his open palm, at the same time as pulling on her clothing for leverage. Her forehead smacked against Andros's cheekbone, hard enough to stun them both. Jack went in for the grapple, wrapping his arm around her neck and locking it in place by holding onto his own wrist.

He tightened his grip, and she finally let go of Andros, who spun away, limp and with limbs outstretched. Her hands came around and she tried to claw him instead, her fingers striving to find a target unseen. He started to strangle her, pressing against the sides of her neck, and her probing weakened. After a few seconds, he felt her whole body, up to that moment as tight as a wire, soften.

Jack relaxed his hold without letting go, and finally someone came to see what the noise was about. Kayla stopped by the axis hatch to take in the scene, then twisted around.

'Arush! Bring the medkit. Stat.'

Then she pulled herself in, trying to avoid the still hovering drops of blood that were now drifting in the air currents.

'Get her out of here,' said Jack. 'Put her somewhere safe for now.'

'Holy crap, Jack. What the hell happened?'

'This is not the time for explanations. Seriously, get her out of here and away from him. She's coming round, and she'll just start up again where she left off.' He pushed Cat towards Kayla, who had no choice but to catch the gallowglass.

Arush bundled in, dragging his big red bag of supplies. 'Ah, there's blood.'

Cat was pulling faces, trying to work out what had happened and why she'd passed out. Kayla shoved her down the axis tube and forced her along it. They began to argue, but she was, at least for the moment, not going to come rushing back through. Jack pulled Andros over into the empty space in the centre of

Control, and for the want of anywhere else to put him, sat him on Runi's pilot chair and strapped him down.

Andros seemed dazed, drunk with confusion. Although the attack had lasted only seconds, Cat had known how to hurt him physically as thoroughly as he'd hurt her mentally.

'Can you patch him up?'

Arush unzipped the bag and snapped on a pair of surgical gloves. 'Be easier in gravity, but sure. Nothing seems to be hanging off.'

'Check he's still got all his fingers before you say that.' Jack swung himself out of the way. 'I'll get rid of the floaters.'

He dug out the little hand-held vacuum cleaner from its charge point and spent the next ten minutes chasing down the coagulating spheres of black blood from wherever they were, either drifting or settling. The splashes he could do little about – they'd have to chip them off later when they were properly dry.

Julia would have to change the air filters, or at least wash them out. The grilles were spattered with sucked-in blood.

'How is he?'

'He can answer for himself,' said Andros.

'Maybe I didn't want to talk to you.' Jack disconnected the collection bag, so he could empty it into the waste disposal. 'You provoked that, and if I hadn't been here, you'd be urging us all to space her right now.'

'What did he say to her?' asked Arush. He was trying to bandage Andros's hands, but the captain kept moving.

'He was being a dick. What he actually said isn't important right now. What he was, was a dick.'

'Do you know how dirty a human bite is?' Arush deliberately hurt Andros, to make him pay attention. 'It's filthy. Any of these could become infected. We only have so many doses of antibiotics, and there's no guarantee any of them will work.'

'What can I do?' asked Jack.

'Get me a light, so I can see what I'm doing, stitch what

191

needs stitching.' He rummaged through his bag. 'I need the local anaesthetic.'

'That won't be necessary,' said Andros.

'You'll do what you're told,' said Arush, then to Jack: 'What happens after that, I really don't know. It's not like we can just ignore this. I'll get Julia to come up and do a damage report. Hopefully none of this stuff is busted.'

Jack caught Andros's gaze over Arush's shoulder. There was no question of thanks, or even an acknowledgement that Jack might just have saved the man's life. Brown eyes stared out of a scratched and bruised face, impassive, blinking slowly.

Was Andros NovaS? He hadn't denied it. The revelation was an added layer of complication to a task that was already far too dangerous. Even while the whole strange, almost-silent struggle had been taking place, it was to a background of vast energies being poured into the rock a couple of kilometres south of the *Coloma*.

What he did see, though, was a man even more out of his depth than he was himself. Someone who had managed to back himself into a corner and had no exit plan. Someone who, from the moment they set sail, was simply trusting to luck as to whether he came home at all.

Jack was going to code some locks into the system, to prevent the laser array being redirected without his knowledge or permission. He felt it was the least he could do. And he didn't particularly feel the need to tell anyone he was doing it, either.

He realised that not all voyages would be like this, but that thought wasn't going to help him in the days and weeks ahead. God have mercy on their souls.

21

The estimated overall change in all natural mortality associated with a 1°C increase in maximum apparent temperature above the city-specific threshold was 3.12% in the Mediterranean region and 1.84% in the north-continental region. Stronger associations were found between heat and mortality from respiratory diseases, and with mortality in the elderly.

M. Baccini et al., 'Heat effects on mortality in 15 European cities', *Epidemiology*, 2008

'Would you have let me be spaced?' he asked in the darkness. The air thrummed, and the mattress they lay on was constantly in motion, a low-value earthquake, every minute of every hour. Exhaustion forced them to sleep, but the vibrations woke them too early. This was not the cradle of the deep, the slow, rhythmic swing between sea waves, but a jangle of white noise.

No one had thought about this in advance.

'You know I can't answer that,' said May. 'You shouldn't even be asking.'

'Does this, any of this, mean nothing then?'

'No. Just that its meaning is orthogonal to the safety of the ship and the crew.' She raised herself on one elbow, and he felt her breath on his skin. 'You have to understand, Jack. You need to put that first. What we do is what we do. It's ... I'm not going to deny it's nice.'

'Nice?'

'Better than nice. I like you. We're good together.'

'But?'

'Yes, you have a nice butt too.'

'That's not what I meant.'

'If I went bat-shit crazy, started to trash the ship and tried to kill you and the rest of the crew, would you stop them from throwing me out the airlock?'

'I don't know?'

'Is the wrong answer. If I was trying to put a hole in the side of Control, or deliberately poisoning the breathing mix?'

'I wouldn't want to space you.'

'No one wants to.' She kissed his shoulder, and he shivered. 'No one ever wants to. But we might have to. You might have to. To save yourself. To save Arush and Julia and Patricio and Marta and Runi and Kayla.'

'And Andros?'

'This isn't about whether I'd space you, or whether you'd space me. We both know that.'

'No one's talking about it.'

'We're all thinking it, though. It's up to everyone to come to their own decision.'

'Shouldn't we – you and me – at least discuss it?'

'No. It's too dangerous. Everyone is open to persuasion. Everyone is malleable. Especially you. You're technically competent. Sometimes brilliant. But emotionally, you're a mixture of a blank slate and a car crash. I could twist you around my little finger with a single word, and I'm not going to do that.'

'Well. Thanks.' Jack rolled onto his back. The deep, chthonic movements made his teeth ache. There had to be some way of damping them. It was the *Coloma*'s points of contact with the surface which transmitted the vibrations: the anchors that held them safely down, the landing shocks which provided them with stability also cursed them. A centimetre above the rock would solve the problem, but they couldn't hover there indefinitely.

'Is Andros NovaS?' he asked.

'I don't know. Probably, yes. It's a complication we didn't

need and can't afford. We can't do anything about it, either. Something happens to him, all our contracts are void, all our pay in jeopardy, all our bonuses lost. We have to line up with all the other creditors, and crew are a long way from the front. Even if we bring in the asteroid, we'll be lucky if we get ten cents on the euro.' She slid one leg over his, and looked down on him from above. 'Whatever you decide, you have to decide on your own.'

He started to speak, and she pressed a finger against his lips.

'And you don't discuss it with me. You're crew. You have those rights and responsibilities independent of anyone else.'

Jack sagged into the bedding. He knew what he was being asked to do. On the one hand, a successful mission would bring them riches and, if not fame, a certain amount of bankable notoriety. On the other, nothing was guaranteed. Something could go wrong in any number of critical systems and their cold, desiccated corpses would continue to orbit the Sun until someone else tried to capture the asteroid for themselves. And on the third hand ...

'Cat owns the mining rights, doesn't she?'

'She's sold the rights to NovaS for a fixed term.'

'And if she dies? If we kill her?'

'The rights will go into her estate. If she has a will, or there's a specific provision for the transfer of the rights in the claim paperwork. I'm supposing her government. Her father.'

'She murdered her friend to get those rights.'

'His heirs couldn't claim because the claim wasn't properly registered. I don't know the law.'

'I'm just wondering. If we space Andros, we lose our contract. If we space Cat, do we also lose our contract? I mean, we know that we had to make every effort to retrieve her from her sleep tank, and Andros was happy to just ignore that. Now, he's doing everything he can to make her fighting-angry, and all he needs to do is repeat that until we can't do anything but space her. Maybe he thinks he gets to keep the royalties that St

195

Ann's were supposed to have.' He scrubbed at his face. 'What a piece of shit.'

'We know that now.' She put her head on his chest, and he idly stroked the velvet of her hair. 'Obviously, the only way we can all get out of this with any dignity is to keep them both alive, and apart, for the five months it takes to drive this thing to L4.'

'I thought we weren't discussing our choices?'

May turned her head slightly and nipped his chest. 'If there's any way we can get home quicker ...'

'We can't. We absolutely can't. I wasn't lying.'

'Well, damn,' she said, with no force whatsoever. 'I can't sleep and I need to.'

'Is there any way of tuning the landing shocks to damp out particular frequencies? Or putting some insulation under them? Feels like a hundred Hertz.'

'I'll look into it. We don't have anything spare. Unless you want to give up your mattress and get three other people to do the same, and then share what's left. Maybe we'll get used to it after a few more days.'

'I hope so. Because the only thing worse than being stuck here with two people determined to kill each other is being here with nine people determined to kill each other.'

'We are moving, though.'

'Yes, how much and how fast will become clear. I'm worried about the rotation speed.'

'What do you mean?'

'That I can spin up or spin down the asteroid at will, depending on whether I focus the beam ahead or behind the centre of mass. A centre of mass which is constantly changing position in three-dimensional space. I could, I think, although I haven't run the numbers, get this thing spinning so fast that all the loose rock will just fly off into space. Or I could stop the rotation entirely, or send it back the other way. I could make it tumble end over end, not that that would be a good thing, as

196

I'm relying on the equatorial trench to guide the exhaust.'

'You're feeling powerful. A god to this little world.'

'It's not like that. Just, after years of not making any decisions of consequence, I can suddenly do all this. Literally move mountains.'

'Would you want to stop the rotation?'

'I've thought about it. We'd have a blast pit, which would be much more efficient. But I'd be worried about the *Coloma*. We don't have a sun-shield, and by turning every few hours, we keep cool. The refinery would prefer a zero rotation, I guess.'

'Don't tell Andros. He'll get all in your face about that.'

Jack hit his head against the pillow. 'It's too loud.'

'That thing you did. The arm around the gallowglass's neck.'

'Kayla told you?'

'She told everyone.'

'Judo. Choke hold. I just remembered it. It's harmless if you do it right.'

'You knocked her out.'

'She was tearing Andros apart.' He'd remembered Mesman. He hadn't thought about her for months, and suddenly, there she was at the moment he'd needed her, teaching him the moves, using her lithe, athletic grace to slam him into the mat again and again and again until he'd learned to fight back. 'And he didn't seem that bothered about defending himself. He's almost twice her size. Twice her mass.'

'It's how much you're willing to bring to the fight.' May rolled onto all fours, and started doing a series of complicated stretches. They'd all lost muscle bulk, and despite everything, there was still never any real effort to do all the exercises they needed to. 'She seems to have more than Andros will ever do.'

Jack knew almost nothing about May, apart from her accent. How old she was, even. 'I couldn't let her kill him.'

'Of course you couldn't. That's before you had to worry about the damage to Control.'

'We can fix that, right?'

'If we can't, we can work around it. Multiple redundancies.'

He should really be doing some exercises of his own, but he just lay there, beached, exhausted. Besides, there was something intimate about just watching May go through her routine without needing to join in or interrupt. Homely. Which was an odd thought, considering how far they all were away from anything that might resemble home.

'Do you think it's odd,' he said, 'that we're here, doing this huge thing, pretty much without supervision or scrutiny? That we're armed with a massive laser, moving asteroids, and no one seems to be looking over our shoulder and making sure we're doing it right?'

'Earth-Moon, that's different, but this is the high seas. OSTO are just a registry. They take notes and keep tabs on stuff, not people: they were set up to do property law because otherwise how else could people turn a profit?'

'So as long as we bring the riches back, no one cares how we got them?'

'This is why crew don't talk about their pasts, Jack. This is exactly why. You think Cat Gallowglass is the only murderer on this ship? She's not. We know that Runi was involved in some pretty serious shit, and as for the others? There are bodies floating in space from the Belt all the way to the inner system, and only some of them got there by accident.' She finished her stretches and sat cross-legged next to him. 'You ran away to space. But space is very big, and very scary, and we're well over the black horizon. I'm going to suggest that maybe next time you should stick in sight of the coast.'

He wanted to ask her about where she came from, how she'd grown up, what had driven her into space, just as he had wanted to a hundred times before. But he knew she wasn't going to tell him, ever. She was crew to the core. So he didn't, and he lay there in the semi-darkness, listening to the sound of her breathing, the circulating air and the damnable rumble coming up from the rock below.

And as he listened, he could tell the sound had changed. And before he could sit up, there was a voice outside the cabin door.

'Jack?' It was Patricio.

'I hear it. I'll be there in a second.' He swung his feet out onto the floor and searched for his clothing.

'What is it?' asked May.

'Don't know. Could just be a geology thing, but I'll need to check.' He pulled on his shorts, and then his flightsuit.

'Shower.'

'I know.' He pulled on his ship slippers and left her. Patricio was waiting at the bottom of the ladder.

'Can you feel it?'

'Just now.'

'Marta's already in Control.'

They were speaking quietly. It added weight to the situation.

'So, let's go.' Jack climbed up to the axis and pulled himself along to his usual seat.

Marta was crouched over one of the workstations, and Julia was at another, her hands in the wiring loom, plugging things in, taking them out again. Jack sat next to Marta and loaded up the screens he needed. He typed in the passkey and Marta pretended not to look, or even acknowledge that was what he was doing.

'Okay. I'll dial the laser back to ten per cent. Keep it warmed up, but not produce thrust.'

The strange new vibrations died away, and the stillness was profound.

Julia looked round, eyes blinking in wonder. 'That feels good. Do you mind if I, you know, put my head down for a bit?'

'I'll keep it off for a couple of hours at least,' said Jack. 'Go ahead.'

She backflipped away from the console, and almost rushed off down the axis.

'Have you found anything?'

Marta brought up the seismic model. The seismographs had

199

continued to record as the laser burned its way through the regolith to the layers below, and the patterns of vibrations had produced a level of detail that was all but photographic.

'The speed of sound doesn't tell us what the rock is made of – we assay for that in the lab. But here, at five degrees north, twenty to twenty-five west, it looks like a low-speed bleb. Whether that's volatiles, or low-density, uncompacted breccia, I don't know.'

'I'll take a look at the ephemeris data. See if the thrust calculations are out.' Jack tracked his guide stars and plotted KU2's course through the heavens. 'We're still on course, more or less.'

'If it's just richer in carbon compounds,' said Marta, 'there's not going to be a problem. You can adjust for increased outgassing.'

'And if it's not?'

'If it's ice? I don't know enough about what happens when you try and melt frozen water or carbon dioxide with a gigawatt laser. Intuitively, I'd say it has a high chance of exploding.'

'My feeling too.' Patricio turned the model and peered at it. 'Ice is solid, though. It would register a high speed of sound, three and a half, four thousand metres a second. This is much lower, two to two and a half thousand. Not ice. Not solid ice anyway.'

'Not solid ice, but possibly still ice, possibly rock with ice?' Jack leaned forward, almost pressing his nose up against the screen. 'Or definitely no ice at all?'

'We can't say with any certainty.' Marta pushed the window aside so that she didn't have to look at it any more. 'If it is ice, it's dangerous. We know the surface cracks extend below the regolith, and if it blows, we run the risk of putting enough stress at a single point to open up a fault-line all the way through an asteroid we're still attached to.'

'At that point, we lose half the mass at least, even if we continue. We'd have to very quickly consider abandoning the mission.' Patricio looked sour. 'Can you just avoid burning that area?'

'Yes, at the cost of thrust, and at some point, it might just become structurally unstable. And the closer we get to the Sun, the more outgassing we'll get, and we'd have strapped ourselves to a comet.' Jack rubbed his face. He was dog-tired. 'If it is ice, we can just deal with it by melting it at low power until the problem goes away, but someone's going to have to go out and take a sample. I'll go, but at least one of you is going to have to come with me, because I'm not the one with the rock drill certificate.'

'The shuttle's repaired and under pressure,' said Patricio. 'Who will be our pilot, though? The one who might suddenly freeze or the one who flies into murderous rages?'

'There's no way of getting to the trench on foot, is there?' Jack already knew the answer. He put his head in his hands. 'This is one hell of a maiden flight.'

'Runi or the gallowglass?' asked Patricio.

'Runi,' said Jack. 'At least, we should ask him first. He hasn't tried to kill anyone in the last twenty-four hours, and maybe getting back behind the controls will settle him. This is simple stuff, right? Go, hang around for us, come back.'

'I agree,' said Patricio. 'But when do we go?'

'I'd rather get this out of the way. The sooner we can put the laser back on full power, the better. I'll get Runi, you get Kayla. We can suit up and decompress in the shuttle on the way over. The laser will be overhead again in six and three-quarter hours. That gives us plenty of time.'

Marta caught his arm. 'No. That's tired Jack speaking. Turn the laser off. If something goes wrong, you're delayed, you spend longer there than you thought, you're then working against the clock. Another clock that runs out sooner than your air. You'll rush something, and you'll make more mistakes. Turn it off.'

He was about to remonstrate with her when he realised she

was unequivocally right. It was a stupid thing to try and do. It was bad enough out there already.

'I, yes. I'll turn it off. Good catch.'

22

Daily numbers of deaths at a regional level were collected in 16 European countries. Summer mortality was analyzed for the reference period 1998–2002 and for 2003. More than 70,000 additional deaths occurred in Europe during the summer 2003.

J. M. Robine et al., 'Death toll exceeded 70,000 in Europe during the summer of 2003', *Comptes Rendus Biologies*, 2008

This was different. This was extraordinary. Jack clipped his belt onto the cable and climbed out onto the outside of the shuttle. Runi hadn't landed it. It was hovering, and the pilot expended a squirt of cold propellant every so often to keep the vessel aloft. It was four, five metres down to the surface, far enough away that the exhaust wouldn't stir the surface debris.

He and Patricio were going to jump to the edge of the burn trench and screw in some anchors. The combination of the light, the shadow, the dull surface and the shining melt of the trench was confusing and difficult to focus on. How far away or how large objects were was lost under the sharpness of the sunlight and the tightness of the horizon.

Jack carried the anchors, Patricio the drill. Jack's earlier fix, to think of the asteroid surface as a vast cliff face, wasn't going to work. Down was down, but at least once they were in the trench the rock was solid, and not going to fly away.

'Ready?'

They weren't going to just step off: it would take them two minutes to fall to the surface, and unless they could manage not to give themselves any horizontal momentum, they'd travel along far further than down. Instead, they were going to climb to the underside of the shuttle and deliberately push themselves in the direction they needed to go. It felt mad, wrong. It was impossible to rationalise that this huge mass of splintered, shattered rock simply wasn't going to behave like a planet. And yet it wasn't. Ever. Not even once.

Patricio led the way, hand over hand, crawling down the hull of the shuttle, head first so he could see where he was going, and avoiding the attitude-jet nozzles on the way. Jack followed, trailing a separate cable, until they were both able to hold themselves in position, feet aimed down, one hand on a shuttle grab bar.

'Now, slowly. Absorb as much of the impact as you can with your knees, and screw the first anchor in as quickly as you can. Doesn't matter that it's not firm. Just firm enough to get a second one in better. Understand?'

'I got it.'

'Do not stab down with the screw end. You'll bounce straight back up again. Turn only.'

'I got it, Patricio.'

'Good. Now all you have to do is do it.'

Jack looked down, with difficulty, as his field of view didn't quite extend as far as his boots. He took a breath and let go, dabbing his fingertips against the strutwork as he did so. He drifted towards the surface, slowly descending, trailing the free cable behind him. As he dropped, he took hold of one of the anchors, both hands on the T-bar at the top, and positioned it between his legs. He bent his knees, and waited for the anchor to register the contact first.

He waited, and while he did, he considered the life choices that had brought him to that moment.

Then there was pressure against his hands and he twisted and twisted as quickly as he could before the counter-rotation set his whole body spinning in the opposite direction. His feet touched rock and he let his legs fold slowly under him. If he pressed back now, he'd float away again.

But the suit was only so flexible, and it pushed him anyway. He lost contact, and his feet started upwards, dragging his hips and torso, and he was left hanging onto an asteroid by only his hands around the crosspiece of a barely fixed anchor screw.

'Jack?'

'It's holding. Just about. Let me get it further in.'

He wasn't going to be able to do it from that angle, so he tentatively reeled his body back in and grounded his feet once more. One more turn. Two more turns. The thread was winding into the regolith. He kept on going until the screw anchor was completely swallowed up. He let go with one hand, and clipped himself on with the other. Then he gathered up the slack on his safety cable and fed that through the loop at the top of the crosspiece.

He gave the anchor a tug. It seemed firm.

'I'm down and attached. I'll put in a second anchor.'

Jack got another anchor from his belt. It took him three attempts to get it to bite: he'd been lucky the first time, when he'd needed it. He screwed it down, tested it, and finally felt able to call Patricio down.

When he was within arm's length, Jack gripped the miner's belt and guided him the rest of the way. Patricio clipped himself on.

'Okay?'

'Okay.' Jack felt his nerves singing with the effort. Everything was tight and jangling. Something, anything could go wrong, break, get tangled, and that would be that. 'Runi? Okay up there?'

'All systems nominal. You can proceed.' He was taking care to be very professional.

'We'll be back as soon as we're done.' Patricio paid out more cable and looked down into the trench. 'Getting an anchor in through the melt is going to be difficult. Anchor to the wall, and I'll drill there.'

'What if what we want to sample is on the floor of the trench?'

'Then we drill that too.'

Jack unfastened himself from the anchor and flexed his ankles. He went up, one metre, two, clearing the bank of abraded material that had built up against the side of the trench. Then after hanging there for what seemed like an age, he started to arc back down again, descending into the shadow below. He tightened his cable and foreshortened his glacial fall, angling over the line of frozen lava and towards the blocky, cinder-lined trench wall.

The heat had fused the rubble together. There would be small pockets of frozen melt, but most of all, there would be a veneer of plasma products, elements torn apart and recombined in a soot-like powder, pressed into crevices and voids and coating every exposed surface.

It was very dark, and he couldn't see where the wall began, so he hit it without warning and bounced off it uncontrollably. He was floating again, but his speed was gradually decreasing. If he did nothing but hang on, he would come into contact with the trench again shortly. He belatedly turned his suit lights to maximum brightness, and found they didn't really help.

'Give me a minute. I'm trying to get under control.'

'Careful. Protect your faceplate and your life support.'

'I'm okay. Just that it's really hard to see.'

He slowly descended again, and this time he was able to get a pinch-grip on a piece of rock jutting from the wall. He groped for an anchor, and used what little leverage he had to get it into the rock. It resisted turning with one hand, but he was reluctant to let go and try with two, so he persisted. The broad screw thread seemed wedged in, and perhaps it would hold. He left it there, sticking out proud, while he clipped onto it and cautiously twisted it in further.

'Fuck.'

'Hard work?'

'The hardest. It's in. Suit lights on full, and be prepared for how black it is in here.'

Patricio dropped over the banked slag, and again Jack caught him and hauled him in so that he could clip himself on.

'This is hell,' said Patricio. He shuddered, before unslinging the drill. 'Let's get to work.'

The older man's momentary show of fear did more to unsettle Jack than the actual environment he needed to be afraid of. But there was nothing either of them could do. They needed the samples, and they could still look out for each other. Patricio shortened his tether to provide some tension, and Jack forced another anchor into the rock face. Everything was coming up black, so fine-grained it was almost greasy, like oil.

The drill bit spun, and a fine mist streamed from the hollow tip. Patricio leaned in, but let the cutting edge do the work. 'It'll take the time it takes,' he said. 'If we're to get a sample from the trench floor, we'll need another anchor. I suggest on the other side, low down.'

Jack turned himself around. The trench was some ten metres across. Barely any distance at all. He fixed his safety line to the second anchor, and unclipped his tether. No different than sliding from one end of the axis to the other. Except there were stars overhead, along with canopies of solar cells and the bright thistledown of the laser.

He brought his gaze down and concentrated on what needed to be done. He paid out enough cable to get him across, and aimed at a point directly opposite him on the far wall. He pushed off and floated over, tilting his hips as he passed halfway so that he could land on his feet. Dust turned like glitter.

He caught hold of the rock and let himself settle, his face-plate millimetres from the carbon-black rime. He felt down for an anchor with one hand, and the other hand slipped. He stayed very still, hoping that he'd fall close to where he'd been, but even the reflexive tightening of his fingers was enough to push him away. He drifted out, and down, falling like a feather towards the glassy ribbon paving the bottom of the trench.

'Jack?'

'It's more difficult than it looks. I'm going to try again.' He reeled himself in using his cable, and arrived back at the anchor. Patricio resumed drilling, and Jack launched himself over the gap once more.

He'd thought he'd done everything right, but when it came to it he still couldn't find any grip on the rock, and he bounced away again.

'This isn't working. I'll have to try closer to the top.' His gloved fingers were black, the white of his spacesuit smeared with dark streaks. He rubbed his hands on his sleeves to try and restore some of the tactility on the pads. He pulled himself back, and rested for a moment.

Patricio's faceplate was spattered with dust. 'Almost there,' he said.

'More than I am.' Jack readied himself, and angled slightly up this time, hoping to find something to hold onto.

He found he was going too fast. He reached behind him for his cable, and used the friction between his hand and the line to slow himself down. Too much. He drifted down at roughly the same height as he was before, just further along. Perhaps there'd be something there, though. He reached out in front of him and brushed the rock face, waiting for a snag.

He found one, and closed his palm around it. Barely daring to breathe, he fetched out an anchor and started the laborious work of screwing it home without so much as pressing down on it. He was sweating – not down his face, where the fans continually circulated the air, but everywhere else. He needed to stay calm, to have a steady hand and absolutely not rush. There was no way to do this quickly.

It was in. Finally. He tethered himself to the anchor, and ran the safety cable through the loop.

'Patricio? I'm putting in another anchor here and then you can come across. You should be able to drill down from here.'

'Rather than do that, you come back and I'll go over. Okay?'

'I won't be sorry not to have to do that again. Deal.' Jack unclipped his tether, fastened onto the safety, then checked it was properly fixed to the anchor. He slid along it, over the trench, and swapped cables after retethering.

Patricio handed him the rock core, a slim cylinder of what looked like concrete, the length of his forearm.

'Bag it,' he said, and started across. Any trace of nerves had apparently vanished. He was concerned only with the job. He stared out over the trench, then glided down the cable to its anchor point. He tethered himself and set to work, drilling down into the trench floor. The frozen melt flung out shards of glass as he applied the drill bit to its mirror-like surface.

Jack was left with nothing to do but wait and watch, and admire the scenery. This was what being in space was about, and perhaps if he'd realised that these moments of terror existed, then he might not have been so eager to pursue them. There might have been other places, on Earth, where he could have hidden and carved out a life for himself, on his own terms, but realistically, everywhere was in reach of his parents. All it took was money, and they had what was essentially a limitless supply of that.

But the moments of terror were also survivable. EVA was like staring into the void, and having the void stare back. It didn't seem to get any easier, and maybe one day he'd be standing in an open airlock door and simply refuse to leave it. Maybe one day he'd be done with it.

Today was not that day. He endured.

There was a glow on the horizon, barely a kilometre away. The Sun was coming over the side of the asteroid, and they would be bathed in pure, harsh sunlight at any moment.

Then he looked at the shadows. The Sun was already up, over his shoulder, behind him and casting darkness across the trench. He watched the glow increase, and realised it had a green tinge to it. That it was making the ground he was attached to shake.

'Patricio. The laser.'

'What about the laser?'

'The laser is firing.'

The column of incandescent plasma grew taller, and the trench between the two men turned briefly hazy. A shock wave, picking up the fallen dust and grit.

'You turned it off.'

'Someone's turned it on. Runi, someone's turned the laser on. Get them to switch it off. Stat.'

'I'm already telling them that.'

'Patricio, you need to stop and get out of the trench.'

'The rotation speed is two k an hour. The laser won't reach us for another, say, twenty minutes. I'll have finished in ten.'

'No. Absolutely not. You told me that. Marta told me that. The exhaust follows the trench, and you need to get out, now. Runi, talk to me.'

'They can't turn it off,' said the pilot. 'It's behind a lock. Which you installed. What's the code?'

'Give me a moment—'

'If you can't remember it now, get out and then remember it.'

'That's what I'm saying. Patricio. You heard the man.'

'*Hijo de puta!*' Patricio pulled the drill clear and waited for the bit to stop spinning. 'All right. Yes. Go yourself, then. We can't both get in the shuttle at the same time.'

Jack freed the safety line from the top of the anchor and made sure it was secure on his belt, then unhitched his tether. He thought about retrieving the anchor itself, then realised what a stupid idea that was. He checked again that Patricio was genuinely coming back: the miner was halfway across the trench, feeding his own line through the running hitch.

Jack took hold of his cable and, in a moment of forgetfulness, jerked too hard on it. It went tight, and he was flying over the bank and out into the free space beyond. He'd given himself far too much momentum: he'd forgotten where he was and what

210

he needed to do for a mere second, and now he was in trouble. More trouble. If he reeled in the safety line, he'd increase his rate of turn, so much so that he might smash into the shuttle, and Runi was flying that shuttle, and loud noises set the pilot off. But if he didn't do something ... he could hit the surface at the same speed.

With Patricio still in the trench, there wasn't any manoeuvre Runi could pull to help.

'I'm moving too fast,' he reported.

'Are you carrying anything?' asked Runi.

'Anchors.'

'Throw them in the direction of travel. As hard as you can.'

He was over the shuttle now, travelling in a line that ended in space far above the asteroid. When the cable snapped tight, he'd transfer some of his energy to the shuttle. It would make it difficult to steer momentarily, and then he'd be bouncing back the way he'd come.

He unclipped an anchor, held it over him like a javelin and waited for his feet to come up to horizontal. Then he threw it, as fast and as straight as he could, past the length of his body and almost certainly into orbit.

The effect was instantaneous. His ground speed all but disappeared. He shortened the length of the cable, and when it did go taut, it was an inconsequential tug. He rebounded towards the shuttle and continued to gather his line, until he looked beyond the shuttle.

The flaring column of plasma was huge. Silent. Brilliant. Patterns shifting and spinning and fading as it rose upwards. Golden light blazed and condensing dust glowed. It was a fountain, a fan, a spray of matter rising from the trench and slowly diffusing across the star-pecked sky.

It marched past at a funereal pace, burning and cauterising as it went. Colours flickered as the elements that had formed the rock were torn apart and flung away.

So close. He could almost reach out and touch it.

An empty safety line snaked by, coiling as it passed him and straightening again afterwards. He didn't recognise its significance until he was bumping along the hull of the shuttle, and remembered to grip onto a handhold. He clung to the skin of the ship and gazed in awe, in terror, as the laser continued to burn.

'Patricio?'

23

We provide observational evidence that sea level acceleration up to the present has been about 0.01 mm/yr^2 and appears to have started at the end of the 18th century. Sea level rose by 6 cm during the 19th century and 19 cm in the 20th century. Superimposed on the long-term acceleration are quasi-periodic fluctuations with a period of about 60 years. If the conditions that established the acceleration continue, then sea level will rise 34 cm over the 21st century. Long time constants in oceanic heat content and increased ice sheet melting imply that the latest Intergovernmental Panel on Climate Change (IPCC) estimates of sea level are probably too low.

S. Jevrejeva, J. C. Moore, A. Grinsted, P. L. Woodworth, 'Recent global sea level acceleration started over 200 years ago?', *Geophysical Research Letters*, 2008

'The code has changed.'

'What does that mean?' asked Julia.

'That means,' said Jack pulling at his greasy hair, 'that I can't turn the laser off, that I can't move the laser, that I can't steer the asteroid, that I have no control whatsoever over where we're going or how we're going to get back. And one of you did this.'

'So we're out of control?'

'That's what I just fucking said. I have no control, and until I do, we are ... God only knows. Thrust will be whatever it is, and at some point in the next few days, it'll start pushing us off course. In case any of you haven't worked it out, an uncontrolled burn is just that. It won't send us home. It'll send us somewhere else.'

'Where else?'

'I don't know.' He wanted to mourn Patricio. He wanted a gap to mourn in, but here he was, in Control, adding his stink to the stink of other humans, trying to fix something that someone else had done that was going to kill them all and had already killed one of them. 'I can't know. We could end up dropping ourselves into the Sun.'

'But you can turn it off.' Julia's voice rose in volume and pitch. 'You can get it back.'

'I can if someone tells me what they changed the passcode to.' He had never known fury like it. As if he'd internalised all of that boiling, seething plasma and he was just a hollow shell around it. What he wanted to do was breathe it out and turn the entire module into a furnace. Instead, he stopped it up, and it consumed only him. 'I put in a passcode because I didn't want anyone using the laser as a weapon. I got scared by the idea and I didn't ask anyone's permission, so okay. I'm owning that part of it. Someone – who isn't me or Runi – has changed it while we were EVA.'

'Why couldn't it have been you?' asked Andros. 'You and the gallowglass. Trying to extort more money from NovaS.'

Jack blinked back tears. 'There wasn't enough of Patricio left to fill a spectrograph sample. And Runi did his absolute best to get me back to the *Coloma*, all credit to him for holding it together, but he's virtually catatonic now. You could have been looking at three deaths, not just one. As accusations go, it's pretty fucking stupid.'

'It still could have been the gallowglass,' said Kayla into the silence that followed. 'If she's got the passcode, then we could do this one of two ways.'

May was matter-of-fact. 'Torture it out of her, or torture the captain to make him pony up more cash?'

'Something like that.' Kayla didn't look anyone in the eye. 'But once we've got the code, there's nothing to stop us from spacing her, right?'

'There's nothing to stop us spacing her now.'

'Except that she might have the passcode.' Kayla unstrapped. 'I'm going to ask her.'

Julia put out her hand. 'Just hold on. We need to work out what our endgame is here.'

'Endgame? Not dying is my endgame, sister.'

'Enough,' said Andros. 'We have a problem. We need a solution. Astrogator, can you get me the laser back without the passcode?'

'Perhaps. If anyone used to be script kiddie in their spare time and can hack the laser's program, then don't hold back.' He stopped, and thought of WhitetailDeer. He would have loved this challenge. 'I can probably write something that will brute-force try every letter and number combination until the heat-death of the universe, but it could take hours, days, weeks or months to stumble on the right combination.'

'How long do we have?' asked his captain, and it took Jack a few moments to realise the question was aimed at him.

He could feel the vibrations due to the mining laser through his seat. He'd been prepared for accidents, for things going wrong, for equipment to break: but not this. Not deliberate interference. Not sabotage. Not ... murder. Not when so much was riding on it.

'We could be careering around the inner solar system until the asteroid falls apart or we hit something, assuming we haven't starved to death, frozen to death or run out of air first, or the laser will end up vaporising the ship, or it'll just break. The end point will be the same. No one will be coming to rescue us.'

This wasn't what he'd imagined when he'd embarked on his ten-year-long plan to escape his parents' well-meaning, cult-like insistence he join them in transhumanism. His had been a future naively filled with shiny spaceships and bright adventures. Instead, he was strapped to a decaying asteroid, in half a ship, with a saboteur, and staring almost certain death in the face.

'We need the passcode,' he finished, lamely. 'And Kayla's right. We have to take spacing off the table, now, or we'll get nowhere.'

'That's not what I said.'

'It's the cold logic of what you said.'

'I will not spend the rest of the voyage with whoever killed Patricio.' Marta was white with fury. 'I will not.'

'Even if it means you die yourself?' said May, 'because that's what we're talking about. I agree with Jack.'

'Well, you would.'

'Julia. Shut the fuck up and think.' May continued: 'Someone on this ship has the password. They are never going to offer it up if they think they'll be straight out of the airlock. Let them deal with Andros. Then we can get the laser back, save our skins and still cash in at the end.'

'What about Patricio?' asked Marta. 'Does his death mean nothing to you?'

'It means less to me than mine.' May brought her head up and her chin out. 'I'm sorry. This is about survival now. My survival.'

For a moment, Jack thought he might need to stand between the miner and the engineer, his lover, his ... he didn't know what. Everyone was right. Marta was right. May was right. The moment passed, though.

Andros moved from his seat towards the axis. 'I will be in my cabin for the next few hours. If anyone has anything to say to me, in private, in confidence, then you know what to do. Astrogator, get me the laser back.'

'Someone's going to have to tell Arush and Runi,' said Kayla. 'I can do that.'

'And the gallowglass.' May shrugged. 'I'll talk to her. Make it plain.'

Jack stared at his screen, his mind racing from point to point to point, and never settling. 'Someone must have seen something,' he said. 'Someone has to know.'

'They've had their chance to say so: if they haven't, it's because they're colluding.'

'Yes, I expect they are.' Jack scrubbed at his face. Who would do this? Not him. He knew that much. Runi and Patricio had been in decompression with him. Cat? She wasn't allowed anywhere near Control since her fight with Andros: someone would have stopped and challenged her, and even if she'd managed to get to a workstation, she didn't know the ship systems.

What if it was Andros himself? That made a perverse kind of sense: blame Cat Gallowglass for sabotaging the mission, get her spaced, then use that as leverage to get her royalties added to his own. In which case, this whole thing was a charade, they were being played, and it was well within Andros's character to do it.

'If anyone can help, then fine. Stay. Otherwise, go. I don't want an audience while I try and fail to do this.'

He did the thing that would take the longest to work first: a quick and dirty password cracker. He knew he'd put in a simple alphanumeric phrase that might, in retrospect, have been easy to guess, but almost impossible to attack by brute force. Whoever had broken it, either through the front door or the back, had changed it to something different. He didn't know how long the new code was, or whether it contained any special characters. The cracker would try everything, every combination of one character, then two, then three, and so on until it found the right combination.

He set it off, and had it grinding away in the background while he inspected the guts of the software they used to control the ship. After a while, he looked up, because he was no longer alone.

It was Cat.

'Do you know what you're doing, or are you just hoping you do?' she asked.

'Astronomy and maths are mostly just programming these days. I can do that, but there's a whole stack of things I've just heard about being done, and I'm trying to work out if I know enough to do them too.' After a moment, where he reamed one of his eyes, he added: 'Was it you?'

'No.'

'As far as you're concerned, it's only been a couple of weeks since you killed someone to get your claim on the asteroid. Now you find out your own father has wasted the money you got him, and of course you're going to want to fix that, and the only way you can is by shaking NovaS down for more. So you, I don't know, guess the password, or use a back door, or you saw me program it in, or ... there's a keylogger?' He was distracted by Cat's hair, which was growing out properly after three years in hibernation, sprouting in loose, dark spirals. They shook like springs in the low gravity as she turned her head from side to side.

'I've never been alone in Control.'

'That's not answering the question,' said Jack. 'I've been doing things on my console while May's been doing things on hers next to me. I've not seen what she's done.'

'It'd be pretty brazen to do something like that, sat next to you.'

'I'm not in the mood for fucking around, Cat. Just tell me straight. Was it you?'

'What? So you can space me?'

'So we can fix it, just you and me, so I don't have to space you.'

They stared at each other. He didn't know any more. It wasn't him. He knew that. Marta? It could have been her. She was there when he turned the laser off. He'd used the code in front of her. Who else could have seen him type it in? Unless there really was a keylogger. Was there a black box system that recorded everything? He needed to look for one.

God, but he was tired.

Cat moved to a console and strapped herself in. 'I know the OS,' she said. 'And from what I can tell, you may as well just put a bullet through it. Killing the process and restarting it won't affect the operation of the laser, and it won't get you past the password.'

'What if,' said Jack, 'I get whoever wrote the software to send me a non-protected version of the program, delete the one we have, and load up a clean version?'

'Where in the system was the password? Was it just on the controller program down here?'

'I don't know. Yet. If it was, that could work. That could actually work. If it comes to it, I could find out what commands the laser is expecting and how they're coded. I could write my own control program and at least turn the thing off.'

'Could you get it started again?' she asked.

'No. It'd just be a kill-switch.'

'We need control,' she said.

'I know.'

'Now.'

'Yes. I know. I've just said all that.'

'I know you're trying to help.'

'Help?' It came out as a growl. 'I'm the only one doing something here. I seem to be the only one able to do something. This is just ...' He gripped the edges of his screen and only let go when he thought he had the anger tamped down again.

'I'm sorry about your friend,' said Cat.

'Thank you. Not that he was my friend, as such. I hardly knew anything about him. If he'd have come when I first called him, he would have got clear, and I should have insisted, shouted at him, told him he was being an idiot and just made him move.'

'You did. We were listening to the transmission. You did all that. He made a bad decision. It cost him his life.'

She was nineteen. He had to keep on reminding himself that she was nineteen and not ninety. Or nine.

'I'm going to call home,' Jack decided. 'Get the laser control program re-sent. Travel time's twenty minutes or so, plus however long it takes to find someone who knows where to find it and send it forward. Who the hell do I talk to in Cis-lunar anyway?'

'Andros won't let you tell anyone he doesn't have control over the laser.'

'Because that'll crash the share price. Fuck. This just gets worse. What if I just do it anyway?'

'I've been asleep for three years. You tell me.'

Jack felt the ship tremble. It was really getting on his already wire-tight nerves. 'The company will no longer be able to finance its loans. It'll go bankrupt, and be liquidated. The *Coloma* will become an asset, and we'll be told by the official receivers to bring it back so it can be sold. We, the crew – and you, the rights holder – won't see another cent.'

'You seem to know a lot about this, Jack Astrogator.'

'We've already discussed this scenario, under different circumstances.'

'Do you see why I'd never have done something like this?'

'Maybe,' he said. 'Maybe.' He lapsed into silence.

'I'll protect my asset,' said Cat, 'no matter what. It's all I have.'

'How? Currently, it's careering through the inner solar system, and until we work out a way of cracking that code, your asset is simply a line of numbers on a virtual balance sheet.'

'I won't let my people down, Jack.'

'If it wasn't you, then someone else wants to fuck our shit up.' He glanced at the cracker. It was working its way through the combinations. He hadn't expected anything, and he wasn't disappointed. He returned to poking the laser guidance program, trying to get it to respond, seeing if there was any way to open it up while it was running and manually edit the passcode out. But it wouldn't have been much of a lock if he could have just done that.

Cat watched his attempts. 'That won't work, will it?'

'No. I don't think it will. It won't stop me from trying, but no, I don't think I can do it that way. I can terminate the process, even delete it, but the laser will keep on burning using the last set of instructions it received. If I can get a new program from somewhere, I can reinstall it and hope that's enough. I'll check the drives, see if there's a clean install on there somewhere. I mean, that's what I'd do.'

He did, and came up blank.

'We have all of the OS, and none of the applications. That's just fucked up. Proprietary software.' Jack wished he had something to throw.

'You could go around your crew and choke-hold them one by one until they tell you the passcode.'

He heard, and ignored, the barb. 'Give it five minutes, and we'll be kicking the crap out of each other anyway. Who did this? Who?'

'If you can work out why they did it and what they want, you might be able to work out who.'

'Money, sex or revenge. That's why anyone does anything, right?'

'Then you have to go through them and find a motive.'

'I've shared air, food, space and more with these people for months, and I know so little about them. That's the crew way. If I wasn't already ... famous? notorious? ... they wouldn't know anything about me either.'

'You're famous?'

'I was, briefly. And no, I don't want you to know, and you don't need to know.' Jack closed his eyes. Normally it helped him concentrate, but he found all he did was remember the glowing, shifting plasma. He looked around Control, at all the lights, at the snaking wires and the shining screens. 'We're sitting on an almost unquantifiable amount of wealth. One tenth of one per cent of that would make anyone the richest person in the world, or off it. You sold out, whatever its name was ...'

'Lithospheric.'

'Them. Perhaps one of us has had a better offer, too. Has anyone come to you since you've been awake and suggested that a different company might offer you improved terms?'

She didn't answer. But she did give him the look.

'Oh crap. Who was it?'

'You wouldn't believe me if I told you.'

'But—'

'I tell you who wants me to dump NovaS, you go to them, and they deny it. Which of us is lying, Jack? My word – gallowglass, killer, angry little kid – against theirs: crew, known, trusted.'

'But they'll know the new passcode.'

'Jack.'

'So this is, what? Blackmail? Either you sell the mining rights on to another new company, or we don't go anywhere?'

'They already threatened me with that, and I turned them down. Now it's a corporate takeover. Without the laser, NovaS is dead. I guess someone back on Earth or the Moon is ready to buy the ship from the fire sale, and suddenly the mission is on again.'

'If you sell them the mining rights.'

'And if you agree to work for them.'

'This is cold.' Jack hunched in on himself. 'Why did you turn them down?'

'Because I thought I could get more money out of Andros.'

'You tore half his face off.'

'I got angry and I lost it. I won't apologise.'

'If you'd said yes to them earlier, Patricio would still be alive.' That wasn't fair, and he knew it. This was eating away at him, one bite at a time. Soon, there'd be nothing left. 'Why tell me you know who it is, and then not give me the name?'

'This is not my fault. If I had said yes, what about your Captain Andros? What would have happened to him? Having the asteroid stolen out from under him?'

Andros appeared to owe too much money to too many awful

222

people to go home without his prize. He'd fight the saboteur. He'd have to be spaced. And they'd still be on board with whoever killed Patricio. Marta had made it plain she wasn't going to stand for that. So perhaps her too. What a mess.

'Presumably, we'll be offered some sort of cash incentive so that we don't just throw the *teringlijer* saboteur out the airlock?'

'If you get to that point, you'll find out. All of this, everything, has happened very quickly. But my first and last thoughts are for my people. I have to save them. If that means we all die, but they live, then I'll do it. I'll sacrifice you all. And myself.'

'How did that work out last time?' asked Jack. The cracker had gone through another million combinations, and still hadn't hit the magic formula. 'I'm just saying, that maybe it's not about the rock at all. That's not where the problem is.'

'I didn't come all this way to hear the truth, Jack Astrogator. You do what you think you need to do. And I'll do what I think I need to do. Just one last thing. Can the *Coloma* go home without the drive unit?'

He instinctively thought no, that it was impossible. The only propulsion that the crew section had was cold-gas thrusters. But their delta-v requirements were genuinely small, and they had got smaller since the laser was burning. Perhaps they could. Not easily, but sometimes the iron laws of physics offered unlooked-for mercy.

'I don't know,' he said.

'If I were you, I'd check,' she said. Then she left to talk to whoever she needed to talk to, and Jack was alone.

Slowly, almost reluctantly, he brought up the astrogation software and started to draw curves.

24

Using average annual conditions from 2005, simulations were performed for 100 years into the future using four different rates of sea-level rise: 0, 24, 48, and 88 centimeters per century. Results from these predictive analyses suggest that the average concentration of groundwater withdrawn at the municipal wellfield will exceed the potable limit after 70, 60, 55, and 49 years, respectively, for the four simulations.

C. D. Langevin et al., 'Effect of sea-level rise on future coastal groundwater resources in southern Florida, USA', *SWIM21*, 2010

Jack called everyone together in Control.

'I've got an announcement to make,' he said, once they were all present – all except Patricio, and there was a hole where he should have been. The way they all looked at him, but couldn't look at each other, told him they'd spent the last few hours working through the implications of not getting the mining laser, and their drive section, back under their control. That one of them was a very good actor, and simultaneously, not very good crew. They were all ready to kill someone, anyone, if they thought it might save themselves.

Had anyone been to see Andros in his cabin? Jack didn't know, but the man didn't look well.

'This is not about the laser, so don't get your hopes up. I can't get it under control. There are no back doors to the program. We can't stop the laser from firing, short of taking the shuttle up to it and tearing its guts out, having avoided the laser beam itself and the three maser beams that supply it with power. And that will also destroy our drive. The cracker is working, in that it's continuing to work, but there's no guarantee that it will ever come up with the right combination. The longer it takes, the less likely it is that we can re-correct the course we end up on.'

He was so, so tired.

'Doing a clean install of the program might get us to where we need to be. However, asking for the software would be admitting losing control of the laser in the first place. The NovaS share price would collapse, the company would become bankrupt, and this ship, and the rights to the asteroid, would be back in play. As crew we'd be looking at cents in the euro, if that.'

Andros was grey, as grey as the rock outside, and Jack felt genuine pity for him. They both knew that the captain wasn't going to get out of this alive.

'Someone would step in and buy NovaS's assets, though?' asked Arush.

'Yes. But they'd need our cooperation, the mining rights and the passcode if they wanted the asteroid. That gets complicated very quickly, but that's not what I want to say.' He took a deep breath. 'I've worked out a way to get the crew section back to a stable lunar orbit, using only the resources we have here on the asteroid.'

'The *Coloma* is not your ship,' said Andros. 'It is mine.'

An admission, at last, that he was NovaS. But it was all too late.

'This is your ship, for now. But in every single possible future, it isn't.' He turned to the rest of the crew. 'I can get you home. For certain. The numbers don't lie. There is a catch, though. Our course is changing rapidly – rapidly for an asteroid – and our launch window closes in twenty-five and a half hours. After that, we'll all have to make a deal with the person who killed Patricio, and hope we can live together without incident for however long it takes to get this mission back on track.'

225

'This is mutiny,' said Andros.

'Yes,' said Jack, because it was. 'I'm sorry. If the crew vote for it, we're taking the ship, and there's nothing you can do about it. I can't speak for everyone, but as far as I'm concerned you're welcome to stay on board, and take your chances with your investors when we get back to Cis-lunar space.'

Runi spoke, in a small, almost childlike voice. 'You're absolutely certain?'

'Yes. I can give you all the figures, the delta-v calculations, trajectory, just how much we'll get off a gravity assist from the Moon: that's the window that closes fastest. I can't get us to the right point in front of the Moon with the gas we have, if we leave it any later than the twenty-five-hour mark. If we hit it right, we go into orbit. Someone will rescue us from there, even if it's just to claim salvage on the ship.'

'That's a hell of a risk,' said Julia. 'You want us to trust you on that?'

'Yes. I want you to trust me. I want you to know that we do have a viable alternative to whatever Patricio's killer has in store for us. It doesn't just get us back home in a few months' time. It gives us something to bargain with right now.'

'So which one of us is it?' Arush asked from the axis hatchway. 'Cards on the table, I don't think it's me, but at some point, they're going to have to show their hand.'

Jack glanced across at Cat. She saw him, but ignored his overture.

'There's no point in trying to work out who it is,' said May. 'Jack's right: they've got this sewn up. They're here to steal the asteroid, aren't they? So let's talk about whether any deal they offer us as crew is good enough to swap sides.'

'I'd still like to get paid,' said Julia. 'I've got my reasons, but if NovaS isn't in a position to give me my wages – and a bonus – then I'm going to talk to whoever has the cash.'

'Does Patricio's death mean so little to you?' Marta's face had gone white and pinched. 'He was crew.'

226

'No. Whoever did that is a bloody liability, and no one is ever going to crew with them again. And a couple of million extra when we dock at L4 is going to go a very long way to make sure I don't have to.'

'I'm sorry about Patricio and all,' said Kayla. 'But like Julia, my principles are for sale. I could have guessed this trip was a bad hit when I signed up, but I came anyway. I want the money that was promised me. If you've got the green, then I'll work for you.'

'Runi? What about you?'

The pilot hunched up. 'They could have killed me along with Patricio, and they still could. Jack's plan is better.'

'What about the money, Runi?'

'Julia, at the moment, no one but NovaS has offered us anything.'

'NovaS, and Andros, is a dead man walking.' She glanced across at the captain. 'No offence, but. You heard Jack. He's toast.'

'How much do you want, Julia?'

'At least as much as I'm getting now.'

'What you're getting now is precisely nothing.' Runi clenched his jaw. 'I can always earn more money. What I can't do is buy another life, and the only person who appears to realise that is Jack. For now, I'm with him.'

'Enough. Enough. I need to say something.'

'Shut up, Andros. You're in charge of jack shit right now.'

'Julia, let him speak.'

'Thank you, Astrogator. The problem you are all trying to solve is not the problem you need to solve. I stole this ship. I stole this ship from NovaS when they wanted to replace me as captain, when I'd done all the hard work sourcing the ship, fitting it out and finding a crew.' He clasped his hands tight to try and still the shake in them. 'The people who invested in NovaS are not nice people. I was terrified for my life for three whole years. Every day, every setback, every delay, I was hanging by

227

a thread. The only thought that kept me going was my share of the profit when we brought the asteroid back. Then when everything was ready, they fired me.'

Even the fans were silent for a moment.

'So we're not the actual crew?' asked Marta.

'They would have arrived eighteen hours later at L2, and wondered where the ship was.'

'And all this shit about investors?'

'A distraction. NovaS went bankrupt and was wound up the day after we left Cis-lunar space. I stole the ship, and was going on to steal the asteroid. Despite this, I would have honoured the agreement I made with you. I would have seen all of you paid, together with all of your bonuses, and you would have been rich. And if the person with the passcode had come to see me, I would have still have kept my word. But I know all too well what waits for me back at Cis-lunar: my only shield would have been my money, and any hope of me seeing a single cent of that is now, apparently, gone. Just remember this in the minutes and the hours to come: there are worse people to crew with than Mikkel Andros, and you are sharing a ship with them.'

With that, he unclipped his belt and pulled himself across to the axis. Arush moved out of his way, and watched him drift all the way to the end.

'Someone needs to keep an eye on him,' said May. 'We don't want him wrecking anything.'

Arush nodded, and followed their erstwhile captain.

'Jesus fuck, I did not see that coming,' said Julia. 'We're a fucking pirate ship. What the hell do we do now?'

'I still want paying,' said May. 'Especially now there's not even any pay in escrow for us, halfway through a mission that we thought would see us seriously wealthy by the end. I've spent that several times over in my head, and I'm not giving up those dreams.'

'You're saying we should do a deal with whoever killed Patricio?'

'That's exactly what I'm saying. Jack's plan is pure. Clean. I'm neither.' She scowled at him. 'You can afford to blow this off: you're young, and your parents. Some of us don't have either of those on our side.'

'I don't even own the clothes I'm wearing,' said Jack, 'and my savings were down to a hundred euros when I left L2. But okay, you want to talk about that? Let's talk about that. My parents own half the ships on Earth's oceans – maybe more than half by now, I don't know – but before any of you think I'm some poor little rich kid slumming it off-world for his gap year, or some other toss, I had to escape from my house and run for the spaceport, helped by the only friends I'd managed to make – and trust – all on my own. One of them died during that, and I still don't know if it was a coincidence.'

'So you're rich?' said Cat. 'How rich?'

'My parents are rich. Point zero one per cent rich. Top hundred. Something like that, but I don't have a pot to piss in.'

'But you could just go to them, and ask them for whatever you wanted.'

'No, I can't do that.'

'But they're rich.'

'My parents are transhumanists,' said Jack. 'I refuse to be.'

Julia looked at him. 'Oh, mate. You will be, one day.'

'Whatever you want to believe about me, that's fine. Currently, we're all marooned, in a stolen ship, on an out-of-control asteroid somewhere just inside the orbit of Mars, our captain's just about to kill himself, one of our crew has been murdered, and we're being held hostage by someone seemingly prepared to see the rest of us die too. So I don't see how much money my parents have changes our position one tiny bit. I'm making my argument on its own merits. I can get you home. For sure.'

Arush returned. He floated through into Control still looking behind him, down the axis to the bottom of the ship. 'He's ... gone,' he said. 'He just stepped into the airlock, pumped it down and that was that. He didn't even make it outside.'

'Jesus,' blurted Julia. 'Talk about rats.'

'Andros never wanted us to retrieve the gallowglass,' said Kayla. 'Perhaps he knew it'd leave him vulnerable, open to this kind of attack.'

'He wasn't stupid,' said May. 'He was all the other things, but he wasn't stupid. He knew he couldn't go home without the asteroid.'

As eulogies went, it was honest, but brief. Jack pressed his fingers into his temples and made small circular motions with them to try and alleviate the stress. An iron band was tightening around his head. 'This whole situation is just ...'

'Yep. Welcome to Shit Creek,' said Julia. 'Tell me someone has the paddle.'

Jack took a swig of water from his bulb, and almost brought it straight back up again. 'Talk to us, Cat.'

'Okay,' said Cat. 'This is not what I expected, and certainly not what I wanted. But I killed to get this asteroid, I destroyed the company that sponsored me by going over to NovaS, Andros stole this ship from them, and I'm not going to get sentimental about another company taking it over. What I care about is the money.'

'Girl after my own heart,' said Kayla.

'It's not for me.'

'Sure, it's for "your people".'

'It is,' she insisted, and Jack felt he should intervene.

'Let's just hear her out.'

'They've already had their pay-out from NovaS, though, and that worked out well, didn't it?'

'Kayla? We've got more important things to discuss than the financial competence of her government.'

'That's just a fancy-ass way of saying what Andros said: they pissed it up against the wall.'

Cat held back. She clenched her fists and ground her jaw, but she stayed in her seat and waited for the moment to pass.

'One of you came to me soon after you retrieved me, and asked me to pull the mining licence from NovaS.'

'They what now?'

'Who?'

Cat stared them all down. 'I said no. I had a deal. I *thought* I had a deal. They kept on. They asked me if I knew how things were going with St Ann's. Said that if I knew, I wouldn't be happy.'

'Arush?' said Julia. 'You told her about St Ann's.'

'Gods, no. She asked me. She came and asked me. I'm not the one. Cat, tell them I'm not the one.'

'He's not the one,' she said. 'Though she did use that to her advantage.'

'She? It's one of you.' Marta jabbed her finger at Julia, Kayla and May. 'Which one of you?'

'It could be you,' said Julia.

'I loved him. I actually loved him,' she screamed back.

Runi covered his head with his arms, hiding from what was now his world, and everyone else had the grace to look shocked and not a little ashamed.

'I will sell my mining rights for twenty billion over the next decade,' said Cat. 'It's not much for a whole nation, but it could be enough. Time is not on our side to do any negotiations, I want it guaranteed and I'm willing to walk away, in case anyone here thinks blackmail is a winning strategy.'

'Walk away?' said Julia. 'Like, where would you go?'

'Back to sleep.'

'We trashed your ship getting you out of it. It won't even seal.'

'It will seal. Foam from the inside will hold a third atmosphere of oxygen. I can get back in the tank and wait for the next ship. However long it takes.' She looked at them, one by one. 'My mining rights. My terms. I won't be pushed around. I have a choice, and if I don't get what I want, you don't get what you want.'

'Arush? What do you think?'

'I don't know. Getting paid is always good. So is going home. I guess that's the one thing left to show. Whoever reset the password needs to prove we can get the laser back. Because if they can't do that, we're wasting air talking about it.'

'He's got a point. So ...' said Julia, looking in turn at May and Kayla. 'Which one of you bastards is it?'

Neither moved.

'Oh, come on. NovaS is long gone. Andros has killed himself. You're the only player left. You're not going to get spaced, no matter what, because you've got the purse-strings now. Doesn't mean we're going to like you, but another mil on top of our agreed bonuses would mean we don't spit in your food on the voyage home.'

'Don't count on it,' said Marta. 'You're selling yourselves to a murderer, but I'm not. I don't know why I'm even here.'

Still no one moved.

'Jesus. Someone.'

Then May loosened her seat strap and twisted around to face the console.

'You have got to be kidding.' Julia bared her teeth. 'You cold-hearted bitch.'

'I've just made more money than you could possibly dream of,' said May. 'And you're angry you never thought of this.'

Marta lunged for May's back, inexpertly knocked off course by Arush.

'Marta,' said Arush. 'No. That's not going to solve anything.'

They struggled in a knot in the middle of Control.

'It'll give her a scar to remember Patricio by.'

'I'm sorry about him,' said May. 'No one was meant to die.'

And Jack was just left there. Empty. He watched Arush try to push Marta back as she was still scrabbling to reach May. He saw Kayla shrink away in disgust. Julia was blinking like she'd just woken up. Runi still motionless. Cat? Cat knew. She already knew and she wasn't surprised. She was the only one looking at Jack with anything approaching sympathy.

May didn't so much as glance in Jack's direction. She stretched out her fingers towards the keypad as he'd seen her do a hundred, a thousand times before. Routine.

And he – he had been discarded. 'I'm going to be sick,' he announced, unstrapping himself and kicking out towards the axis.

Arush twisted aside, and Jack hurried to the junction and went head-down the shaft to the toilets. He fell off the ladder, landed awkwardly on his forearms and crawled the rest of the way. He just managed to get his head over the bowl before his stomach contents came heaving up. He kept on going until there was nothing left but sticky strands of mucus.

He coughed and spat, spat and coughed. His throat was raw, and the taste like hot iron in his mouth.

The crew code she'd taught him was nothing but a blind to hide behind. She'd sabotaged the ship. Patricio had died because of it. She'd nearly killed him. She'd known he was out there, in the trench, and she'd done it anyway. And now? She was going to expect him to guide the asteroid to the refinery, and take the money she offered him, and she'd probably have to pay off Patricio's relatives, and give the crew a larger share, and cut Cat a bigger slice of the royalties, but that would be easy because there was so much money swilling around. The company she worked for – secretly worked for – would have factored all that in. They might even protect her from NovaS's aggrieved investors.

Maybe it was some kind of resurrection of Lithospheric, rising up from the grave to stab at NovaS like a vengeful ghost. Or maybe it was the African nation that Cat had condemned to annihilation by killing her friend, their gallowglass. Or maybe it was just one predatory corporation preying on another, as they always had. Nothing but business, all about the bottom line. No hard feelings.

Money. It all came down to the money. She'd never been anything but honest about that. They'd shared a bed, and more, for the better part of a year, and he'd been ... what? A distraction? Convenient? It came down to just not being enough: not enough for her to stay her hand or change her course.

He spat one last time, and rocked back on his knees.

Then Julia appeared at his shoulder, and knelt down next to him. She handed him a water bulb and rested her hand gently on his back.

'You'd better come. There's a problem.'

25

We find strong causal evidence linking climatic events to human conflict across a range of spatial and temporal scales and across all major regions of the world. The magnitude of climate's influence is substantial: for each 1 standard deviation (1σ) change in climate toward warmer temperatures or more extreme rainfall, median estimates indicate that the frequency of interpersonal violence rises 4% and the frequency of intergroup conflict rises 14%.

S. M. Hsiang, M. Burke, and E. Miguel, 'Quantifying the Influence of Climate on Human Conflict', *Science*, 2013

May was typing in the password over and over again, and the program was rejecting it with the same frequency. Sweat beaded on her forehead, and her face was flushed with ... what? Fear? Guilt? Frustration?

Jack reached past her, over her rapidly moving fingers, and closed the window.

'The cracker is trying thousands of combinations a second. You'll never get in while it's still running.'

She finally looked at him, and it was almost as if she didn't recognise his face: her gaze skittered over him in blank incomprehension. Then she snapped back to the screen, pushing her hand across her hair. Trails of liquid bounced and bobbled free.

'I forgot. I just forgot. Close it.'

Jack settled into his habitual seat next to May and strapped himself in. He felt preternaturally calm, as if this was always how he was going to be, and he just needed some extreme trauma to unlock it. 'I could do, but if I need to restart it, it'll go from the beginning again. I don't think I can pause it without it losing its number-count.'

'Think?'

'I wrote it quick and dirty. I hadn't thought about this scenario at all.' There was still acid in his mouth, and he took a swig of water. It stuck in his throat, and he had to gag it down.

She had the grace to look momentarily troubled. 'Do what you can.'

He worked out a way of suspending the cracker – it hung, mid-operation, and Jack refreshed the laser control program's access page. He ported it across to May's screen. 'Try it now.'

She took the offered window and typed out the password.

The program made a blep sound and told her it was the incorrect password.

'It's still interfering,' she said. 'You'll have to terminate it.'

'It's not—'

'Just kill it.'

'That seems to be your answer to everything,' he said. The silence in Control was profound, the crew waiting for what might happen next. But he opened a command line and forced the cracker to shut down. 'There. Done.'

'Thank you,' she said. She typed out the passcode again. The program rejected it again. She tried once more, this time pecking out the numbers and letters one at a time. She entered the combination, and got the same disappointing result.

'You do remember it, don't you?' asked Julia.

'Of course I do,' said May. She cleared the screen, and punched out the passcode slowly, deliberately. She'd done it often enough that Jack could see what it was supposed to be: BlackHorse587PrioryBell. He had no idea what that meant or why it was significant to her, only that there was clearly a problem with the way she'd keyed it in in the first place.

'She doesn't remember it. Holy shit, she doesn't remember it.'

May looked at Jack. For help? 'There's ... a problem.'

'So Julia told me.' He stared at his lap for a moment, wondering what to do, what to feel. Then he reached across and closed the program down on her screen, before opening one on his own. He typed in the password, and it wouldn't let him in. 'It's not that. Whatever it is, it isn't that.'

'It has to be that.'

'It might be close to that, but it's not that. I've tried it, you've tried it, and it's not worked.' Jack flexed his fingers. 'What else do you have?'

'What do you mean?'

'I'm not the one who sabotaged the mission, killed one of their crewmates, drove the captain to suicide, and is prepared to take everyone else out for a bigger sack of cash. I'm just plain old naive, stupid Jack Astrogator who doesn't believe a person even when they tell me exactly who they are.' He took a deep breath, and it lodged like a stone in his chest. 'So. What else do you have?'

'It has to work,' she said.

'And yet, it doesn't.'

'You've done something to the program.'

'I haven't been able to get into the program to do anything to it. If I could, we wouldn't be where we are now. You don't get to blame this on me. I had a perfectly good password that I could type in, and it worked.'

'You used my name.'

'I hold my hands up to that, as I do to setting a password protect in the first place, but I did write it down and put it in my locker along with my spare pair of pants and a phone that no longer works so that someone would find it if I died.' That was it, wasn't it? 'You found it.'

'Of course I did. And you used my name.'

'Was that when you decided you should kill me?'

'She's forgotten the password,' jeered Marta. 'She can't get into the system. She killed Patricio, and she can't even finish the job.'

'I can do this,' said May. It came out more pleading than she intended. 'I can do this. It's just a glitch.'

'How long do we give her?' Julia looked over May's head at Jack. 'How long will it take to prep the crew section for flight?'

'I can do this!'

Julia screwed her face up. 'Shut up. Shut up, or God help me, you're following Andros out of the airlock this very second.'

'That's another conversation we need to have,' said Kayla.

Jack didn't pick up the import of the sentence straight away, but when he did, he felt broken all over again. How far down were the pieces going to fall? 'She's our engineer.'

'Doesn't mean we can't space her,' said Marta.

'I can't vote for that.'

'She has you by the balls.'

'He's too decent.' Cat interposed herself between Marta and May. She still looked tiny, but she was at least a distraction. 'He hasn't voted for any of us to die, and he won't. It's a character flaw. We can't hold it against him, but we can't let that get in the way of a decision.'

'You don't get a say in this. You're not even crew.'

'No, I'm not crew,' Cat said. 'But I still take my responsibilities seriously. None of you is getting my asteroid without paying for it, and if I leave here with you, the rights will lapse before I get the chance to return, if ever that happens. If she's not in a position to give me a deal, a good deal, one that means St Ann's is safe, then I'm staying.' She pulled herself towards the axis. 'I'm going to get ready. Get the supplies I need. Foam. Air. My suit. If I'm going, I'll need to decompress, but I'll delay that for a few hours. Let me know if she can deliver. The rest is your business.'

When she'd gone, Julia managed a stiff shrug. 'Okay. She's right. We've got some decisions to make. Jack, can you unlock the laser?'

'Maybe.' He didn't look at anyone. He didn't dare, in case they saw just how insubstantial he'd become, just a shadow, going through the motions, while he gazed down on the scene from elsewhere, a disinterested third party. 'I can use the password cracker, and set it going again using May's password as a base, and noodle around it. If it's just a mistyped character, it'll find it.'

'How long will that take?'

'I don't know.'

'How long will it take to cover the likely combinations around the passcode?'

'A couple of hours?'

'You've got one.'

'Julia,' said Arush, 'we need to talk about this.'

'What's there to talk about? Little Miss Engineer has fucked up big time. Not only has she killed someone, she's cost every single one of us seven, eight figures minimum. If she can't come up with a replacement deal, she's toast.'

Jack recoded the cracker, using BlackHorse587PrioryBell as the seed. If it was the numbers that were wrong, the cracker would take bare seconds to find the right combination. If it wasn't, and if there was something more fundamentally flawed, then it might never break its way in. Everything was so very finely balanced. She had so very nearly killed him, and yet he was still trying to save her.

'We need to call Earth,' he said. 'Get them to send the new program anyway.'

'We don't even know who to call,' said Kayla. 'There hasn't been a NovaS for the better part of a year.'

'If this used to be a Lithospheric ship, maybe we can find someone who worked for them.'

'Lithospheric are even deader than NovaS, Jack.'

'Then we try whoever May's working for.' He was clutching at smoke now and he knew it. 'May, you need to contact them, get the program sent.'

239

She stared at her screen.

'May. Contact your company. Tell them we need this program.'

'There …' She stalled.

'Oh, God. There's no company, is there? You're working on your own too. She's gone freelance, just like Andros.' Julia smacked her forehead. 'Fuck my life, there really is no one at the end of the phone.'

'I can get half a dozen buyers lined up with a couple of calls,' May said. 'One of them will win the auction, and then everything else will happen. I promise.'

'You can't negotiate a new deal, because you can offer them jack.' Kayla finally snapped. 'You're nothing. You've locked us out of the laser, and you can't get us back in. We don't need you. We can make any calls ourselves.'

Jack dragged his fingers up through his hair, and made fists. He pulled at his scalp so hard that he might actually feel the pain. He remembered back to May showing him her watch. The watch she was still wearing. Its utility had outlasted his. 'What did you think was going to happen?'

'It was Patricio's idea,' said May, making Marta growl. 'You know what he thought. He said as much.'

'Patricio would never have agreed to this. He was for the crew. And you killed him.'

'That was never meant to happen.'

'Wasn't it? You nearly took Jack, too, and Runi.'

'We just needed to get rid of Andros and NovaS, and we'd have it all.'

'You mean you'd have it all. There's no way back from this.'

'So we're fucked,' said Julia. 'It's Jack's way or not at all.'

Jack noticed that Runi was sobbing. Quietly, trying not to give offence or draw attention to himself, but his body was quaking with the effort. Jack unstrapped and took himself across to the pilot and clung onto him.

'I just. Want. To go. Home.'

'I know. I know. You will. I promise. You will.' Jack twisted round and looked at the faces of the remaining crew, May last of all. 'I can take you all home. Everyone. Even now.'

'You know that's not going to happen, Jack,' said Julia. 'She's out of here.'

'I vote to space her,' said Kayla.

'So do I,' and Marta tensed her body, ready. 'Arush?'

'She has to go.' He clenched his jaw. 'Sorry, Jack.'

'Runi's excused,' said Julia. 'But we need to make this legit.'

'Jack,' said May.

'Shut it now. Jack, you know this has to be done.'

He could save her. The cost, though: he had a job to do, guiding the ship home. If she stayed on board, they'd never make it back. They'd kill each other first.

And that still might happen, even if he voted to space her.

He wasn't decent. He was weak.

'I can't,' said Jack. And he couldn't. He was too shattered to do one thing or the other.

The inevitable, initially tentative scuffle turned quickly into something more serious, but Jack held onto Runi, and he didn't intervene and he didn't look. He was a coward and a fool and he hated what he'd become and the steps he'd taken to get there, and still he wanted it to just be over. So he shut his ears and his eyes to the fight and buried Runi's face in his shoulder. The pilot needed his navigator as much as the navigator needed his pilot.

The shouts and the screams and the grunts and short-breathed barked commands suddenly shut off with the slamming of the outer airlock door. She would be in there, trapped with the body of their captain, and under no illusion as to what was about to happen.

Someone hit the switch to pump the air out, and there were fail-safes inside the airlock itself to prevent it being used for murder, and May would know them all. The battle to override

241

them, to purge the air into the vacuum outside, was as intense as the one to counter each move.

And maybe someone got fed up with the lethal games, and reopened the airlock and bludgeoned May into unconsciousness with a fire extinguisher or a ground anchor or a wrench, then closed the door again and vented the air away.

The ship's nerve-jangling vibrations continued. They – the remaining crew – were in no better state than they were before, and now they had no engineer, so were arguably in a worse position.

Julia came up through the axis into Control. She was bleeding, and had been bled on. Her face was speckled with drying drops of crimson. 'What do we need to do?'

Jack disengaged himself from Runi and pushed himself back to his workstation. He blinked and scrubbed at his face, and for a moment nothing would come.

'Jack. No one's angry with you, Jack. No one blames you. That part is over. But we need you right now. You need to concentrate on the task of saving yourself and the rest of us. Okay? Tell us what we need to do.'

He looked at his hands as if they belonged to someone else. 'I ... Lighter. We need to make the ship lighter. Whatever we don't need, just ... dump it.'

'We need an inventory,' she said.

'Right. Okay.' He swallowed hard. 'There's equipment we'd use on the surface: lines, anchors, drills, everything from the lab section. Food. Don't ditch all one flavour. If we need to ration, we will do. Water: we can't do without it, even if our recycling is nearly perfect, so go easy on that. Take out Cat's share, too. If Andros had a spacesuit, throw it.'

'If we get rid of all that, is it going to be enough for you and Runi to hit the window?'

'Telemetry will give us the answer a few hours into the flight. If we're coming up short, we can only correct if we have fuel reserves. The lower our dry mass, the better chance we have.'

'I'm sorry, Jack,' said Julia.

'Let's just talk about the plan for now. In fact, let's only ever talk about the plan. We don't need to talk about anything else.'

'Yeah. Got it.' Julia withdrew.

'Runi, I'm going to send you my data. If you think it's impossible, then say so. I'm convinced we've enough fuel for this, but if there's any other way of getting more delta-v out of this thing, we should probably do that now.'

Runi nodded, and wiped his sleeve across his cheeks. 'I'll take a look.'

'Don't think about anything else. Just that. I'm going to talk to Cat. Let her know what's going on, because no one else has remembered to.'

He found her in the galley, and sat opposite her at the table.

'I'm sorry for your loss,' she said.

'How long do you need to get ready?' he asked her, ignoring her condolences. 'We could do with some help clearing things out of the ship, cutting the lines, making sure we don't get fouled.'

She made the calculations in her head. She'd already piled cans of foam and two black-ringed oxygen cylinders by her feet. 'I can carry this to my singleship in one go, store it there, and come back and prep for you. An hour? The rest of the time is yours, given the air supply in the suit.'

'The sooner we go, the less delta-v we need to find.'

'Can you do it?'

'Yes, I think so.'

'They're lucky to have you.'

'Really?' He stared at the tabletop for a moment. 'You know there's nothing I can do for St Ann's, don't you? That my parents, for all their billions, haven't lifted a finger to stop any of this happening: to St Ann's, and all the other St Ann's.'

'I will get them a home, Jack. I owe ... I owe Castor that at least.'

Jack wasn't in any position to say whether or not her dead

friend would have agreed with her. 'You can still come with us.'

'You need the mass. What would happen if you were centimetres a second out, and I was still aboard? Your crew have a taste for killing now. It wouldn't take much for them to do it again.'

He had to acknowledge that it was true.

'We're down to the cold equations of life and death,' he said. 'We're saving ourselves and leaving you behind.'

'You go,' she said. 'This asteroid and me. We're bound together. I'll make it work for me, for us. One day.'

Part 3

Kessler Syndrome

Part 3

Kessler Syndrome

26

Among the future trends that will impact our national security is climate change. Rising global temperatures, changing precipitation patterns, climbing sea levels, and more extreme weather events will intensify the challenges of global instability, hunger, poverty, and conflict. They will likely lead to food and water shortages, pandemic disease, disputes over refugees and resources, and destruction by natural disasters in regions across the globe.

Climate Change Adaption Roadmap, US Department of Defense, 2014

The *Anubis* had crashed in Nansen crater, 13 October 2075, killing its crew of three and taking out an automated He-3 scoop-loader. OSTO had made the wreck safe, recovered the dead and fined all concerned, but the debris was left for Jack's team to salvage.

Nothing about the *Anubis* crash had been delicate. The vessel had come down hard at an oblique angle, and had kept on disintegrating until there was only the bones of it left. The groove it had made was a new stark feature at the north pole of the Moon, and the Sun, low on the foreshortened horizon, blacked out the shadows. It would be there permanently, had already picked up a local name, and would probably gain IAU recognition in due course: for now, Jack and three others picked their way across the edges of the unofficially titled *Anubis* Scar with electric carts and metal detectors, scooping up wreckage and tossing it into plastic cages.

The team's floodlights only partly compensated for the contrast between blinding light and utter darkness, and there was a certain laziness about their search. Big pieces were easy to find. Smaller pieces took more effort, but were more abundant. One-sixth gravity spread things far from the impact site, and at some point it was going to become uneconomic to trawl further afield using manual labour. There might be a case for letting simple cleaning robots loose, if someone could make them, power them and get them to pay their way, but a tidy Moon wasn't as important as a productive Moon, and humanity seemed intent on despoiling another planetary body.

The skeleton of the *Anubis* itself had already been cut up and sent to the refineries on rail-gun sleds. They were yet to tackle the damaged loader, which, although an insurance write-off, stood a decent chance of being made to work again, even if the chassis currently ran closer to the regolith than it used to. Jack occupied a peculiar economic niche – scavenger, rather than predator – and it was one that it was difficult to turn a profit in, as the cost of air, water and food fluctuated almost daily. But they called themselves Selenites and they managed.

Despite the inherent contradictions in his work, despite the cold and the dark and the constant gunpowder smell in his nose, Jack liked his work. He skipped forward, watched the dust spill like liquid under his ridge-soled boots and ran his detector across the surface. He'd already found an iron-nickel meteorite, and for that alone a collector or a museum would pay enough to keep someone breathing for a whole week: anything else that went into his cart that shift was a bonus.

The line worked its way up the five-hundred-metre block, reached its virtual end, and then turned around to comb the next twenty-metre strip. The loader was a kilometre further on, and they – or rather Jack's boss, Yao – had hired a lifting body to scoop it up and dump it next to their dome in Challis, on the Earthside. That was next week. This was now. The week after, there'd be something else to retrieve – material of significant value discarded simply because it wasn't worth the owner's trouble to pick it back up again.

He didn't need the detector to point him to the frayed slab of foil-backed insulation. He bent his knees, checked for sharp edges, and finding none, tossed it into his cart. Before the slab had even arrived there, he spotted something that had been hiding under it. He kicked the dust away, and found what could have been part of an aerial.

The detector spiked, the tone running up and down the scale as he passed the loop over the object, and he bent a second time. He pulled at the exposed end, and the regolith shifted down a whole two-metre length. A low-gain omnidirectional antenna, ripped from the *Anubis*'s hull as it ground its way into the crater's bedrock. The connecting coax box at the far end was still seemingly intact. That would pay for dinner, plus more, when it had been refurbished.

The cart trundled on its big sprung wheels behind him, dumb as a rock and slaved to his suit location, following him around at a respectful distance. The antenna wouldn't quite fit in the bed of the vehicle, but if he hung it out the back, he wouldn't be likely to poke himself in the helmet with it. It was light – most things were – and he secured it to the plastic cage with a Velcro tie.

Some crews he'd worked with liked to chat, but Yao thought that unnecessary talk was dangerous, distracting talk, and that suited Jack just fine. The airwaves were clear most of the time, and if his earpiece beeped, he knew that the information coming in was worth listening to. It might even save either his life, or someone else's, as it had done already twice before.

And Yao would never normally interrupt an EVA unless it was important, because concentrating on this particular job in hand was more than enough for the human brain to cope with. Daydreaming was a factor in far more spacer deaths than anyone wanted to acknowledge.

'Jack Jack Control over.'

'Jack receiving over.'

Yao was an absolute stickler for radio protocol, too.

'Switch to channel two. Over.'

Jack clicked the dial round with his fat, gauntleted fingers.

'Control Control Jack over.'

'Receiving. I have two OSTO operatives here. They want to talk to you. Over.'

Jack paused in his search. He guessed that this was about the *Coloma*, and also that it needed his full attention. 'I filed my final statement with them two years ago. I've nothing left to add. Over.'

'I've dispatched a transport to Nansen. It'll bring you here. Over.'

'After my shift, or now? Over.'

'After. Straight after. Over.'

'This sounds serious, Yao. You sure about this? Over.'

'They haven't offered to recompense me for your time, so yes, after your shift. You've got some sweet junk already. Keep going. Over.'

'That wasn't what I meant, Yao. Am I going to need a lawyer? Because if this is about what I think it's about, I'm definitely going to need a lawyer. Over.'

The signal popped for a moment.

'They assure me you won't need a lawyer. But that you do need to be on that transport. Out.'

The other three members of the team were now twenty metres ahead, but Jack took a few more moments. The *Coloma* was the gift that kept on giving. His reputation as the navigator that got the ship back from KU2 had earned him significant kudos, but the circumstances surrounding what happened on the asteroid had also made him highly suspect as crew. He'd not crewed again since, to anywhere.

That was okay, too. He'd done enough in one trip to last him a long time, if not a lifetime. He'd found a place in Yao's company. It kept him off-Earth, and below the radar, although if OSTO could find him, he was certain his parents knew where he was and what he was doing. They could play the long game. Whether he could too would remain to be seen.

Deep breath, loud inside his helmet. He switched back to the main channel and resumed his search pattern. Bound, visual check, sweep, move on. The fragments, he'd pick and choose; if they were interesting to look at, or high in metals or plastics, he'd scoop them. The big pieces all went in regardless – once they were in an atmosphere, they could sort them by hand. Even the rubbish could be macerated and sorted at the main facility. That was where Yao was really scoring: waste disposal for the big corps. Junk farming was just a sideline, more a public service to keep him sweet with OSTO than a get-rich-quick scheme.

He thought about the trillions in KU2, about the millions that had been due to come to him. What he had now was a suit, enough air and water and food and somewhere to lay his head. He was accumulating pay somewhere, but he hadn't looked recently because he'd not been anywhere where he could spend his money. Neither did he get stuff sent to him. He paid subscriptions for various online services, and had reconnected with The History of the Decline and Fall of the Roman Empire. TBone had vanished, suddenly, six months after the *Coloma* set sail. Jack hoped that wherever they were, they were happy, and not dead like WhitetailDeer.

History was barely a teenager any more, and not even in Rio. At twenty-three degrees south, life in the barrios had become untenable. In the face of water shortages, heatwaves and intermittent power, fires in the hills and flooding across the city, he'd bailed for cooler climes. He'd got stuck at the Uruguayan border, but made it to Rivera. He didn't say what he did for a living. Jack supposed it wasn't legal, but he wasn't in a position to help.

The world below was falling apart, sometimes slowly, sometimes quickly. The population of St Ann's had become fragmented, lost, degenerating into factions and fighting over what was left of the fortune gifted to them by Cat. He thought of her often. He wondered if she'd managed to re-enter her sleep tank. He wondered if it had managed to keep her alive for the three years since the *Coloma* had left. It seemed unlikely: she had had unshakeable hope, but the mechanics of hibernation were far from perfect.

Then he realised he was doing that thing that killed. He'd been going through the motions of searching for pieces of the *Anubis*, all the while thinking about other people, other places. He needed to be in the now. It was what Yao was paying him for, and his boss wouldn't thank him for cutting his suit, or running out of gas, or falling over and cracking his faceplate.

Jack dragged his mind back to looking for ship parts amongst the bone-grey dust of the Moon, and keeping in line with his colleagues.

'Radio check,' he said. 'Over.'

'Emma receiving. Over.'

'Noah receiving. Over.

'Sumana receiving. Over.'

'Check complete. Out.'

He was in charge of these people. He was the most experienced of the team, and dear Lord they were all so young. He felt ancient, a veteran, and he was, because there were no old, bold spacers. He'd survived a mission that had ended the lives of three people, and could have easily claimed them all. His was the voice of reason. He was the grown-up. And these kids would move on to better, safer things in a year or two, but he had to get them there first, past the point where they were no longer going to make the stupid mistakes that would kill them – just the regular mistakes instead.

Even while he was still making the same mistakes.

They still had an hour on the surface, and he recognised that he was in no fit state to be outside, let alone be in any position of responsibility. Damn Yao. He knew what effect he'd have. Now he'd get to dock Jack's pay, because it wasn't the boss calling time.

'All crew all crew Jack over.'

They called in, one by one.

'We're finishing early. I've got a bad case of drift. Head back to the hopper. Out.'

Maybe they guessed it was the private conversation he'd had with Yao, so they didn't argue. But they did stand and stare at him, because this was the first time he'd ever pulled this on them. Micrometeorite strikes, faulty valves, broken fans, thermo-regulation problems were all part of the mix, but he was the one who was always focused and insisted that his team were too.

They all turned around and loped back towards the skeletal hopper that had brought them to the site, and would return them to their temporary dome near the final resting place of the *Anubis*. Their carts bounced along behind them, rattling over craters old and new and leaving more tracks in the already criss-crossed and trampled plain. The passing of the ship had thrown bright dust over dark, and the further disturbance of the surface gave rise to patterns and shades that might pass for colour on that monochromatic world.

They attached their carts to the underside of the hopper, and Jack made sure they were fixed securely in place by the time-honoured method of giving them a shake. The plastic carts wobbled silently, but nothing fell off. UV exposure and micrometeorites degraded the structure of the mesh, and the dust, the ubiquitous dust formed from countless tiny impacts and having the properties of microscopic knives, stuck to every-one and everything.

Things broke all the time, and Yao's Selenites weren't im-mune to that. But today, everything was still holding together.

'All crew all crew. Strap in. Prepare for departure. Out.'

What could OSTO want with him after all this time? What

had happened on KU2 had been outside not just their jurisdiction, but anyone's jurisdiction. He hadn't even been obliged to answer their questions, but there were lessons to be learned, and he'd felt compelled to unburden himself. He could have found a priest for free, or a barman for the price of a few drinks, or a therapist for considerably more, but OSTO got to him first and that was that.

He pulled down the ladder, locked it in place, and waited while his crew clambered up.

The hopper body was like a bow-topped wagon – a flatbed and a hooped roll-cage. Underneath were spring-suspension legs and an array of cargo straps and cold thrusters. They were all limited by traffic control to a maximum altitude of ten metres, and a speed of ten kilometres an hour, and like all transport regulations, that was honoured more in the breach than not. They were designed to do work, to move loads and people, not look pretty or be pressurised. In that, they were all alike, even if they did differ in their particulars.

By the time he too had reached the level of the flatbed, the others were in their bucket seats and strapping in. He hadn't rolled one yet, but had been in one rolled by someone else. That had been ... interesting, and the wait for another hopper to rescue them worryingly long. He'd never been that low on air, before or since.

He sat in the driver's seat – no pilot's licence required at ten metres – and ran through the systems checks as he secured himself down. There was no gentle way to fly a hopper. The name was completely descriptive as to the nature of its trajectory across the lunar surface. The navigation screen came online, and even though he could see the temporary Selenite dome across the crater floor, with its aerial mast and three red lights aglow on top, he logged the journey with traffic control and waited for the proceed signal to come back.

It did, moments later, and after one last routine check that everyone was ready, Jack popped some gas into the thrusters and the hopper lifted off. He nudged the thrusters while in flight to aim towards the dome, and just as the hopper's legs were about to alight again, he fired the thrusters a second time. Now they had both vertical and horizontal movement. The arc was graceful, travelled in perfect silence, and some twenty metres later, he had to do it again.

The dome slowly resolved, the reflective silver coating of the double-walled inflatable skin glowing in the late lunar evening sun. Nansen passed below, while the black sky above was dotted with fast-moving lights. Satellites, habitats, factories, stations, shipyards, and then the ships themselves, along with rail-launched automated cargo. Objects rose and fell above and below the horizon, flickering with exhaust.

And they had arrived. The hard body of the airlock extended out from the inflated dome like a finger, and Jack brought the hopper down with one last jump, near enough the regulation ten metres away. Dust blew outwards and fell, but not before giving the dome, and the sub-orbital transport parked next to it, another coating of fine, grey dust.

'Jack Jack Emma over.'

'Receiving over.'

'Do we have visitors? Over.'

'Negative. I've been called back to Challis. You'll have to manage the next shift on your own if I can't make it back in time. Over.' He could have said Out, but he left space for her to say something else, if she wanted to.

'Who's in charge until then? Over.'

He hadn't given it much thought, his mind being occupied by other matters, so he made a snap decision. 'You are, over.'

She was sitting behind him, and it was such a chore to look around, but he guessed that she was blinking and the others frowning. She was competent, had her certificates, and did things by the book. She was good crew: they all were, and any of them could have stepped up, but he needed to deputise, so why not her?

255

'Okay.' She didn't sound certain, but she didn't turn it down. 'What do you want me to do with the cargo? Over.'

'You decide. You know where and how it's stored, and you know how to get ready for the next EVA. I'm on the transport. Any questions, direct them at Challis. Jack out.'

He shut down the hopper, and while his crew were unloading the carts, he skipped across to the transport and opened the airlock door. He'd talk to OSTO, and then he'd ask Yao why he'd thought the summons was so urgent.

Then he'd come back to Nansen, where the crew knew not to bother him with questions about the *Coloma*.

27

The Tribunal had found that Mr Teitiota could not bring himself within either the Refugee Convention or New Zealand's protected person jurisdiction on the basis that his homeland, Kiribati, was suffering the effects of climate change.

Teitiota v Ministry of Business Innovation and Employment,
New Zealand Supreme Court, 2015

The triple airlock at the Selenite dome in Challis took off almost all of the dust from his suit – electrostatic grid, pressurised air jets, high-gauss magnetic wand – but Jack could still smell it. Inside the changing room, he stowed his suit on the hanger and plugged his life support into the regenerator, found a flightsuit that fitted and slipped on some ship slippers.

The logo on his left breast was a patch for some company he'd never heard of. Yao was big on reuse, less so on branding. For a moment, he stood in front of the pressure door that led on into the dome and looked at his reflection in the circle of glass, moon-made, embedded in it. He lifted his hand to his head and passed it over his shaved scalp. The stubble rasped slightly. His long hair had gone even before he'd left KU2. It had been a ridiculous affectation, and he'd dumped it out the airlock to symbolically save weight.

His razor cut made him look reborn, even if he felt about a hundred years old.

Then he realised that Yao was looking back at him through the porthole.

The bulkhead door was an automatic closer, pneumatic on CO_2 rams that kicked in on sensing a pressure drop either side. It had a manual override, but there was never much chance of staying conscious long enough to operate it. At all other times it was on a handle and runners, and it slid back easily enough.

'A welcoming committee,' said Jack. 'Yao Selenite.'

'Always pleased to see you, Jack Recycler. I shouldn't have favourites, but there you are.' Yao passed Jack a lanyard with his name, face and QR code.

Jack dropped it over his head. 'Why you didn't tell OSTO to bother someone else?'

'Come on, Jack. Half my business comes from OSTO. They're friends, not enemies.'

'What's this about, Yao? What are you not telling me?'

Yao, normally so genial and accommodating, stood awkwardly and wouldn't look Jack in the eye. 'It's more like, what have you not told them? They're twitchy, Jack. Makes me think you've not come clean with me either.' Yao's own scalp shone darkly under the sharp lighting. 'I took a risk taking you on.'

'As you remind me every time we talk, but I'm still not sure what risk you think it was.'

'Reputational, Jack.'

'I was a hero, for all of five minutes. That somehow justifies paying me less for the rest of my life, and I take it gratefully, just as long as you keep me busy and away from people like ...'

'Like OSTO. I know. But I don't even know it's the *Coloma* they want to talk to you about, because they sure as hell won't tell me.'

'What else could it be?'

Yao spread his hands wide, and he side-eyed Jack for a second. 'Parents?'

If it wasn't the *Coloma*, maybe? It might be part of their long game to drag him back into the suffocating embrace of the Van der Veerden family, getting OSTO involved in ... what? The Organisation was pretty toothless, most of the time.

'You've got my back, right? Tell me you've got my back.'

'I've got you. You want to carry on working for me, then we just carry on as before.'

'And you're not thinking of selling out to some vee-cee consortium or shell company that's a thinly veiled front for a couple of billionaire shipping magnates?'

'I own the stock.'

'For now.'

'We don't know what tomorrow brings. If someone makes me an offer, I'll consider it, but if I wait five years, they'll have to make me a bigger offer. Or maybe I'll make them an offer and buy them out. Who knows? I do this because it needs doing, and I want to make sure that someone keeps doing it.' He shrugged. 'They're in my office. Be careful, okay?'

'I will. And,' Jack screwed his face up. 'Thanks. They're not the only ones who get twitchy.'

'You can always just walk out again. It's not like they can arrest you. Fuck the police, Jack.'

'I'll take your advice on board. How long have they been here?'

'Hour or so.'

'They've probably waited long enough.' Jack dug his hands in his pockets and found a plastic business card at the bottom, left by the previous wearer. He fished it out and read the name.

Park Min-gyu.

It wasn't the name he recognised so much as the holographic image of the man's face next to it. The space lawyer he'd talked to at Transit, all those years ago.

'How come you get to see a lawyer, and I don't?' Jack flipped Yao the card, and the man unerringly caught the spinning rectangle with an ease that came with experience.

'I see him when I need to. Though I will have to tell him to stop leaving his cards around.'

'Don't worry about the escort.' Jack passed Yao in the doorway. 'I know the way.'

259

The Selenite dome was small by lunar standards, but it was perfectly functional, and one of a nexus of habitats in Challis. There were good reasons to cluster – to share resources and personnel – but there were no towns on the Moon, and no councils organising anything. If someone needed a service or essential supplies, they paid for them, either in barter or hard currency. That extended to air and water.

People who couldn't pay died, and so a charity was set up to repatriate indigent spacers. People still died. Jack knew that Yao helped as he could, and knew that Yao wanted that kept quiet. Working for Yao was better than working for a lot of other companies.

Jack arrived at the central core and took the steps down, through the inevitable series of pressure doors, until he was metres below the regolith and in amongst the living quarters and life support machinery that sat cheek by jowl in the depths. Yao's office was little more than a broom cupboard with a desk, but this wasn't the headquarters of a manufactory or a primary resource extractor, or even a high-end service provider.

He opened the door, without knocking, and there were two OSTO agents in their own dark blue flightsuits, name tags and everything, wedged into the only two chairs present, staring at tablets dense with text.

'You wanted to see me.'

If they had, then they shouldn't have been so startled by his presence in the doorway. One of them, the man, seemed particularly inept at recovering his flying tablet, and Jack guessed he'd not been long off-Earth, what with the fumbling, and the longer hair. The woman was a suede-head, like him, and she at least managed to not bounce around the tiny room like a leaky balloon.

He looked at them both. There was more room in the corridor or the gym or the galley, but any conversation they had there was more likely to be overheard or interrupted. There was a surveillance jammer on the desk, and the agents had most likely swept the room for listening devices already. This was definitely about the *Coloma*.

'I've just pulled a full shift, so it'd be nice if one of you gave up your chair, rather than have me stand,' he said, and waited while a brief tussle of wills took place. In the end, the woman stood and sat on the desk, back to her colleague and partly obscuring him. Jack didn't know what that signified.

He took the chair, and jammed it up against the door before sitting in it. One-sixth gravity made it difficult to look bored or louche, and he'd much rather the interview was just over rather than affecting some kind of attitude.

'Just to confirm,' said the agent on the desk – Peary was what was on her tag, 'you are Jaap van der Veerden, also known as Jack van der Veerden, currently employed by Selenite as a ...'

'Recycler. That's me. And you are?'

'Sonya Peary. He's Santiago Dominico. We're with the Outer Space Treaty Organisation.'

Jack squashed the urge to reply with 'no shit', and just nodded.

'Before we can proceed, I need you to sign a non-disclosure agreement.' Sonya Agent found the page on her tablet after a brief search and proffered it towards Jack.

Jack sat on his hands.

'That's not going to happen,' he said. 'You're going to have to give me more than that before I sign anything.'

Santiago Agent peered around his colleague. 'Jack, we can't go any further until you do.'

'Then we've all had a wasted journey. I hope OSTO are going to pay Selenite for my time, because I'm not losing money over this.'

'We know how much you spend, Jack. It's just building up in your account.' Sonya Agent offered him the tablet again, and again Jack refused.

'If this is about the *Coloma*, then I don't care about disclosure. You've had all I can say on that anyway, and it's in the public domain.' He shrugged. 'I'm here as a courtesy to Yao.'

'Okay, Jack.' Sonya Agent put the tablet down next to her and crossed her ankles. Had they picked her because of her superficial resemblance to May? Would OSTO go to such lengths? 'Me and Santiago have both read the *Coloma* report. We know you have scars from that.'

'You didn't bring me halfway around the Moon to sympathise with my broken psyche. Just ask your questions so I can go back to Nansen and try to concentrate on looking after my crew.'

'Jack. We need your help,' she said. And maybe she slipped a little, because for a moment, Jack could have sworn she looked scared.

'It's true. We need to ask you a big favour,' said Santiago Agent, peering out from behind his colleague. 'But before we can do that, you need to sign the form.'

Jack looked up at Sonya Agent, then held out his hand for the tablet. There was something ... off. He made his digital mark without glancing at the boilerplate, and handed it back. He slowly sat up. 'Go on then.'

'It's not what you think, Jack,' said Sonya Agent. 'Although you should probably know that with the death of Marta Jepsen six weeks ago, in what Danish police are calling an assassination, you're the last surviving crew member of the *Coloma*.'

Jack ran his thumb over his chin, rasping at the fine stubble that grew there. 'And you're telling me you're here to talk about something more important than me potentially being on a hit list?'

'I'm afraid so. All the same, how's your personal security?'

'I'm on the Moon. If someone wants to kill me, then there are a thousand ways of making it happen. I still manage to sleep at night. Sometimes I even sleep well.' He pursed his lips. 'I don't even know who I'm supposed to be protecting myself against. Is Marta's death a matter of public record?'

'Yes, but no one's reporting the connection between her and the *Coloma*,' said Sonya. 'Yet. Had you kept in touch with the other survivors?'

'The crew,' corrected Jack. 'We didn't crash, we didn't break down. The mission was sabotaged. We were able to bring it home. And no one died on the way back.'

'But did you keep in touch with them?'

'No. They all went home, back to wherever on Earth. We spent six months nursing half a ship back to Cis-lunar. We'd had enough of each other by then.'

'After all you went through, that seems a shame. You could have at least given yourselves some warning about was happening.'

'We were crew. We were there to do a job. When the job changed, we did that too. Then we went our separate ways.' Jack hunched over. 'You could have warned us if you'd known. But you didn't know, did you? You've only gone looking for us in the last few weeks, because of whatever this is.'

'You've not flown since the *Coloma*, have you?'

'If you're here to make me an offer, then I'll listen to you.'

He'd meant it as a throwaway remark, but neither agent treated it as such, and Jack sat more upright.

Santiago moved his chair so he could be more in Jack's eyeline. '1998 KU2,' he said. 'Do you know where it is now?'

'No.'

'Do you want to hazard a guess?'

'You know what? I hate these sorts of games. Just tell me.'

'You're familiar with the Torino scale?'

'Ah, fuck.' Jack's heart skipped a beat, and when it resumed, it was hitting a different rhythm. 'I know now why you want to talk to me.'

'We're trying to keep it a secret, but if we make it to the end of this week without something leaking, we'll be surprised.'

'When will it hit?'

'Eight months. It's just come out from behind the Sun, and KU2's orbital characteristics are under close analysis. Currently, we are at Torino seven. We expect to be able to say for certain if we need to upgrade it to Torino ten within ten to fourteen days.'

'Or Torino one.'

'We might. But that's one of the things we need to talk to you about.'

'A four-and-a-half-k mostly stony asteroid. It's going to make a hell of a mess.'

'If it hits land, a crater seventy kilometres wide and one kilometre deep. Blast effects fatal in the range of seven, eight hundred kilometres from the impact site, continent-wide wildfires. If it hits ocean, there'll be a wall of water five hundred metres high that will spread out from the impact site and circle the globe twice. The water vapour alone could put Earth into an ice age.'

'So, there is an upside to it.' Jack scrubbed at his face. Was he responsible for this? As the last man standing from the *Coloma*, he supposed he was. And Cat was still strapped to the rock, asleep, unaware. Not that she could do anything but watch even if she was awake.

Santiago put his tablet down. 'Casualties are estimated at between a half and two billion from the immediate impact effects. Secondary effects such as starvation, disease and war could well kill ninety to ninety-five per cent of the rest. Civilisation will go back to the Iron Age, if we're lucky.'

Jack waited for one of them to continue. When they didn't, he asked: 'Why are you telling me this? So I can go and do the decent thing and space myself?'

'Do you want to stop it?' said Sonya. It was as mild as an invitation to dance, but Jack felt long-dormant anger surge inside.

'That implies you already have a plan to stop it, and that you're going to go ahead with it whether I say yes or no. Seriously. If you have something meaningful to say, say it. Otherwise, leave.' He considered walking out himself, but was only halfway off the chair when he decided he'd let them have both barrels.

'For fuck's sake, this was inevitable, eventually. If not me, then some other unsupervised idiot with the ability to drop a megatonne asteroid on people's heads. Why have you not put a stop to this? I made absolutely certain that at every point in the manoeuvre we weren't Earth-crossing. I took my responsibilities stone-cold seriously, but I was the only one on the *Coloma* crew who even thought about that, even though it made the job harder.

'Then we lost control of it. It still looked okay. It was decelerating. Apoapsis was moving inwards all the time. It'd miss Earth. It'd fall into an orbit between Earth and Mars. And maybe, since it was valuable, someone else would go and fetch it back, now that we'd proved in practice we could move it.' He ran out of steam. It wasn't their fault. It was his fault. But they had a plan. They had a plan. He slumped forward and rested his elbows on his knees. 'What do you need?'

'You've been to KU2. You've been on the surface. You directed the laser. You were privy to the seismic data—'

'Haven't you got that?'

'No.'

'Why the hell not?'

'Because the company that salvaged the *Coloma* won't hand it over. Commercially sensitive.'

'You have got to be fucking kidding me.'

'And we need you to negotiate with Catherine Vi, if she's still alive.'

'Cat. Cat Gallowglass?'

'Yes. Apparently we have to have her permission to divert the asteroid away from a potential extinction-level event.' Sonya looked around at Santiago, then back at Jack. 'If the mission is successful, whichever state or multi-state organisation is responsible will be liable for a trillion-dollar lawsuit, brought by St Ann's, for violating their mining rights.'

Jack blinked, and tried to get his mind around the concept. 'There's a word for this.'

'Kafkaesque?'

'Fubar. Fucked up beyond all recognition.'

'If she's dead, then we could have to deal direct with St Ann's, as Vi's lawful heirs and successors, or the rights become void. We're looking into that. And yes, before you ask, an attempt to divert the asteroid will happen, no matter what. But our lawyers have asked us to make this as simple as possible, so that in the event there is an afterwards, we don't spend the next two decades in court. The law allowing us to just do this doesn't exist. The *Coloma* crew interviews all say that of everyone, it was you who got on best with Catherine Vi.' Sonya recrossed her ankles the other way.

'Okay. If that's what they say. It wasn't much of a relationship. I trusted her when the rest didn't so much. When it got difficult, I helped keep her alive. We did talk.' He huffed, and gave in. 'I take it you have something to offer her in return.'

'Not yet,' said Santiago, eventually.

'For fuck's sake. You expect her just to hand over the wealth that could save, could still save, her nation? I don't think you realise who you're dealing with.'

'It's being discussed. At the highest level. By the time you get there, there'll be an offer on the table.'

'Wait, what? By the time I get there?'

Sonya glanced around at Santiago again, then said: 'You mistake our intentions. You'll be part of the crew. You're going back to KU2.'

28

When potential storm climatology change over the 21st century is also accounted for, Sandy's return period is estimated to decrease by ~3x to 17x from 2000 to 2100.

N. Lin, R. E. Kopp, B. P. Horton, and J. P. Donnelly, 'Hurricane Sandy's flood frequency increasing from year 1800 to 2100',

PNAS, 2016

The agents had gone, replaced by Yao. Jack felt hollow, like a bubble. One prick and his skin would burst, revealing him to be insubstantial. He'd inadvertently steered a potentially planet-killing asteroid into the path of the Earth. As mistakes went, it was right up there with a microbiologist dropping a flask of highly contagious virus just as they're about to take an international flight.

Months of night. No harvest for two, three years. Acid rain stripping what was left of the boreal forest away. Heavy snowfalls at high latitudes. Landslides diverting the course of rivers. A layer of ejecta metres thick over a continent, covering farmland and cities alike. Air full of smoke, and once the sky cleared, no ozone layer to mop up the ultraviolet. Cancers, cataracts, plant damage, for years.

It took what humanity had already done to the climate and doubled down on it.

There were nearly eight billion people on the planet below. Arguments had swirled for the last century as to how many was too many, or whether talking about ways of reducing the numbers was just a way of suggesting that there were too many brown or black or yellow people. There weren't enough of the right kind, that was for certain. Not enough pale-skinned immortal billionaires.

'You okay, Jack?'

It was about the hundredth time Yao had asked him that, and all he could do was grunt.

It could have been worse. It could have been even bigger. An asteroid that would punch down into the mantle with enough energy to melt the entire crust, throw the atmosphere into space and evaporate the oceans, would have left nothing but a few objects on the Moon for alien archaeologists to discover.

Sure, it could have been worse, but not by much. And it was his fault. At least, he was responsible for not locking out that future. At the time, it hadn't occurred to him that the sacrificial and entirely credible thing to do would have been to take the crew section of the *Coloma* and deliberately crash it into the laser – avoiding the beam – disabling both parts and providing some certainty as to KU2's orbit. It would have killed, quickly or slowly, everyone on board, but better that six die than billions.

He'd concentrated on getting the *Coloma* home, while KU2 burned and sputtered like a firework in the far, cold reaches of outer space.

'Jack?'

The thought of being back on that slowly shifting pile of debris, held together by nothing more than static and ill-will, made him cold to the core. And there was Cat to deal with. To reason with. To convince that her best interests lay in not trying to threaten the Earth with near-total destruction in order to leverage a better deal for her homeland.

He could almost taste the irony.

'Say something, Jack.'

'Okay, Yao. I know you're there.'

'And are you?'

'Just about.'

'What did they say to you? You look like a ghost.'

'I signed an NDA. I can't afford to break it on what you pay me.' He stopped staring at the ceiling. 'It turned out it was and it wasn't about the *Coloma*. Also, I quit.'

'You quit? Selenite?'

'Yes, Selenite. I appreciate, more than you can imagine, what it meant when you gave me a job. That I could stay up here and not have to slink back to Earth while struggling to keep my own body weight upright against the gravity and simultaneously hiding from my parents. And, apparently, a corporate hit squad.'

'You're shitting me.'

'No. But I have to break cover now.'

'Are you coming back?'

'I mean, yes. I hope so, but I don't know.' What he wanted to say was he didn't know if there'd be anything to come back to, but the panic was going to be almost as bad as the actual impact, and he didn't want that on his conscience as well.

'You working your notice?' asked Yao.

'Not going to happen. We'll have to invoke that penalty clause on the contract. I'll pay you whatever it takes.'

'So who are the new guys? At least tell me that.'

'It's not OSTO, if that's what you're thinking. And you run a clean operation, so it's not like there's any dirt to turn over to the Organisation anyway.'

Yao clicked his tongue against the roof of his mouth. It was the most annoyed Jack had ever seen him. 'You're a good worker, Jack.'

'You mean I don't complain.'

'I have my bottom line to worry about, same as everyone else. I have to haul air and water, keep you in patches and food. None of it comes free. You gave value. If you need a reference, you got it, but I don't like the way you're just going. Leaves me short, and the *Anubis* isn't going to collect itself.'

'I'm on a time-limited offer. If I don't take it, the opportunity's gone. Launch window, and all that.'

'Back out into space?'

'Back out into space.'

'You were ... content. I won't say happy.'

'Yao, it's not about you, or the job. Something just came up.'

'And you won't tell me what it is.'

'Because I signed an NDA. I could have just walked, and you'd have found out later, but I owe you as much honesty as I can give. Which is why we're having this conversation now. Check the rosters, see if you can get a rookie in. This company doesn't depend on me. It depends on you.'

'If you'd had the capital, I'd have made you a partner.'

Jack thought about that. 'I'm flattered?'

'Junior partner.'

'I'm still flattered. But I'm never going to be able to access that sort of money.'

'Never?'

And at that moment, Jack realised that his name was still a millstone around his neck, and he'd never be free of it. He stood up and proffered his closed fist.

'Let's part on good terms, Yao, and leave what's unsaid, unsaid. Thank you for everything, and I wish you well.'

Yao – did he look disappointed with himself, too? Maybe. He dapped, but he also folded his other hand over Jack's.

'Give me a call, okay?'

Jack nodded, all the while knowing that he'd never do it. If he came back, if there was something to come back to, then someone else would be looking for an experienced spacer with all their certificates, and hopefully the taint of the *Coloma* would have finally dissipated. He took off his lanyard and coiled it up on the desk between them and left, heading for the airlock.

And if they failed? If they came back and Earth was shrouded in dirty clouds from pole to pole, lit from below by fires so vast they shone through? He was pretty certain that the lunar settlements were unsustainable in the long run, and that there'd be no terrestrial space capability for two or three centuries, if ever. Those above would stretch it out as long as they could; given another hundred years, another fifty even, they might have made a go of it. But today, everything was fragile, and everything would break. One day, one vital component would be missing, and that would be that.

He hoped that whoever was making preparations for pushing KU2 out of the way were good at their jobs. Professionals, and not like those in the movies.

He took off his flightsuit, put it back on a hanger and attached a fresh life support from the rack to his spacesuit's backplate. He heaved himself into his spacesuit, leg, leg, arm, arm, and finally body and head. He thumbed his suit closed, and all the systems kicked in: oxygen, fans, temperature control, lights, comms, and all the tell-tales that would warn him if something wasn't working. It was still in his nature to check everything, but it was now routine. His life depended on that second skin, whether he was outside for hours or for minutes. And he loved it. It was so simple, even though it was complicated. Whether he was in or out of the suit or inside a dome or a transport, his existence was reduced to the essentials. All the things that needed to work either did or didn't, and he could fix most of those that didn't himself.

He needed to fix this, too.

Jack cycled the airlock, one, two, three doors, and felt his suit stiffen around him as the air thumped and faded away. Outside, over Challis, it was closer to midday than it was at Nansen. The shadows were less oblique and the regolith a bright grey sea, walked on and walked over again and none of it pristine. OSTO had managed to declare a few square kilometres around the Apollo 11 site off-limits while they worked out what to do with it, but every tourist that made it to the Moon wanted to see it up close, and they wanted it with all the privilege that a six-figure ticket bought.

271

He loped over to the OSTO transport that was waiting for him, and made it through the airlocks. They even had a flight-suit the right size for him, the arrogant bastards being so sure of his cooperation. Yes, he had a choice, but no, he really didn't.

Santiago Agent was presumably up front with the pilot, but Sonya Agent was in the cargo bay with him. Seats were lined up along the sides of the hold, and she was already strapped into one. Jack deliberately picked a place across the aisle from her and buckled himself in.

'You've already convinced me,' he said. 'You don't have to nursemaid me as well.'

'This comes under "looking after our asset".' She then spoke into her lapel, where she presumably had a microphone: 'We're good to go.'

'Is that what I am now? An asset?'

'Primarily, yes. When we're done, you can pick another identity.'

Which was refreshingly honest, at least. The overhead speakers rumbled 'acceleration acceleration', and the thrusters kicked hard and long.

They weren't headed for anywhere on the Moon, and it felt momentarily that he was being shanghaied all over again, to join a ship of dubious provenance and doubtful legality. Just as he'd agreed to his first trip sight unseen, he'd done the same again.

'So where are we going?' he asked when the thrusters had stopped.

'L2,' she said. The semblance of gravity had all but dis-appeared. 'The less contact you have with other people, the better.'

'If people are disappearing all over Cis-lunar, you think no one's going to put it together?'

'It's not like that.'

'Then there's a rapidly assembled ship at L2 that's got shut-tles coming and going all the time.'

272

'When was the last time you talked to someone about something that wasn't to do with junk, Jack?'

He rummaged around in his memory, and came up with nothing.

'Fair point. But other people aren't as incurious as me.'

'Granted. But we've managed to get a dozen nuclear warheads into orbit without arousing suspicion, so give us some credit.'

'Isn't that in direct contravention of the Outer Space Treaty?'

'Well spotted. We don't have much choice if we want to save the world. Painting one side of the asteroid white will take too long, and the window for using solar sails has already closed.'

'Mass driver?'

'We're trying to reduce the amount of uncontrolled debris in Earth-crossing orbits, not increase it.'

'What about the laser?'

'Arguably, yes. The one you used isn't working and will take an indefinable time to repair. If we bought or commandeered an asteroid tug, we'd still need to take the nukes along for insurance. So we cut to the chase. Nukes will work. They represent certainty, and that's what we, and everyone else, will need.'

'And you're not worried about the precedent?'

'Not as worried as I am about my home planet being set on fire.'

'We've been doing that for two hundred and fifty years, and it hasn't stopped us yet.'

'There's nothing like a five-kilometre mountain bearing down on you at thirty kilometres a second to concentrate the mind.' She looked wistful for a moment. 'Who knows? It might even help.'

'They'll forget about it five minutes after KU2 sails by.'

'Then we should do something about that.'

'We? I'm just another poor spacer going from gig to gig.'

'You never thought about changing the world?'

'I had enough – have enough – trouble changing my own.'

273

Jack pushed against his harness and stretched his legs out. 'As important as this is, I've gone straight from being on shift, to hauling around the Moon, being told the world is ending, quitting my job, then being dragged out to L2 for a second round with a killer asteroid. I'm trying to make the best decisions I can, but I'm not planning on anything beyond that. Don't get distracted. Do the job. Come home.'

'You—'

'Sonya, you need me to avoid an expensive lawsuit, not divert an asteroid.'

'There's a chance this won't work. That we'll drop the rock and it, or part of it, will end up hitting Earth.' Sonya clenched her jaw.

'I understand that. I'm going to do everything to help you remove the threat, and ...' He stared at the forward bulkhead. 'I have precisely one friend and two parents on Earth. And my relationship with my parents is, well, complicated. I haven't talked to them for nearly five years now. But since they're going to live for ever – global catastrophe notwithstanding – that'll be just an eyeblink in history to them.'

'I did the background check on you. Your whole life.' Now it was her turn to fix her attention on the grey wall ahead. 'I contacted them.'

'Oh.'

'I wanted to find out what you were like when you were younger. I didn't get to talk to them, let alone see them. Far too busy to meet a junior OSTO agent.'

'I could have saved you the trip,' he said. 'Did you get a response?'

'They're concerned about your ongoing welfare. I think that might be a direct quote.'

'I might give it another five years, then.' He hesitated before asking: 'Look. I don't know if you can do anything, but my friend, my one and only friend, is stuck in a border town between Brazil and Uruguay. This is not a demand, please don't

274

take it that way, but I'd like to do something for him while I have the chance. Get him across. Get him settled.'

'I thought you were going to ask me to warn your parents about KU2.'

'If anyone is going to survive, then it's them. History? Not so much.'

'Give me their details. I can't promise anything.'

He took that. 'Thank you.'

'Shall I tell you about the mission now?'

'Are you allowed to do that?'

'Protecting the asset covers making sure the asset doesn't talk to anyone,' she said. 'So, you're heading for an ESA ship, the *Aphrodite*.'

'That the one that was supposed to go to Jupiter next year?'

She nodded. 'It was ready. We asked. They offered it to us with the commissioning crew. The warheads we got from the French, three hundred kilotonnes apiece. The flight profile is for two gravities boost and deceleration, by which point the *Aphrodite* will have about a week to ten days to place the warheads, then pull back and detonate them.'

'Two-g?'

'Boosters on top of the plasma drive. The intercept orbit can't be made any other way.'

'Will it take two-g? It's a deep-space vessel.'

'I've been told there's been a lot of welding of extra struts going on. Nothing is supposed to fall off.'

'And if it does?'

'I guess the crew will have to fix it.'

'This isn't supposed to be Hollywood. This is supposed to be certain.'

'The ship has to make a delta-v of some sixty thousand metres a second. I know you steered the *Coloma* back with less than two hundred, but this is different. They've run the numbers, and that's what it has to do. You can go over it if you want, but we can't wait for the most efficient window. Neither do we have the luxury of building a ship specifically for the purpose. Maybe we should have, but we barely have enough budget to pay for office staff.' She stared at her hands, then shrugged. 'It's not like the corporations are falling over themselves to pay taxes.'

'Insurance?'

'This is the insurance.' Sonya glanced at Jack from under her brows. 'It's literally the best we can do.'

29

The rate of change is 10 times faster now than during the last event, which was 56 million years ago and resulted in the mass extinction of many benthic species, and the Great Dying 300 million years ago, when over 90% of the ocean species on planet Earth became extinct. Basically, evolution kicks in at each of the events and marine organisms re-evolve. Life on the planet will go on. Whether we are part of it or not is another matter.

C. Turley, Plymouth Marine Laboratory, oral evidence to the Parliamentary Committee on Science and Technology, 2017

If the *Coloma* looked like thistledown, the *Aphrodite* was some kind of nuclear-powered brick. Somewhere under the temporary scaffolding of strutwork and solid-fuel boosters was a ship, but one that wouldn't be revealed until after the deceleration phase of the mission and its arrival at KU2. The toroidal gravity section was clear, and turning already, and the docking port was sited ahead of Control, as it had been for the *Coloma*. The transport locked on, after waiting for an earlier shuttle to disengage, and Jack tethered his suit behind him. Sonya Agent stayed in her seat.

'God speed,' she said.

'Very traditional,' said Jack.

'Wishing you luck doesn't seem appropriate.'

'No. Not in the circumstances.' His hand hovered over the airlock button. 'I've not got anything to say. I'm disappointed.'

'Great lines from poets or playwrights?'

'Look on my works, you mighty, and despair?' He punched down, and the door slid aside. 'Thanks for the lift.'

He pulled his suit behind him into the airlock and cycled through into the *Aphrodite*, into the quiet busyness of a ship getting ready to leave. In Control, the consoles had actual seats with screens on retractable skeletal arms and foldaway keyboards, and where Runi would have sat there was a central pit with a holographic display, sited so everyone could see it.

There were two crew on deck. They both looked up from their screens as he entered, and both went back to their lists straight after.

'Captain's down the axis,' said the man. Now, he looked like a proper astronaut: square-headed, lantern-jawed, clean-shaven and high cheekboned. In truth, he looked like a cosmonaut, a living representation of Soviet-era art. The woman was an elf, slight and other-worldly. Neither resembled Jack: bald, shiny, with a spacer's pallor. They were the right stuff, and he, for all his genetic inheritance, was several steps below them.

'Sure,' said Jack, and headed for the shaft.

'You can leave your suit by the airlock.'

'Where does everyone else keep theirs?'

'Down in the EVA bay.'

'Then that's where I'll have to stow mine.' Perhaps they hadn't realised. 'I've been ... co-opted onto the crew.'

The cosmonaut stopped what he was doing and swivelled in his chair – the chair turned too, which was fancy. Jack could read his embroidered name badge now: M. Tamm.

'OSTO said they were sending a specialist,' he said, clearly not believing that Jack could be that person.

'I wouldn't have used that word, but okay.'

Now the elf – R. Suonpää – stopped too. 'You're the special-ist? Our oversight?'

'I don't know what you've been told by OSTO, because no one said anything to me about oversight.' Jack readjusted his grip on his spacesuit, finding odd comfort from it. 'I'm here to help, in any way I can.'

He didn't know what they were objecting to, because they hadn't said: his obvious spacer heritage, his age, or simply that he was there, breaking up their established dynamic, that he represented an outside authority, or that they were already deeply and unavoidably frightened of failure. Unless it was because they recognised him.

Perhaps he should just tell them. Their gazes were skittering all over his flightsuit – navy blue, compared to their royal blue, unadorned apart from the letters OSTO on the sleeve. They were looking for his name. Jack hoped that the *Aphrodite*'s captain had had a little more advance warning of his arrival, but if he had, he hadn't seen fit to tell his crew. Or perhaps the OSTO had dropped them all in the shit by not informing anyone.

'Jack,' he said, 'Jack ... Agent.' He'd been Jack Recycler for long enough. It was time for a change. 'You've read the *Coloma* report?'

'Yes. Of course.'

'I was Jack Astrogator in that.'

There followed a long moment while the pair of ESA astronauts recalibrated their responses. 'This is your fault' was on the tips of both their tongues. Neither seemed willing to go first, though.

'So I guess I'm not the person you were either expecting or wanting. And this whole scenario is, yes, my fault – I was on a crew that moved an asteroid into an Earth-crossing orbit. I'm not trying to escape any responsibility for what happened, and I would very much like to be responsible for fixing it. Which is why I'm here.'

'You shouldn't be,' said the cosmonaut.

That was final enough.

'I know that. But everyone else from the *Coloma* is dead. I'm literally the only person left alive who can tell you about the debris ring, the conditions on the surface, where the gallow-glass is, what the seismics said, and potentially where to place the bombs. I haven't done ten years in astronaut school, I haven't got a PhD, I'm not a mission specialist, I'm not a fast jet pilot, I'm not any of those things that you are. I'm not here to interfere with any of the mission-critical roles or events. I'm here to tell you what it was like, so that you can be prepared. And primarily, I'm here to try and stop you from being sued, so that you can concentrate on the job. That's all. That's what I'm here to do.' He didn't mention the five thousand hours of EVA he'd clocked up. 'I'll stow my suit, and find the captain.'

He pushed off down the axis like he'd done a hundred times before, pulling his suit behind him.

Jack passed the entryways to the rotating section, and headed further down to the technical and mechanical modules. The *Aphrodite* was newer than the *Coloma*, but it felt more solid. Its Jupiter mission profile was measured in years, not months, and there were plans for resupply ships to join it, if they weren't already on their way by a slower transfer orbit. Jack hadn't so much lost interest in wider events, as he hadn't dared to become invested in them.

And being here, in a place that only superficially resembled the interior of the *Coloma*, was enough to force a knot into his stomach. He remembered that feeling all too well. What could he do about that but swallow and breathe, swallow and breathe, and trust that it would pass, or at least fade into the background where he could deal with it privately?

As he hesitated and hovered, he became aware of being watched. A man, ESA crew, older and balder than the cosmonaut, was hanging off a curved bulkhead door down near the far end of the axis. The man stopped watching, and with a twist of his body, headed up the tunnel towards him.

Mariucci. L. Mariucci.

'You must be Jaap van der Veerden,' said the man. 'Thank you for coming.'

The nausea started to recede.

'You okay? Want some water?'

'Give me a moment,' said Jack. 'Memories. I didn't think it'd be like this.'

'Sure. Take your time.'

Jack screwed his face up and blinked back the pain. If this man knew his name, then he was going to be in charge.

'You can call me Captain, or Commander Mariucci, or the Old Man, or O Captain my Captain. What do I call you?'

'Jack. I introduced myself as Jack Agent up in Control. That's my role here, right?'

'More or less. Although we call it Command.' The captain regarded Jack with curiosity. 'It will be said that you caused this whole situation.'

It had been said already. 'Will we be under way before the news gets out?'

'The timing of that is out of my hands, as we're not the only people with telescopes and an interest in KU2, but I think we might.'

'I won't be listening to the news, and there'll be nothing anyone can do to bring me back. The only thing I'll have to worry about is the rest of your crew.'

'You have some spicy sauce, Jack.'

'I didn't know that you hadn't briefed them before I'd arrived. So I ended up walking into a wall of blame in *Command*. I blame me, so there's no reason why they shouldn't, but it's not going to help anyone concentrate.'

'We have twelve hydrogen bombs on board, and yet you are the most volatile thing we carry.'

'That might be true, but I won't be the one going boom.'

'No. You won't, and neither will anyone else. The crew are professionals: however, they are also human. They have family and friends on Earth they're worried they'll never see again. When I formally introduce you, I will lay down the law.'

Jack caught the implication. 'And before then?'

281

'I cannot stop people talking to each other, Jack. A good captain knows when to permit dissent and when to prevent it. And how. You're a "spacer", yes? You don't mind being disliked, just as long as everyone works together? I can't make them be your friends, but I will tell them to leave you alone.'

'That's probably the best I can expect. I have to be here, no matter what. Do the job, go home.' Jack listened to the fans for a moment. 'You don't want me on board, do you?'

'You are our specialist, and as such we welcome the insights you bring.' He tried to sound sincere, but he failed. 'This is a complication and a disruption, but there's no other way. We're all going to have to make the best of it. Jack, I am content with OSTO's decision to send you, but I cannot make anyone like it. Is that understood?'

'Crystal clear.' Jack had accepted that he wasn't there to win hearts and minds, but the stark reality was sobering. 'Where do I put my suit?'

'I'll show you. Your kit goes next to your bunk.'

'Unless OSTO want to freight out the spare pairs of shorts I've left in my locker, this is it.'

'Nothing?'

'I can remember the few passwords I need. Otherwise, no.' Jack pulled his suit towards him, and took hold of the upper right arm. 'This is all I've needed for the last few years. I've worked every day of that, and today was no exception. I'll stow my suit and get some rest.'

Whether Mariucci found the tang of lunar dust distasteful, or respected the labour required to pick up the scent, he didn't say. But he did smell it. His Roman nose twitched, and his gaze took in the scratched visor and the well-worn outer integument. Jack was no dilettante, whatever his family name suggested.

'Follow me. I'll show you where.'

The EVA module had an airlock on the inside as well as the outside.

'Pressurising up to fifteen psi?'

282

'Standard procedure. You're used to five?'

'All the time. The *Coloma* was at fifteen, but that's been the only environment I've worked in at one atmosphere. Otherwise, it's been lunar standard atmosphere.'

The captain pointed to the racks. Pristine white spacesuits were displayed, almost like museum exhibits, behind perspex doors. Jack did a quick head count. Six suits. His would be the seventh, although there was room for a good dozen. His suit, and specifically his life support, were a commercial brand, and definitely not ESA standard.

'My LS sockets aren't going to fit your regenerator,' he said.

'Adaptors?'

'You'll need to find them, or a whole new suit for me. But you'll need to get them for Cat Gallowglass's suit anyway, which is the same style. Neither of us can hot-swap our backpacks.'

'I'll put them on the list.'

'It's a Chinese clone of a Z8, with a PLSS manufacture date of 2070.'

'Got that.'

'I can order the parts myself. Or I can make them out of a flight manual, some duct tape and a couple of socks.'

'I'll get you the adaptors.' Mariucci almost smiled. 'You're going to have to trust me, just as I'm going to have to trust you.'

Jack hung up his suit in one of the lockers, and left his life support in the unit for now. 'That's going to be a big ask for some.'

'We'll survive, Jack. Now, I won't be rostering you. You don't know the ship, and the commissioning crew do. They don't need your help, although they might ask for it. If you're bored, we have a full entertainment suite, and gymnasium, and Il Dottore will want to give you a medical for a baseline, and expect you to comply with his regime for the rest of the flight. You'll be required to lecture the crew on KU2, aid us in image interpretation, and lend general assistance on an ad hoc basis.

Otherwise, your time is yours. You may find that uncomfortable, for which I apologise in advance.'

'So I'm supposed to do … nothing? While everyone else is working? You know how that's going to look to them, don't you?'

'Your work ethic is admirable.'

Jack pressed his hands to his face and dragged them down his cheeks. 'Do you want them to hate me even more?'

'There will be considerable media interest in this mission,' said the captain. It seemed a digression, but Jack went with it.

'Yes, okay.'

'The crew will be on camera some of the time. How do you feel about that?'

'I … I haven't thought about that at all.'

'This will be very different to what you're used to, either with the *Coloma* or with Selenite. People will know you're on board. They'll want to talk to you, interview you, demand to know what the hell you thought you were doing putting a live asteroid on a collision course with the Earth and threatening billions with death.' Mariucci cocked his head. 'Would you be okay with that?'

'No.' Jack felt his insides shrivel. 'That wouldn't be okay. That …' He couldn't think of the words to describe just how awful it would be.

'Then we'll have to agree that there will be give and take. You get some of the things you want, and we get some of the things we want. We must succeed, for the sake of the planet. My job is to maximise the chances of us doing so, and I will use you to that end. Your free will is a thing of the past, Jack van der Veerden: it is suspended until I say otherwise.'

Jack took a moment. The last time he'd felt this intimidated was when he'd faced Mesman in the spaceport. But he felt that same cold-water wash now. 'I will do what you want.'

'Good. Because if I thought otherwise, you would be back on the transport, along with a strongly worded letter to OSTO.

You are here because you add something to the mission. Outside of that something, you detract a greater amount.' Mariucci checked they were alone in the module. 'I will have to fight for your presence here, against my own crew. You have already put me in a position I do not want. I do not say this unkindly, but we have no room for personal feelings. There is no room for hurt, for regret, for anger, for petulance. We need unity of purpose, clarity and focus. For now, I own you. In return, I will give you your chance at redemption. Whatever we do, however we do it, you will not let me down. *Capisce?'*

30

Two gravities was what the space plane had pulled when it left Peenemünde. Jack had managed it without a problem. Now, four years later, it was unbearable. Twenty-five minutes of continuous acceleration, simply to break themselves out of the solar orbit and drive in towards the Sun. The ship's plasma drive would take care of the course corrections, but at the other end the *Aphrodite* would place itself between the onrushing asteroid and the Earth and force another burn, timed precisely so that by the time KU2 caught them up, they would be moving at the same speed and in the same direction.

The shining gods that were ESA-trained astronauts had been subjected to far worse and were far better prepared for the crushing weight and the feeling of suffocation that came with it than he was. Two gravities was nothing. People regularly had far more on roller coasters. Fast jet pilots pulled five as a matter of course. But for Jack, who had grown used to lunar gravity, two gravities was killing him. It was twelve times what he'd call normal. He was weak. He was unfit. He was dying.

If he lived, he was going to hit the gym hard. Weight-bearing exercise, sustained effort, cardio work: the lot. If this was all it took to reduce him to a useless, boneless mess, then he'd have to do something about it.

If he lived: he couldn't currently move. His seat in Command was digging holes into his fragile skin, and even the folds in the cloth of his flightsuit had turned into blunt knives. His legs were canted forward in the direction of travel, but there was no blood left in them. His head was fractionally lower than his heart, and everything was pooling there. His headache was threatening to turn into a stroke.

The clock on every screen told him how much longer he had to go. Twenty minutes. Somewhere outside, the Moon had receded and the Earth swelled briefly before shrinking and becoming a binary system, blue and white points of light together against the dark. A solid-fuel booster, strapped to the scaffolding, burned white-hot and pushed them further away.

Momentary respite came when the first booster exhausted itself. Gravity fell to zero. Jack gasped at the pain in his head and his feet. The *Aphrodite* shuddered as explosive bolts kicked the empty canister away, and for a few brief seconds all was quiet except the sounds of breathing.

'Acceleration acceleration.'

Bang.

Jack was forced back against his seat padding. It hurt even to blink, but he couldn't stare at the forward bulkhead until the clock hit zero. The throbbing in his temples was impossible to ignore, and precluded any of the mind games he might play to distract himself. He was in hell, and reliving the worst moments of his life on a loop. All the indignities of childhood, of his teenage years, of more recent times. The death of friends. Of WhitetailDeer. Of Patricio. Of Andros. Of May. The thumping of a fist on an airlock door matched the pulse in his veins.

And that rock, that damned rock, haunted by the ghost of a gallowglass he'd never met with a name he'd forgotten until now: Castor. The friend that Cat had betrayed and murdered, throwing an entire nation into the fire at the same time. This was his revenge: making the fortresses of the rich in the north and the south experience the same existential fear as his people on the equator had. If his parents, his aunts and uncles, his brothers and sisters were going to be allowed to burn, then why not make that experience available to everyone?

How was he going to talk Cat round? Could he persuade her to give up her claim? What if she rejected the OSTO-brokered offer? Her own people were already reduced to stateless refugees, divided and dispersed, but she was proud: she'd hold out for everything she could get.

It was impossible. It was all doomed to failure. The bombs on board would be insufficient. The asteroid would fall, and the world would be utterly changed in the blink of an eye. They were cursed by a dead gallowglass and held to ransom by a live one. It was over, it was over already.

'Acceleration acceleration.'

The pressure fell away, and Jack looked at the clock. Minus one. Minus two. Minus three. It was over. He raised his hands to his face and pressed his palms against his eyes, his fingers digging into his scalp. It was over, and he'd survived.

Almost immediately, the rest of the crew started doing things: checking systems, calibrating sensors, training telescopes on distant stars and matching their angles against the ephemeris. All Jack could do was lie in his chair and breathe heavily. The pain was slowly receding, but the memory of it remained.

'Life support nominal.'

'Plasma drive online.'

'Sensor array active.'

'High gain at forty-five decibels.'

'Power at one hundred and thirteen per cent. Preparing to deploy radiators.'

'Spin up the torus.'

'Spinning up on my mark. Three, two, one. Mark.'

'Burn complete at T-plus twenty-four fifty-seven.'

'Astrogation?'

Jack raised his head, but the call wasn't for him, and he let himself drift back. He wasn't there to provide mundane checks on navigation, let alone heroic feats. The thing he was best at, he wasn't allowed to do. He was in space again, but more as a passenger than crew. He had some insights. He could talk to Cat. Otherwise, he was a spare part.

He reached down and punched the buckle on his harness. The cool ship's air flowed across his back, chilling the hollows where sweat had pooled. He wondered if the ESA astronauts did anything as uncouth as sweat. They looked perfect.

He felt the stubble on his head, and on his face. That had started to happen only recently. He'd never had a fast face, but now he had to run a clipper over his cheeks and chin as often as he did over his head and the nape of his neck. Clippers were standard on commercial crews: someone was always willing to play barber, male or female or whatever, it didn't matter. It was the only physical contact he'd had in months.

If there weren't any on board, then ... scissors, he supposed. There were things that he just took for granted now. Including being all but bald.

He shrugged his harness off and peeled his moisture-darkened flightsuit away from his sticky skin, and left the crew, the real crew, to finish their post-burn checklists. He was going to head to the torus, and ... he didn't know what. He'd spent the last few days watching people engage in purposeful activity while they ignored him. He'd listened to music, he'd read some books, he'd watched some old movies – the newer ones all had the spectre of unfolding climate disaster in the background, and he found he couldn't bear it – and he absolutely had stayed offline, not even talking to History. He didn't trust himself not to say anything early. He still didn't know if the news had broken yet.

He wondered what his parents would think. All that planning, all that self-denial, and they could die just like anyone else.

Would it shock them into changing, or did they have a plan for this scenario too? He guessed they had, and he also guessed that the sheer scale of the catastrophe might overwhelm any preparations they could have made.

The ground would ripple and break, the tsunami would be vast, the darkness would be for a decade. If they did live through it, they'd emerge into a world where their wealth would be useless. The survivors would value more basic things than gold.

Part of him was drawn to that. Just so he could confront them and ask them if it had been, in the end, worth it.

This was why he so desperately needed something to do. To distract him, and take his mind away from the apocalyptic thoughts that were swirling around him. Ghosts, flying rock, black space, white light, and the thump-thump-thump of a fist against a heavy door.

He made it into the axis and pulled himself as far as the transit tunnels. The crew quarters wrapped the *Aphrodite* in an unbroken ring, so unlike on the *Coloma* it didn't matter which tunnel he used, he'd get to where he was headed eventually. The torus was running on a one-third-g spin, and the acceleration from the plasma drive wasn't even a couple of per cent of that, not enough to throw him off balance.

The whole design brief was different to the *Coloma*. The *Aphrodite* was a science ship, a collaborative, collegiate endeavour, where everyone was expected to share not just their working hours, but their lives. The dozen cots were still separate cubicles arranged around the circumference, but much more integrated into the rest of the furniture – the desks, the gym equipment, the entertainment and games areas, the galley and the wet rooms.

The commissioning crew had taken cots near each other. Jack had found an unoccupied one ninety degrees spinward. He didn't have anything to put in it to mark it as his, but it became his nevertheless. He opened the door, checked his bedding was still in the place where he'd left it strapped down. It was.

He closed the door again, and stood in the middle of the ring, looking up at the arc of the floor curving around to meet him, and then behind him, at it soaring away. He'd run around it a few times, just to say he'd done it, just to say to other people that he'd done it, but it wasn't that interesting, and every revolution he'd see the same off-duty astronauts narrow their eyes as he passed by. No one needed that.

One-third gravity was twice what he was used to, but it wasn't a chore. It made him tired, and that was okay, because then he could sleep a lot, in the dark, with ear plugs in, and he didn't have to get up for anything specific. Not being tired was his enemy.

'Three months. Thirteen weeks. What the hell am I going to do between now and then?' He said it out loud, and there was no one around to answer him. The acceleration phase had scared him in a way that nothing much had recently. He needed to hold onto that raw, naked emotion and channel it into something constructive.

He collected one of the tablets from the rack and tapped it open, navigating through the files and icons until he got to the flight manuals. First up, configuration of the ship, systems and functions. He slipped it into the holder on top of a treadmill, fastened the elastic straps around his waist that would hold him down better against the moving road, and started the machine up.

After a while, he stopped, stripped down to his shorts and resumed. He wasn't moving quickly, a gentle jog rather than a serious run, but he was at least moving. And while he moved, he read. He looked away to see if he could recall information, and looked back to check he had it correctly before scrolling on.

He kept going long after his legs had told him he should stop. And when he finally turned the machine off and the rollers glided to a halt, he found he had an audience. He leaned on the arms of the treadmill, sweat running down his body, and he felt abruptly self-conscious. He was being examined.

His watcher threw him a towel, which spun and opened in mid-air, folding itself over one shoulder. Jack made no attempt to catch it, just calculated its passage and waited for it to land.

'Thank you.'

'You're welcome.' L. Rossard. He had a French flag on his left arm. 'I'm your doctor,' he said.

'I'm not sick.'

'I've talked to the captain. I know you're expecting me.'

'I can refuse.'

'You can refuse me. You cannot refuse the captain. And since he has already said you require a medical, you cannot refuse me either. Not in this.' He cocked his head to one side. 'It will take only a little of your time. Shower first. Then find me in the infirmary. Yes? We could fight over this, but you would lose, and there seems little point in expending our energies over something so futile.'

Jack dragged the towel across his face. 'I had a medical when I joined Selenite.'

'Then you know what to expect.'

To forestall any further argument, the doctor walked away around the torus, leaving Jack to rerack the tablet and stand under the shower for longer than was strictly necessary. He'd review the ship's systems later, and see if he couldn't access the astrogation software. He might even remember how to use it.

If he was feeble physically, he was a mess emotionally. He should probably acknowledge that to himself, even if he wasn't going to tell anyone else. He'd run away to space with only a vague idea of what to do, had ended up, entirely by chance, with a job that could have made him if it had gone right, and instead, it had broken him. Even then, he'd used every gram of his skill to get them back home despite the horror of what had gone before. After that, working for Yao? It was the only job he could get. His name was toxic because he'd done nothing while May had been killed. He hadn't prevented it, but neither had

292

he participated: he'd put his own feelings in front of what had been best for the crew.

His lover, his saboteur, his traitor. If she'd killed him along with Patricio, would she have dreamed of his body expanding in a cloud of plasma? If she'd succeeded in hijacking the mission and its prize, would she count her millions as nothing but dust and ash because she'd sacrificed him to get them? Probably not. Those calculations had already been made.

He turned the water off, towelled himself dry and let the automated dryer reclaim the rest of the moisture. He pulled on his shorts, flightsuit and ship slippers, and presented himself for examination.

'What do I call you?'

'You can call me Doctor, or Laurent, or Laurent Doctor, after the fashion of commercial space crew. It's up to you.' He brandished a blood-pressure cuff. 'Do you prefer Jaap, or Jack?'

'Jack. I've been Jack for a while now.'

'I need to see your body. I'm not a tailor.'

The examination room could double as a tiny operating theatre, and most of the equipment was still wrapped in protective plastic. Jack's first instinct was to wonder if any of it was going to be recycled for its volatiles: long- and short-chain hydrocarbons carried a premium in the Cis-lunar economy.

He unzipped his flightsuit and threw it to the floor, and stood there in all his pale glory. Only his face was tanned.

'How old are you?'

'What's the date?'

'2076. January.'

'Twenty-seven. Twenty-eight in April.'

'How long have you been in low-gravity environments, cumulative and consecutive?'

'Four years, and four years.'

'You've not returned to Earth once?'

'No.'

'Why not?'

293

'I don't intend to ever go back.'

'The effects of long-term exposure to low gravity are becoming apparent. Almost all of them are deleterious to the human body. Your life expectancy is likely to be reduced quite drastically.'

'I realise that. I have, in fact, factored that in.'

That earned him a sideways look from Laurent. 'Very well.' He slipped the cuff over Jack's hand and slid it up past his elbow. He pressed some buttons on the box, and it whirred and beeped. The cuff inflated to its maximum. Jack's face twitched at the discomfort, but a few seconds later the cuff began to deflate again. 'These readings are low.'

'I know. I'm in twice my usual gravity.'

'That you are young and active and reasonably fit may have so far saved you from the worst effects. From a brief examination of your body, you've lost muscle, and that will include heart muscle. You're potentially suffering from nutritional deficiencies, too. I can do some blood work, but it'll be easier to assume the findings and put you on a high-protein diet with supplements. Regular, increasing weight-bearing exercise and tests of cognitive functions should also follow.' The doctor canted his head to one side again. 'You haven't looked after yourself, and your previous medicals would have picked that up. I'm supposing you ignored both the results and the recommendations.'

'You don't have to be a highly trained specialist in peak physical condition to do useful work in space. No one expects that any more.'

'Useful work? You call what you did useful work? You pushed an asteroid towards our only home!' He dropped his hands by his sides, and went back to a bench and tidied everything away that he had been going to use, but now clearly wasn't. 'I'm sorry, that wasn't very professional of me,' he said. 'My husband is back on Earth. I worry about him.'

'And you blame me.'

294

'I blame the lack of regulation that permitted this to happen. That it was you is the least important fact about this. We should fix this, and then take steps to ensure that it could never happen again.'

'Agreed.'

'You do?'

'No one should be in this position. It shouldn't be possible to be in this position. But we find ourselves in this position all the same.'

Rossard leaned on the counter, then he began to retrieve his instruments, one by one. 'With your permission, perhaps we could begin again?'

'Yes. That would ... yes. Okay.'

31

Number of displacements due to weather-related events 2008–2016: 195.7 million.

Global Report on Internal Displacement, Internal Displacement Monitoring Centre, 2017

The meeting was held in Command, not in the torus, because Captain Mariucci wanted to make use of the holographic plotter. Jack wasn't the first nor the last to arrive. There were more seats than crew, but Jack had observed that every crew member had their particular favourite, so he avoided those, choosing one of the others more or less at random.

The air had thawed very slightly in the week they'd been in flight. He knew their first names, and knew whether they wanted him to use them or not. They all disliked the commercial naming convention, but they did use Jack Agent to his face. He had no idea what they were calling him behind his back, let alone what people were saying about him on Earth, but some of that seemed to be leaking out in the attitudes of those on board. The benefits of a news blackout was something ESA could learn about.

They assembled. There was no captain yet. Colvin, the astrogator, talked quietly with Suonpää, the pilot, while the atomjacks – the nuclear demolition technicians – stared pointedly at the empty plotter. Rossard was the only one to acknowledge Jack.

He strapped himself in, and was just adjusting his buckles

when the captain entered, hand over hand, like a man in a hurry. He'd tethered a tablet to his forearm, and it clattered around on the end of its coiled cord before he brought it under control.

'I won't keep you waiting,' he said. 'There is good news and there is bad news.'

The plotter flared, and the lasers drew shapes in the air: curving lines and rotating spheres.

'Current predictions show that KU2 will pass Earth at a distance of three to five thousand kilometres. It will break up due to tidal forces. The orbit of any potential fragments will change: all of them are expected to achieve escape velocity, but at least some, and potentially all of them, will strike the Moon in multiple impacts, three and a half hours later.'

He let the scenario play out in coloured lights, and left the final outcome turning and winking, motes of dust surrounding a grid-drawn planet.

'Anyone on the lunar surface will most likely be killed. Any structure on the lunar surface will be destroyed. Ejecta will achieve lunar escape velocity, but not terrestrial escape velocity. Anyone in lunar orbit will also most likely be killed. Any structure in lunar orbit will most likely be destroyed. The debris will coalesce in a loose planetary ring, which may take in the region of a thousand to ten thousand years to dissipate. Most of it will fall to Earth, causing localised damage. Some of it will re-accrete on the Moon, increasing the impact rate there for millennia.'

Rossard stirred, and circled his finger in the air. 'And for those without a background in astrophysics?'

'Earth will not be hit by the main mass, but there will be repeated minor impacts caused by deorbiting debris. Minor being in the kilotonne to low megatonne TNT-equivalent range. Which we would essentially have no warning of. We would lose most, if not all of our satellites, over a period of days and months. We would be able to replace the LEO satellites, but anything beyond that, including our communications and GPS hardware, would be impossible, as those orbits would lie within the debris ring. Space flight will be rendered impractical for centuries. We will be essentially Earthbound for as long as the disc persists.'

'And if we fail to divert the asteroid, how would we get back home?'

'There would be no infrastructure remaining to allow for that journey.'

The doctor leaned forward and frowned at the display, falling silent.

'Anyone else?'

'We've avoided immediate execution, but not imprisonment and torture,' said the pilot. She tightened the band restraining her ponytail. 'A different sentence for our meddling.'

She didn't look at Jack, but the atomjacks did, briefly, before looking away.

'Does this alter our mission profile?' she asked. 'Do we have to push the target harder to avoid this scenario? And how many fragments, and of what size, are we expecting?'

'I will tell you plainly,' said the captain. 'This scenario is far more complex than simply making sure the asteroid doesn't hit Earth. The chances of the Moon being in the wrong place at the wrong time were quantifiable but very small. It is unfortunate that that is what we have to deal with. However, once the asteroid is within the Roche limit, it will begin to lose integrity. At that point, it turns from a bullet into a shotgun shell. The orbital deflection caused by the mass of the Earth will separate the fragments out, increasing the arc of potential collisions. We cannot predict either the mass or the number of the fragmentation products, because we don't have the seismic data from the *Coloma*.'

Now they did all look at Jack. He cleared his throat, tried to speak and cleared his throat again.

'You,' and he still couldn't get the words out. The animation in the projector was terrifying. He tried again. 'You're looking at potentially three major fragments, two stony, one an iron-nickel mass under the north pole. I would say seventy to eighty per cent by volume is in those three masses. The rest is just rubble, anything from dust to car-sized boulders, but there's nothing holding it together. So, three impactors, plus the rest.'

They continued to stare.

'You want more? I can put all this in a document, circulate it. The asteroid is a tumbler. It may have got worse. The surface is lethal. I haven't even told you about the debris ring yet. Basically, it's a mess.'

'Your mining laser,' asked Colvin. 'How did you operate it?'

'The laser was on station at twenty-five k altitude. Fixed point, held by thrusters, so that we could drive the asteroid continuously, firing at the surface over the centre of mass. As the asteroid rotated, the laser dug a trench, the sides sintered, and it kept its shape. We had one area which burned erratically. We were looking for volatiles when Patricio died. It's all in the report. We never did find out what was causing the vibrations.'

It was probably the most he'd spoken since his deposition to OSTO.

'I don't know what happened after we left. How long the laser burned for, whether the laser, or the solar panels, are still there in orbit. When we get a model of the asteroid, I can fill in the seismic details as best as I can remember. Anything else you need to know, I'm not going anywhere.'

The silence that followed wasn't one filled with awe at his knowledge, but neither was it as hostile and scratchy as he'd feared.

'Thank you, Jack,' said Mariucci. 'We have sufficient to work with for now. So there you have it. Our task is to save the future. While Earth no longer faces an existential risk, it remains in extreme danger. We had a plan to steer all of the asteroid away from the Earth. Now we need a different plan to steer all of the asteroid away from the Moon. That will take delicate judgement and skill. Take a moment to digest the importance of the task, then be about your work, please.'

The crew dispersed, back to the torus, to talk things over. Jack knew he wasn't wanted, and he was much more comfortable in zero-g, so he dallied. He didn't have anything explicit to do – more reading, more exercise – and his speech had been the first time he felt he'd actually contributed. Still, being a passenger sat uneasily about his shoulders.

Mariucci looked up from behind the holographic display. 'Come closer, Jack. Come closer and tell me what you see.'

Jack unclipped himself from his seat and pulled himself to the edge of the pit. The lights danced within the display and reflected against his face.

'Wind it back?' he asked.

The asteroid re-formed, leapt from the surface of the Moon, coalesced into a single mass and retreated around the Earth.

'What's the error on this? Three thousand k isn't much of a miss ... it's too close.'

'The figure of three thousand is the closest possible approach at a confidence of ninety-five per cent. The mean statistical average from the simulations is four and a half thousand. That will still break the asteroid apart and put it in the path of the Moon.'

'Do we have enough delta-v to push the asteroid beyond the Roche limit?'

'Eighteen thousand kilometres? No. In the time we have, with the weapons we have, we can move it laterally just over one lunar radius.'

'Enough to save the Earth. Not enough to save the Moon.'

'Ironic, yes?'

'I wouldn't call it that. Not out loud, anyway.' Jack let the orbits speak to him. 'Three and a half hours from closest approach to Earth, to when it reaches the Moon. That's enough time to identify which fragments are going to hit, and not enough time to do anything about them.'

'I'm looking for something extraordinary, Jack.'

'How many bombs would it take to break the asteroid apart early?'

'Go on.'

'Blow it up as soon as we get there. If there are three pieces that aren't going to fall apart, then we can concentrate on them and plot their courses accurately. See if there's any we can safely leave, and nudge the rest out of the way with the bombs we have left. The asteroid will shatter anyway when we try and move it.'

'So your suggestion is to disrupt the asteroid as soon as possible, identify potential impactors and leave, disrupt or move them as necessary?' Mariucci pursed his lips and regarded the display. 'There is a minority report from the ESA taskforce that proposes the same thing. They believe, like you do, that disrupting the asteroid prematurely makes good sense. More senior members of the taskforce disagree, and their plan to simultaneously detonate the entire payload carries considerable weight.'

'This idea gives you more control.'

'If I send you the minority report, will you read it and give me your comments? In private?'

Jack looked at the captain over the mass of glowing light. 'You want me to keep this secret?'

'Yes. For reasons you well understand.' Mariucci touched the display console and the dot that was the asteroid approached the Earth, broke in sparks and tore off chunks of the Moon.

'The crew blame me for all this.'

'Of course they blame you. In the absence of anyone else to blame, they blame you. Il Dottore tells me little, but I understand even you blame yourself.' He switched the display off. The lights faded and died, but Jack could still see them. 'That we agree on this is good, but not essential. I know my crew, and know that some of them disagree with me on important matters. But I want them to disagree with me, and not you.

301

This is not a democracy, as you might be used to. No one has a vote. Not you and not me. I do have influence, and I need that undiluted. So, in the event of you being asked your opinion on how best to deflect the asteroid, you will be non-committal, lukewarm. Yes?'

'I get it.' He did. He didn't have to like it, but he understood it.

'I'll send you a link to the proposals. Read them, and delete the link.'

'Okay.'

'Good man.'

Jack took that as his cue to leave. He pushed off for the axis.

'Are your certificates up to date?'

He hung off a handle. 'Yes, captain.'

'Thank you.'

He pushed himself along to the transfer tubes and descended into the torus. The rest of the crew were already there, clustered in one of the recreation areas, leaning forward and talking urgently with each other. Two of the voices were raised, angry, accusatory. The doctor was playing peacemaker, but some weren't having it. If they'd realised that their job had become far more complicated, with less chance of success, then this was the fall-out.

Jack avoided them, collected a tablet and signed in, and waited for the report Mariucci had promised him to turn up. He made himself a coffee – hot coffee that tasted like coffee, not the tepid brown drink that was common to lower-pressure environments – and was heading for his cot when someone shouted his name.

'Van der Veerden. You were in there a long time. What did the Old Man say to you?'

So it was back to Van der Veerden now, and he wondered how he should respond. 'He was just making sure I had my certificates. Asking about my EVA experience.'

He started to turn away, when the voice – it was Tamm, the

Estonian atomjack – called out: 'We see you, Van der Veerden. We see you.'

'Okay. I'm not here to fight. I was co-opted to help. If you've got questions about the mission, I'll answer them. Otherwise, I'm just going to go and take a nap.'

'How can you sleep, Van der Veerden?'

He turned back. 'Honestly? Badly. I worked hard, every day, so I was exhausted enough that I would pretty much pass out. These last couple of weeks haven't been so good for me.'

They were watching him, judging him. Hating him, even. Dr Rossard seemed ready to intervene, but he too had conflicting loyalties. They were unified, and Jack was the outsider, and a problematic one at that.

'Why are you even here?'

His tablet decided to beep with a notification. Incoming message. The report.

'ESA wanted me here,' said Jack. 'I left everything and came.'

'We don't need you.'

It was good they were having this out now, rather than later, but it still got under his skin and made him itch. 'What do you want me to do? Go and take a hammer to the nuclear warheads? Shut the O$_2$ valves off? Try and put a hole in the hull? Smash up the screens in Command? Is that what you want? You want an excuse to space me? Throw me out the airlock without my suit? You want to hear me banging against the door, begging you not to pump it down? Is that it? Is that where we're going with this?'

They had all read the *Coloma* report. They all knew what he was talking about, and Tamm didn't have an answer. Perhaps he hated Jack more because of that, but Jack didn't care.

'We're all crew. We're all here to get the job done. My job is to brief you about the asteroid, and try to talk Cat Gallowglass round. And when we're done, we can go our separate ways. If you've got anything else to say, take it up with the captain. I'm not doing this again.'

303

If they did want to space him, and the captain didn't, and that fact was the only thing keeping him alive for the moment, then he'd take it. He glared at them all, individually, even Rossard. They'd do their duty, even though they knew they were in space because they were special, worthy, the elect. Not like those grubby spacers, toiling in workshops and refineries and shuttles and ships. They were above all that.

'You're supposed to be better than me. Remember?' He took his cooling coffee and his tablet and went to his cot. When he'd stopped shaking, he read about how it might be possible to stop a loosely bound asteroid from striking the Moon at thirty kilometres a second.

32

2018 was 1.5 degrees Fahrenheit (0.83 degrees Celsius) warmer than the 1951 to 1980 mean, according to scientists at NASA's Goddard Institute for Space Studies (GISS) in New York. Globally, 2018's temperatures rank behind those of 2016, 2017 and 2015. The past five years are, collectively, the warmest years in the modern record.

NASA Goddard Space Flight Center, press release, 2019

Mariucci announced they were going to run through the possible scenarios. He included one where they were left with a choice as to which of the Moon-impacting fragments of asteroid they would move, and which they would have to leave.

'All of them have to be wargamed, and we have to be ready for whatever happens,' said the captain. 'In those cases where we cannot move everything, we will have already decided what to move and what to leave.'

'I'm not comfortable with that,' said Colvin, the astrogator.

'None of us is.' The other atomjack, Vrána, took the display's controls and rotated the asteroid. They had good images of it now. The laser-burned equatorial trench was easily visible, and although the resolution wasn't yet good enough to see detail, there were clear hints of spiralling tracks across the rocks where the laser had gone off course before failing.

They couldn't yet tell if Cat's ship had survived, and that would be only the first step in establishing whether Cat herself had survived. If she had, it would be considered a miracle; but in the current situation, whether she'd lived or died was going to barely warrant a footnote.

Jack had filled in the interior of the asteroid from memory. He'd sat for hours at a time, trying to match the shapes he drew to what he'd seen, going back and refining the model again and again, until he couldn't be sure that he wasn't just fooling himself.

It was as good as it was going to get. Reality would prove the ultimate test, and if he'd got it all wildly wrong, then people were going to die.

Jack asked whether the Moon was being evacuated, whether the refineries and orbital manufactories were being shut down and mothballed. The answer was a terse yes. But whether they were or whether they weren't wasn't going to make any material difference to what they did on the *Aphrodite*.

Instead, he circled his hand at the display. 'Can anyone use the sandbox?'

'Yes,' said Mariucci. 'There are no prizes for the best answer, but there's no harm in everyone trying. The working group at ESA are all running the numbers on the same software: if anyone comes up with what they think is a solution to a particular problem, then send it to me and I can get Earth to check it.'

'Thanks.'

'If the ship's computer starts to run slow, then I'll have to limit the processing time,' said Suonpää.

Was she warning him off? Perhaps. It wasn't going to stop him: Jack had some ideas that he wanted to explore, even if other, more qualified people were running the same simulations.

'Will we also be modelling the effects of any potential lunar impacts, Captain?'

'Off-ship, but yes, because that will directly influence our decisions here.'

'And will that include a potential death toll?'

Not so much warning him off as beating him down, and the Old Man could see that.

'Yes. Of course. We will be following an entirely utilitarian ethic here. What brings the most benefits to the most people is the course we will steer. Everybody understands this, yes?'

Everyone did, eventually.

'When the time comes, which it surely will, we will already have decided what to do. If this happens, then this. If that happens, then that. I have previously explained this to some of you,' and he had the grace not to look directly at Jack, 'but it bears repeating. You do not have free will. You will do as I say, when I say it, according to plans we have already agreed on and practised. You will know what to do, each and every one of you. No egos. No heroes. I expect no more nor less of you than that you play your part when called to do so.'

That quietened the pilot down. She was, as far as Jack had gleaned, a fast jet pilot, a war veteran, an incredibly safe pair of hands, but he couldn't help thinking that someone else would be better in this situation. Someone more cautious, more willing to listen, more able to feel their way through the problems. There was a lot to be said for not believing that you had all the answers before you asked any of the questions.

'We will be ready. When we fire the remaining boosters, there will be no more time to try things out. We execute the plan, we work our way through the decision tree, and we make certain we have done the very best job we can. Use this time wisely. There will be new scenarios to explore every day, sent by the working group. You should submit your own, too. That is all.'

The crew were very good at knowing what to do when dismissed. They all had roles to play, checklists to work through and equipment to maintain. Jack had nothing but his self-imposed routine.

'I suppose it's out of the question that you've managed to find me a job on board?'

'Sadly, yes,' said the captain.

'I'll go back to the torus and carry on making my way through your coffee stocks, then.'

307

'The crew are giving you a hard time?'

'When they can be bothered to talk to me at all.'

'When we arrive at KU2, you'll have more than enough to do. You'll be on the EVA team to retrieve Catherine Vi. We have brought an inflatable hab, at your suggestion, which can be constructed around the gallowglass ship to make that transition easier. It will need to be anchored to the surface, but once it's inflated Il Dottore will revive her if that proves possible, and you will be there to greet her.'

'You know she won't sign the asteroid over unless we offer her something?'

'It's in hand, Jack.'

'I was promised it'll be here before we revive her.'

'I was told the same.' The captain equivocated. 'Do not put your faith in that.'

'So just what am I here for? I'm grateful that I am,' Jack gestured at the simulation, 'that I have a chance to do this, but how am I supposed to persuade her to take an offer that might not even exist?'

'You're here because you're someone she recognises. And trusts, to some degree. You may be the only one alive that she does. At least, you gave her a chance when no one else was prepared to.' Mariucci leaned back in his chair. 'You ran away to space, didn't you?'

'I studied hard, did a degree, took some extra units, and managed to divert enough money from my allowance to pay for a seat on a space plane. Only then did I run away to space.'

'There were, most likely, easier ways of getting up here.'

'Not for me. Captain, I've worked continuously since I left Earth. I've got more time in space than anyone on this ship, and I've done more roles. You think it's a big thing to do a multi-hour EVA, but for me, that's where I work, every day. I don't want you thinking that I'm just some poor little rich kid, slumming it until he's had enough and goes home to Mam and Pap.'

308

'Can you go home?'

'Probably, yes. The temptation is always there. You have a crappy day at work, some idiot puts a hole in their suit, the hopper doesn't start up, the job isn't as advertised. Your lover tries to kill you and accidentally throws an asteroid at the Moon ...' Jack shrugged.

'I think the time has come to talk to the crew. I wanted to avoid doing so, but I see now that it was a miscalculation on my part. You are completely right: you are, by any metric, the most experienced astronaut on the ship.' Mariucci hunched forward, looking at the lights of the display. 'But we're all a lot more than just the job, Jack. There are always new relationships to be made, new skills to learn, new stories to hear and old ones to tell. And this is why you're here.'

'I don't understand.'

'I want you to save Catherine Vi's life.' He looked up at Jack, through the destruction and the chaos. 'That is all. All the other lives, you can leave to us. But hers? Hers will be the first. She will reach a point of crisis. Everything she has worked for will be, one way or another, at an end. It is up to you to get her through that to the other side. Your trajectories may have started off very differently, but you are on matched courses now.'

'What if the deal she gets from OSTO is some crappy bare-minimum thing that she won't take? We put her on the *Aphrodite*, and look, I know better than you do what happens when things turn bad on a ship. How many heavy sedatives has Rossard got? How many are you prepared to use before you have to space her?'

'These are difficult questions. I had thought you would be the biggest risk, but no. She will be. If she doesn't accept the offer as it is? We have to be prepared. What about this other gallowglass? The one she killed: Castor, yes? Can we presume his ship is still on the asteroid somewhere?'

'We didn't look for it. We probably had images of it, but

they've gone, along with the seismic data. You'd have to re-acquire all that. But why are you bringing this up now?'

'Imagery will be taken as a matter of course when we arrive. Jack, we may not receive her offer until the very last minute. In order to get her to accept it, when her first instinct might be to reject it, we might need to remind her that she doesn't completely occupy the moral high ground.'

'You want me to guilt her into giving you the rights? That's low.'

'Jack,' said the captain. 'I'm not in a position to change any part of this process. My destiny is fixed. Yours and hers are not.' He spread his hands wide. 'I won't order you to do this. I leave it to your judgement. Do or not do. But if we can revive her, she will be your responsibility from then on, and I would very much like her to return to Cis-lunar with us, at the end of a successful mission.'

They stared at each other for a while. Jack felt confused and outplayed and not a little angry, while Mariucci seemed sombre and reflective.

'Can I go, sir?'

Mariucci dismissed him with a wave, and Jack spun towards the axis.

He slid down the access tunnel to the torus, and went to the galley to make himself some coffee. The crew had already clustered in one rest area, and were, from what Jack could overhear, splitting up the tasks and laying out schedules, before separating and doing their ship-work.

Jack found a seat away from them, signed in to a tablet and found the modelling program. He loaded up the data he'd seen used in Command, most of which he'd provided anyway, and just watched it for a while: hard, bright colours in a translucent envelope representing what were the cores of the asteroid, and what was the agglomeration of debris around them.

His mind was everywhere. He couldn't use Castor's death against Cat, surely? But the asteroid was going to be diverted, no matter what she said. It was better that she lived, rather than destroy herself in some last act of defiance, but who was he to choose that for her?

He looked back at the screen propped up on his knees, at the asteroid, at the cores. He needed to put what to do with Cat to one side for now, and concentrate on making sure that none of the main masses reached the lunar surface. And if he could do that, then what about the loose rock? It would potentially spatter the leading edge of the Moon with projectiles sized from dust to boulders, and most of them more than able to tear a hab roof open or put a hole in a ship. Projectiles that would number in the millions. A whole lot of infrastructure would be lost. If there was anyone there during zero-hour, they'd likely die, either directly from the impact or from the loss of air that would follow the storm.

But infrastructure could be rebuilt, and people were being evacuated. He frowned, then opened a scratchpad and worked out the minimum energy he'd need to redirect each of the three cores. Then he looked up the maximum theoretical energy he had at his disposal.

He pulled a face. The margins were in his favour, but they were closer than he liked. He was going to need to get creative, and orbital mechanics were notoriously unforgiving. He caught himself for a moment: he was in the problem, grazing on the numbers, tasting them and chewing them over.

The iron-nickel mass was nearly forty per cent of the total. A fragment of planetary core, it was never going to break apart. It would have to be shoved aside in one big lump, which was going to take a hell of a lot of bombs. However, it was the most predictable part of the entire mission. He could calculate with a reasonable degree of certainty how many kilotonnes he'd need, and put a ring fence around that number.

Seven bombs left.

It didn't look like enough. He'd need at least one to disrupt the asteroid and clear out the loosely held debris. But he

311

didn't want to get distracted: two sub-twenty per cent of the total masses of light rock, density somewhere in the region of three point four. Two bombs apiece? The question was, would they fracture? If they did, their momentum would be divided between the parts. Some parts would move quickly, and some would move too slowly to avoid hitting the Moon.

But what about the practicalities?

A separate EVA for each bomb. The *Aphrodite* couldn't land like the *Coloma* had, so every time they wanted to plant a bomb, someone was going to have to go down to the asteroid, anchor the warhead to the surface – no one had ever mentioned missiles – and come back for the next one. Every time they wanted to detonate, the ship was going to have to retreat to a safe distance, and he didn't even know what that might be, and then press the firing button. Each and every time.

He thought he ought to look up that safe distance. There were no figures for three hundred kilotonnes, but through extrapolation he decided that the ship would receive a lethal dose of radiation as far away as two hundred and fifty kilometres. The actual safe distance was going to be at least double that, if not three times.

He laid the tablet down and pinched the bridge of his nose. The whole scenario was based on a false assumption, that they could place their bombs how and when they wanted, when they were going to be nearly a thousand k off-station every single time they wanted to blow something up. And he knew how long it took to navigate back through the debris field to the asteroid, because he'd done it before. Doing it this way was simply going to take too long. Every day meant a day closer to Earth, and a larger angle of deflection required to make the asteroid bits miss. They couldn't take a month laying the bombs because they didn't have a month. They had a week.

He closed his eyes and tried to imagine what it would be like attempting to conduct an EVA in an irradiated blender, hanging off a microgravity rock half a kilometre across while

312

silica shards as sharp as daggers milled about. Working to plant a nuclear bomb in those conditions? Making sure the bomb survived in those conditions long enough to be detonated?

And even then, what was going to happen to all the loose material, not just the surface and subsurface stuff, but what was in the debris ring, too? They might get lucky and survive the first explosion, but there was no guarantee they wouldn't get holed by something significant, which would put paid to any further detonations. They'd end up being too busy saving themselves to save the Moon and the planet around which it circled.

Even if they could do simultaneous detonations, that still meant at least two cycles of plant and retreat, and the risk of disintegrating the rock cores grew exponentially.

There had to be an answer somewhere in there. They had enough bang, but they had to put it exactly where they needed it, when they needed it, or it wasn't going to work.

The brief he'd been given was to assume KU2 had first to be disrupted into its component parts before those parts were then nudged aside. He should really work on that, find a way to make it possible within the next couple of weeks. Except that was what everybody else was doing, and he'd simply be replicating their efforts, trying to beat them to the best solution of what looked like being an impossible situation.

How was he going to make this thing work? How was he going to exploit what he already knew about the asteroid, to give him extra leverage?

He had two weeks, and nothing else to do. He took a deep breath and dived in.

33

We reconstruct the mass balance of the Greenland Ice Sheet for the past 46 years by comparing glacier ice discharge into the ocean with interior accumulation of snowfall from regional atmospheric climate models over 260 drainage basins. The mass balance started to deviate from its natural range of variability in the 1980s. The mass loss has increased sixfold since the 1980s. Greenland has raised sea level by 13.7 mm since 1972, half during the last 8 years.

(J. Mouginot et al., 'Forty-six years of Greenland Ice Sheet mass balance from 1972 to 2018', *Proceedings of the National Academy of Sciences of the United States of America*, 2019

Jack was almost late for that last meeting. He'd stayed awake for nearly twenty-four hours and was drunk with lack of sleep when he finally crashed in his cot. When he woke up, tablet beginning to slide off his chest, he thought he was back on the *Coloma* and May was by his side.

It wasn't the *Coloma*. It was three years later and he was on the *Aphrodite*.

He didn't know what time it was, what day it was even. He stroked the tablet into life, saw he had several messages, and, dragging the cursor over them, discovered he should already be in Command. It was today. It was now.

He rolled out of his bed, stumbled blinking out into the brightly lit torus, and of course no one else was there, and no one was going to come and get him. He didn't have time to make a coffee, and in any case, his whole body was completely wired. More caffeine could send his heart into palpitations, and he didn't want to cause a medical emergency, not just before deceleration. He grabbed a water bottle, tucked it into a pocket and climbed up to the axis, the tablet strapped to his forearm by its elastic carry-straps.

They were all there. They hadn't waited for him, and there was no reason why they should. Tamm was talking, and Colvin was asking questions: things seemed difficult, if not fractious. Tamm glanced at Jack as he entered, then carried on as if he wasn't there. The holographic display glowed with objects and vectors, and it looked so complicated and sophisticated. Jack scrubbed at his face and drank some water – noisily, according to the set of Suonpää's shoulders – as he tried to settle into attentive, listening mode.

Tamm had taken the dead-end scenario to its logical extreme. He couldn't make it work, and told everyone that because he couldn't, no one could. Colvin was just the latest in a line of interlocutors who couldn't make it work either, but didn't see why. Mariucci presided over the bear-pit, and eventually he'd had enough.

'The working group have met all these problems, and more. We have to concede that there is no solution to this particular problem. All we can do is hope that the geology is different to what we've been led to believe, and that our base scenario might conceivably work. We've all tried very hard, both here and on Earth.'

'Can I?' ventured Jack, and Command fell silent. 'Can I load something up, because I might have something, but I don't know. I need ... other people.'

Suonpää snorted. 'This better be good.'

But Rossard glowered at her. 'Anything is better than nothing,' he said. 'None of you has solved this.'

'It has no solution,' said Tamm. 'The perfect Kobayashi Maru.'

'I know what that is, and I don't think this is it.' Jack ported his model to the display. 'The sandbox won't even let me model this properly, so I've had to make some off-program calculations. This is sort of Plan A, the base scenario where we use everything at once, but not configured in the way it's set out.'

'Do we really have to listen to this?' asked Colvin of the captain.

Mariucci did nothing to reprimand her, not even a twitch of his eyebrows. But he did say 'Yes.'

Jack pressed the heel of his hand against his breastbone. He could feel his heart making big, deliberate beats.

'Okay.' He paused to let the acid wind pass. 'As much as we'd like to place bombs individually, it simply takes too long to retreat to a safe distance each time. Even two separate bomb-laying missions is out, because after the first we have an even more hostile environment than the one we have now. If I thought we'd live long enough to place the things, then it might be worth it, but we won't be able to carry out a second round at all, and that's that. It's all or nothing.'

The others had reached the same conclusion, but it still left a bad taste in the mouth.

'Given that we have to place all the bombs on the surface of KU2 at once, we have to work out the most beneficial position for them. We know that we're going to fracture the asteroid, and once it has fractured, we can't control where the fragments go.'

'Get on with it,' muttered Tamm.

'For fuck's sake,' said Jack, 'it's not like you had a single workable idea between you. And I'm not looking for your approval. I'm looking for his.'

Mariucci grunted, and folded his arms.

'Which means,' continued Jack, 'we have to push as much as possible out of the way while making what might remain as harmless as possible. If we believe the seismic data, and if I've remembered it right, there are three main cores. Two are stony, undifferentiated, chondritic parent-body type material, one is differentiated, iron-nickel core. My suggestion is we essentially slam the iron-nickel core through the middle of the other two. What we push, we push. What we disintegrate, we disintegrate. What's left of the cores will miss the Moon. What's left of the debris will fan out in a more or less predictable pattern, but none of it will be big enough to strike the lunar surface hard enough to produce ejecta of sufficient velocity to form a debris ring around the Earth.'

He ran his simulation. The program couldn't cope with the deformation or the jet of metal plasma roaring back out into space.

Vrána leaned forward. 'Orion. You're using the asteroid as an Orion ship.'

'Yes. Yes I am. We know, theoretically, that it works, but no one has ever modelled using bombs this big against a pusher-plate of proto-planetary mass. But if we can get even close to the same effect, we can drive the asteroid aside in one vast shove, relying on the loose debris between the cores to act as a shock-absorber, at least initially, as the iron core tries to pass through the centre of mass. What little gravity there is might even take some of the debris field with it.'

'And you've modelled this?'

'It's rough. It's very rough. If the ESA working group can run it through their supercomputer, then we'll get a better idea of what might happen.'

'What if the alignment's all wrong?' Colvin was trying to find fault, but her face had hope written on it for the first time in a long time. 'This will only work if the asteroid cores are along a very particular vector.'

'Every seventy-six point four hours. If the readings are accurate. The asteroid is tumbling more than when we left it. Its precessing angle is close on sixty degrees now. We place the bombs where the iron-nickel core is closest to the surface, more or less where the *Coloma* landed, and wait for the tumble to come around. Which it will.'

317

'This is ridiculous,' said Tamm.

Vrána waved him down. 'It has …' He steepled his fingers and pressed them to his lips. 'Possibilities.'

'As long as everything is moving in the right direction to start with, it'll keep moving in that direction. I don't know whether it's enough. I mean, I think it is, but there's a lot of work to be done.' Jack let go of his tablet, and it floated free on its tether. He watched the cable extend and stretch, then bounce back. He frowned at it.

Colvin and Suonpää got into a heated argument about the divergence of the resulting debris, but Jack didn't listen to that. He was looking at the tablet, looking at the cord that held it to his arm, and desperately trying not to force the idea that was on the very edge of his conscious mind.

'Jack?'

He blinked. The captain was talking to him.

'Sorry, what? Sir.'

'Is there anything else you'd like to add?'

'Yes. We left maybe fifty, a hundred kilometres of mono-filament-cored cable on the surface – we just ditched everything to save weight – and I was wondering if we couldn't use that to hold the asteroid together. For long enough to keep most of the debris in a narrower arc. Maybe. There are anchors on the surface, too. We'd have to make a net of it, somehow. I don't know how that would even work, but it might be worth a look at.'

Mariucci turned his gaze on his crew, one by one, until they acquiesced to his will. Some were easier to bring into line than others: Tamm being the most resistant, and his colleague Vrána the least. 'We have two days to prepare the *Aphrodite* for deceleration. I'll pass this on to ESA, and get them to run the numbers. If it gains their approval, it doesn't matter who devised this, only whether it can succeed. We need to throw everything, our whole selves at achieving that outcome. Is that clear?'

It was clear, but it took a few moments to wrest a verbal commitment out of everyone.

'You have work. Begin, please.'

Again, the crew scattered, and again, Jack was left alone with the captain. But there wasn't going to be any lengthy conversation between them this time.

'You did well today. Go and sleep, Jack.'

Jack acknowledged the compliment, but he was too tired to make anything of it. He reeled in his tablet and released himself from his seat, drifting free for a moment before heading down the axis. He was starting to crash, and there was no point in denying it. Too much coffee, and too much coding, and watching too many pixels rearrange themselves on a small screen, had meant he'd managed to scramble his brain into new and interesting patterns. He had two days to reset himself, then came deceleration and the important task of saving the space-going future he'd found himself part of.

He arrived in the torus to a tableau of conflict. The antagonists, and their supporters and conciliators, were frozen in the act of squaring off in the main trackway by the gym equipment. The five of them stared at him as he stepped off the bottom of the ladder. It took Jack a moment to realise what was going on, that the doctor was standing between Tamm and Vrána, that Colvin and Suonpää had picked a side each, and that Mariucci's coerced agreement had lasted as long as it took to get from Command to the torus.

The thing was, he understood it completely. He would have been feeling the same: his home, his family, his one friend, his civilisation, all under threat from an implacable natural force that knew no compromise or negotiation, and recognising only raw brute strength was sufficient to turn it aside. Having believed for weeks, if not months, that the extinction of the entire human race was possible, then to be told that this interloper, this untrained, uneducated spacer who'd caused the problem in the first place, was coming on board with them, tasked with helping them clear up his mess?

He'd be pissed, too. In fact, he was surprised no one had tried to take a pop at him before now. Just because he'd cut off every part of his former life didn't mean that anyone else had. Breaking point had finally come, and not because he'd suddenly done something wrong, but because he'd done something right, ahead of them, ahead of those whose jobs it was to come up with the ideas and win accolades.

He didn't say anything. It would be stupid to even try. They needed this moment in a way that he didn't, and that suddenly struck him as singularly peculiar, because he'd lose everything too. There wouldn't be the infrastructure in orbit to land him back on Earth – where he'd be weak and useless – nor enough in Cis-lunar to keep him alive. He'd die. And he was okay with that.

He'd done what he'd meant to do. He'd run away from his parents, from their philosophy of endless life, and he'd embraced mortality so fully that he'd picked literally the most lethal job going outside of arsenic mining. His first mission had killed three of the eight people on board. His second could well see seven out of seven.

He would die, and that would be the ultimate liberation, the ultimate raised middle finger. Oh, that was fucked up.

And the crew were still staring at him.

He slowly unstrapped his tablet from his wrist and walked the short distance to the dock, where he plugged it in. Then he walked over to the kitchen, and tried to remember how everyone took their drinks, not that he'd ever made them any before, or vice versa.

Plates. There were plates. He extended the table, and put down six, no, seven place settings. Cutlery – fork and spoon, because space food didn't really see the point of knives. Glasses, plastic, seven, and they had a jug which he filled from the spigot, and the water was cold and condensation collected on the outside because the engineers had made sure that the atmosphere wasn't too dry. The *Coloma* had been too dry.

Food. What the hell did these people eat? He'd never eaten with them: they were over there somewhere, and he was over here, or whichever combination meant he was sitting on his own. The ship had a menu of vegan and vegetarian meals from cuisines around the world, so he picked mainly Mediterranean meals, be they north, south or east, and started feeding them through the heater units. Some of them were designed to be eaten cold, so he just tore the lids off and placed them in the middle of the table.

Arms lowered. Chins dropped. Muscles relaxed and insults faded. They had no idea what he was doing and, frankly, neither did he. Only that these should be his people, that they all breathed the same air and ate the same food, so why shouldn't they do it together, just once? It could turn out to be a monumentally terrible move, but his addled mind was telling him that this was what he ought to have been doing all along.

It wasn't an awful thing, to reach out to someone who had every reason to hate you. If they didn't take the offer, then okay, but someone had to go first, and this time it was going to be him. At least they weren't trying to kill each other now. He'd confused them, and confused himself.

He laid out the trays of food, and assigned the hot drinks to a place setting at random. Then he just sat down and stared dumbly at what he'd done. There was a set table, and whatever a person's background, it was magnetic. He felt it himself. The invitation was invisible, but irresistible.

He reached out and took one of the miniature flatbreads and dipped it into what he presumed was hummus, and put it on his plate, then some of the brined, vacuum-sealed olives – olives, on a spaceship – and there was a warm pasta dish of fusilli and a tomato sauce flavoured with basil, and he helped himself to some of that.

A chair moved, and Jack looked up. Rossard sat opposite him.

He scowled, and in sharp, angry motions, put some food on his plate. He drank a glass of water first, then started spearing squares of what looked like feta, one at a time, and biting down on them.

'This is difficult for all of us,' he said.

'I know that. If you want to call me a piece of shit, that's fine. After this mission, you'll never see me again. You'll get schools named after you, while my life for the next decade or two will probably be more hearings and investigations, where we get to ignore the system that permitted this to happen and concentrate on my small part in it.'

'You don't know that.'

'We both know that.'

Vrána fell slowly into the chair next to him. 'You're still a piece of shit,' he said.

'Thank you.'

'But you're a smart piece of shit.'

'Thank you?'

'We shouldn't be in this position in the first place.'

'I realise that.'

'And we have to change all of that.'

'Yes.'

'You agree?'

'Yes. There's a place for private companies in space. That place is where they can at least do no harm.' Jack picked up an olive, stared at it for a moment, then popped it in his mouth. It was salty and bitter. 'Don't be so surprised. I've had a lot of time to think about this.'

'But you work for OSTO now.'

'I have no idea if I work for them, or whether this flightsuit is just for show. We might talk about something more permanent when we get back.'

Colvin placed herself next to the doctor. 'Just one question: do you think it'll work?'

Jack picked up his water and stared at the reflections in the

322

trembling surface. The lower gravity made the liquid slow and oily. 'Yes. I mean, yes, it'll work, which is all that matters, but there'll be consequences that are going to be hard – if not impossible – to predict, and there'll be consequences of those consequences. We won't let the Moon be destroyed. Not this time.'

'You cannot say that. You cannot say that with any confidence at all.' Tamm was leaning over the table, jabbing his finger at Jack.

'Then tell me where I've gone wrong.'

'All of it. All of it is stupid.'

'Tell me where I've got my maths wrong. Argue with the numbers, not me. Your captain's right. No one need care who came up with a working solution. Just that it works. You want the idea? It's yours. Take it. If it doesn't work, then, well, you can just give it back.'

'It's not stupid,' said Vrána. 'It's something. It's not nothing. It's better than nothing.'

'We already had better than nothing.'

'Let's not do this again,' said Rossard. 'Markus. Sit. Sit down.'

'His better than nothing is better than our better than nothing. He can be right this time.' Vrána spun his empty fork. 'Let him have this.'

'I will not sit down and eat with him.'

'You can and you will,' said Mariucci. Suonpää stood by his side. 'No apologies are necessary, or even wanted. We each know what has brought us here, what roads we walked in on. Some of those paths were smooth. Some of them less so. We are all pilgrims on the way. We join together to share this meal, we depart to go about our tasks. Simple. Who could possibly object?'

He kneaded Tamm's shoulders with his heavy fingers, and eased him into a seat as far away from Jack as possible. He took the odd seventh place for himself. Suonpää sat somewhere between Tamm and Jack, leaning forward slightly to shield him from view.

Mariucci smiled down the table at everyone, and raised his glass. '*Per cent'anni*,' he said.

34

When hurricane Sandy wreaked havoc in New York in 2012, stranding low-income and vulnerable New Yorkers without access to power and healthcare, the Goldman Sachs headquarters was protected by tens of thousands of its own sandbags and power from its generator.

Climate change and poverty, UN Report of the Special Rapporteur on extreme poverty and human rights, 2019

He was fitter than he was before, but two gravities still hurt. The feeling of being crushed and suffocated remained the same, and although he could rationalise it away, the anvil on his chest was still very real. When it was over, when the rocket exhaust had cleared and the glow of burning gases faded, they got their first proper look at KU2.

It was even more of a mess than when he'd first encountered it. The debris ring had been pulled out of shape by time, distance and the new rotation of the body below. Rather than a diffuse disc, it was more an enveloping cloud of slowly turning dust and rock. The poles had fewer bodies crossing them, but not none.

'We're going to have to go through that,' said Suonpää. 'No alternatives.'

The debris was orbiting closer to the surface as well, down to a minimum of seventy-five kilometres. It was going to get noisy, and potentially dangerous. And there was the laser, what was left of it. The solar panels had gone, presumably pushed

325

away by light pressure as the asteroid had rounded the Sun, leaving a fat white cylinder, slowly rotating in the dark, holed and scarred and silent.

Jack asked for an image of the old north pole, and after a few minutes' searching found Cat's ship, still tethered to the rock. A laser scar had passed within a hundred metres of her, a glassy arc and one of many burned sinuous lines that patterned the surface with baroque geometry.

'She's still there.'

'She could be dead,' said Rossard. 'The sleep tanks are – were – far from perfect, and she's using one that's seven, eight years old now. Even if she is alive, the brain could have deteriorated to the point where she doesn't have capacity.'

'Some might find that convenient,' said Jack. 'But I'm betting on her surviving through sheer force of will.'

'You're right about that rock being a dangerous mess, though.'

'Yes. Yes, I am.' Jack looked at the display, and all the radar-bright targets. Although the *Aphrodite* was a deep-space exploration ship, the sheer number of reflections it was trying to track overwhelmed the computer, and Colvin had to turn off the facility in order to maintain the rest of the systems. 'And you, and me, have to EVA onto it.'

'As long as it's just the once.'

'It'll be fine. Can we centre on the *Coloma*'s landing site and zoom in closer?'

It was difficult to tell if they had gone to finer detail, since the features were almost fractal, the landscape repeating at smaller and smaller scales. But there were the drums of cable, and the spare anchors they'd ditched, along with all the lab equipment they could strip out, and the food and the suits. It looked like a rubbish tip.

'So much for a pristine world,' said Suonpää.

'We were going to disassemble it and smelt it down for alloys. There would have been nothing left of it.' Jack checked for the things he knew ought to be there on the surface. 'The kit's mostly there. We dumped a few hundred litres of water. Some of it might have frozen into the subsurface, but I'm guessing it's mostly boiled off.'

'As long as you can get the gallowglass out of the way,' said Vrána. 'Markus and I can do our jobs.'

'Getting her out of the way will be straightforward. Getting her consent, though ...'

'I don't care about that,' said Tamm. 'When it's time to press the button, it gets pressed.'

Mariucci intervened. 'We are descended from those who made her islands uninhabitable. We should remember that.'

'I refuse to be held responsible for the sins of my fathers.'

'None of us was responsible, but all of us have benefited,' Jack said, then added pointedly: 'And I'm still waiting to hear about whatever offer I'm supposed to give her.'

'You're a billionaire.' Tamm turned in his seat. 'Why don't you offer her something?'

'If I could, I would.'

'Jack's personal finances are not a discussion point, Markus, any more than yours are.' Mariucci was ignoring the question of the missing OSTO deal. 'We need to prepare for descent. The ship will be pumped down over the next two hours to five psi and the atmosphere replaced by pure oxygen. All O_2 atmospheric protocols will be strictly adhered to. The halon fire suppression system will go live. Everyone needs to know where their nearest breathing assist station is at all times, and during insertion through the debris ring we will be suited and sealed. We make the arrangements, then we manoeuvre.'

For once, Jack had something to do. He followed Rossard down to the rear of the ship and retrieved the inflatable hab from the stores, along with the bottles of gas they were going to use to inflate it. The doctor had to get his medical supplies ready too: chemicals for his auto-injector, easily digestible food, water, eye drops, swabs, sensors and a set of spanners and screwdrivers in case the sleep tank wouldn't open.

Jack readied his spacesuit, and two compatible life support systems: one for him and one for her. This deep in the ship, he could feel the tremor of the plasma drive. He put his hand against a panel to feel it properly: a hum of a different quality to the air scrubbers and water filters and the torus motors. Work. He put the spare life support in a bag with straps, and fastened it against a cargo net near the airlock. He moved everything else there too – the hab, the medical kit, the gas – and made sure he could carry it all, as he'd be wearing most of it down to the surface.

'If we've got everything,' he said, and checked the ship's clock, 'we should suit up.'

Rossard looked up and down the axis, and wiped his sleeve against his forehead.

'Okay?'

'I've done this before.'

'How often?'

'In a swimming pool, lots of times.'

'And in space?'

'Twice.' Rossard rubbed the back of his neck. 'There's not much a doctor can do to a patient in a vacuum.'

'You're barely certificated?'

'You spacers measure things differently.'

'No one would have employed me to pick litter on the Moon on the basis of two short EVAs.' Jack unhooked Rossard's suit from its hanger. 'But on the other hand, Andros took me on as an astrogator on the basis that I was the only warm body he could get. I learned on the job. You can too.'

The ESA suits were fancy: articulated joints, lightweight armour outer covering, plugs for sensors and tools, top-notch environment controls and a helmet that was closer to a transparent bubble than not.

His own Chinese knock-off seemed tired and worn in comparison. Which it was. But it also looked old, while Rossard's spacesuit looked like the future. He could wear it, rather than it wearing him. 'I wouldn't mind one of these,' Jack said. 'I bet they don't chafe.'

'No, it's very comfortable. Considering it's designed to have a hard vacuum on the other side of it, it's almost not enough. I'd feel happier with a bit more ... how do you say?'

'Bulk?'

'Yes. More substance.'

'Any time you want to swap yours for my Z8.' Jack powered up the ESA suit and watched how the lighted panels front and back bloomed into life. The motorised back hatch opened up and Jack peered inside. The internal garment seemed untroubled by use, and even had that new-suit smell. He held it up. 'In you get.'

Rossard had practised enough to remember how to put his suit on: he stripped off his flightsuit and then leg, leg, arm, arm, and that shimmy which pushed his head through the neck seal and his torso into position. Jack fetched a life support pack and slotted it into place. He got all of the green lights and gave Rossard the thumbs up. The suit controls were on the left sleeve, and he closed it up for him.

The hatch sealed. The helmet fans came on, and evaporated the sweat forming on the doctor's forehead.

Jack could suit up in less than twenty seconds if he had to, but there was no need for crash protocols. They had air pressure, and time, and making sure everything was tidied away before acceleration was important. He folded Rossard's flightsuit up and stowed it next to his own, then shook out his suit and fixed his own, technically inferior but still perfectly serviceable life support pack into its cradle. He climbed in, feeling all its familiar hard edges and constrictions as he did so. Had he saved up enough for a new suit, one that fitted a little better than the one he had? Potentially, yes.

But a lot depended on him getting another job after this, and that depended on how much damage KU2 did to Cis-lunar.

One thing was for certain: there'd be plenty of scrap for Yao to recycle afterwards.

His own controls were on his chest. He thumbed his hatch closed and listened to the suit respond around him. Everything was nominal. Everything was fine.

'You okay in there?' he asked Rossard.

'It's good,' said Rossard, even though his face told another story.

The ship looked and felt different from the inside of the spacesuit. All the usual sounds were blotted out, and replaced by the close-breath cocoon of the helmet. They made their way gracelessly, hand over deliberate hand, along the axis to Command, and installed themselves in their seats. Rossard first, Jack manipulating the straps for him, and then Jack, made awkward by the clash between his suit and his chair's geometry.

They waited for the others to join them. Jack's earpiece slowly filled with chatter, and Command with spacesuited crew.

'If everything is ready,' said the captain, 'then we can proceed. Cease rotation.'

'Ceasing rotation.'

'Retract radiators.'

'Radiators retracting.'

'Pilot? You have the helm.'

'Controls to manual. Dead slow ahead.'

'Acceleration acceleration.'

The *Aphrodite* was never meant to enter a debris field. It had no pushers or gas guns or nets to protect its hull. Anything it encountered, it was simply going to have to knock aside. The crosswise velocity was tens of centimetres a second, less than crawling speed, but a fist-sized rock was still going to bang hard, and knock into other rocks, causing a chaotic cascade. And in that churn, any damage done was going to have to wait until later to be assessed and repaired.

Runi would have hated this. But then Runi was dead, along with everyone else from the *Coloma*'s crew.

The central display picked up the largest pieces of debris in front of them. The hologram was bright with obstacles, all very slowly rotating about the asteroid at the heart of the cloud. All reason said to go into reverse, yet their needs demanded the opposite action.

Suonpää moved them closer. Then she vectored the ship in the direction of the rotation of the debris field. They spiralled down over the north pole in ever tighter circles.

Muffled by the suit, it was difficult to hear the scratching on the hull, the sound of hundreds of taps and scrapes as the grit and gravel left over from the formation of the solar system collided with the white paint made by its only civilisation.

But the larger, more solid impacts set the ship ringing. Although the bulkheads were closed, and a hole somewhere wouldn't evacuate all the air, every moment was a moment where the consoles might light up to indicate a breach and the alarms might sound. They relied on the sensors fixed to the outside of the hull, and it was the sensors that were taking the brunt of the collisions. They weren't necessarily fragile, but neither were they designed to be hit by pieces of rock. They could afford to lose some, but the critical ones, the radar and the cameras and the radio antennae that connected them to Earth? No. Absolutely not.

'Altitude three hundred and fifty kilometres.'

'The radar's getting too many reflections. We're flying blind.'

'I have not trained for this,' said Suonpää.

Mariucci cleared his throat. 'Nevertheless, you are trained. I trust you implicitly to get us below the debris.'

'We know where we are in relation to the surface through intermittent lidar. That is all.'

'It is sufficient. Turn the radar off if you wish.'

'I still need it. If we get a clear space, then I can drop through it.'

Had it been like this the first time? The debris ring had been much more defined, and it had had moons to order it. Now those moons had gone – one brought down because it had been Cat's ship, the other lost in space somewhere – and the ring was dispersing, less dense but less defined.

After a while, Colvin called 'Three twenty-five.'

The central display was less bright, and more diffuse. Dust, not rock. Jack opened his mouth to say something, then closed it again. It wasn't his call. Pilot and navigator, Suonpää and Colvin: it was their decision. They would have seen it for themselves, and had their own opinions about how quickly they could descend.

'This is ridiculous,' said Colvin. 'Can you give me a thrust-neutral burn from the attitude jets? Try and clear some of this away.'

Suonpää twitched her fingers. 'In three, two, one.'

The ship shook slightly. The dust stirred and made vortex patterns in greens and yellows.

'I have radar lock on the surface.'

'I'm calling it. Acceleration acceleration.'

They sank, lower and lower.

'Collision warning.'

'I see it,' said the pilot. A reflection, something the size of a suitcase, was closing on their position. So slowly, that in any other situation it would be laughable. But if it hit them it might break something critical. It could even kill them. Suonpää slowed the rate of descent enough for it to pass harmlessly beneath the ship, and then she resumed.

'Three hundred k.'

Eventually, 'Two hundred and fifty.'

'Acceleration acceleration.'

The space between them and the asteroid was clear, and they could fall the rest of the way without constant concern. Jack checked the time. It had taken them three hours to get below the debris ring. Something to remember: it was going to take them the same amount of time coming back up.

'Descend to twenty-five kilometres altitude over the pole,

332

restart the torus and deploy the radiators,' said Mariucci. 'Then we go lower. Laurent? Jack? As soon as we arrive on station, you'll begin your retrieval of Vi. Suits off, get something to eat, and be ready to EVA in ninety minutes.'

'Captain.' Jack punched his harness, and went to help Rossard with his. Back down the axis to the airlock, and the relief of unsealing his suit. He felt the cold air across his stubbly hair and scratched the places where he couldn't previously reach, and it felt good. It always did.

Rossard didn't look so happy. He seemed drained, exhausted already, both physically and emotionally. Like he'd been stretched tight for too long and was now sagging and slack.

'I'm worried that I have to keep asking you if you're okay,' said Jack. 'You're the doctor.'

Rossard grimaced, then worked his jaw, as if he'd spent the last few hours grinding his teeth. 'Just ... stress. If I didn't feel that way, it'd be abnormal. Right?'

'You're the commissioning crew, not the astronauts they were going to send to Jupiter. And suddenly you find yourself in a save-the-world situation, and sure, that's stressful: but once we get outside and down to the surface, you have to be absolutely certain that you want to be there and you can do your thing. There's not much of a margin for error, and rescuing Cat is going to be hard on both of us.'

'I'll be fine, Jack.'

'We should get a third to come with us.'

'It's not necessary.'

Jack pulled out their flightsuits from storage, and pushed Rossard's towards him. 'I've been a team leader for a bunch of rookie spacers on the lunar surface: I was responsible for making sure their equipment was up to code, that their certificates were valid and they were in the right frame of mind to work in hard vacuum for hours at a time. And yes, there've been times when I've had to card someone because one of those three things didn't happen. Either you tell the captain, or I will.'

Rossard snatched his flightsuit out of the air. 'I thought you and I were getting along.'

'This isn't whether we get along, this is about safety. This is too fucking important to bring anything else but our A-game to. We can go back to ignoring each other later if you want, but you know you'd fail your own medical right now. You *know* that. Go to the captain, tell him you want a third hand. Shit, tell him you don't trust me to do it, I don't care if I look bad. This is not about us. You have to understand that.'

The doctor dressed in a silence that stretched on towards breaking point.

'Please?'

Then Rossard turned his back on Jack and hauled himself up the axis. But he didn't stop at the torus, and went on towards Command.

Why did everything have to be so complicated?

35

The permafrost feedback is increasingly positive in warmer climates, while the albedo feedback weakens as the ice and snow melt. Combined, these two factors lead to significant increases in the mean discounted economic effect of climate change: +4.0% ($24.8 trillion) under the 1.5°C scenario, +5.5% ($33.8 trillion) under the 2°C scenario, and +4.8% ($66.9 trillion) under mitigation levels consistent with the current national pledges.

D. Yumashev et al., 'Climate policy implications of nonlinear decline of Arctic land permafrost and other cryosphere elements', *Nature Communications*, 2019

Falling from two hundred and fifty metres up over KU2 wasn't how Jack ever anticipated his reacquaintance with the asteroid. He had a line at his waist, and an absolute assurance that Suonpää would keep the *Aphrodite* on station at that height, for as long as it took.

He wasn't at all convinced, but there was no other way of getting to the surface. The ship was never meant to get this close to another body. If the crew on its intended mission ever wanted to explore, they'd deploy one of the remote-controlled survey drones that they'd take with them, but those hadn't been packed yet. No shuttle. No easy trip down. Head first over the tumbling rock, it would take him twelve minutes from perfect rest to touchdown, and he'd land at seventy centimetres a second.

Twelve minutes was a long time. The ground beneath him

was continually turning, and what was his marker before he'd let go of the airlock was already sliding out from underneath him.

He wanted very much to visualise the rubble surface as a cliff again, but there was no way around it: he was falling, slowly, almost imperceptibly, downwards. He'd undoubtedly kick up debris on landing. What he then had to do was make his way to the easiest-to-reach anchor point and tie on the life-line. Rossard would then descend, at a much faster rate, and use a friction brake to slow his speed.

Then Mariucci would do the same. Quite why the captain had decided he was going to be the third leg of their tripod, Jack didn't know, just as he didn't know what Rossard had said up in Command. Mariucci was either coming along for the ride, or he was properly keeping an eye on things.

Jack had the inflatable hab and the gas bottles, Mariucci the medical kit and Cat's life support. Rossard carried only his expertise and his fear. Their loads were more or less equal.

And still he fell, though he had no sense of falling. No wind noise. No rushing of the ground. As if he was a snowflake, back from when they had snow, drifting downwards.

'Fifty metres, Jack.'

'Copy.'

Just over a minute to go. He bent his knees and waited. Back on Earth, he'd be moving faster if he'd just misfooted on a set of steps. It was difficult to look down at his feet in his suit: the neck didn't articulate, and the bottom edge of the faceplate occluded them. No matter. He'd know when he had contact.

'Twenty.'

'Ten.'

'Five.'

Something pressed against the soles of his boots, and he crouched down. There was nothing to hold him on the surface, and nothing to hold the surface together. Rocks spalled and spun, and he started to rise up again. He had time, plenty of time, to calculate his next move, even though his brain was telling him to act now. There was an anchor dug into the regolith five metres distant, and the guideline from it ran straight to the gallowglass ship. He put his hand down and just flicked his fingers behind him. A tiny gesture, but enough to redirect him. He was going up, but he was going across faster.

He reached out, closed his fist over the fixed line and held on. The cable stretched, then eventually pulled him back. Jack clipped himself on with his diamond-patterned tether, and hooked the line that attached him to the *Aphrodite* directly to the anchor.

'Laurent? Line's secure.'

Jack pulled himself along to the next anchor and secured his second clip. Up above, the doctor pushed himself away from the airlock and moved rapidly down the invisible line towards the asteroid.

He braked too early, and was momentarily left stranded a couple of metres clear of the anchor. He disengaged the friction lock and pulled himself the rest of the way down.

'Clip onto the anchor line, clip off the ship line,' said Jack.

Rossard complied. His hand was shaking, but the carabiners locked on the line no matter how tentative the push-through. He twisted around to unclip from the ship, and his feet grazed the surface. Jack watched the rock move. One fragment came towards him, turning end over end. It would have been easy to catch, but it looked sharp, so he pulled on his tether and sank below its trajectory.

'Keep your feet clear.'

'Yes. Yes, of course.'

Rossard managed to unclip from the ship line, and pulled his way towards Jack. Jack turned and started down towards the gallowglass ship, unclipping and clipping his tethers as he went. It hadn't changed much since he'd seen it last, over two years previously, and it still appeared to be firmly tied down. He climbed up on top, using the tension in the line to press his feet to the hull.

The hatch had been pushed up tight, and sealed with foam. She had, at least, got that far. They had literally left her there on the rock, lifting off into space and taking their long way back home. She had watched them diminish to a pale speck, and then she would have turned to her own ship, stranded and abandoned, plasma jetting from the trench and steering the asteroid to ... here, apparently. Right here.

He opened the bag containing the hab. This was, for him, the most difficult part of the EVA. He needed it centred on the gallowglass ship's hatch, with an airtight seal around the hull. He ran a hose from a cylinder strapped to his hip to the inlet valve and injected a tiny amount of gas. The hab shuddered and unfolded like a flower, the ribs stiffening and dragging material out and away from the densely packed mass.

He was left holding something that resembled a weather balloon, with a ring-shaped opening. It was easy to manoeuvre, despite its size, but it had an inertia that was all its own and threatened to drag him free of his perch and send him bouncing across the hull surface, and potentially right off. He held it up over his head to inflate it further. The ribs became rigid, and the structure settled.

Mariucci was on his way down the line, and Rossard climbed up to join Jack, bent over, clinging to the restraining cables. That was okay, as long as he was also tethered. Then Mariucci was up with them, and Jack remembered what it had been like with Patricio, Marta and Arush. Different. Very different.

Jack lowered the hab down around them. 'Hold it down. I'll inflate the double-wall, then seal it.'

Each section of the double-wall was isolated. He squirted nitrogen into each one, then made his way around the circumference again, this time with the foam spray, first applying it in blobs, and then a continuous line. Twice, to make sure.

'Give it a minute to set.'

The foam was aggressively sticky. He'd tried not to get any on his suit, but there were blebs of it on his faceplate, and up his arms and across his chest, like yellow scabs. He didn't pick them in case he damaged the outer integument.

'Everyone good? Everyone happy?' asked Mariucci.

'Ecstatic,' said Rossard, then reassessed what he needed to say. 'Everything is fine. Suit is nominal. I'm ready to extract Vi from the sleep tank.'

'Good. Jack?'

Jack checked his suit's readings. 'Nominal. Ready to pressurise.'

'Go ahead.'

He checked twice that he had the right tank – oxygen, not nitrogen – and twisted the tap on. His external sensor told him the pressure was rising, but so did his ears. He could hear little creaks and pops from the hab as the material strained against the vacuum outside. No high-pitched squeaks to indicate a leak. The seal was holding.

'Three psi,' he reported. 'Three and a half. Four.'

His suit was relaxing around him, but he was glad he wasn't going to be taking it off.

'Four and a half. Five.' He closed the tap, and started to unstrap the cylinders from his sides. 'Let's get the hatch open.'

A knife in a vacuum took on a significance that it didn't have before: a totemic symbol of just how fragile human life in space was. The blade on the saw wasn't particularly sharp, but it would, used with enough force and carelessness, cut through a pressure suit and kill the wearer. Jack wasn't going to be that person. He kept his hands and everything else behind the blade, and knelt down next to the sealed hatch.

He pushed the tip of the saw into the foam, and started working the serrated edge along the hatch rim. The hatch was never meant to be closed from the inside – though Cat had done her best – and the foam was only designed to provide a temporary seal. If it had lasted long enough for her to get out of her spacesuit and into her tank, then it would have done enough. But when he broke through, there was a hiss as the pressure equalised from the inside out, carrying dried foam shavings on the lessening jet of air.

'That's a good sign,' Mariucci observed.

Jack sawed around the rest of the hatch, then put the guard back on the blade before returning it to the kit bag.

'Ready, Laurent?'

'I'm ready.'

Jack pushed down on the hatch. His lights immediately struck the faceplate of Cat's spacesuit, and for a moment he thought she was in there, mummified, but there was nothing behind the plastic. His breathing returned to normal, and he pushed the hatch all the way through.

The doctor reached in and pulled the empty suit out, passing it to Mariucci, and now that there was enough room for him to enter, he slid in so that he sat opposite the sleep tank.

'It still has power. Checking the read-outs ... all within tolerances.'

'She's still alive?'

'Her life functions have been preserved, at least. How much of her is there remains to be seen.'

'We need to retrieve and revive her,' said Mariucci. 'That is the beginning and the end of the matter.'

Jack hadn't been party to the discussions either within the crew or without it, but he did know that hardly anyone would have been upset if the inside of the gallowglass ship had been an unpressurised tomb. It was difficult to gauge from the captain's tone which side of the argument he held to, and whether he had overruled or been overruled. But Jack hoped that he wasn't the kind of person to leave anyone to die in space.

Then he saw that the pressure was dropping. Slowly, nothing to indicate that he had a catastrophic leak, but enough to give him concern.

'We're down to four point seven psi. I'll top it back up.' He opened the oxygen cylinder and watched the pressure build back up.

340

'Cause?'

'Seepage, maybe. I can go around with the foam again.' He looked at all the numbers. 'Okay. Temperature is registering as minus fifteen. Are we going into shadow?'

The dome was opaque, but the unfiltered sunlight was extraordinarily bright. 'Potentially.'

'Then it could get really cold in here, very quickly. We should have thought of that. Can we do anything to mitigate? Heater in the ship?'

'I have my back to the main controls,' said Rossard. 'I don't have the space to turn around.'

'Then be quick.'

'There's no such thing as quick where a sleep tank is involved. Pass me the medical kit.'

Mariucci lowered the bag through the hatch, and Jack now had more than just his own suit's environmental controls to keep an eye on. He buffered the air with nitrogen, even though it diluted the oxygen, just to give himself some leeway.

Mechanical sounds, motors and pumps, came out of the ship. Rossard moving around, his arms reaching out with instruments, retreating for more items in the bag across his lap.

Then a cough in the cold, sharp air.

There wasn't enough power left in Cat's suit to open the back hatch, so Jack did it manually, swapping out the old life support pack for the new one that Mariucci carried. He pushed it home and waited for the systems to load up. Lights. Air. Heaters. For all the advantages of the newer suits, the old ones really were bombproof when it came to longevity.

Rossard was better at reviving Cat than Arush was. Or perhaps she was better at being revived. This time there was no panic, no unruly disorientation, no forgetting who she was or who these people were. She was alive. Conscious. Responding to external stimuli. Jack caught Mariucci's purposeful stare. Looking after her was now his job. Convincing her of the legal niceties of waiving her interest in billions of euros of mining rights was his goal.

He absolutely should have something else to offer her by now, and he still didn't. No one stayed warm, dry and well fed on gratitude. She was going to refuse. He knew it.

Rossard climbed out and held onto the edge of the hatch, his feet rising into the air before his body fell slowly back down to the hull. He reached in, and Cat's brown hand gripped onto his forearm. She emerged squinting into the inflatable hab, lit only by suit lights.

She saw him. She recognised him. She tried to turn herself towards him, even with Rossard on one side and Mariucci gripping her shoulder on the other. She reached out and pressed her splayed hand on his faceplate, so that Jack could see the whorls of her fingertips.

He shook out her suit, manoeuvred it so that she could climb inside it. She stared at it, then at the ESA suits, and Jack's different one, and put on hold her questions as to how much time had elapsed until this second awakening and where they were now. One familiar face was enough. With help, she pushed her legs in and then her arms, and finally her head. Jack closed the backplate and the suit bloomed into life.

The men held her upright long enough for her teeth to stop chattering and her eyes to settle in their orbits.

'You remember me?' Jack asked. 'You remember who I am?'

'Jack,' she said. 'Jack Astrogator.'

'And you remember who you are?'

'Cat. Cat Gallowglass.'

'The ship is a European Space Agency deep-space explorer called the *Aphrodite*. Something has gone very wrong, and we need to get you on board so we can explain everything. It's too dangerous to do it here. Do you understand, Cat?'

'Why are you even here, Jack?'

'The Outer Space Treaty Organisation asked me to come along.' Asked, told, it didn't really matter. He would have done it anyway. 'I'm here because you are. You have to come with us now.'

'Where are we going?'

'The *Aphrodite*,' said Jack. 'It's on station above us, but it can't land. It's not built that way.'

'Okay.'

'Good.' Jack took the saw, uncovered its blade and drove it through the hab wall. It was tougher than he anticipated. He thought it was going to be a like a soap bubble, one prick and it would be gone, but instead, when it burst, the edges of the rent flapped and chattered. The roof collapsed on them, and Jack had to slice hard against the reinforced material, then push it out of the way to reveal space and the ship as if drawing a curtain aside.

The air from the hab glittered away in an expanding pale mist, and then it was gone, and all that was left was black sky and black rock, and the only illumination came from their suits.

'Does the *Aphrodite* have navigation lights?'

'No. Where it was going, it didn't need lights. However. Captain to *Aphrodite*. External cameras turn to my location, please.'

Four bright stars winked on above, and grew in intensity, enough to cast faint shadows. The surface of the asteroid resolved, and the lines that would take them back to the ship glistened like ropes in the rain.

'Are we ready?' The captain untethered himself from the gallowglass ship and stepped across the deflated hab still attached to the hull by its foam collar. 'Miss Vi, are you ready?'

'I ... yes.'

'Tether yourself to Jack. I'll go ahead, the doctor will follow behind. Slowly and safely. *Aphrodite*? Four to come aboard.'

36

We note that the scientific community has already tried all conventional methods to draw attention to the crisis. We believe that the continued governmental inaction over the climate and ecological crisis now justifies peaceful and non-violent protest and direct action, even if this goes beyond the bounds of the current law.

Scientists' Declaration of Support for Non-Violent Direct Action Against Government Inaction Over the Climate and Ecological Emergency, 2019

They stared at each other across the width of a table, like they had on the *Coloma*. They both had coffee cups in front of them, just like on the *Coloma*. He was wearing an OSTO flightsuit instead of a StarLift; she was in a borrowed ESA one that was too big for her.

He kept on forgetting how small she was, because in his memories, and his dreams, she seemed always so much larger. He'd spent the last three years orbiting around her, a satellite to her star.

While they sat in the rotating torus, Tamm and Vrána were down on KU2, anchoring the first warhead in place. Each one came in a protective box that could be screwed down: no one wanted them to become detached or damaged before detonation. After that, of course, it wasn't going to matter.

He still didn't have an offer from OSTO to present to her. Mariucci didn't know what the delay was. Neither did he. He was just winging the entire conversation with Cat, and he had no idea where they were going to end up. He was nervous, and despite his efforts not to show it, he knew he was failing.

'So that's where we ended up,' said Jack. 'The laser's still up there, with something burned out. The solar panels are probably on their way out of the solar system, driven by the wind.'

'And you never went home.'

'I said I wouldn't. And I didn't.'

'And your parents?'

'If you believe you're effectively immortal, what's a few years? I'll break before they do.'

'Will you?'

'I don't know. The doctor here doesn't think much of my self-care, and any time spent outside Cis-lunar increases my cancer risk. I don't have a dosimeter, so it's anyone's guess.'

'You could be dying now.'

'Yes. But space isn't a place for sick people. Sorry, space isn't a place for penniless sick people. Either I go back to Earth, or I space myself. That's as much healthcare as I can afford right now. I feel fine. Yao lets his workers self-certificate, whether or not they've seen an actual doctor and had all the tests.'

'And Earth?'

'I'm not the best person to ask,' said Jack. 'I can't honestly say I'm that up on the news. There are wars and rumours of wars. Things like that.'

Cat rested her elbows on the table at him and Jack shrugged, embarrassed by both his lack of knowledge and his not caring.

'Everything is difficult. I hear other people – crew – talking. Parts of India are gone. Just … gone. I think Arush went back there, but there's only so many fifty-degree summers you can stand before it all breaks down. I know they cancelled the Hajj last year. That's literally never happened before.'

'Apart from that one time.'

'That was before either of us was born. I'm sorry, I don't know. I just don't know.'

'How do you not know?'

'What do you want me to say? That I'm selfish, stupid, self-absorbed, narcissistic, sociopathic, misanthropic? Okay.' He felt like throwing his coffee across the torus, but he drank it instead. It was already cold, the consequence of not being properly hot in the first place. Then he hated himself for being more concerned about the temperature of his drink than about the wash of refugees across the planet. 'I'm fucked up. I thought that was taken as read.'

'You've heard nothing about St Ann's?'

He had. A little. But he was going to deny it. 'No. I've not looked. Why would I look? I don't want to look.'

'You're scared to look.'

'Yes, I'm scared to look. There's only so much horror anyone can take before their minds just turn away. I have friends down there—'

'You have friends?'

'One friend, and he reacts exactly the same. There's nothing we can do about any of this. There's nothing we can say, there's nowhere we can go. And you're as much a victim in all this as I am.'

'I am not.'

'Cat. You got bought and sold. The idea that you owe these people, your father, loyalty is ... ridiculous. They stole your childhood.'

'And what do you think being herded onto boats while your country sinks is? Do you think about their lives, their child-hoods?'

'This is impossible.' Jack stood up and walked away. 'You're impossible.'

'You can't run away from this. There's no "away" any more.'

'You didn't plan this,' he shouted from up the slope.

'No. But to quote you, that's where we are.'

He came back, leaning across the table at her. 'They're going to do it anyway.'

'Not without my permission. Which I do not give.' She raised her own voice, tired and weak through lack of use. 'Do you hear me, Captain whatever your name is? I do not give my consent.'

'They're planting the bombs on the asteroid. Right now.'

'Don't you think I know that?' She jabbed a finger into his chest, rocking him back on his feet. 'Don't you think I know what it is that you're doing?'

'You've been in a tank for most of the last seven years. How the fuck do you know anything?'

'And you've had your head up your arse for the same length of time. All of your energy has gone into saving yourself. Do you think you should be congratulated for that?'

'What? No. I survived, that's all.'

'So what about other people?'

'I'm here, aren't I?' He stared at his feet. 'I'm here because of you.'

Cat looked at her coffee. She cradled the cup in her hands, then she held it up to Jack. 'Make me another one.'

Jack took the cup wearily and tracked over to the kitchen. He recycled the old drink through the waste-water management system, used the water boiler to make her another and took it back over. He sat down again. He knew what he had to do: he just wasn't doing it at all well.

'Things have moved on,' he said, and she waved him down.

'If this asteroid was going to just sail past out towards Mars, then you wouldn't be here. Neither would they, and neither would anyone. There are easier targets out there now, and most of them don't come with prior claim. You're here, they're here, because KU2 is a threat to their whole economic system.'

'We're here because it's a threat to the Earth, to the Moon: people will die.'

'Jack, people are dying already. But they're poor, from poor countries. No one gives a shit about them now, or in the future. If they all died tomorrow, that'd be mostly okay. No, you're

347

allowed to be here because the asteroid is a threat to rich people, not to poor people. People like us.'

There wasn't much he could say to that, because it was true.

'You killed your friend over this,' he managed eventually.

'That we were forced into that position passes you by, doesn't it? That there was and is enough money to save everyone, but the people with the power and the wealth want the rest of us to fight amongst ourselves. So we did, and we do.' She sighed, and scrubbed at her face with both hands. 'I know. There could only be one winner, and I wanted to save my people so much, I thought it justified anything. At that moment, maybe it did. Now? I don't know any more.'

'And you'd rather watch it *all* burn if you don't get your way?'

'You've offered me nothing in return for my rights. Nothing.'

'How about life? The people you want to save will die at the same time as everyone else.'

'They're dying now, Jack. This is the point you're not getting. They're dying at sea, dying on land, they're dying poor and hungry and exploited and dispersed and alone. A world with no access to space, with random death from above, with no weather or communications satellites: how is this different to what they already have? This way, at least some of the right people get punished for what they've done.' She looked up at him. 'Tell me you haven't thought of that too.'

'That my parents might suffer? No real-time ship tracking. No instant unloading at port. Ships lost at sea. Tsunami, storms, collisions.' Jack shrugged. 'I might have done. They won't really suffer, though. They'll probably be just fine, unless there's a direct hit on the house. One of the houses, that they happen to be in at the time. I don't think you appreciate just how much security hundreds of billions of euros can give you.'

'Then maybe the laser should have burned for longer, or shorter, so KU2 would smash into the Earth. See how secure they felt then.'

'You really do want them to burn.'

'Look at what they've done, Jack. Look at what they've done: they've blocked every attempt at fixing things, and now even when it's actually happening they still want me to hand this over for free. And there are hundreds, thousands of millions of people like me, who they want to go away and just die quietly, without making a fuss. Well, this is me making some noise. They will hear me now.'

'This is academic. They're going to move the asteroid anyway. They're going to blow it up and shove it to one side and send it into deep space.'

'If they do, they have to pay me for it. And I'll use that money to buy my people a homeland.'

'They're not going to pay you,' said Jack. 'They're just not.'

'Then I'll take them to court.'

'The lawyers will bleed you dry. You won't see a cent.'

'I'll fight them. I'll fight them and I'll win.'

'But when? Ten years' time? In that decade, what little money you had will be gone, and so will your people.'

Cat worked her jaw. 'It's not my plan to give in.'

'You had a plan: I'm not saying it wasn't a good plan to start with. A deal with Lithospheric. Money up front for St Ann's. Royalties later.' He doubled down with Mariucci's suggestion. He had nothing left. 'Your friend—'

'Castor.'

'Castor's people had the same plan.'

'And then I killed him, dropped Lithospheric and went with NovaS.'

'Your plan was not the problem. The problem was back on Earth, not up here in space.' Jack scrubbed his scalp with his fingernails. 'Your plan was never going to work. Whatever you'd done, whoever you'd cut a deal with, the money was going to end up in the same ridiculous, incompetent hands.'

Her fingers tightened around the coffee cup. 'I did the best I could.'

'Did you? You let your greed – the thing you seem to hate the most in other people – dictate what you did. And continue to do.'

'It's not greed if I do it for other people. My people.'

'You killed Castor for this.'

'I know I killed him. I know I did. You know I did. Why do you keep on saying that?'

Jack was done. He'd failed. He could keep on at her like this. 'I don't know what else to say. It's over, that's all. It's over.' Then: 'Perhaps the asteroid is cursed after all.'

She stared at him. 'What?'

'I don't believe this for a moment, but it makes as much sense as anything: KU2 has been cursed by Castor's ghost. He's looking for revenge on everyone who comes here. He killed Patricio, made May forget the password, made Andros kill himself, made the crew kill May, and he kept you close, didn't he? What do you suppose the chances of something else going wrong are? Someone's tether breaks, and they're lost to space. One of the bombs goes off too soon, and kills us all. Or not at all, and the asteroid hits the Moon anyway. Or any number of scenarios where we end up dead and there's a ring of rock around the Earth.'

'That's stupid,' she said eventually.

'I should really go and tell the captain.'

'That the asteroid is cursed?'

'Does that sound better than "We fucked up"? You should get on board with the haunted asteroid theory. It'll make you feel better.'

'This is not my fault.'

Now it was Jack's turn to stare her down. 'That's like me saying it isn't mine. Look, we've gone as far as we can with this. I don't have a deal for you, and I don't know why. ESA are going to reduce this asteroid to radioactive rubble and kick it across the solar system. You won't waive your rights, so I guess they'll see you in court.' He got up from the table and took his empty mug with him over to the kitchen. 'We should look for Castor's ship while we still have time.'

'Why?' she asked. Her voice seemed diminished.

'Because his parents, his brothers or sisters, if they're still alive, if we can find them, might want his body back, and this is the last chance anyone's going to have to do that.'

'Why are you doing this?'

'Doing what?'

'Tormenting me.'

'It's not just about you. It's about Castor's family.'

'You don't care about your own family.'

'It's not about me either. You knew him. Do you think he cared about his family? Did they care about him?'

She pressed her lips together and refused to answer. Jack cleaned his mug and stowed it in its holder in the cupboard. He unracked a tablet and brought up the best photographic images they had of KU2, and started blocking out a search pattern.

The cameras on an exploration ship were far more powerful than those on the *Coloma*. There was a chance the laser had passed over the other gallowglass ship, or it had broken loose in the same event that had put Cat in orbit around the asteroid; if so, there'd be nothing for him to find. But if it was even partially intact and still on the surface, and they had a picture of it, then he was going to spot it. It was just going to take time.

Who was he doing this for? Was it for Castor? Why the hell not? The man – the boy – deserved better than to be barely remembered as an also-ran.

After a while, Cat drifted over, her hands dug deep into her pockets. He carried on his study of the grid square, and only when he finished did he look up from the sofa.

'Can I call home?' she asked.

'I don't know. You'd have to check with the captain.'

'He can't stop me.'

'Of course he can. I don't know if it's even possible. The

debris disc is moving. Comms may be intermittent or down completely.'

'I need to talk to home.'

'Then check with the captain as to how you can do that. And how often. I'll have to come with you.'

'Am I a prisoner?'

Jack put the tablet on the seat next to him. 'No. But I have to accompany you wherever you go on the ship. The crew are busy with their duties, so I have to make sure you ...' He rubbed the end of his nose. Saying it sounded harsh, but they were past that now. 'Make sure you don't compromise the mission in any way.'

'You mean break stuff.'

'Pretty much.'

'Or you'll throw me out the airlock.'

'I have no idea of the flight profile back, but we've a lot of delta-v to kill and we're out of solid-fuel boosters. It's going to take months, whatever course we steer. Rossard's got some sedatives he can use, or we could tie you up, but ultimately, yes. We're in space. What do you expect? It's standard operating procedure.'

'You never used to be this cruel.'

'Of course not. The idea of spacing someone was unthinkable. But I was wrong: what are you supposed to do in a fragile ship full of complicated machinery that needs constant maintenance and is months from anywhere? It's a practice that's evolved out of necessity, not because people enjoy it.'

'Some will.'

'Yes. I'm sure that's true. But no one here would. Least of all me.'

'You voted in my favour on the *Coloma*.'

'Yes.'

'Why?'

'I didn't understand the rules properly then. I voted out of reflex. No good person would send someone to their death just

352

because, and I wanted to be that good person. When they came for May, I did nothing. I didn't help her, but I didn't help them either. I found out I wasn't that good person, but neither was I ever going to be *them*. I changed at that moment, and I'm still trying to figure out who I am. Having said all that, I would still vote to keep you. We should all have one last chance.'

The torus rose up to their left and their right and met unseen on the other side of the circle, and Cat looked like she was about to say something else, but her open mouth closed and she stalked away.

Jack fastened the tablet to his wrist and was compelled to follow her.

37

What will make a difference is the power of the people – through regulation, divestment, consumer choice and public protest. Public surveys emphasise that, throughout the world, deniers are in the minority. The worried majority doesn't need to win over everyone in order to win on climate change.

D. Hall, 'Climate explained: why some people still think climate change isn't real', *The Conversation*, 2019

'You're here and she's not,' said the captain.

'Rossard – Laurent is giving her another series of neurological tests.' Jack looked behind him, down the spine of the ship. 'He's convinced there's a scientific paper in it: something-something long-term effects of induced sleep hibernation. They're going to be a while.'

Mariucci swivelled in his chair and faced the holographic display. The asteroid was annotated with floating tags marking the placement of the bombs, and the stretches of cable they were using to keep the cores together post-detonation. The more Jack looked, the more preposterous it seemed, but it was his plan, albeit confirmed as viable by better minds and more powerful computers.

'And how is she?'

'I'm not really—'

'If I wanted a professional opinion, I'd ask Il Dottore. I'm asking you, Jack Agent.'

'Like glass,' said Jack. 'She won't bend, but she might break. I'm going to ask you again where the deal OSTO promised me at the start of this mission actually is.'

'It's still being discussed.'

'Is there genuinely going to be a deal, or is everyone just blowing smoke here?'

'It's in everyone's best interests for her to rescind her claim,' said the captain.

'That's a party line if I ever heard one. Give me something to persuade her that it's worth her while. Something. Anything that might start a negotiation.'

'All I can do is pass on your concerns, Jack. I have my mission, and this part of it is, sadly, out of my hands.'

'I feel as if I've been repeatedly lied to. Prove me wrong.'

'I'll go back to them again, and I'll tell them that Vi's agreement is as important as any other mission-critical element.'

Jack grunted in frustration. They were running out of time. 'By the way, I found him.'

He unstrapped his tablet and dabbed at the screen to wake it up. The image showed – slightly pixelated – a circular object, cracked like a tapped egg, but still intact enough to resemble the ship that it was. It was almost exactly the same colour as its background, but once seen, it was obvious.

Mariucci took the tablet and satisfied himself that what he was seeing was what Jack said it was. 'Does she know?'

Jack nodded.

Mariucci zoomed out to determine where on the asteroid the target was. 'There are many reasons why this retrieval idea of yours shouldn't happen. If the RTG was breached, then the area will be highly contaminated with radioisotopes. Then there is the time it will take, the unnecessary EVA and consequential risks. Then there is the retrieval itself, the preparation of the body for long-term storage, and its repatriation afterwards.'

'You encouraged me to look.'

'You would have done it anyway.'

'I mean, yes—'

'You know why we did this. And it may or may not have served its purpose, but its course has run.' He handed the tablet back to Jack. 'I'm sorry, Jack. I can't allow this.'

'If it was your son?'

'I would like to think I could put my personal feelings aside and try and make my decision based on what was best for the success of the mission and the safety of the crew.'

'You're more sentimental than that.'

'Am I?' He considered the matter. 'I suppose I am.'

'So?'

'There's no one to accompany you. The crew are all engaged in purposeful activity: we need to prepare for acceleration. If it had been earlier, then possibly. Now? No.'

'Cat will come with me.'

'You've asked her?'

'Not yet, but I'm sure of her answer.'

'And you trust her?'

Jack hesitated for just a moment too long. 'Yes.'

'She's still refusing to give up the mining rights. If she gets to the surface, she could potentially sabotage the lines or compromise the bombs. There's very little you could do about that. What advantages of size and skill you have onboard would be largely negated outside. I cannot – will not be permitted to – risk that.'

'The wreck is away from the bomb sites. Away from any of the lines, too.'

'The asteroid is only four and a half kilometres across. Nothing on the surface is far away from anything else.' Mariucci tried a different argument. 'What if she decides to, say, go down with the ship?'

'Stay on the asteroid?'

'Let me talk you through a scenario: you and she descend to

356

the surface and make your way to the wreck of this gallowglass vessel. You retrieve whatever remains are present, and bag them to bring back to the *Aphrodite*. But she refuses to return. You cannot force her – it's too dangerous for you to fight in such an environment. You have two choices: the first, is that you leave her there, and give her de facto control of what happens on the asteroid for however long her air supply lasts. Call it six hours, conservatively. What do you think she might do in those six hours? The *Aphrodite* will have to depart KU2 to make minimum safe distance, but will have no assurance that, once it has done so, the bombs will still be in place.'

Jack swallowed. He knew what was coming next.

'The second sees you stay with her, to prevent her from interfering with our infrastructure. The *Aphrodite* will still have to go, but without you on it. Now, I've been studying you, getting to know you while you've been aboard, and I think you would sacrifice yourself to stop her. Am I right?'

'Probably.'

'This asteroid has claimed life after life, and now you want to give it yet more? I like you, Jack. I think you and Catherine Vi – once you sort out what sort of people you want to be – will achieve much, for the benefit of many. Remember your task, your solemn task. You must keep her alive, and to do that, you must stay alive yourself.' The captain dipped his head. 'I refuse your request. I'm sorry. This is not an easy decision to make, or accept, but it is the right one.'

'I was sent here to get her agreement over the mining rights. In the absence of an actual deal, this is the only thing we have. You understand that, don't you?'

'Captain . . .'

They both turned to see the doctor in the axis, a darkening wad of bandages and dressings pressed to his temple.

'Fuck,' said Jack. 'Where is she?'

'I don't know.'

Behind him, both pilot and navigator started to unclip themselves from their chairs.

'Remain on station,' ordered Mariucci. 'Close bulkhead doors. Breach procedure.'

Klaxons barked.

'Bulkhead doors closing.'

'Call Markus and Pavel. Emergency return.'

'Roger.'

'Cameras. Find her.'

'Airlock has been activated.'

'Shut it down.'

'I don't think I can.'

'Pull the power breakers.'

'Manually? They're in the axis.' Then, 'I can isolate the supply to the pump. Manual override is going to beat that.'

'Then cancel that.'

'I've got a visual. She's in the airlock.'

'Suited?'

'Yessir.'

'That's something at least. Open the bulkheads. Deirdre, see to Laurent. Ronja, maintain position. Get the away team up to the ship.'

'They can't enter if she's in the airlock.'

'I know that. Jack: with me.'

The bulkhead swung aside and the captain pulled himself down the axis towards the far end. Jack followed Mariucci's feet. There was blood on the walls where Rossard had planted his free hand, but no signs of damage to the ship.

They moved quickly down the axis, ignoring doors and hatches off it, and arrived at the EVA module. The airlock door was shut, and the space inside partially pumped down. The automatic system couldn't open the internal door against the air pressure, but neither could it open the external door to the vacuum.

'We have two astronauts coming back to the ship. Their lines are tethered to the outside of this airlock. They can go around to the secondary airlock, tethering as they go.' Mariucci hung off a handhold. 'Getting them back inside is not the problem.

'It's getting her out.'

The shipwide intercom buzzed. 'Pressure in the primary airlock is falling. Manual valve is open.'

'She's going to go down to the surface,' said Jack. 'Can the away team stop her?'

'They're not near the airlock yet.'

'Someone has to stop her.' Jack slammed his fist on the airlock door. 'This is all going wrong.'

He pushed away from the door and through into the module where the suits were. He grabbed his life support pack from the recharger and let the momentum carry him across the room to his suit.

'I can't permit you to do this,' said Mariucci.

'You told me I have to keep her alive.' Jack pushed his life support into position and powered up the suit. 'So you could help me do just that.'

Jack shucked his flightsuit, and Mariucci took hold of the torso of the spacesuit, bracing his leg against a rail.

'I'm waiting for a message,' said the captain. 'From the EU. Regarding refugee status for the people of St Ann's. There's a final ratification meeting today.'

'And you were going to tell me this when? Get on to them. Tell them we need a result. Now.' Jack tucked his head in and his face reappeared in the faceplate. 'Closing suit.'

He could hear the radio chatter between Tamm and Vrána. They were fifty metres away from the airlock door, climbing up the lines from the surface to the ship.

'Outer door open.'

'She's in the doorway.'

'*Kurva drát!* She's going to jump!'

'No line. No line.'

'She's out. Repeat, she's out.'

359

'Cycle this fucking airlock,' said Jack. 'I'll get her back.'

Mariucci leaned on the intercom. 'Power to primary airlock. Prepare for EVA.'

The pumps chugged, and it was slow, too slow.

'Where did she go? I need a trajectory.'

'Not straight down,' said Tamm. 'Oblique. I can see her. She's moving at a couple of metres a second, down range, towards the south.'

It was in the direction of Castor's ship. But escape velocity was barely more than her speed. If her path didn't intersect with the surface, then she was going to head out into space, into the debris cloud.

'Someone get her on camera. Plot a course.'

'Van der Veerden. Jack. Listen to me.' Suonpää's voice was calm, but her message urgent. 'You will not be able to replicate her vector. If you're out by even one degree, you'll miss her. You have no way of manoeuvring. Wait to see where she ends up. I'll do what I can with the ship.'

'Do we really not have any way of manoeuvring?'

'Tethered EVA only. I've got her on external view. This perspective. Difficult to tell. Wait.'

'Pavel and I are at the airlock.'

'Tether to the ship. Unclip the descent lines. Prepare for acceleration.'

Mariucci grabbed hold of Jack's shoulders and forced him around. 'Do not go until I give explicit instructions.' Then he headed back up the axis towards Command.

Jack waited for the green light at the airlock, and the second it came on, he punched the door button. It opened for him and he stepped inside, slapping at the closer, and then the cycler. Everything was taking so long. He clipped onto the rail inside the airlock and waited, his rapidly exhaled breath misting the lower part of his faceplate. His suit tightened around him.

'Jack, can you hear me?' It was the captain.

'Affirmative.'

'Vi is coming down five hundred metres south of our current location. There are no warheads in that location. There is a line that crosses some fifteen metres to spinward, right in your orientation. She will bounce, but her vector after initial contact is unpredictable. Exit the airlock, but remain tethered to the hull. Understood?'

'Affirmative.' Jack opened the outer door. There was the darkness of space, the brightness of the rock. He eased himself out and tethered on, unfastening himself from inside the airlock. Tamm and Vrána were clinging to the outside, and now he was too. He looked down, the direction he immediately thought of as down.

'Jack, I want to make this clear to you. If she goes into orbit, if she holes her suit, breaks her life support or is otherwise incapacitated, we will not be retrieving her. Only if she represents a threat to the successful conclusion of this mission will I ask you to intervene. Likewise, if you disobey me and attempt a rescue of your own outside of that limited scenario, we will not be retrieving you either. Tell me you understand.'

'Affirmative. Is there a line I can use for descent?'

'Cable drum C is good to go.'

'Thank you, Pilot.' Jack located the hatch near the open door, pulled on the cable to release it and clipped his spare tether to it.

Cat was slowly falling towards the asteroid, arms and legs splayed as if she were parachuting, although she was probably just trying to control her rotation. She wouldn't strike the surface straight on: she'd hit it with a glancing blow. Some of her momentum would be transferred to the loose rock, which would fly outwards from the point of impact. She herself would rebound upwards, and potentially into the debris field kilometres above.

She moved her arms, and her body slowly turned until she was travelling feet first, facing down towards the surface.

'Acceleration acceleration.'

The ship, with the smallest of flares of cold gas, nudged itself southwards. The disengaged lines snaked, waves travelling up and down to the anchor points below.

'Target impact in five seconds.'

Cat bent her knees and touched the surface with the toes of her boots. She tried to kill as much of her momentum as she could, but perfection was impossible. Even so, she almost stopped dead, rock spinning away, flashing light and dark shadow. But she lost contact with the ground even as she reached down to try and find a solid handhold. She slowly rose up again, and again she splayed her arms and legs, waiting for the ephemeral gravity to take effect.

'Her lateral velocity is ten centimetres a second. She'll re-contact with the surface in four minutes.'

'Once she gets within touching distance, she can go in any direction she wants. If you're going, go now.'

'Can she hear any of this?'

'If she's on the right channel, then every word.'

'Well. In that case, I'm on my way.' He pulled himself into position, head down over the bone-grey asteroid, then pushed himself off, arms and legs wide, just like she had. The line spooled out behind him, and ahead, the jagged, hateful pile of rubble that was KU2.

Four minutes later, Cat was able to settle on the surface again, this time staying in contact with it, resting tremulously on all fours. If she moved, she'd float free again.

'Cat. Cat Gallowglass. It's Jack. Can you hear me?'

'Yes. I can hear you.'

'Listen to me. There's a line ten metres directly ahead of you. It's anchored. Can you reach it?'

'Jack, where is he?'

'Where is who? You mean Castor?'

'Where is he? He's here, isn't he?'

'Yes, he's here, but he's still another half a kilometre further on.'

362

'I killed him, Jack.'

'I know you did. You killed him and claimed the asteroid for your people. That's why you did it.'

'I did it for them. Then they threw it away.'

'You knew that three years ago. *Aphrodite*, what's my ETA?'

'Seven minutes thirty. You're coming in faster than before.'

'Copy that. Cat, listen to me. We're not going to be able to get to Castor. We don't have time to retrieve him. It's not going to happen. You have to let him go. You have to let it all go. It's gone. All of it.'

'Then what's the point? Everything I've done, all the good, all the bad—' She broke off, and Jack continued falling.

'Cat?'

Silence.

'Cat. I'm coming down near the line. Meet me there. Ten metres. Just glide to it. It's right in front of you, about twenty, thirty centimetres above the surface. Catch it and hold on.'

It took her a while to react, but eventually she straightened her arms and reached out. Her gauntlets dabbed at the rock and she started to move.

'Six minutes, Jack.'

'Copy that, *Aphrodite*.'

38

This monument is to acknowledge that we know what is happening and what needs to be done. Only you will know if we did it.

Monument to the disappeared Ok glacier, Iceland, 2019

He grabbed at the ground line like he was coming in to land on an old-style aircraft carrier. It stretched and flipped him over, and he dug his heels in. Rock and dust spurted away at a low angle, fanning out and dispersing, rising up and refusing to fall back down. He scraped his back, and its precious life support, across the ground for a moment before rebounding.

The only thing connecting him with the surface was his left hand. The cable he held went taut, and it started to pull him back across the asteroid. If he wasn't careful, he'd foul the line up to the *Aphrodite* too, and that would be that. He snagged the ground line in his other hand, and hauled himself towards the distant anchor, trying to counter his side-to-side movement by swinging his feet left and right.

Cat was already there, clinging to the upright post as if it was the only safe place in the middle of a stormy sea. She reached out for him and pulled him in. The anchor rocked. Its solidity was an illusion. It could work its way loose with the next movement. Jack waited for everything to damp down, before clipping his second tether to the ground-based line.

'If you let go, you'll be lost,' he said. 'I'm going to use your tether to clip to me. Is that going to be okay?'

She looked at him, and up at the *Aphrodite*, which was slowly precessing overhead, and at the line that connected the two.

'I don't want to go back, Jack. I've failed. I killed people – Castor wasn't the only one, he was just the last – to get here, and that was only the start of it. But this rock was Castor's. It belonged to him. I took it away from him, so how can I complain when someone tries to take it away from me?'

'The time to have discussed this – to have realised this – was before you smacked Rossard around and jumped overboard. What the hell went on?'

'He ... just. I don't even know. I think he said it was time, and it is time, isn't it? I had to do something. But I've failed. Everything I've tried so far has failed. I can't go back in the sleep tank again. I just want it to stop.'

'No one is going to make you go back into the tank. Give me your tether. I'll hook it to me.'

She started to stand up, a lethal manoeuvre. Jack reached through her arms and tightened his fist around one of her loose tethers. The anchor twisted, rising upwards before jerking to a halt.

'I'm fifteen. I'm twenty-two. I don't even know any more.'

'Get back down here. No sudden moves.' What Jack wanted to do was reach around behind him and take hold of the line that had spooled out from the *Aphrodite* and try to fix her to that. They could reel them both in, no matter how much she fought him.

But that wasn't really the answer. If he stopped her from her self-destructing this time, there was no guarantee he could stop her the next, and that might be on the ship. If it was going to be decided, it would be here, on the asteroid. He clipped her carabiner onto the ground line and let go of her.

'Cat. You get to make your own choices. And so do I. Captain Mariucci has his mission to complete, and the *Aphrodite* needs to leave here in the next few hours. His crew should all be going with him, but he absolutely cannot risk leaving you here on your own, where you might try to damage the warheads before detonation.'

Her face, now level with Jack's, was shiny with sweat. Whereas he was unnaturally calm, like this was always meant to be.

'If you're going to stay, then I have to stay too. Make sure everything stays intact, until it doesn't have to.'

'You'll die.'

'Yes. That is the consequence. It'll be over very quickly, if that's any comfort.' He carefully twisted himself around so that he could see out into space. It took him a moment to find the Earth and its moon. 'We're getting close, Cat.'

'It's too late anyway. Too late for St Ann's. Too late for the Dutch. Too late for Bangladesh, for Florida, for Venice, for Rio. Too late for anyone living near the equator, or relying on the rains, or the glaciers. We're up here, and all we're doing is finding new ways to break the planet. We should have done better, Jack. Our parents should have done better.'

'My parents are too busy trying to live for ever, and yours are too busy trying to live for now. Neither of us can do anything about that from an asteroid loaded with twelve nuclear warheads, moving at thirty kilometres a second towards the Moon.'

'This wasn't supposed to be our future.'

'But it is. This is exactly what was predicted. Only not enough people who could have done something about it wanted to change what was coming. It'd be nice to believe that something good will come out of this. Cis-lunar space is being evacuated. Most of what's there will get trashed. Yet we both know they'll be back – the corporations, the investors, the lawyers – and they'll try and carry on exactly the same as they did before because there's so much money to be made. And the next time someone drops an asteroid, maybe that one will hit the Earth, and maybe it won't, and no one will have learned any lessons from this except that someone will be on hand to bail them out. There'll be no systems in place, no laws or safeguards to

366

prevent it happening again. If you've got a few billion in the bank, you can pretty much buy all the law you want.'

'So what do we do? We can't hurt them. Unless we both decide that throwing the warheads into space is something that we should do. What do you say, Jack? Together. Let KU2 hit the Moon. Make them suffer. No one's going to stop us.'

Jack looked up again at the *Aphrodite*. Tamm and Vrána were still on the hull, either side of the airlock. 'They probably would. And they might have guns, knives, hammers, other weapons. I don't know what captains are issued with, but I know what's in a toolkit. That's beside the point. I'd stop you. This isn't the right path either.'

'What about revenge? What about justice?'

'I've lived with what happened on the *Coloma* for three years, every day, thinking about what I should have done, what I should have said. But for you it was barely three hours between Castor dying and you finding out your father had squandered the money you got from NovaS, and you've had less than two months awake in total in the last four years. It's raw for you in a way that it's not for me, or the rest of the human race. Justice is good, but the world has turned.'

'Can they hear this, up on the ship? What we're talking about?'

'The same way you could hear us.'

'What do they think?'

'I don't know. I suppose they would want us to leave the warheads alone and let them detonate them at the right time. Other than that? They blame me in varying degrees for where KU2 ended up, think that instead of plotting a course back to Cis-lunar, I should have used the fuel to get to the laser and disable it. We'd have all died, but at least we wouldn't have an Earth-colliding asteroid.'

'And it would be business as usual.'

'Until someone else dropped another rock.'

'Something has to change, Jack.'

367

'And despite being at exactly the right place at the right time, we know that nothing we do here will change anything. There's nothing you can do for St Ann's from here. There's nothing you can do for Castor from here. There's nothing I can do for May, or Andros, or Patricio, or Runi, Arush, Kayla, Marta or Julia. Neither of us can bring any pressure on any parent, government, agency or corporation from here. The future can go on either with us, or without us. You get to choose which.'

'So what do I do? What's left for us?'

'For me? I don't know. Neither of us is anything special. If you choose to die here, we'll get a line in the history books, and that's about it. If we choose to live? I'm wearing an OSTO flightsuit, so maybe I'll apply there, shake things up a little. For you? It's up to you. There aren't that many ex-gallowglasses around as an example. Politics? Lead your people, wherever they've got to. They'll follow you. You can't be any worse than your father, at least. Give them hope. Keep their stories alive. Or you can stay in space, assuming there's something left for us spacers to do. Your certificates are a bit out of date, but getting them up to code shouldn't be too much of a problem.'

He stopped to drink some water from his suit's dispenser. He felt that if he kept her talking, something might give. He didn't know what. It wouldn't take much for her to unclip herself from the line and just leap. She'd achieve escape velocity. If she passed through the debris field without putting a hole in her suit, then she'd be in deep space. She'd become another piece of debris that might impact the Moon, or might end up in orbit around the Sun. She would die when her suit exhausted its oxygen supply. Her body would be preserved potentially for ever.

He'd return to the *Aphrodite*. They'd pick their way through to make the minimum safe distance, and perhaps a bit more, and light up the asteroid. With Cat dead, there'd probably still be some messy legal business to take care of, but who knew?

Jack saw that she'd lost heart. All of the fire and adamantine

368

resolve had gone. She had finally acknowledged that everything she'd intended to achieve was now impossible. There was nothing left for her here. She was looking for a way to finish it. Finish herself. The only question remaining was how many people she might want to take with her.

Jack wasn't interested in giving the ESA directors sufficient wriggle-room in court. That wasn't enough for him. Mariucci had given him his solemn task: keep her alive.

'Are you prepared to give up your claim?' he asked.

'What's it worth now?' She reached down and picked up one of the rocks from the ground. She threw it, and the transfer of momentum caused her tether to tighten and loosened the anchor just a little bit more. The thrown rock turned and spun and disappeared into the distance. It would be back, in about two or three hours. 'Nothing. Trillions of dollars of metal and volatiles. Billions in royalties. If I could spit on it, I would. I killed, for this?'

'Cat. Give it up. Come back with me to the ship.'

'I wish I'd never been talked into it. I was the Prime Minister's daughter. I was the champion of our people. I was going to go into space and get the biggest asteroid I could find and save our island from the sea. As if I could do that. As if anyone could. The sea was coming whether we liked it or not. Did you know, did you, that at one point they were talking about cutting my legs off to save weight? The only reason they didn't was because I might get complications during the flight. It might have killed me before I got them their money. And they spent it on, what? I don't know. I don't want to know.'

She grew agitated again, and the anchor lifted up the rock around it. She didn't notice that, and neither did she notice Jack taking hold of the ground line and twisting the slack around his wrist. She was essentially adrift.

'The bastards. My own father. The whole cabinet. They pissed it away while I was out here, asleep. Unconscious. Dying.'

'I know.' He wondered what they were all making of this up

369

above. Holding their breath, or shouting at them. He asked for a third time: 'Do you give up your claim?'

'It's not done anyone any use. Not Castor, not me, not St Ann's. I give it up. I give it all up.' She panted with the effort for a few seconds. Then she kicked.

The anchor didn't – couldn't – hold. It lifted out of the regolith, dragging dust and rock behind it, and the two of them soared upwards from the surface. She was tethered to the ground line. He was tethered to the ship line. The only thing holding them together was the loop of cable around the back of Jack's gauntlet.

Her carabiner ran through the line and rammed up against the anchor. Her trajectory altered as the slack rose from the asteroid. Where were the next anchor points? Were there any, or was it just free cable at either end? The twist of line tightened on his wrist.

'Let me go, Jack.'

'I don't think I can.'

She started to reach for her tether, but such was the geometry of their combined ascent that it was below her, and her hand couldn't initially find it. She twisted around, head down.

'I've nothing to go back to.'

'Neither have I. But we don't have to go back. We can go forward.'

Her fingers pushed the gate on the carabiner, while the line grew increasingly tight around Jack's gauntlet. He swung his free hand around and tried to slacken it off. It wasn't happening. As if he weren't in a serious enough situation already, he was in danger of losing his hand before he died of anything else.

'Are you ... ?'

'I'm caught,' he said.

And rather than finish unclipping herself, she reached for the line either side of Jack's trapped wrist and brought her hands together. She grunted with effort. The loop slowly opened, and eventually he could pull free.

They started to move apart. Centimetres at first, still travelling side by side, but the gap increasing every second. They stared at each other, wondering what was going to happen next.

Then, almost too late, she held out her hand, and he snatched at it. Their hooked fingers closed on each other's, and gave enough momentum to bring them together again.

Jack grabbed her arm. She clutched at his. 'So what do I do now?'

'For now, give me your tether,' he said. 'We can work out the rest later.'

She tentatively reached to her waist and ran the strap through her fingers to the carabiner. She held it out to him. He took firm hold of it, and clipped it to his own belt.

'Now, slowly, unclip from the ground line. *Aphrodite*, do you copy?'

'Receiving.'

'Can you spool up drum C on my mark? Slow revolutions.'

'Copy that.'

'Unclipping.' Cat freed her other tether, and the line and the anchor it was attached to simply floated free.

'Take in the slack. Stop on my mark.'

Jack and Cat gradually pulled away from the gyrating anchor, with its sharp edges and glittering point. Their upward progress was still unimpeded, and it was going to cause problems both for them and for the *Aphrodite* very shortly.

'Jack. Do you copy?' It was Colvin.

'Receiving.'

'Your current vector is going to put you above amidships. I can keep reeling in the line, but we're going to get a significant rotational component at some point.'

'You mean we'll spiral in, slam into the hull and dent it and us.'

'Affirmative.'

Suonpää interrupted. 'I'm turning the ship. This isn't going to be pretty, so everyone hang on. Acceleration acceleration.'

371

Pale gas flared at the corners of the *Aphrodite*. The vessel turned around its long axis, so that the airlock now pointed into space. Tied to the line and each other, Jack and Cat passed by the white hull between the torus and the radiator panels.

'Drum C to free running. The moment it starts to pay out, apply the friction brake. Gently.'

They were ten, then fifty, then a hundred metres over the ship.

'Jack?'

'It's fine. Just hold tight and wait until we stop moving.'

They were beyond the radius of the radiators. The line went tight, and more cable paid out, bringing them to a gradual halt. They were now hanging over the ship, which was hanging over the asteroid, and everything was very slowly falling down.

'Reeling you in, fifty cents a second.'

More cold gas flared to keep the *Aphrodite* above the rock, and the airlock moved from their below and right towards their centre. Both Tamm and Vrána were there, double-tethered, ready to receive them. The drum continued to wind in the line.

'Put your feet to ship,' said Jack. He turned his hips. The tether between him and Cat tightened, and put both of them into a spin. He tried to correct, but so did she.

Then there was the ship again, a white wall with a black rectangular opening.

'Brace.'

He wanted not to close his eyes, but did anyway, briefly. The part he really needed to protect was his faceplate, and he brought both arms up, elbows in, and tried to cover as much of the plastic as possible. The collision was chaotic: being hit by a few hundred tonnes of spaceship was going to leave bruises, but he took the brunt of it on his shoulder. He bounced away, but only so far: the two atomjacks were grabbing and holding onto any part of him that came within reach.

Tamm dragged him back down, and Cat followed him like a balloon on a string.

'Elegant,' he said.

'Effective.' Jack managed to clip onto a hand rail, and then attached Cat's spare tether. 'Cat?'

'I'm okay. I'm okay.'

Jack unhitched himself from the safety line, and it spooled the rest of the way onto its drum. 'We're by the airlock,' he said. 'Coming aboard now.'

He moved aside for Cat to pass through the airlock door, clipping and unclipping as she went, and he took a long last moment to look out into space with his own eyes. Below them, the asteroid turned, oblivious as only a dead accumulation of rock could be to what was about to happen. Good riddance. It had become a symbol of hubris, avarice and wrath. It might become something more, but that would take effort and sacrifice, and he would be fought every step of the way.

So be it.

He closed his tether around the rail inside the airlock, and undid the one on the hull. He pulled himself into the airlock and pushed the cycler button. Cat was facing him, her face reflecting the blue-white of the suit lights.

The door closed behind them. It was over. They were done. But they were both finally free.

Credits

S.J. Morden and Gollancz would like to thank everyone at Orion who worked on the publication of *Gallowglass* in the UK.

Editorial
Rachel Winterbottom
Brendan Durkin

Copy editor
Elizabeth Dobson

Proofreader
Jenny Page

Audio
Paul Stark
Amber Bates

Contracts
Anne Goddard
Paul Bulos
Jake Alderson

Design
Lucie Stericker
Loulou Clark

Joanna Ridley
Nick May

Editorial Management
Charlie Panayiotou
Jane Hughes
Alice Davis

Finance
Jennifer Muchan
Jasdip Nandra
Afeera Ahmed
Elizabeth Beaumont
Sue Baker

Marketing
Lucy Cameron

Production
Paul Hussey

Publicity
Will O'Mullane

Sales
Laura Fletcher
Jen Wilson
Esther Waters
Victoria Laws
Rachael Hum

Ellie Kyrke-Smith
Frances Doyle
Georgina Cutler

Operations
Jo Jacobs
Sharon Willis
Lisa Pryde
Lucy Brem